The empty canvas.

The Empty Canvas

BY ALBERTO MORAVIA

The Woman of Rome

Two Adolescents

Conjugal Love

The Fancy Dress Party

The Time of Indifference

Five Novels

A Ghost at Noon

Bitter Honeymoon

Roman Tales

Two Women

The Wayward Wife

The Empty Canvas

ALBERTO MORAVIA

The Empty Canvas

TRANSLATED BY
Angus Davidson

FARRAR, STRAUS AND CUDAHY
New York

138701

The Empty Canvas

Prologue

I remember perfectly well how it was that I stopped painting. One evening, after I had been in my studio for eight hours, painting for five or ten minutes at a time and then throwing myself down on the divan and lying there flat, staring up at the ceiling for an hour or two—all of a sudden, as though at last after so many feeble attempts I had had a genuine inspiration, I stubbed out my last cigarette in an ashtray already full of dead cigarette butts, leaped cat-like from the armchair into which I had sunk, seized hold of a small palette knife which I sometimes used for scraping off colors and slashed repeatedly at the canvas on which I had been painting, not content until I had reduced it to ribbons. Then from a corner of the room I took a blank canvas of the same size, threw away the torn canvas and placed the new one on the easel. Immediately afterward, however, I realized that the whole of my—shall I say creative?—energy had been vented completely in my furious and fundamentally rational gesture of destruction. I had been working on that canvas for the last two months, doggedly and without pause; slashing it to ribbons with a knife was equivalent, fundamentally, to finishing it—in a negative manner, perhaps, as regards external results, which in any case had little interest for me, but positively, in relation to my own inspiration. In fact my destruction of the canvas meant that I had reached the conclusion of a long discourse which I had been holding with myself for an interminable time. It meant that I had at last planted my foot on solid ground. And so the empty canvas that now stood on the easel was not just an ordinary canvas which had not yet been used; it was a particular canvas that I had placed on the easel at the termination of a long job of work. In effect, I thought, seeking to console myself against the sense of catastrophe that was throttling me, this canvas, similar in appearance to so many other canvases but for me fraught with meaning and consequence, could be the starting point from which I could now begin all over again in complete freedom, just as if those ten years of painting had not gone by and I myself were still twenty-five, as I was when I had left my mother's house and had gone to live in the studio in Via Margutta in order to devote myself in complete leisure to painting. On the other hand, it might well be—in fact it was highly probable—that the empty canvas now flaunting itself on the easel was the outward sign of a development no less intimate and no less necessary but entirely negative, a development which might lead me, by imperceptible stages, to complete impotence. That this second hypothesis might well be the true one appeared to be borne out by the fact that slowly but surely boredom had come to be the companion of my work during the last six months, until finally it had brought it to a full stop on that afternoon when I slashed my canvas to tatters; it was rather like a deposit of lime in a spring which, in the end, blocks the passages and brings the flow of water to a complete standstill.

It may be opportune at this point for me to say a few words on the subject of boredom, a feeling which I shall have reason to mention frequently in the course of these pages. However far back into the years I probe in memory, I recall having suffered always from boredom. But it is important to understand what I mean by this word. For many people boredom is the opposite of amusement; and amusement means distraction, forgetfulness. For me, boredom is not the opposite of amusement; I might even go so far as to say that in certain of its aspects it actually resembles amusement inasmuch as it gives rise to distraction and forgetfulness, even if of a very special type. Boredom to me consists in a kind of insufficiency, or inadequacy, or lack of reality. Reality, when I am bored, has always had the same disconcerting effect upon me as (to use a metaphor) a too-short blanket has upon a sleeping man on a winter night: he pulls it down over his feet and his chest gets cold, then he pulls it up on to his chest and his feet get cold, and so he never succeeds in falling properly asleep. Or again (to make use of a different comparison) my boredom resembles a repeated and mysterious interruption of the electric current inside a house: at one moment everything is clear and obvious—here are armchairs, over there are sofas, beyond are cupboards, side tables, pictures, curtains, carpets, windows, doors; a moment later there is nothing but darkness and an empty void. Yet again (a third comparison) my boredom might be described as a malady affecting external objects and consisting of a withering process; an almost instantaneous loss of vitality—just as though one saw a flower change in a few seconds from a bud to decay and dust.

The feeling of boredom originates for me in a sense of the absurdity of a reality which is insufficient, or anyhow unable, to convince me of its own effective existence. For example, I may be looking with some degree of attentiveness at a tumbler. As long as I say to myself that this tumbler is a glass or metal vessel made for the purpose of putting liquid into it and carrying it to one's lips without upsetting it—as long as I am able to represent the tumbler to myself in a convincing manner—so long shall I feel that I have some sort of a relationship with it, a relationship close enough to make me believe in its existence and also, on a subordinate level, in my own. But once the tumbler withers away and loses its vitality in the manner I have described, or, in other words, reveals itself to me as something foreign, something with which I have no relationship, once it appears to me as an absurd object—then from that very absurdity springs boredom, which when all is said and done is simply a kind of incommunicability and the incapacity to disengage oneself from it. But this boredom, in turn, would not cause me to suffer so much if I did not know that, although I myself have no relationship with the tumbler, such a relationship might perhaps be possible, that is, because the tumbler exists in some unknown paradise in which objects do not for one moment cease to be objects. For me, therefore, boredom is not only the inability to escape from myself but is also the consciousness that theoretically I might be able to disengage myself from it, thanks to a miracle of some sort.

I mentioned that I have always been bored, let me add that it is only in fairly recent times that I have succeeded in understanding with any measure of clarity what boredom really is. During childhood, and later too, during adolescence and first youth, I suffered from boredom without explaining it to myself, like someone who suffers from continual headaches but never makes up his mind to consult a doctor. Especially when I was a child, boredom used to assume forms that were entirely obscure both to myself and to other people, forms which I was unable to explain and which others, not infrequently my mother, attributed to upsets in my health or other similar causes—just as the crossness of infants is often attributed to their cutting teeth. During those years, I would suddenly stop playing and remain motionless for hours on end, as though in astonishment, in reality overcome by the uneasiness inspired in me by what I have called the withering of objects; the obscure consciousness that between myself and external things there was no relationship. If at such times my mother came into the room, and seeing me dumb and inert and pale with distress, asked what was wrong with me, I answered invariably:

"I'm bored," thus explaining a vague and indefinite state of mind in a single word of clear, narrow significance. My mother, taking my statement seriously, would lean down and kiss me and then promise to take me to the motion pictures that afternoon, or suggest some kind of amusement which I knew perfectly well was neither the opposite thing to boredom nor yet its remedy. And I, though pretending to welcome her suggestion with delight, could not prevent myself from having the same feeling of boredom—the boredom that my mother claimed to be driving away—at the touch of her lips on my forehead, at the placing of her arms round my shoulders, as well as at the thought of the pictures that she held like a dazzling mirage in front of my eyes. Neither with her lips, nor with her arms, nor yet with the pictures had I any sort of relationship at that moment. But how could I explain to my mother that the feeling of boredom from which I was suffering could not be alleviated in any way? I have already observed that boredom consists chiefly of incommunicability. And now, being unable to communicate with my mother, from whom I was cut off as I was from every other kind of external object, I was in a way forced to accept the misunderstanding and lie to her.

I will pass quickly over the disasters caused by my boredom during adolescence. At that period it was my worst trial at school and was attributed to so-called "weaknesses," in other words to a congenital incapacity in one subject or another, and I myself accepted this explanation for lack of any more valid one. I now know for certain, however, that the bad marks which fell upon me thick and fast at the end of each scholastic year were due to one cause only—boredom. Indeed I felt acutely, with my customary deep distress, that I had no relationship whatever with all that enormous jumble of Athenian kings and Roman emperors, of South American rivers and mountains in Asia, of Dante's hendecasyllables and Virgil's hexameters, of algebraical processes and chemical formulae. All these unending pieces of information did not concern me, or concerned me only in order that I might establish the fact of their fundamental absurdity. But I did not boast, either to myself or to others, about this purely negative feeling that I experienced, in fact I told myself that I ought not to experience it, and I suffered from it. I remember that this suffering, even then, inspired in me a desire both to define and to explain it. But I was a mere boy, with all the pedantry and ambition of a boy. The result, therefore, was a project for a universal history "according to boredom," of which, however, I wrote only the first few pages. My universal history according to boredom was based on a very simple idea: the mainspring of it was neither progress, nor biological evolution, nor economic development, nor any of the other ideas usually brought forward by historians of various schools; it was simply boredom. Burning with enthusiasm at this magnificent discovery, I went right to the root of the matter. In the beginning was boredom, commonly called chaos. God, bored with boredom, created the earth, the sky, the waters, the animals, the plants, Adam and Eve; and the latter, bored in their turn in paradise, ate the forbidden fruit. God became bored with them and drove them out of Eden; Cain, bored with Abel, killed him; Noah, bored to tears, invented wine; God, once again bored with mankind, destroyed the world by means of the Flood; but this in turn bored Him to such an extent that He brought back fine weather again. And so on. The great empires —Egyptian, Babylonian, Persian, Greek and Roman—rose out of boredom and fell again in boredom; the boredom of paganism gave rise to Christianity; that of Catholicism, to Protestantism; the boredom of Europe caused the discovery of America; the boredom of feudalism kindled the French Revolution; and that of capitalism, the revolution in Russia. All these fine discoveries were noted down by me in a kind of summary, then I began with great enthusiasm to write the true and proper history. I do not remember exactly, but I don't think I went any further than a highly detailed description of the atrocious boredom from which Adam and Eve suffered in the Garden of Eden, and how, precisely because of this boredom, they committed their mortal sin. Then I grew bored with the whole project and abandoned it.

Actually I suffered from boredom between the ages of ten and twenty to a perhaps greater extent than in any other period of my life. I was born in 1920; thus the time of my adolescence was spent beneath the black banner of Fascism, that is, of a political regime which had been erected into a system by the incommunicability both of the dictator toward the masses and of the individual citizens between each other and toward the dictator. Boredom, which is the lack of a relationship with external things, was in the very air one breathed during the period of Fascism, and to this social boredom must be added the boredom of dull sexual urgency which, as is liable to happen at that age, prevented me from making contact with the very women who I believed could afford me relief. But my boredom saved me from the civil war which was to devastate Italy for two years. This was how it happened. I was in the army, in a division stationed in Rome, and as soon as the armistice was declared I took off my uniform and went home. Then a proclamation was made bidding all soldiers rejoin their units on pain of death. My mother, characteristically obsequious to the authorities, who at that moment were Fascist and German, advised me to put on my uniform again and report to headquarters. She was anxious for my safety, but in reality she was urging me toward deportation and probably death in a Nazi concentration camp—as happened to many of my comrades in arms. It was boredom, and boredom alone—that is, the impossibility of establishing contact of any kind between myself and the proclamation, between myself and my uniform, between myself and the Fascists—it was boredom from which I had suffered for twenty years, and which now caused the great empire of the fasces and the swastika to be entirely non-existent in my eyes, which saved me. Despite my mother's prayers,

7

I took refuge in the country, in the villa of a friend, and there I spent the whole period of the civil war, painting—which is as good a way of passing the time as any other. It was then that I became a painter; that is, I hoped to be able to re-establish contact with reality, once and for all, by means of artistic expression. In the first sense of relief brought about by my enthusiasm for painting, I did indeed almost convince myself that my boredom had been nothing more than the boredom of an artist ignorant of his vocation. I was wrong, but for some time I deluded myself with the idea that I had found a remedy.

At the end of the war I went back to live with my mother who, in the meantime, had acquired a big villa on the Via Appia. I had hoped, as I said, that painting had overcome boredom once and for all, but I realized almost at once that this was not so. I started suffering from boredom again in spite of my painting; in fact, since boredom automatically interrupted painting, I became conscious of the intensity and frequency of my old trouble more acutely than before I had started painting. Thus the problem of my boredom presented itself again, unchanged. I started asking myself what could be the reasons for it, and by process of elimination arrived at the conclusion that perhaps I was bored because I was rich and that if I were poor I would not be bored. This idea was not as clear in my mind as it appears now on paper; it was a question, not so much of an idea, as of a kind of haunting suspicion that there was a connection, obscure but indisputable, between boredom and money. I do not wish to linger too long over this exceedingly disagreeable period of my life. Since I was bored, and when bored could not paint, I began to hate with all my soul both my mother's villa and the comforts I enjoyed there; it was to the villa I attributed my boredom and the consequent impossibility of painting, and I longed to leave it. But since it was a question of a mere suspicion, I could not bring myself to say clearly the one thing I ought to have said to my mother: I don't want to live with you because you are rich, and being rich bores me and boredom prevents me from painting. Instead, I sought instinctively to make myself intolerable, in such a way as to hint at and to some extent to force my departure from the villa. I recall those days as days of unending ill-humor, of obstinate hostility, of determined non-compliance, of almost morbid antipathy. I have never treated my mother worse than I did during that period; and thus, to the boredom that oppressed me, there was added on top of everything else, a feeling of pity for her, incapable as she was of finding any explanation for my rudeness. Worse than anything, I suffered from a kind of paralysis of all my faculties, which made me mute and apathetic and dull, so that I felt as if I were buried alive inside myself, in a hermetically sealed and stifling prison.

My sojourn at the villa and my consequent state of mind would have probably been far more prolonged if, luckily, my mother had not come to believe that she recognized in my boredom a feeling analogous to that which had ruined her relations with my father.

My father was a born vagabond—from what I have been able to make out, putting two and two together. He was one of those men who fall gradually silent when at home, lose their appetite and in fact refuse to go on living (rather like birds which cannot endure to be shut up in a cage); but who, on the other hand, once they find themselves on the deck of a ship or in a railroad train, recover all their vitality. He was tall, athletic, fair-haired and blue-eyed, like me; but I am not good-looking because I have become prematurely bald, and my face, generally, is grey and gloomy; he, however, was a handsome man—at least if one can believe the boasts of my mother, who insisted on marrying him willy-nilly, in spite of the fact that he kept telling her that he did not love her and that he would leave her as soon as he could. I saw him only a few times, because he was always traveling, and the last time I saw him his fair hair was almost grey and his boyish face was all furrowed with fine, deep wrinkles; but he was still wearing the carefree butterfly bow ties and check suits of his youth. He came and went, that is, he ran away from my mother with whom he was bored and then came back again, probably in order to get a new supply of money so as to run off again, for he himself had not a penny, although, in theory, he was in the "import and export" business. Finally he came back no more. A violent gust of wind in the sea off Japan overturned a ferryboat with a hundred passengers on board, and my father was drowned with the rest of them. What he was doing in Japan, whether he was there in connection with "imports and exports" or for some other purpose, I have never known. According to my mother, who loved scientific or seemingly scientific definitions, my father suffered from "dromomania," in other words the passion for movement. It was perhaps this mania, she used to remark thoughtfully, that explained his passion for stamps—those small, brightly colored evidences of the vastness and variety of the world—of which he had gathered together a fine collection, still preserved by her, as well as his talent for geography, the only subject he had seriously studied at school. As far as I could understand, my mother looked upon my father's "dromomania" as a purely individual and therefore fundamentally insignificant characteristic, but I could not help feeling a kind of fraternal pity for that pathetic, faded figure, more and more faded as time went on, in whom I seemed to recognize—at least in his relationship with my mother—certain features in common with myself. But these were external features, as I realized on thinking the matter over: my father, it was true, had also suffered from boredom; but in him this suffering had been dissipated by happy wanderings in one country after another; his boredom, in other words, was the ordinary kind of boredom, in the sense in which the word is normally used, the boredom that asks no more than to be relieved by new and unusual sensations. My father, in fact, had believed in the reality of the world—in the world of geography, at any rate; whereas I could not manage to believe in the reality even of a tumbler.

Anyhow, my mother did not indulge in any great subtleties; she believed she could recognize without any possible doubt, in my boredom, the superficial tedium which had previously made her relations with her husband difficult. "Unfortunately you take after your father more than after me," she finally said to me one day, in a brisk manner. "I know that, when this thing attacks you, the only remedy is to send you away. So go away, go wherever you like, and when you've got over it you can come back."

I answered, with relief, that I had no intention of going away; traveling did not interest me in the least. I merely wanted to leave the house and set up on my own. My mother objected that it was absurd for me to go off and live on my own when I had the full use of a big villa like the one we lived in, where I could do just as I pleased into the bargain. But, having by this time determined to take advantage of the opportunity, I answered with some violence that I would leave next day, not a moment later. My mother then understood that I was serious. All she did was to repeat, with carefully studied bitterness, that my reply reminded her of my father, even to the tone of voice: I must therefore do whatever pleased me best, I must go and live wherever I liked.

There remained the question of money. We were rich, as I have said, and up to this time I had enjoyed more or less un-limited credit; I drew upon my mother's bank account when-ever I needed it. But now my mother, foreseeing a repetition with me of the experience she had already had with her husband, to whom she had always given enough money for him to run away but never enough to stay permanently away from her, informed me dryly that from now on she would give me a monthly allowance. I replied that I asked nothing better; and when, with a kind of angry remorse, she announced the amount of the sum she intended to allow me, I told her at once that I would be satisfied with half of it. My mother, who had been expecting an argument of the sort that she had formerly carried on with my father, to whom the money she offered had never been enough, was very much surprised at this unforeseen disinterestedness on my part. "But you can't live on as little as that, Dino," she exclaimed almost involuntarily. I replied that it was my affair, and in order to avoid giving myself the airs of an ascetic, I added that in any case I hoped soon to succeed in earning a living by my painting. My mother looked at me with incredulity; she did not believe in my artistic abilities. A few days later I found a studio in Via Margutta and moved there with my belongings.

My change of dwelling caused no alteration in my state of mind. Once the initial relief due to change had worn off, I started to be bored again at intervals as in the past. I ought to have foreseen that boredom would not disappear simply owing to my moving house; in any case I was rich not because I lived in the Via Appia, but because I possessed a certain amount of money. The fact that I did not want to make use of it mattered, fundamentally, very little; there are rich people who are miserly and who spend a very small part of their income and live poorly, but no one on that account would think of calling them poor. And so my first idea, or rather my first obsession, that my boredom and consequent artistic sterility were due to living at home with my mother came gradually to be replaced by a second and more serious obsession; that it was impossible to renounce one's own wealth. Being rich was like having blue eyes or an aquiline nose; a subtle compulsion bound the rich man to his money, and gave the color of money even to his decision not to make use of it. In short, I was not a poor man who had been rich, I was simply a rich man who was pretending, to himself and to others, to be poor.

I proved to myself that this was true in the following way: What does a really poor man do, if he hasn't any money? He dies of hunger. What would I do in such a case? I should go and seek help from my mother. And even if I did not do so, I should not on that account be considered poor; not at all, I should merely be considered mad. But, I reflected, mine was not an extreme case. It was an intermediate case, since it was true that I allowed myself to be supported by my mother, even though I limited such support to what was strictly necessary. Thus, in comparison with the really poor, I found myself in the privileged, treacherous position of the rich gambler in relation to the poor gambler: the former can lose to an unlimited extent, the latter cannot. But—even more important—the former can really "play," that is, amuse himself; whereas the latter can only set out to win.

It is difficult to say what my feelings were as I thought over these things. There was a sense of some kind of petty witchcraft, against which I could do nothing, because it was impossible for me to tell when or how or where the spell that enmeshed me had been woven. Sometimes I thought of the saying in the Gospels: "It is easier for a camel to go through the eye of a needle, than for a rich man to enter into the kingdom of God," and I wondered what being rich meant. Was one rich because one possessed a lot of money? Or because one had been born into a rich family? Or because one had lived, and still lived, in a society that placed riches above all other good things? Or because one believed in riches, desiring to become rich or bewailing the fact that one had been rich? Or because—as in my case—one did not want to be rich? The more I thought about it, the more difficult did it seem to me to define precisely, in my own mind, the feeling of compulsion, of predestination, that wealth aroused in me. Of course this feeling would not have existed if I had succeeded in freeing myself from my initial obsession that my boredom resulted from wealth, and my artistic sterility from boredom. But all our reflections, even the most rational, originate in some obscure basis of feeling. And it is not so easy to free oneself of feelings as it is of ideas: the latter come and go, but feelings remain.

It may be objected at this point that when all was said and done I was nothing more than an unsuccessful painter who—which is perhaps unusual—was conscious of his own failure, and that was all there was to it. Quite right, but up to a certain point only. Certainly I had failed, but not because I was unable to paint pictures that other people liked; it was rather because I felt that my pictures did not permit me to express myself, in other words to deceive myself into imagining that I had some contact with external things—in a word, they did not prevent me from being bored. Now the fundamental reason why I had started painting was to escape from boredom. If I went on being bored, why go on painting?

I left my mother's villa, if I remember rightly, in March 1947; a little more than ten years later, as I have related, I took a knife and slashed my last picture and decided not to paint any more. Immediately my boredom, hitherto kept at bay to a certain extent by the exercise of painting, attacked me again with incredible violence. I have already observed that boredom consists, fundamentally, in a lack of contact with external things; during those days it appeared to me that there was a lack of contact, not only with things, but with myself. I know that these matters are difficult to explain; I will not go further than to suggest my meaning by use of a metaphor. During the days following my decision to give up painting, I closely resembled, in relation to myself, some individual, for various reasons intolerable, who is found by a traveler in his own railroad car at the beginning of a long journey. The car is of the old-fashioned kind, without any communication with the other coaches; the train is not going to stop until the end of the journey; and so the traveler is forced to remain with his hateful companion without hope of escape. In reality, and leaving metaphor aside, boredom had thoroughly corroded my life during those years, down below the surface of my job as a painter, leaving nothing unimpaired; so that once I had given up painting I felt I had been transformed, without noticing it, into a kind of shapeless, truncated fragment. And the main feature of my boredom was the practical impossibility of remaining in my own company—I myself being, moreover, the only person in the world whom I could not get rid of in any possible way.

And so at that time my life was dominated by a feeling of extraordinary impatience. Nothing that I did pleased me or seemed worth doing; furthermore, I was unable to imagine anything that could please me, or that could occupy me in any lasting manner. I was constantly going in and out of my studio on any sort of futile pretext—pretexts which I invented for myself with the sole object of not remaining there: to buy cigarettes I didn't need, to have a cup of coffee I didn't want, to acquire a newspaper that didn't interest me, to visit an exhibition of pictures about which I hadn't the slightest curiosity, and so on. I felt, moreover, that these occupations were nothing more than crazy disguises of boredom itself, so much so that sometimes I did not complete the errands I undertook. Instead of buying a newspaper or drinking coffee or visiting an exhibition, after taking a few steps I would return to the studio which I had left in such a hurry only a few minutes before. Back in the studio boredom, of course, awaited me and the whole process would begin over again.

I would take down a book—for I had a small library and have always been fond of reading—but very soon I would let it drop: novels, essays, poetry, drama, the whole literature of the world—there was not one single page that succeeded in holding my attention. In any case, why should it? Words are symbols of objects, and with objects I had no relationship at all in moments of boredom. So I would drop my book, or perhaps in an impulse of rage fling it into a corner, and turn to music. I had an extremely good record player, a present from my mother, as well as about a hundred records. Who was it who said that music always acts in some kind of way, that is, makes itself listened to forcibly, so to speak, by even the most distracted person? The man who said that was incorrect. My ears refused not merely to listen but even to hear. Besides, when it came to the point of choosing a record, I was paralyzed by this thought: what sort of music is it that can be listened to in these moments of boredom? And so I would close the record player, throw myself down on the divan and start thinking of what I could do.

What struck me above all was that I did not want to do simply anything, although I desired eagerly to do something. Anything I might wish to do presented itself to me like a Siamese twin joined inseparably to some opposite thing which I equally did not wish to do. Thus I felt that I did not want to see people nor yet to be alone; that I did not want to stay at home nor yet to go out; that I did not want to travel nor yet to go on living in Rome; that I did not want to paint nor yet not to paint; that I did not want to stay awake nor yet to go to sleep; that I did not want to make love nor yet not to do so; and so on. When I say "I felt" I ought rather to say that I was filled with repugnance, with disgust, with horror.

I used to ask myself, between these frenzied bouts of boredom, whether perhaps I did not want to die; it was a reasonable question, seeing that I disliked living so much. But then, to my surprise, I realized that although I did not like living I yet did not want to die. Thus the inseparable alternatives which filed through my mind like a sinister ballet did not halt even in face of the extreme choice between life and death. The truth of the matter, I sometimes thought, was not so much that I wanted to die as that I wanted not to go on living in my present manner.

Chapter 1

After I had moved into the studio in Via Margutta, I managed to overcome the irrational and almost superstitious repugnance that the villa in the Via Appia aroused in me and to establish fairly regular contact with my mother. I went to see her once a week, to lunch, which was the moment of the day when I knew I should find her alone; and I would stay a couple of hours, listening to her conversation, which I knew by heart, on the only two subjects that interested her: botany, that is to say, the flowers and plants which she grew in her garden, and business, to which she had devoted herself ever since she had reached years of discretion. My mother, in truth, would have liked me to visit her more often, and at other times of the day too, for instance when she was entertaining her friends or the people of her own social set, but after a couple of invitations which I refused firmly, she appeared to resign herself to the rarity of my visits. Her resignation was, of course, a forced one, ready to vanish at the first opportunity. "Some day you'll discover," she was accustomed to say, speaking of herself in the third person, which in her was always an indication of a feeling strong enough for her to wish to conceal it, "you'll discover that your mother is not just an ordinary lady whom one visits out of

17

politeness, and that your real home is here and not in Via Margutta."

One day, not long after I had given up painting, I went to my mother's house for the usual weekly luncheon. Actually it was rather a special luncheon; that day was my birthday, and my mother, in case I had forgotten this, had reminded me of it that same morning, giving me her good wishes by telephone in her strangely official and ceremonious manner: "Today you reach the age of thirty-five. I convey to you my sincere good wishes for your happiness and success." She informed me at the same time that she had prepared a "surprise" for me.

And so, about midday, I got into my old, dilapidated car and went off across the town with the usual feeling of uneasiness and repugnance that seemed to increase steadily as I drew nearer my goal. My heart more and more heavily oppressed with a weight of anguish, I at last turned into the Via Appia between the cypresses and pines and brick ruins which line its grassy banks. The gateway to my mother's house was on the right, halfway along the Via Appia, and I looked out for it, half hoping, as usual, that by some miracle I should find it was no longer there, so that I could go straight on to the Castelli and then go back to Rome and return to my studio. However, there the gate was, thrown wide open especially for me, one might have thought, so as to stop me as I passed and swallow me up. I slowed down, turned sharply, and with a gentle, noiseless lurch entered the graveled drive, between two rows of cypresses. The drive rose gradually toward the villa, which could be seen at its far end; and as I looked at the small black cypresses with their dusty, curled foliage, and at the low, red house crouching beneath a sky full of fluffy grey clouds like lumps of dirty cotton wool, I was again conscious of the horror and consternation that assailed me each time I went to see my mother. It was a horror such as might be felt by a man who is preparing to commit an unnatural act; it was almost as though, as I turned into the drive, I were actually re-entering the womb that had given me birth. I sought to rid myself of this disagreeable feeling of retrogression by sounding my horn to announce my arrival. Then, after making a half circle on the gravel in front of the house, I stopped the car and jumped out. Almost immediately the glass door on the ground floor opened and a maid appeared on the doorstep.

I had never seen her before that day; my mother, who persisted in keeping a staff at the villa which would barely have been sufficient for a five-room flat, was for this reason frequently compelled to make changes. She was tall, with ample, robust hips and bosom and curiously short, badly cut hair, like the hair of a convict or a convalescent, and her pale, slightly freckled face had a sly expression, possibly owing to the huge pair of black-rimmed spectacles that concealed her eyes. I particularly noticed her mouth, which was shaped like a crushed flower and was of a delicate geranium pink. I asked her where my mother was, and she in turn asked me, in a very gentle voice: "Are you Signor Dino?"

"Yes."

"The Signora is in the garden, over by the greenhouses."

I started off in that direction, not without first giving a surprised glance at another car which was standing on the open graveled space near mine. It was a sports car, low, powerful-looking, with a top that opened back, and of a metallic blue color. Had my mother then invited someone else to lunch? Turning over this disagreeable doubt in my mind, I walked round the villa, along the brick pathway in the shade of laurels and holm oaks, and came out on the far side of the house. Here was a large, formal, Italian garden, with flower beds in the form of triangles, squares and circles, small trees clipped into spheres and pyramids and cones, and numerous avenues and paths, graveled and box-edged. A wider, straight path, covered by a white-painted iron pergola twined round with the branches of vines, cut the garden into two parts and stretched from the villa to the far end of the property where, against the boundary wall, could be seen the glistening panes of the greenhouses in which my mother grew flowers. Halfway between the villa and the greenhouses, underneath the pergola, I caught sight of her walking alone, her back turned toward me. For a moment I refrained from calling to her and watched her.

She was walking slowly, very slowly, in the manner of someone who looks around and is pleased with what he sees and prolongs his contemplation as much as possible. She was wearing a pale blue two-piece dress, the jacket very tight at the waist and very wide at the shoulders, the skirt extremely narrow, a veritable sheath. She always dressed like this, in very close-fitting clothes that made her small, fragile figure look even more meager and rigid and puppet-like. Her head was large, on a long, sinewy neck, her hair a crisp, dull blond and always elaborately waved and curled. The pearls around her neck were so big that I could see them perfectly clearly from a long way off. My mother loved to adorn herself with showy jewelry: massive rings that danced about on her thin fingers, enormous bracelets, laden with charms and pendants, which looked as if they would slip off her bony wrists, brooches too elaborate for her scrawny bosom, earrings too big for her ugly, fleshless ears. I noticed too, with a mingled feeling of familiarity and distaste, how the shoes on her feet and the handbag that she held under her arm seemed to be too big. Then I pulled myself together and called to her.

Characteristically mistrustful, she stopped immediately, as though somebody had placed a hand on her shoulder, and then turned without moving her legs, with the top part of her body only. I saw her long, pointed face with the hollow cheeks, the pinched mouth, the long, narrow nose, the glassy blue eyes which were looking at me obliquely. Then she smiled, turned right around and came to meet me, her head bowed, her eyes fixed on the ground, and saying as though it were a matter of duty: "Good morning and many happy returns of the day"; and although her intention was affectionate, I could not help noticing that the sound of her voice remained as it always was, dry and croaking, like the caw of a rook. She said again as she came up to me: "Many happy returns of the day. Come on, give me a kiss!" And then I stooped down and hastily planted a kiss on her cheek. We walked off side by side toward the far end of the path. Pointing to the vines that covered the pergola, my mother suddenly said: "Do you know what I was looking at? At my bunches of grapes here. Look!"

I raised my eyes and saw that the grapes all looked as if they had been nibbled or sucked, some more and some less.

"Lizards," said my mother, in the curiously intimate, affectionate, and at the same time scientific tone of voice that she used when speaking of her flowers and plants. "Those nasty little creatures climb up the posts of the pergola and eat the grapes. They ruin my pergola; the black clusters among the green leaves and tendrils look so beautiful, but if the grapes are half nibbled away, the whole effect is spoiled."

I said something or other about a ceiling by Zuccari in a palace in Rome, in which the subject of the painting was, in fact, a golden pergola with clusters of black grapes and vine leaves, and she went on: "The other day a hen belonging to the peasants close by somehow found its way into the garden. One of these lizards was on the pergola, and was, of course, sucking at my grapes. Then, for some odd reason, it lost its footing and came tumbling down. Just imagine—it didn't even touch the ground: the hen caught it in its beak and positively drank it down. Yes, I really mean that—it *drank* it."

"Then you must take to keeping hens," I said. "They'll eat up the lizards, and the lizards, of necessity, having been eaten, will stop eating the grapes."

"For heaven's sake, no! Hens, besides eating lizards, destroy

21

everything, wherever they go. I'd rather keep the lizards."

And so we went on around the garden, going down the long path underneath the pergola to the boundary wall and then walking through the greenhouses. My mother would stoop down and touch the corolla of a flower that had opened in the night, holding it between two fingers against the palm of her hand; or she would stand enraptured (there is no other word for it), glassy-eyed, in front of an earthenware flower pot from which a fleshy plant, like a green, hairy snake, curled right down to the ground, so that you almost expected it to hiss at you; or again, in a dry, didactic manner, she would provide me with a quantity of botanical information, culled from the detailed reading of horticultural manuals as well as from her long conversations with her two gardeners, very patient because very well paid, upon whom she inflicted her company the whole time they were working in the garden. As I have said, her love of flowers and plants was the only poetical thing in my mother's otherwise completely prosaic life. It is true that, in her way, she loved me; and that she introduced an unbelievable passion into the management and the enlargement of our property. But, both in business matters and with me, the predominant influence was her own character, authoritative, unscrupulous, self-interested, mistrustful. Flowers and plants, on the other hand, she loved in an entirely disinterested way, with unrestrained enthusiasm and no ulterior motives. And my father, how had she loved *him?* As usual, the idea came back into my mind that my father and I resembled one another at least in this one point: that we did not want to live with my mother. I asked her abruptly:

"By the way, I should very much like to know why my father was always running away from you."

I saw her wrinkle up her nose, as she always did when I spoke to her about my father. "Why *by the way?*" she said.

"Never mind, answer my question."

"Your father wasn't running away from me," she answered

22

after a moment, with icy dignity, "he liked traveling, that's all. Look at these roses, aren't they lovely?"

I said peremptorily: "I want you to tell me about my father. Why then, if it's true that he wasn't running away from you, didn't you go traveling with him?"

"First and foremost, because somebody had to stay here in Rome to look after our interests."

"You mean *your* interests."

"The family interests. And then, I didn't like his way of traveling. I like to travel with every sort of convenience. To go to places where there are good hotels, and people that I know. For instance to Paris, London, Vienna. But he would have dragged me off to goodness knows where, Afghanistan or Bolivia. I can't bear discomfort and I can't bear out-of-the-way countries."

"But tell me," I persisted, "why did he run away from home, or why, as you say, did he travel? Why didn't he stay with you?"

"Because he didn't like staying at home."

"And why didn't he like staying at home? Was he bored?"

"I never took the trouble to find out. I only know that he used to become gloomy, and never say anything, and never go out. In the end it was I who gave him the money and said to him: 'Here you are, go away, it's better for you to go.'"

"Don't you think that if he had loved you he would have stayed?"

"Yes, exactly," she answered in a disagreeable voice that seemed to take pleasure in telling the truth, "but he didn't love me."

"Then why did he marry you?"

"It was *I* who wanted to marry *him*. He, perhaps, wouldn't have done it."

"He was poor, wasn't he? And you were rich?"

"Yes, he had nothing at all. He came of a good family. But that was all."

"Don't you think he might have wanted to marry for money?"

"Oh, no. Your father wasn't mercenary. In that respect he was like you. It's true that he was always in need of money, but he didn't attach any importance to money."

"Do you know why I'm asking you all these questions about my father?"

"No, indeed I don't."

"It's because it occurred to me that, in one respect anyhow, I'm like him. I'm always running away from you."

She stooped down and, with a little pair of scissors that I hadn't noticed before, neatly cut off a red flower. Then she straightened up again and asked: "How is your work going?"

At this question I was suddenly conscious of a tightening of the throat and of a feeling of grey, icy desolation spreading all around me, issuing from me in steadily widening waves, as happens in nature when a cloud comes between the sun and the earth. In a voice that in spite of myself sounded strangled, I replied: "I'm not painting any more."

"What do you mean, you're not painting any more?"

"I've decided to give up painting."

My mother had never been in sympathy with my painting. In the first place because she understood nothing about it but disliked admitting this or hearing it said to her, and also because, not unjustly, she thought it had been my painting which had taken me away from her. But once again I was forced to admire her power of self-control. Anyone else in her place would at least have shown some satisfaction. She, however, received the news with indifference. "And why," she inquired after a moment, in a tone of polite, idle, almost mundane curiosity, "why have you decided to give up painting?"

By this time we had almost reached the villa, and there was a smell of cooking, of very good cooking, in the air. At the same time I felt that my despair, instead of lessening, was increasing, though I kept repeating furiously to myself: "It's getting better now, it's getting better now." And then a recollection rose to the surface of my mind, a memory of myself as a child of five, with my knee bleeding, sobbing despairingly as I came up through another garden and ran toward my mother, into whose arms I threw myself impetuously; and of my mother bending over me and saying to me in her ugly, croaking voice: "Now, now, don't cry, let me look at it, don't cry, don't you know that men don't cry?" And now I looked at my mother and it seemed to me that, for the first time after a long period, I had a feeling of affection for her. Then, in answer to her question, I said: "Don't know," speaking as briefly as possible, for I was ashamed of my despair and did not wish her to be aware of it.

But I realized at once that it was no use saying "Don't know"; the feeling of desolation did not cease on that account; it made my flesh creep and my hair tingle, and around me the whole world seemed discolored and shriveled. Then a light puff of wind brought that smell of good cooking to my nostrils again, and I felt a desire to throw myself sobbing into my mother's arms, as I did when I was five, with the same hope that she would console me for my abandoned painting just as she had done then for my wounded knee. Suddenly I said unexpectedly: "Oh, by the way, I forgot to tell you that I'm leaving the studio, which serves no purpose now, and coming back to live with you." I paused a moment, astonished at these words which I had had no intention of uttering and which issued from my mouth for no explainable reason. Then, realizing that I could not now withdraw again, I added with an effort: "Provided you want me to."

In spite of the amazement into which I had been thrown by my own proposal, I could not help admiring once again my mother's capacity for dissimulation, the capacity that she, in her "society" idiom, called "good form." I had said the thing she had been waiting to hear for years; the only thing, perhaps, that could give her real pleasure; nevertheless not a sign appeared on her wooden, expressionless face or in her glassy eyes. Slowly she said, in a more than usually disagreeable voice, almost in the tone of someone reciprocating a compliment of no importance whatsoever: "Of course I want you to. In this house you'll always be more than welcome. When would you come?"

"This evening or tomorrow morning."

"Better tomorrow morning; then I'll have time to have your room got ready for you."

"Tomorrow morning, then."

After these words we said nothing more for some time. I was wondering what it was that had happened to me, and whether my true vocation now might not be to stay at home with my mother and accept the fact of being bored and administer our property and be rich. My mother, on her side, appeared by this time to have got beyond the phase of surprise and complacency at her unhoped-for victory; and was already devoting herself, as could be concluded from the thoughtful expression on her hard, set face, to the organization of that victory—that is, to plans for my future and her own. Finally she remarked, in a casual tone: "I don't know if you did it on purpose, but anyhow it's a good omen. Today is your birthday and today you've decided to come back and live here. I told you this morning that I've prepared a surprise for you. Now it'll do to celebrate both occasions."

I asked without thinking: "What's the surprise?"

"Come with me and I'll show you."

I said, cruelly: "In any case let's celebrate only one of these two occasions today—my return home. That's the real cause for rejoicing today."

Did my mother notice my sarcasm? Or was she unaware of it? Certainly she said nothing. In the meantime she was walking in front of me around the walls of the villa, toward the open space at the front. I saw her walk in a deliberate fashion up to the beautiful sports car standing near mine and then stop, one hand on the hood, more or less in the attitude of a girl being photographed for a car manufacturer's display poster. "You once told me," she said, "that you would like to possess a very fast car. At first I thought of buying you a real racing car, but they're dangerous things and so I decided on this convertible. The dealer told me it was the very latest model, only a few months out of the factory. It'll do a hundred and twenty miles an hour."

I approached slowly, wondering how much this car that my mother wanted to give me could have cost: three million lire, four million? It was a foreign car and the coach work was sumptuous: I knew that cars of this kind were extremely expensive. My mother was now talking about the car in the same detached, scientific, curious, almost affectionate tone that she adopted when discussing the flowers in her garden. "I like this particularly," she said, pointing to the instrument panel which had a black background against which the various switches and polished metal controls sparkled like diamonds on black velvet in a jeweler's shop. "I would have bought it simply for this. And then I like it also because it has the solidity of a good pair of strong shoes, handmade and specially designed for long walks. A reassuring solidity. Well, would you like to try it? We've time to take a little turn before lunch, only for a few minutes, however, because there's a dish that can't be kept waiting and the cook is very anxious that you should appreciate it, she's done it specially for you."

Staring absent-mindedly at the car, I murmured: "Just as you like."

"Yes, do try it, especially as I have to confirm my purchase of it with the dealer."

I said nothing; I opened the car door and got in. My mother got in beside me and, as I started the engine and lowered the gear lever, she informed me in her usual intimate, scientific tone of voice: "It has a convertible top. The dealer assured me that in the winter not the smallest breath of wind can get in. In any case, there's the heater. In the summer you can put the top down; it's more amusing to drive without the top."

"Yes, it's more amusing."

"D'you like the color? I thought it was lovely, so much so that I didn't even want to see any other. The dealer told me that the metallization of the paint is an expensive process but the effect is smarter."

"It's much more delicate," I said vaguely.

"When it's tarnished, you can have it repainted."

The car gave a very loud roar, just like a racing car; then I drove around the open space and moved off swiftly down the drive. The car was very powerful and very sensitive, as I could tell when I felt it leap forward beneath my feet at the slightest pressure on the accelerator. We went out through the iron gates, and I could not help recalling the sensation I had had a short time before when, on my way up to the villa, I had felt I was re-entering the womb that had given me birth. And now? Now I was inside that same womb and I should never leave it again.

Outside the gates, I turned to the right and went up the Via Appia in the direction of the Castelli. The dull, sultry day had caused a dark, shifting, volatile ring of thundery-looking clouds to form thickly over Monte Cavo; all along the Via Appia the pines and cypresses, the ruins, the hedges, the fields were dim with dust and burnt up by the heat of summer. My mother went on praising the car to me in a casual, conversational manner, as though she were gradually discovering its merits. Without saying a word, I drove on up the Via Appia as far as the fork, bore to the left, very fast all the time, went down to the Via Appia Nuova, turned around at the traffic signals and came gack again.

"What d'you think of it?" asked my mother, as we came again into the Via Appia Antica.

"I think it's a splendid car in every way. Anyhow, I knew it already."

"What do you mean, when it's a new type that's scarcely been out a month?"

"I mean, I already knew cars of this make."

We reached the gates, the drive with the cypresses, the villa with the open space in front of it. I did a half turn, stopped, pulled up the hand brake, and then, after sitting motionless and silent for a moment, turned abruptly to my mother and said: "Thank you."

"I bought it," she answered, "mainly because I liked it so much. If I hadn't bought it for you, I should have bought it for myself."

It appeared to me, however, that she was expecting something more—to judge, at least, from her discontented, exacting expression. "I do really like it very much; thank you," I said again. And, leaning forward, I lightly touched with my lips the dry, rough make-up on her thin cheek. In order, perhaps, to conceal the satisfaction that my affectionate gesture gave her, she said: "The dealer suggested that before using the car you should read the instructions for driving and maintenance," and she opened a compartment in the instrument panel and showed me a yellow handbook; "because these cars are delicate and easily damaged."

"Yes, I'll read it."

"With this car you could go touring. For instance, when the autumn comes, you could go to Spain, or to France."

"I'll go in the spring, I can't go this autumn."

"Yes, of course, in the spring too. The car has a big luggage compartment. It'll take three suitcases."

My mother seemed now to be really satisfied; so much so that some of her "good form" had given way and it could be seen distinctly—which was most unusual—that she was content. As we walked across to the house my mother pointed to the left, to a long, straight path, narrow and flanked by tall laurel bushes, at the far end of which one caught a glimpse of a small, red, building. "Your studio," she said. "It's remained exactly as it was. Nothing has been touched. If you like, you can go and start painting there tomorrow."

"But I've already told you I've decided to give up painting."

She made no reply; perhaps she had pointed out the studio to me merely in order to make me repeat that I had in truth given up painting. By now we had arrived at the front door. My mother preceded me into the hall, saying in an authoritative tone of voice: "Now go and wash your hands, because lunch will be ready at once."

She opened a small door which led into a passage to the kitchen. I went by another door to the cloakroom. Surrounded by the four blue walls of the bathroom, I automatically looked at myself in the mirror above the wash basin while my hands twisted and turned in the soapy lather, under the jet of warm water. Just at that moment the door behind me opened and I saw in the mirror the head, with its short, badly cut hair, of the maid who had greeted me on my arrival a short time before.

Looking at her reflection and without turning, I asked: "What's your name?"

"Rita."

"I've never seen you before."

"I've only been here a week."

I bent down and vigorously soaped my face, although there was no need to do so: I felt I was dirty because of the thoughts that oppressed me. While I was washing, I heard Rita's soft voice telling me: "I've put the towel here," and I nodded my head. When I lifted my face, the girl had gone. I left the bathroom and, crossing the hall, went toward the drawing room, or rather toward the four or five sitting rooms, anterooms and drawing rooms that occupied the ground floor of the villa.

These rooms, used by my mother both for living in and for entertaining, communicated with each other by means of arches or doorways with no doors in them, so that they formed, almost, a single large room; and they were furnished in an entirely impersonal manner, with the opulent, tedious impersonality of furniture that has been chosen solely on account of its commercial value. You could be sure that in those rooms there was not a single object that was not the most expensive, or anyhow among the most expensive, in the category to which it belonged. My mother had neither taste, nor culture, nor curiosity, nor love of beauty; her one criterion in any sort of acquisition was always its price, and the higher the price the more completely was she persuaded that the object possessed the qualities of beauty and refinement and originality which otherwise she would have been incapable of recognizing. My mother, of course, did not throw money down the drain; on the contrary she was always extremely careful, and more than once I had heard her exclaim, in a shop: "No, it's too dear, it's not even to be thought of." But I knew that this exclamation on her part referred to her own financial position and not to the real value of the object in question, about which she understood nothing and which, though out of reach of her purse, nevertheless remained desirable precisely because it was expensive.

The result of this criterion of choice was, as I have already said, a collection of furniture without character and without intimacy, but robust and imposing, for my mother laid great importance not merely on money value but also on solidity and size, these being two other qualities that she was capable of judging and appreciating. And so everything in these rooms—deep sofas, enormous armchairs, gigantic lamps, massive tables, heavy curtains, monumental fittings—conveyed the idea of a luxury that was substantial and of good quality. And in every darker corner of the rooms light was reflected from waxed floors, from surfaces of well-kept wood, from gleaming brass and silver; extreme cleanliness was another characteristic of the house. I noticed that as usual there were a number of large vases here and there, filled with slightly funereal bunches of

31

flowers which my mother, as I knew, went to pick early every morning in the greenhouses. I realized that I was looking at all these things with an eye that was different from usual, less absent-minded, less detached, as though I were trying to discover the effect they made upon me, now that I had decided to come back and live with my mother. And I found that I had a feeling of mean and disgusted complacency, as if faced by an old temptation, now victorious but still as repugnant as ever. I went over to the antique, heavily framed mirror that hung above a console table at the far end of the drawing room, looked at myself and suddenly felt a need to shout an insult at myself, whether from hatred or joy, I did not know. "Idiot!" I cried. Almost at the same moment I heard a rustling sound behind me.

I turned and saw the maid Rita standing a few paces from me beside a wheeled bar-table and looking at me with a questioning air through her thick black-rimmed glasses. I wondered whether she had seen me while I was hurling insults at myself; I looked at her pale, sly face and could tell nothing. After a moment's silence she said: "The Signora will be down in a moment. She told me to offer you a drink in the meantime. What would you like?"

Again I wondered whether her voice contained the irony that was not shown in her face. But no, it was a serious, or at the least a hypocritically serious, voice. I said I would like some whisky and with precise movements she took the whisky bottle, poured some into a glass, added a chunk of ice and some water and handed it to me, asking: "Is there anything else you would like?"

I said I wanted nothing more, and watched her go noiselessly away in her felt-soled shoes. Then I sat down with my whisky in one of the vast armchairs; I lit a cigarette and started to ponder. Why had I abused myself like that in front of the mirror? Obviously, I concluded, the danger of this sort of prodigal son comedy was that, when I least expected it and, as it were, in spite of myself, I might be suddenly tempted to utter profanities or create a scandal. In other words, I was a prodigal son of a particular type who, at the very moment when he was clasped in the embrace of his aged parent, felt a temptation to give the latter a good kick in the shins, and who, after devouring the festive banquet, went out and vomited it up in a corner of the garden. I had no time to go deeply into this interesting speculation as my mother came suddenly into the room. "Did Rita give you a drink?" she inquired.

"Yes, thank you. But who is this Rita?"

"She's new here, she had very good references, she'd been with some Americans who have left. Really she was a sort of nursery governess, but as there aren't any children here I said to her: 'My dear girl, I'm forced to demote you into a parlor maid. You're free to accept or not as you like.' Naturally she agreed, of course she did, with all the unemployment there is. . . ." My mother went on talking about Rita even after we had gone into the dining room, where Rita herself was standing at the sideboard, with cotton gloves on her hands, a lace cap on her head and a little oval apron at her waist. I wanted to say to my mother: "Be careful, you're talking about Rita and Rita is here," then I looked at the girl's sly, bespectacled face and I was absolutely sure that she had seen me when I leaned forward in front of the mirror and called myself an idiot. I felt that this idea was not altogether displeasing to me, as though from that moment a kind of complicity had been established between myself and Rita. I sat down, and my mother, as she also took her seat, said: "Rita, Signor Dino is my son and tomorrow morning he's coming to live here. Now don't forget: if anyone asks on the telephone for a gentleman called Dino, that means my son."

We were now sitting facing one another at a small round table in a room which was not large but which had a very high ceiling. On the Florentine lace tablecloth were plates of German porcelain flanked by spoons and forks of English silver and glasses of French crystal. Behind my mother's chair the golden inlay of a Dutch dresser gleamed in the half-light; behind me, as I knew, stood a Venetian sideboard. The French window giving on to the garden was wide open but the curtains were half drawn because my mother did not wish, in her own words, that some gardener or other should count the mouthfuls as she was eating. My mother herself helped me to wine from a crystal and silver carafe, then told Rita that she could serve the lunch. The girl took from the sideboard a porcelain dish standing on a salver and went across to my mother. The latter said sharply: "Serve Signor Dino first."

"Why? You first," I said.

"No, I. . . ."

"Rita, serve the Signora first."

"But I eat practically nothing," said my mother, and she served herself a tiny portion of food with the point of the spoon. Rita came over to me and then I understood the good smell of cooking I had noticed when we were in the garden— a macaroni pie. "I knew you liked it," said my mother, "I had it made specially for you."

"Good, good, good," I said with masochistic satisfaction, and I deposited an enormous helping of it on my plate. As a rule I ate little, and this type of food, particularly, I did not eat at all. I could not help thinking that this was a continuation of the comedy of the prodigal son, and I burst out laughing. My mother asked in alarm: "Why are you laughing?"

"I remember having read somewhere," I replied, "an amusing parody of the parable of the prodigal son—you know, the one in the Gospels."

"What was that?"

"In the parable, the prodigal son returns home and his father welcomes him with all sorts of attentions and kills the fatted calf for him. In the parody, on the other hand, the fatted calf runs away in terror as soon as the prodigal son comes back, knowing well what his fate is to be. So they wait for him to return. The fatted calf keeps them waiting quite a long time and then decides to come back. In the intensity of his joy the father, in order to celebrate the return of the fatted calf, kills the prodigal son and makes a feast of him for the calf."

My mother believed in nothing—except money. She did rely, as I have already said, upon what she called "good form," and this required, among other things, that she should be a practicing Catholic, or anyhow that she should respect things connected with religion. So I saw her assume a wooden expression, and then she said in her most disagreeable voice: "You know I don't like you to make jokes about sacred things."

"On the contrary, I'm not joking. What, in fact, does my return signify, if not the sacrifice of the prodigal son—that is to say, myself—for the advantage of the fatted calf, which is all this?"—and I gave a wave of my hand to indicate the expensive furniture all around me in the room.

"I don't understand you." My mother was not lacking in a curious, rather gloomy, mechanical sense of humor; without smiling, she added: "Anyhow I think that after the macaroni there happens to be some veal coming—whether from a fatted calf or not, I don't know."

I said nothing, but started devouring my helping of pie with a mixed feeling of joy and remorse, because I was really hungry and the pie was good and yet at the same time I felt angry at liking it. Then I looked up at my mother and saw that she was watching me with disapproval. "You ought to chew your food more thoroughly," she said. "The first stage of digestion takes place in your mouth."

"How very disgusting! Who told you that?"

"All doctors say so."

Her blue, glassy, utterly expressionless eyes brooded over me in an indefinable manner above the two crossed, ring-laden hands upon which she supported her chin. I finished clearing my plate in a mad hurry; then my mother, in her cold, toneless voice, said: "Offer Signor Dino some more," and Rita, who all this time had remained standing with her back to the dresser behind my mother, took up the dish and came over and handed it to me. I helped myself with one hand only, leaving my other hand where it was, resting on the edge of the table. Then I felt the hand with which Rita was supporting the dish press lightly upon mine, in a way that might or might not have been intentional. I did not stop more than an instant to consider this possibility, but resumed eating. Finally I asked my mother, in a tone of slight amusement: "What do you do all the time?"

"What do you mean?"

"I mean exactly what I say: what do you do all the time?"

"Oh, my life is the same as ever, you know."

"Yes, but in all these years that I've been away from home I've never asked you what you did. Now, perhaps because I'm on the point of coming back, I'm curious to know about it. Why, it's quite possible that everything's changed."

"I don't like changing anything. I like to think that I live now as I lived ten years ago, and as I shall be living in ten years' time."

"But, all the same, I don't know how you live; let's see now, what time do you wake up in the morning?"

"At eight o'clock."

"As early as that? But I've often telephoned at nine and been told the Signora's still asleep."

"Yes, sometimes I sleep later because I've been up late the evening before."

"And when you wake up, what do you do? Do you have breakfast?"

"Yes, of course."

"In your room or in the dining room?"

"In my room."

"In bed or at a table?"

"At a table."

"What do you have for breakfast?"

"Tea and toast, as I always did, and orange juice."

"And after breakfast what do you do?"

"I have a bath." My mother answered my questions in a tone which was slightly resentful and at the same time both dignified and surprised, as though I had been seriously in doubt as to whether in fact she breakfasted or washed.

"A bath or a shower?"

"A bath."

"Do you wash yourself or do you get the maid to help you?"

"The maid sees to the temperature of the water, puts in the bath salts, and then, when the bath is ready, helps me to wash the parts of myself that I can't reach."

"And then?"

"Then I get out of the water, dry myself and dress."

"Does the maid help you to dress too?"

"She helps me to put on my stockings. But not my clothes; I prefer to dress myself."

"Do you talk to the maid while you're having your bath and dressing?"

My mother suddenly started laughing, unwillingly, it seemed, with a kind of nervous irritation. "Do you know, you're very odd, with all your questions? After all, I might not wish to answer them. My private life has nothing to do with anyone but myself."

"I didn't ask you what you think but what you do. Do try and understand me. I'm coming home after an absence of almost ten years. It's quite right that I should want to reacclimatize myself. Well then, do you talk to the maid?"

"Of course I talk to her; she's not an automaton, she's a human being."

"When do you put on your jewelry, before or after dressing?"

"I put it on the last thing."

"In what order—that is, which pieces first and which afterwards?"

"Do you know what you remind me of? A policeman in a detective story, investigating a crime."

"The fact of the matter is that I have to investigate something too."

"What?"

"I don't know, something or other. Well, in what order do you put on your jewelry?"

"First my rings and bracelets, then my necklace and then my earrings. Now are you satisfied?"

"After you're dressed, what do you do?"

"I go downstairs and give the cook her orders for the day."

"You mean you write down the menus for her—for lunch and dinner?"

"Exactly."

"And then?"

"Then I go into the garden, I pick flowers and bring them into the house and put them in vases. Or I walk about and talk to the gardeners. In fact, I busy myself in the garden."

"After the garden, what then?"

I saw her look at me for a moment, and then she answered, almost solemnly: "I go into the study and attend to the management of our affairs."

"Every day?"

"Yes, every day, there's always something to be done."

"What do you do?"

"Well, I write, or I see people."

"You mean that lawyers, tax collectors, stockbrokers, trustees and people like that come to see you?"

Suddenly she started laughing again, but this time in a self-satisfied, almost sensual way, showing that I had touched a sensitive spot. "Perhaps you imagine," she said, "that what I do is an easy job? It's not like painting, I admit, but all the same it's a most exhausting job and it keeps me busy the whole morning and sometimes the afternoon as well."

"Oh well, it's a good thing to be busy, isn't it?"

"Some days I get a steady pain, here, at the back of the neck."

"You ought to try and spare yourself."

My mother considered me for a moment—with affection, it may have been—and then said, in her ugly, croaking voice: "It's for you I do it, so that your property may be safeguarded and increased."

"*My* property? No, no, *yours.*"

"When I die it will be yours."

"You're quite young still; I shall certainly die first. Of boredom. Anyhow, let us say, *our* property. How's it getting on, then, our property? How's it getting on?"

"You know, you really are very strange. It's getting on well, thanks to my efforts. Certainly, if it hadn't been for me, we shouldn't have a penny left by now."

"We're very rich, then, aren't we?"

To this question my mother made no answer at all; all she did was to look at me with a wooden face and glassy eyes. Then she said: "Rita, what are you doing standing there like that? Why don't you go and see if the second course is ready?" Rita shook herself as though she had been dreaming and went out. My mother immediately went on: "I do beg of you, as I've always told you, not to speak of money affairs in front of the servants."

"Why not? I could understand, if I had spoken of something obscene. But money affairs? Perhaps money affairs are obscene, are they?"

My mother shook her head, her eyes lowered, as though rejecting my argument without discussion. Then she said: "They are poor, and it's not fair to flaunt riches in front of poor people."

"But you never want to talk about money affairs even when we're alone. You put on a certain face and anyone would think you were shocked, just as if I had started talking about sexual affairs, instead of money."

Another shake of the head. "No," she said. "I like to talk about them at the right time and place; in fact, since you're coming back to live here, we *must* talk about them. After lunch we'll go into the study and I'll provide you with all the information you want."

At that moment Rita came in again, carrying a long oval dish upon which, among small mounds of various kinds of vegetables in season, were arranged slices of the veal that my mother had announced. Urged on by some kind of spiteful demon, I said lightly: "Well, you haven't yet answered my question: are we very rich, or are we not?"

This time she did not merely answer me with silence: I was suddenly aware of her foot seeking mine under the table and then pressing it strongly. Then she said to Rita: "Serve Signor Dino, I don't want any meat."

The feeling of my mother's foot on mine filled me with despair. She was pressing my foot under the table in the way that lovers do; except that we were mother and son and the bond that united us was not love but money. Moreover I could not repudiate this bond, because to repudiate it would mean also repudiating the bond of blood which was implicit in it. So there was nothing to be done: willy-nilly, I was rich; to refuse to be rich was equivalent to accepting the fact of it.

My despair, however, took an unexpected direction. Rita was handing me the oval dish of veal, bending toward me her well-formed bosom and her sly, freckled face with its pretty mouth the color of a pale geranium: under cover of the dish, I turned back my hand as it lay on the edge of the table and took hold of her wrist, then ran my fingers up to her forearm. I finished helping myself with the other hand and, putting the fork back on the dish, once more persisted in asking my mother, coldly: "Well then, are we rich or are we not?" For the second time I felt my mother's foot trampling upon mine. Then I said: "One moment, Rita."

Rita obediently turned back and held out the dish to me

once again. Again I used only one hand, taking the fork to go around the dish picking up some meat and vegetables. Meanwhile I ran my other hand, which I had left dangling beside my chair, up Rita's leg, right up to her thigh. Through her ample dress I could feel the muscles of her leg quiver beneath my hand, like those of a horse when its master strokes it. Nothing, however, was visible in the expression of her face, which now not merely looked, but certainly was, hypocritical. She turned away and I, catching—or anyhow so I thought—a fugitive glance of understanding behind her glasses, could not help reflecting that now, even before coming back to live in my mother's house, I found myself in a situation worse than that of ten years before. At that time, whatever might have been my reasons for doing so, I would never have thought of laying my hands on a servant girl. My mother, in the meantime, had stopped treading on my shoe, just at the exact moment when I removed my hand from Rita's leg and with an odd sort of synchronization, as though she had been acting in agreement with me. Resuming our interrupted conversation, I said: "So you work until one o'clock or later, every day?"

"Every day except Sunday."

"On Sunday what do you do?"

"I go to Mass."

"In which church?"

"San Sebastiano."

"What do you do in church?"

"I do what everybody else does, I hear Mass."

"And do you go to confession sometimes?"

"Certainly I do, of course. And I receive the Sacrament, too."

"And when you've made your confession, does the priest give you absolution?"

"I never have very serious sins to confess," said my mother with a touch of coquettishness. "You know, Don Luigi sometimes says to me: 'Signora, you finish where other people only begin.' Anyhow, what sins do you imagine I can commit, at my age?" And she looked at me, as much as to say, it's a long time since I gave up the only thing that could make me commit sins.

I was silent for a moment, then I went on: "Let's go back to your day. On weekdays, then, you work in the mornings, and then what do you do?"

"I have lunch."

"Alone?"

"Yes, I always lunch alone. Sometimes, but rarely, I keep the lawyer to lunch; but that is only when we haven't finished and have to go on working in the afternoon."

"What lawyer is that? De Santis?"

"Yes, he's still my lawyer."

"And after lunch?"

"After lunch I go for a walk in the garden."

"And then?"

"I go and rest."

"You mean you go to sleep?"

"No, I don't sleep, I take off my shoes and lie down on the bed fully dressed. But I don't go to sleep, I give myself up to my thoughts."

"What do you think about?"

She started laughing again, in a nervous, diffident way, like a young girl who is tempted to speak about a love affair. "That depends. Do you know what I think about at the present time?"

"No, what d'you think about?"

"I think about a house that is for sale on the Lungotevere Flaminio. A very good business proposition, if it was for the location alone. Alas, at the moment I can't afford it, but I think about it all the same. At times I think about things that I *can* afford—this, for instance," and she held out her hand and showed me a ring with a big emerald surrounded with diamonds; "I thought about it for a long time, weighing the pros and cons, and in the end I made up my mind and bought it."

"And after your rest, what do you do?"

"Well really, why this cross-examination?"

"I've already told you, I want to reacclimatize myself."

She spoke unwillingly. "There are plenty of things I do. For example I go and see friends."

"Who do you go and see?"

"Oh, that depends. There's always some reception or other, or a cocktail party, and besides, I have various women friends."

"Have you many women friends?"

"I've kept nearly all the friends I had when I was at school," said my mother, with a thoughtful air. "After that, I don't know why, I never made any more friends."

"What do you do with your friends?"

"What do you suppose we do? We do what married women always do when they're together. We chatter, we have tea or a martini, we play cards."

"What games do you play?"

"How tiresome you are! Why, bridge, or canasta, or even poker. Sometimes I organize bridge or canasta tournaments here, in the evening."

"Ah, yes, I remember; charity tournaments, aren't they? And for whose benefit?"

"The last one I had was for men blinded in the war."

"Blinded in the war. We were all, in a way, blinded in the war, weren't we?"

"Frankly, I don't understand you. But if this is some sort of joke, it's not in very good taste."

"Never mind. And do you go and visit dressmakers?"

"Seeing that I don't go about naked, of course I do. In fact I'm glad you reminded me, otherwise I should have forgotten; there's Fanti's dress show tomorrow."

"Ah, Signora Fanti! The same as ever. Will she never die?"

"Poor thing, why should you want her to die? Not merely is she not dead, but she remembers you, from the time when you were a little boy and used to go with me to see her. She always asks me what you're doing and how you are, and she hopes you'll get married and send your wife to her."

"Well, what do you do in the evening?"

"I have dinner. Often someone comes to dine with me. Sometimes I give a dinner party of six or eight people, and others come in after dinner. Or I go to the theatre or the pictures with friends, always the same ones. But more often I watch television."

"You've bought a television set, have you? I didn't know."

"Oh, hadn't I told you? Yes, and I've had it arranged in a little sitting room upstairs. Some neighbors of mine come in and we watch it together. And often I watch it alone. I like television; it's better than the films; there's no need to leave the house, you can see it sitting in a comfortable armchair and you can do something else at the same time. Just imagine, I've taken to knitting again, after not doing any for years and years. I'm making a cardigan."

"And after television, what then?"

"I go to bed. What do you expect me to do?"

"Oh well, you might read a book, for instance."

"Yes, I do read, in order to put myself to sleep. At the moment I'm reading quite an interesting novel."

"Who's the author?"

"I don't remember who the author is, it's an American novel. About life in a small provincial town."

"What's its title?" I saw an expression of uncertainty come over her face, and hastily added: "I was forgetting, never in your life have you remembered either the name of the author or the title of the books you read. Isn't that so?"

I had spoken in a tone of voice which was perhaps almost affectionate; anyhow, the fact of my having remembered something connected with her seemed to give her pleasure. She gave a modest laugh. "That's not true," she said. "But really, how can one be expected to remember some of these names? Besides, what matters to me is to pass the time, more than anything else. One author or another, it's all the same to me."

"Exactly. Do you still take camomile before you go to sleep?"

"How did you come to remember that? Yes, I do."

"Do they bring it up to your room? Do they put it on the bedside table?"

"That's right, on the bedside table."

I fell silent, with a sense of satiety, of futility. I might, I reflected, go on questioning my mother for hours and still not come to a conclusion about anything: her life, and she herself, had by now attained a degree of utter meaninglessness which amounted, in the long run, to a sort of mystery at the same time both dull and impenetrable. My mother asked: "Is the cross-examination over, then? Or do you want to know what dreams I have while I am asleep?"

"I'm satisfied."

There was silence again. Then my mother unexpectedly said: "Your mother is a woman who lives alone and who has no one but you and is happy that you are coming back to live with her."

I realized, from the fact that she spoke of herself in the third person, that she was moved. I thought of saying something affectionate, but I couldn't find anything to say. Luckily Rita, at that moment, handed me a dish containing a very elaborate pudding which I pretended to admire. "What a wonderful pudding!" I said.

"It used to be your favorite."

I helped myself and was aware that Rita held back a small distance from the table. I did not know whether she was doing this from aversion or from that special kind of coquettishness which simulates aversion. My mother, who had not touched the pudding, gazed at me fixedly and implacably the whole time I was eating it. Finally she made a sign to Rita which I did not understand. The girl went out and a moment later re-

45

appeared with a bucket in which was plunged a bottle of champagne.

"Now let us drink a glass of champagne to your health."

I watched Rita as, with movements which bore witness to a long-established habit, she drew the bottle from its bucket, undid the silver paper and, almost without any sound or gush of foam, pulled out the big cork. She poured champagne into our glasses and then hurried out of the room, as though she did not wish to disturb the festive rite with her presence.

There was I, then, champagne glass in hand, standing opposite my mother, who had also risen to her feet and was holding out her glass toward me. "Many happy returns of the day!" I exclaimed, not knowing what to say.

My mother started laughing. "It's I who ought to say that to you," she said. "You're forgetting that it's *your* birthday, not mine."

I could not help replying: "The real celebration is yours. I've given up painting, I'm coming back to live with you, and so—many happy returns of the day!" And I bent forward and clinked glasses with my mother, who, this time, pretended not to have heard what I said. Then, after drinking, she placed her glass on the table and said: "It's not cold enough."

"Why? It seems to me very good."

"Yes, but it hasn't been long enough on the ice."

She took up her glass again and emptied it completely. Then she pressed a bell on the table. Rita reappeared. My mother made the same remark to her about the champagne not being cold enough, without receiving or, apparently, expecting, any reply. Then she added that we would have our coffee in the study. Luncheon was over.

We left the dining room and went into the study, a not very large room occupying a corner of the ground floor. I had never willingly gone into the study, in fact I avoided entering it because it was a kind of temple of a religion which certainly was not mine. Indeed in this room my mother, seated in a big, leather, gilt-studded chair in front of a large baroque table of carved oak, and against a background of bookshelves in which there were few books but many rows of files, devoted herself, either alone or in company with her men of business, to the ritual, so deeply moving to her, of the management of her affairs. That day, too, I followed her unwillingly: and, once we were in the study, I could not help asking her: "Why here? Couldn't we go into the drawing room?"

My mother appeared not to hear me. She installed herself behind the table, beckoning to me to sit down opposite her in the armchair usually reserved for those who came to talk to her on business. Then she fumbled in her bag, pulled out a key, drew back slightly, opened a drawer and took out a long, narrow ledger which struck me as looking like a book to be used in church, or anyhow connected in some way with religion. However, as I suddenly recollected, it was the ledger in which a list of all our property was kept, tidily and in order. My mother closed the drawer, put down the ledger on the table in front of her, looked intently at me for a moment with eyes glassier than ever, and then said: "A few minutes ago you asked me if we were rich, and I preferred not to answer because the maid was present. All the same, I'm glad you asked me that question. And now I'll give you all the information you wish—partly because," she added at this point in a reasonable tone of voice, "partly because I should very much like you to help me in the management of our affairs and to gain experience and take my place in a number of ways. As you've given up painting, you'll have plenty of time to do this."

I could not repress a shudder at these last words. How serenely, how complacently my mother had pronounced the phrase, "as you've given up painting"—without the least idea that, for me, it was equivalent to hearing someone say, "as you've given up living." With an effort, but this time without any spiteful intent, I asked: "Well then, are we rich or are we not?"

For a moment she sat silent, looking at me with a strange solemnity. Then, leaning toward me and lowering her voice, she said: "We are not rich, Dino, we are very rich. Thanks to your mother, you are a very rich man."

"What does 'very rich' mean?"

" 'Very rich' means something more than merely 'rich.' "

"But less than 'extremely rich' ?"

"Yes, less than 'extremely rich.' "

My mother this time answered me a little absent-mindedly. She had put on a pair of nunlike spectacles, rimless and with gold arms, and was turning over the pages of her black ledger: "Anyhow," she said, "there's nothing better than figures to make you understand, and so . . . and so . . . where is it? . . . ah, here we are . . . to make you understand, as I was saying, what being very rich means."

I realized that she was on the point of providing me with the statement she had promised me, and all at once I was filled with an uncontrollable repugnance. "No, no, please," I exclaimed eagerly, "I don't in the least want to know what being very rich means. I'll take your word for it."

My mother raised her eyes from the ledger, took off her spectacles and looked at me. "But you've got to know," she said, "if only, as I said before, so that you can help me with the management of our property."

I was on the point of crying out violently: "But I don't want to help you with the management," when fortunately Rita came in with the coffee tray. My mother, at the sight of her, seemed to retreat into herself, like a priest at the approach of an unbeliever. She closed the ledger with a sharp snap and said: "You pour the coffee, Rita." Then, while Rita, standing beside me, was pouring the coffee, I kept wondering how I could possibly escape this intolerable thing: the explanation of what it meant to be very rich. Rita was close to me again now and—whether on purpose or not, I did not understand—was lightly touching my knees with her leg. Then she turned toward me and held out my cup. Almost instinctively I jerked my arm. The cup upset in the saucer and the coffee slopped on my light-colored trousers so that I felt it warm and wet on my skin. Pretending to be alarmed, I exclaimed: "Oh hell, my trousers!"

"Rita, why can't you be more careful?" said my mother reprovingly, having neither seen nor understood anything of what had happened.

"Rita had nothing to do with it," I hastened to say, "it was my fault. But now my trousers are a mess."

"It's nothing," said Rita; "there was no sugar in it. I'll bring some water and wash out the stain."

This solution did not please my mother, who at once protested authoritatively, in her most unpleasant voice: "Not at all, stains can't be washed out of clothes when people are wearing them. Signor Dino must take off his trousers, then you can wash out the stain and iron the trousers."

I looked at Rita as she stood beside the table, her face set in an expression of obsequious patience. Then, in a serious voice, she asked: "Is Signor Dino going to take off his trousers at once, or am I to wait?"

"Coffee leaves a mark," said my mother; "better take them off at once, Dino."

"But I can't take them off here, in this room."

I noticed that Rita turned her head aside, perhaps to hide a smile. "Go upstairs then, to your own room," said my mother. "Take off your trousers and give them to Rita. Then put on the dressing gown which is in the cupboard and come down again. In the meantime I'll be getting ready some papers that I want to show you."

So we went out, Rita and I, she almost running in front of me and saying: "I'll go on ahead because that room has been shut up for a long time and at any rate I can open the windows," and I following her and reflecting, with some degree of astonishment, that everything was working out according to the unwritten but inflexible rules for situations of this particular type: the mother who herself provides the son with a pretext for retiring with the maid; the maid and the son going off to the bed upon which they will lie together, each pretending to the other to take seriously the pretext provided by the mother; the maid excited and obsequiously eager; the son also excited but at the same time humiliated by stooping so low. With these thoughts in my mind I reached the first floor and went to my room, whither Rita had preceded me. I found her leaning out of the window, opening the shutters; when she turned around, rather red in the face from the effort, and from running, and also, perhaps, from excitement, I said to her abruptly: "Wait outside a moment and I'll call you."

As soon as she had left the room I went slowly to the window and for a moment stood there, my back against the window-frame, gazing dreamily at the Italian garden which lay below. I am not given to remembering the past nor becoming emotional over places connected with the past, but that day I had decided to come back and live with my mother after an absence of ten years, and I could not help comparing my present state of mind with that of ten years earlier. And then, looking first at the fine Empire furniture in the room and then at the geometrical design of the Italian garden, all of which had remained exactly the same, I realized that I felt a sort of dismal relief at the idea that, fundamentally, I too was unchanged. No, I had not changed, and now I was coming back to live with my mother and I should resume the old habits of ten years ago; perhaps, gradually, I might even begin painting again, down there in the studio at the bottom of the garden, which had also remained unaltered. In fact it might even come about that, just as at one time going to live in Via Margutta had served, for a little, to renew my confidence in my work, so now, coming back to my mother's villa would inspire in me once again—even if only for a short time—the illusion offered me by painting: life, in essence, consisted merely in this continual change of position; it was like being in an un-comfortable bed in which it was impossible to sleep for long on one side. But when my eyes came to rest on the bed in-side the room and I saw that it had neither blankets nor sheets and that the mattress was rolled up, as is always done in uninhabited rooms, I became suddenly aware that the un-changing quality in things and in myself was not after all so positive as, for a moment, it had appeared to me. It was true that nothing had changed, but I was again going to find myself face to face with despair, with the same despair, also un-changed, that had formerly made me run away. Nothing was changed, but since time does not pass to no purpose, everything had become a little worse, even though remaining substan-tially unaffected. And so, while my mother was waiting for me downstairs in the study in order to explain to me, her papers ready in her hand, what it means to be rich, Rita was waiting outside the door for me to call her in and jump on her: two things apparently very remote from one another but in reality connected by a secret, rigorous mechanism. This mechanism was not unknown to me, indeed I had always sus-pected its existence; but I had never seen it with such clarity as I did now—just as you can look at the window display of an airline company and see a section of an airplane engine, with all its numerous and complicated parts. It was, in fact, the mechanism of despair, which, if I returned to live with my mother, would cause me to recoil from money into a state of impotence, from impotence to boredom and from boredom to Rita or to some other degradation of a similar or parallel kind. Better to go back to the studio in Via Margutta, where despair expressed itself, at least, in the empty canvas upon which I would never paint.

At this point in my thoughts I heard a discreet, but ob-viously impatient and confidential scratching at the door; and before I realized what I was doing I had undone my belt, slipped off my trousers, then thrown down the mattress and laid myself flat on the bed. Then I called to Rita to come in.

She came in immediately, assured herself by a quick glance that I was on the bed, and then turned to close the door. I lay with my whole body quite still, except in that place to which desire sent a surge of excited blood: I stared fixedly at my belly, my chin glued to my chest, just as a corpse lying on a catafalque seems to be staring at its own body after it is laid out and ready to be carried to the cemetery. Rita, meanwhile, had come forward and was standing close against the bed; she appeared to be contemplating me, through her hypocritical glasses, as one contemplates an object which one has never seen before and which is worth studying. Then I put out my hand and took hold of her hand which was hanging at her side and pulled it forward in the way one pulls at the bridle of an animal that is not so much recalcitrant as timid; and I felt her whole body following the direction of her hand. I guided her hand toward the center of my body, and as soon as I was sure that her hand had closed, I let go of it. She was now standing quite still, bending slightly forward, her arm stretched out over me, a lively red in her cheeks below the two dark circles of her glasses. Then she said in a slow, contented voice: "How disgusting!" and I was surprised because those were the words I would have used myself to express the mingled feeling of repugnance and excitement that I had at that moment.

I heaved a deep sigh and asked, finally, in a low voice and without looking at her: "Why did you come here?"

She said nothing; she seemed incapable of speaking.

"To take the stain out of my trousers? Well then, go and do it. What are you waiting for?"

I saw her give a start, as though I had hit her in the face. Reluctantly, she opened her fingers, one after the other, then she went out of my field of vision. I realized she had gone out of the room too, for I heard the sound of the door opening and shutting. As soon as I was sure she had gone, I jumped off the bed and went and opened the wardrobe. As I was hoping, beside the silk dressing gown which, according to my mother's advice, I ought to be putting on, there was hanging in a cellophane bag the only suit I had not taken away with me when I had gone to live in the studio—my dinner jacket and trousers. I took out the trousers and put them on. They fitted me pretty well, though perhaps a bit large in the waist; I had been fatter ten years ago, for my mother's food was richer and more nourishing than that of the modest restaurants I had been frequenting recently. I looked at myself in the glass; with my brown linen jacket and black trousers I had the appearance of an unemployed waiter. Very slowly I opened the door and, seeing that there was no one there, ran hurriedly downstairs and, avoiding the reception rooms, went along the passage into the hall and so out of the front door.

The two cars, the old and the new, were standing there side by side in front of the house. The cloudy sky, the trees, the villa were vaguely reflected in the clear glossiness of the new car; the old car, on the other hand, looked dull and dim—with the same kind of dullness, I could not help saying to myself, with which boredom usually veiled the world around me. I tore a page out of my pocket notebook and wrote on it: "Thank you, but I would rather keep my old car. Your most affectionate son, Dino." This I inserted under the windshield wiper, in the place where policemen put parking tickets. Then I got into my car, started the engine and went away.

Chapter 2

In the same building in Via Margutta in which I lived, an elderly painter called Balestrieri had a studio three doors beyond mine on the ground floor corridor. I used often to meet him and had exchanged a few words with him, but was not in the habit of visiting him; like all men who think of nothing but women, Balestrieri behaved with extreme, almost insulting coldness toward persons of his own sex, whatever might be their condition or age, evidently seeing them as just so many potential rivals. Balestrieri was a small man with very broad shoulders and very large feet—two disproportions which he took no trouble to conceal; in fact he drew attention to them by wearing enormous check sports jackets and old-fashioned pointed, patent-leather shoes. Balestrieri's face had in it a strong look of the carnival mask or the Pompeian satyr: the hair silvery white, the skin a hectic red, eyebrows black as coal, a prominent nose, a large mouth, a pointed chin. The expression of his face was slightly doll-like, and yet, underneath, there was a look of uneasiness. I had heard from one or two elderly painters who knew Balestrieri well that he was very erotic, and that he had begun painting in his youth solely in order to attract women to his studio, under the pretext of painting them. Afterward however, the habit of painting, so to speak, had remained with him—which for him meant, above all things, painting the female nude. Balestrieri, who was comfortably off, did not depend on his work for a living; he never exhibited and, in a way, painted for himself only; his friends told me that, so great was his affection for his pictures, on the rare occasions when he decided to give one of them away he used to make a copy and give it in place of the original. As for their quality, all his friends were agreed that he was an extremely bad painter. Once or twice, seized with curiosity, I tried to get a glimpse of Balestrieri's pictures from the courtyard, through his big window; and I caught sight of a few large, dark canvases upon which could be distinguished, with some difficulty, enormous female nudes with exaggerated forms, in attitudes far from natural.

Balestrieri's studio was continually visited by a large number of women. I could see them through my own big window as they crossed the courtyard and then disappeared into the door leading to the ground floor corridor. I knew it was Balestrieri they were going to see, because the other two studios were inhabited by two painters who lived in them with their families and who, in any case, did not make use of models because they painted abstract pictures. Balestrieri's women bore witness to a great variety of tastes: they were young and middle-aged, of the working and the upper class, young girls and married women, fair and dark, thin and fat, short and tall, and it became clear that Balestrieri, like all Don Juans of a not very refined type, did not go in for subtleties but was a collector of adventures concerned more with quantity than quality. It was very rarely that Balestrieri had what is called a relationship, that is, a lasting affair with any one woman; and even when he had, it did not interfere with other less important adventures. Especially during the first years that I lived in Via Margutta, Balestrieri's appearance and the life he led filled me with so much curiosity that I went so far as to spy upon him to some extent. I drew up statistics of the women who visited him: as many as five different women in a month, that is, one new woman every six days, and on an average two visits a day. When I saw Balestrieri for the first time, he was fifty-five; at the time the events I am writing about took place, he was sixty-five; yet during those ten years I never observed any change in his habits: I saw always the same number of women, more or less, as though time, for him, stood still.

Or rather, to be more precise, there was a change, but it showed itself, not in a diminution of feminine visits as one might have expected, but in an increase. Balestrieri's eroticism, which I compared often to a volcano in continuous but quiet activity, in fact went through a phase, when he was about sixty-three, which I can only describe as a paroxysm. The women who filed through the courtyard and knocked at the old painter's door appeared to be more numerous; furthermore, I noticed that they were now almost always very young girls; like all vicious men, Balestrieri, with the years, inclined toward adolescents. I spoke of a paroxysm in his love life; it would be more correct to say that it was a fixation, probably unconscious, upon one single type of woman to the exclusion of all others. Balestrieri, without realizing it, was at that time ceasing to be the Don Juan, the collector of adventures, that he had always been, and was for the first time devoting himself, or wishing to devote himself, to one woman only. The numerous girls, all more or less of the same age, were therefore nothing more than progressive experiments in a type which, little by little, was becoming precisely defined; tentative approaches toward an ideal figure which, some day, would become flesh and blood. And indeed, all of a sudden the flow of adolescent girls to Balestrieri's studio ceased, giving place to a single feminine visitor for whom, evidently, they had prepared the way and who, in herself, summarized them all.

I was able to observe her with some attention, if only because I became aware, almost at once, that she was observing me. Dressed always like a little ballet-dancer according to the fashion of the moment, in a light puffy blouse and a very short, wide skirt that appeared to be supported by a crinoline, she looked rather like an inverted flower with a crooked, oscillating corolla, walking about on its pistils. She had a round face like a child; but it was a child that had grown too hastily and been initiated too soon into the experiences of womanhood. She was pale, with a slight shadow underneath her cheekbones which made her cheeks look hollow, and a mass of thick, brown, curly hair all around her face. Her small mouth, childish both in shape and expression, reminded one of a bud that had withered prematurely on the bough without opening, and its corners were marked by two thin furrows, which struck me particularly because of the feeling of intense aridity which they suggested. Finally her eyes, her best feature, were large and dark, and they too were childish in shape beneath a rather prominent forehead. Their glance, indefinably remote, indirect, unsteady, was lacking in innocence.

Unlike Balestrieri's other women, who walked straight and with bent heads to the old painter's studio, this one crossed the courtyard with what appeared to be a studied slowness, letting herself be drawn along, so it seemed, by the indolent, meditative movement of her hips. She looked not so much as though she were going unwillingly to see Balestrieri, but as though while on her way she were searching for something else that she herself could not have defined. And almost always, as she crossed the courtyard, she would look up toward my studio, and if—as often happened, since I had my easel close to the window—I were visible, she would never fail to accompany her look with a smile. For some time I was uncertain about this smile, which was so slight as to make me doubt whether it was intentional. But later, when I happened to meet her at closer quarters in the corridor, I was forced to the conviction that the smile was for me and that a very precise meaning was attached to it.

This mute invitation on her part inspired in me an obscure feeling of aversion which I will try to explain. In the first place, I am not given to such adventures, especially if the adventure is suggested and almost imposed upon me by the woman; in fact the very persistence of the smile aroused in me an almost spiteful impulse not to return it and to pretend not to have noticed it. In the second place, the girl did not attract me: I had never made love to any but mature women, and this girl, who could not have been more than seventeen, looked less than fifteen, owing to the slenderness of her figure and the childishness of her face. Finally, there was a third reason, a more valid one even if less clear and easy to define, and that was the feeling of nausea that assailed me every time I imagined myself approaching her, speaking to her, and—inevitable consequence—making love to her. This feeling of nausea was not inspired by a direct physical repugnance: the girl did not attract me, it is true, but she was not actually repugnant to me; rather it came from my imaginative picture of the experience in which I should be involved by accepting her invitation. It was, I reflected, the same feeling of nausea that probably everyone experiences when on the threshold of some unknown, vague reality; or perhaps, more simply, of reality unadulterated, if one has become accustomed, over a long period, to not facing it. It was a feeling of disgust mingled with apprehension; and it astonished me because the girl, childish and insignificant as she was, did not seem to justify it in any way.

But when one is bored it is not easy to give continuous thought to anything. Boredom, for me, was like a kind of fog in which my thought was constantly losing its way, catching glimpses only at intervals of some detail of reality: like a person in a thick mist who catches a glimpse now of the corner of a house, now of the figure of a passer-by, now of some other object, but only for an instant, before they vanish. In the fog of boredom I had caught a glimpse of the girl and of Balestrieri, but without attaching any importance to them and with my attention being constantly drawn away from them. And so it happened that for weeks I forgot the existence of these two, who were living and making love only a few steps away from me. Now and then I would remember them, almost with astonishment, and say to myself: "Why, they're still there, they're still making love together!" I forgot Balestrieri to such an extent that, the morning after my flight from my mother's villa, coming back to my studio after having a cup of coffee near by, and noticing in Via Margutta, right in front of my door, a black and gilt hearse with the usual gilt angels at the four corners and the usual black horses in the shafts, but still empty and without any flowers, I never imagined that it might be waiting there for someone I knew. I went around the hearse, which was blocking the way, and into the entrance hall, and since I was walking, as I habitually do, with my eyes on the ground, I ran straight into the coffin, which four men were at that moment carrying out on their shoulders, bumping my forehead against its lower edge. I immediately jumped back, while the four bearers glared at me reprovingly, then the coffin passed close to me, followed by only two persons; a brutal-faced, pock-marked young man in a blue cloth suit and a woman with her arm in his, of whom I could see nothing as she was smothered in black veils from head to foot. The young man made me think of Balestrieri, possibly because he too had a rather red face and very black eyebrows; at the same moment I heard the caretaker of the building murmuring some comment on how sudden some deaths can be, coupled with the name of the old painter. And so I learned that Balestrieri had died, probably the previous day, that this was his funeral and that the woman in mourning was the wife from whom he had been separated for many years and the young man in the blue suit the son whom he had had by her.

As I have already said, my mind at that time had been distracted by boredom to such a degree that I had forgotten the existence not only of Balestrieri but also of the girl. Therefore it was without surprise that I realized I had been in my studio during the last two days without knowing that, three doors further on, Balestrieri had been taken ill, had died, had been watched over through the night, had been placed in his coffin, had been carried away. Heaven knows, I thought, someone may have spoken to me of Balestrieri's illness, and I, while hearing, had not listened, lost in boredom as I was; just as it sometimes happened that I read carefully the headlines in the newspapers and discovered a moment later that I had no idea of what they said. It had required the coffin, or rather the painful blow from the coffin on my forehead, to make me remember the painter's existence, at the same moment when I became aware of his death.

Balestrieri's death, moreover, had not been so simple a matter as might appear at first sight. That same day, partly through the shocked allusions of the caretaker, partly through the more explicit comments of a group of friends whom I met at the café, I was able to reconstruct the old painter's end. It seemed that Balestrieri had died at a very special moment, that is, while he was in the act of making love with the girl who had so often smiled at me. Furthermore, this love-making had not been of a normal kind—meaning by "normal" the act which leads to procreation—but rather a distortion of it, an erotic speciality, so that Balestrieri had been killed not by love-making but by the manner in which he had done it. The caretaker refused to be explicit, she merely alluded to the matter with indignation; my friends at the café, on the other hand, had been cheerfully liberal with details, as though they had been present in Balestrieri's studio at the moment of his death; but, as I finally managed to establish, this was all a question of supposition. In reality Balestrieri had felt sick and had died under the frightened eyes of the girl; that was all that was known for certain. The fact that the girl was his mistress, that he had been found half-naked on the bed, and that the girl herself had run out and called the caretaker, wearing a dressing gown with nothing underneath—all this seemed to confirm the gossip about a sudden death which had taken place at the moment of pleasure. But those who were unwilling to believe this pointed out that the girl was in a dressing gown because she was a model and was sitting to Balestrieri, and that the latter, in the summer, always used to work in a sleeveless vest and a pair of swimming trunks. On the other hand, in support of the "love-death" gossip, there was the reported statement of the doctor who had been summoned to the death bed: "If this man had realized that there are certain things that cannot be done at his age, he would still be alive." Others, however, maintained that, after examining Balestrieri, all the doctor had said to the girl was: "Signorina, you killed him," adding immediately afterwards: "Or rather, you helped him to kill himself." But no one knew who this doctor was nor where he was to be found; he might have been called in through one of the numerous drugstores in the neighborhood; nor did I trouble to track him down.

That same day, after having lunch in a little restaurant in Via Margutta, I went back to my studio and found a parcel with a note from my mother. In her note, my mother gave me a lesson in good manners: "Another time, instead of running away like that, do at least come and say good-bye to me." In the parcel were my dinner jacket and the light trousers which the good Rita had cleaned and ironed. I threw the whole lot onto the floor, lay down on the divan and lit a cigarette. I was suffering as usual from a cruel sense of boredom, and it seemed odd to me that other people did not notice my boredom—they did not realize that, for me, they and the whole world did not really exist. It seemed odd that, like my mother, they should continue to behave toward me as though I were not bored. As I lay there smoking, I gradually began to reflect upon my situation, which was obviously going from bad to worse every day; and finally I asked myself what there was left for me to do, now that I had given up painting and had nevertheless not had the courage to accept my mother's money. I realized that there was little to be done, in the sense of any action that would introduce some really substantial change; but that I could always do what many people do when they find themselves in an unendurable situation: accept it and adapt myself to it. Fundamentally, I thought, I was like some scion of a noble but decayed family who obstinately tries to go on living on the same sumptuous scale as his ancestors. The day he accepts a situation which hitherto has seemed to him unendurable, and which, on the other hand, is the normal situation of an immense number of people, he ceases to suffer and realizes that everything which seemed intolerable at one level is no longer so at a lower level. In reality, what made me suffer was not so much boredom itself as the idea that I could, and should, *not* be bored. I also belonged to a noble and very ancient family which had never been bored, which had always had a direct and concrete relationship with reality. I had to forget this family and to accept, once and for all, the position in which I found myself. But could one live in a state of boredom, could one live without any relationship with anything real, and not suffer from it? Here was the whole problem.

As I meditated thus I became drowsy and fell heavily asleep, with a sensation of drowning rather than sleeping. I had a very vivid dream: I seemed to be standing in front of my easel, my palette in one hand and a brush in the other. On the easel stood the usual empty canvas, and beside the easel—a curious thing, because it was several years since I had done any figure painting—stood a model. She was a young woman with a sage, bespectacled face very reminiscent of Rita's, and with a curiously flat, unsubstantial body against whose bloodless whiteness the twin dark spots on the breast, like big, dark coins, and the black pubic triangle, stood out startlingly, like those of a corpse. I was, supposedly, painting the model; and indeed my hand, armed with a brush, was moving and evidently painting on the invisible surface of the canvas. I went on painting with care, with concentration, with assurance; the picture was going well, the model did not breathe or move and would have seemed to be really dead if it had not been for the gleam of her spectacles and the faintly ironical smile that curled her lips. Finally, after a very long sitting, the picture was finished and I moved back a step or two so as to contemplate it at leisure. To my amazement, the canvas was empty, blank, clean; no female nude was visible upon it, either drawn or painted; I had certainly been working but I had done nothing. Frightened, I seized the first tube of color that came to hand, squeezed out a jet of paint on to the palette, dipped the brush in it and frantically flung myself upon the canvas again. Nothing: the canvas remained blank and meanwhile the girl was smiling more and more mockingly at my vain efforts, all the time retaining the sage, hypocritical expression imparted by her big tortoise-shell glasses. Then a hand was placed on my shoulder; Balestrieri— Balestrieri and none other—a fatherly smile upon his red face, took the brush and palette from me and planted himself in front of the canvas, turning his back toward me. He was wearing a sleeveless vest, and a pair of swimming trunks, and his get-up reminded me of Picasso, to whom I suddenly found he bore some resemblance. Now Balestrieri was painting and I was looking at the back of Balestrieri's neck over which fell his thick, silvery hair and I was thinking that Balestrieri was painting whereas I had not succeeded in doing so. Then Balestrieri's picture was finished; Balestrieri had gone; and I was standing in front of the picture. I did not know if it was good or bad, but anyhow it had been painted; the canvas was no longer blank and empty as it had been when I myself had finished painting, it was covered with marks and colors. Suddenly I was seized with an overwhelming rage; I snatched up the small knife that I always use for scraping colors and struck at the canvas violently and methodically, from the top to the bottom, in such a way as to cut it down its whole length. But I found to my horror that it was not the canvas I had been striking but the model; she was now bleeding from a large number of thin, vertical wounds, starting from the breast and going right down to the legs. Blood, red and abundant, was gushing from the wounds, secondary streams of it were forming and joining together, and now the entire body of the girl—who nevertheless went on smiling—was covered with a network of blood, while I still went on striking, violently, methodically; until finally, with an inarticulate cry of distress, I awoke.

It was a cloudy day and the studio was filled with a subdued, grey, melancholy light. I jumped off the divan and, acting as though I knew what I was doing, rushed to the door, opened it and went out into the corridor. It was empty and the four doors were closed, but as I looked more carefully I noticed that the door of Balestrieri's studio was ajar. Without thinking, and still acting in an almost mechanical way, I went to this door, pushed it and walked in.

I had never before penetrated into the old painter's studio; so I was now able to imagine that it was merely curiosity which brought me there. The curtains were drawn and the studio was almost in darkness; a lamp with a red shade, on a carved and gilded wooden stand—a piece of church furniture, probably—stood burning on a table covered with purple damask. In the blood-red light from this lamp I was able to see that Balestrieri's studio was very different from mine. In the first place it was larger, with a staircase leading to a wooden gallery on to which two small doors opened. Furthermore, my studio had the look of a real painter's studio, sparsely furnished and very untidy, but Balestrieri's, I noticed with a vague feeling of repugnance, was furnished and decorated like an old-fashioned middle-class drawing room of forty or fifty years ago; nobody could have imagined that a painter had lived there, had it not been for the famous nudes hanging close together on the walls from floor to ceiling, and for a monumental easel placed in a good light near the big window, with an unfinished canvas upon it. I was struck particularly by the gloominess of the furniture, most of it antique or sham antique, in the Renaissance style. The walls behind the pictures were hung with red damask; on the floor, in confusion and one on top of another, were Persian carpets of dark, close design. I closed the door behind me and then, looking about me and sniffing in the curious smell that hung in the air, a mingled smell of death chamber and domestic interior, I walked slowly across to the easel. The unfinished picture could only be the one that Balestrieri, just before his death, had been painting of his youthful mistress; and I was seized with curiosity to see what her figure was like. But when I stood in front of the canvas I had a feeling of incredulity and disappointment. Balestrieri had made a charcoal sketch of a figure which I found very difficult to connect with the slender body and childish face of the young girl who had so often smiled at me. It was one of his usual exaggerated nudes, portrayed, into the bargain, in a strained attitude, squatting down on folded legs but with hands clasped behind the back of the neck in such a way as to give the greatest prominence to the breast and hips, two parts of the female body for which Balestrieri seemed to have a special partiality. I was particularly struck by the amplitude of the loins and the heaviness of the breast which I did not remember having noticed in the model. The slim waist, on the other hand, and the slender shoulders and arms might well have been hers. It was significant that Balestrieri had forgotten, or not troubled, to draw the face, so that any identification, for me at any rate, was impossible.

I looked for a long time at the canvas, reflecting that Balestrieri was really an extremely bad painter, even according to the remote naturalistic tradition to which, in a vague way, he was related; then I turned back into the studio and started to examine the pictures hanging on the walls. They were all nudes, all female nudes, most of them posed in unnatural, strained attitudes; and the first thought that occurred to me was that Balestrieri, although he was an extremely bad painter, was nevertheless a very careful painter, accurate, in fact, to the point of pedantry. It was obvious that he did not rely on inspiration and worked rather in the manner of the old masters, by means of successive glazes, coming back again and again to certain details until he was completely certain that he had exhausted all their possibilities. The result, alas, was that special sort of naturalism, photographic, labored and too highly finished, that you can see in the paintings shown in so-called art exhibitions at very commercial galleries. These pictures were perfect of their kind, with the hideous perfection that belongs essentially to pornography. In other words, Balestrieri's world was a concrete, coherent world without any cracks or pollutions in it, and little did it matter if it gave the impression of madness. Balestrieri himself had been perfectly happy in this world, right up to the moment of his death, without ever doubting it or trying to get out of it. Perhaps he had indeed been a sort of madman, but he was a madman whose madness consisted in an illusion of having a relationship with reality, that is, of being a wise man, as his paintings bore witness; whereas I—as I could not help saying to myself—was possibly a wise man whose wisdom consisted, on the contrary, in a profound conviction that such a relationship was impossible, that is, a wise man who believed himself mad.

As these thoughts were passing through my mind I had been going all around the walls, looking at the canvases one by one and not finding any in which it was possible to recognize the features of the girl with the childish face. I said to myself that it must have been like that: Balestrieri had never painted his little mistress, he had been content merely to make love to her; exactly the opposite of what might have been expected in view of his advanced age. I was on the point of going away when a sound from above made me raise my eyes. Balestrieri's girl came out of one of the small doorways leading on to the balcony and started down the stairs, in a leisurely manner and evidently unconscious of my presence; her eyes were cast down, she had one hand on the banister and the other up to her chest, supporting a large bundle.

When she reached the foot of the stairs she raised her eyes and seemed to be frightened at seeing me standing there in front of her, beside the table in the middle of the studio. But only for an instant; immediately afterward a look of relief and calm spread over her round face, as though the encounter were no surprise to her and she had in fact been prepared for it for some time. I said, in embarrassment: "I live in a studio close by; perhaps you may have seen me sometimes. I came in to have a look at the pictures."

Indicating her bundle, she answered: "And I came to get my belongings, before the studio is let. I was his model; he had given me a key, so I was able to get in."

I noticed her speech was completely devoid of any kind of accent that might make it possible to guess where she had been born or the social class to which she belonged. Her voice was colorless and neutral, with a preciseness and economy of tone that suggested a certain reserve. Not knowing how to go on, I asked casually: "Did you come and see Balestrieri often?"

"Yes, almost every day."

"But when did he die?"

"The evening of the day before yesterday."

"Were you there when he died?"

She looked at me for a moment with her big dark eyes that seemed not so much to observe things as to reflect them without seeing them. "He was taken sick while I was sitting for him," she said.

"He was painting you?"

67

"Yes."

I could not help exclaiming in surprise: "But where's the canvas on which he was painting you?"

"That's the one," she said, pointing to the easel.

I turned, glanced quickly at the canvas and then, more lingeringly, at her. In the half-darkness that seemed to dissolve and absorb her contours, her figure appeared more than ever slender and childish, with the wide skirt hanging over the thin legs, the narrow torso and the pale face swallowed up by the great dark eyes. I asked incredulously: "Was it really you who sat for that picture?"

She, in turn, appeared astonished at my astonishment. "Yes," she said. "Why? Don't you like the way he's painted me?"

"I don't know whether I do or not, but it's certainly not like you."

"He hasn't drawn in my head because he always did that last. So how d'you know it isn't like me?"

"What I mean is that the figure drawn by Balestrieri doesn't look like yours."

"You don't think so? And yet it *is* mine."

I was aware of the utter futility and falseness of this pseudo-artistic discussion, over a picture of such a kind and on a question of resemblance, into the bargain. But even though I felt ashamed, just as if there had been a tacit collusion which I ought to reject, I could not refrain from answering in a lively fashion: "It's not possible, I can't believe it!"

"You don't think so?" she said again. "And yet my figure *is* like that." She put down her bundle on the table, went to the easel, contemplated the canvas for a moment, and then turned and went on: "Perhaps there's a little exaggeration, but on the whole I'm just like that."

For some reason, as I saw her standing beside the picture, I recalled my dream of that afternoon. I asked casually: "Is that the only picture Balestrieri did of you, or did he do others as well?"

"Oh, he painted me over and over again." She looked up at the walls and began counting, pointing as she went: "That's me, and that too, and that one up there, and that one there too." She added conclusively: "He was always painting me. He kept me posing for hours."

I was conscious of an obscure impulse to say something nasty about Balestrieri, perhaps in order to force her into a more personal, a more confidential key. I said unkindly: "A great deal of effort for a very poor result."

"Why?"

"Because Balestrieri was an extremely bad painter, in fact he wasn't a painter at all."

She did not react in any way; she merely said: "I don't know anything about painting."

I persisted. "Actually Balestrieri was simply a man who liked women very much."

She agreed, with conviction. "Oh yes, there you're right."

She had now taken up her bundle again and was looking at me with a questioning air, as much as to say: "Am I to go now—why don't you do something to stop me?" With a sudden gentleness of tone, which surprised me because I had neither intended it nor foreseen it, I suggested: "Won't you come to my studio for a moment?"

Her face lit up with a prompt, naïve hopefulness. "D'you want me to sit for you?" she asked.

I felt embarrassed. I had had no intention of lying to her, and now here she was suggesting an artifice which was doubly humiliating to me, partly because it was an artifice, partly because it was the last artifice I should have had recourse to—that of the painter who invites a pretty girl to his studio under the pretext of wanting to paint her; in a word, an artifice worthy of Balestrieri. I asked, rather scornfully: "Did Balestrieri invite you to his studio the first time under the pretext of painting you?"

"No," she replied seriously. "No, I went to him to take

drawing lessons. Then he wanted to paint me, but that was later."

For her, then, the painting artifice was not an artifice at all but a serious thing. She went on: "I've nothing to do now. If you like, I could sit for you until dinner time."

I wondered whether I ought to explain to her that I was a painter who had given up painting; and that furthermore, during the time when I was painting, I had never painted figure studies. But in that case, I reflected, I should perhaps have to look for another excuse for inviting her to my studio, since it appeared that she required an excuse of some kind. One might as well accept the excuse of wanting to paint her. So I said, in a light, vague sort of manner: "Very well, let's go to my studio."

"I used always to sit for Balestrieri at this time of day," she told me, relieved and contented, taking up her bundle from the table. "He painted every day from four till seven."

"And in the morning too?"

"Yes, in the morning too, from ten till one."

Meanwhile we had moved toward the door. I was aware that she was seeing, for the last time, the studio in which she had spent so large a part of her life, and I was expecting that, if only out of pity for the old painter who had loved her so much, she would say something or at least look back as she went out. But she merely asked me, with a glance at the walls: "Now that he's dead, what will happen to the pictures?"

I answered, again unkindly: "Why, I should think they'll try and sell them. And then, when they see that no one wants them, they'll put them away in some cellar or other."

"In a cellar?"

"Yes, they'll throw them away."

"He had a wife from whom he was separated. The pictures will go to her."

"All the more reason for her to throw them away."

Indifferent, reserved, she said nothing. Now she was walking in front of me along the corridor, and seen thus, from behind, carrying the big bundle in her arms and moving in that characteristic way which appeared so spontaneous and reluctant whereas it was really so strongly and sensually deliberate, she gave the impression of a mere house-moving. Yes, she was moving from Balestrieri's studio to mine—that was all. I caught up with her, opened my door for her and said: "As you can see, this is a very different studio from Balestrieri's."

She did not reply, just as though she found no great difference between my studio and that of her old lover. She simply went to the table, put down her bundle on it and then turned and asked: "Where is the bathroom?"

"There, that door over there."

She went over to the bathroom and disappeared. I went over to the divan and rearranged the cushions upon which I had slept that afternoon; then I started collecting the numerous cigarette butts I had thrown on to the floor after smoking them. While I was doing these things I thought about the girl, wondering whether she attracted me and whether I wanted to do what she expected me to do, and I realized that I had no desire at all. In the end I said to myself that I would question her further about Balestrieri and her relations with him, about which I felt some curiosity, and that I would then send her away.

I was so calm and so deeply absorbed in the consciousness of my calmness that I forgot the pretext of painting which the girl had suggested and which I had absent-mindedly accepted. I was startled when the door of the bathroom opened and the girl appeared on the threshold. She was naked, completely naked; she was holding a large towel with both hands against her chest and walking on tiptoe. I realized that Balestrieri had not exaggerated when he depicted her with the well-developed form which had aroused my incredulity. She had in fact a magnificent bosom, full, firm and brown, which did not, however, seem in harmony with her torso—the slender,

71

thin torso of an adolescent girl—and had almost a look of
being detached from it. Her waist also was that of a young
girl, incredibly slim and supple; but the adult quality noticeable in her bosom was again apparent in her powerful, solid
hips. As she walked she thrust forward her bosom and pulled
back her belly, and her eyes were fixed almost greedily upon
the easel that stood near the window; and when she arrived
in front of the canvas she asked, without turning around, in
her strangely expressionless, dry, precise voice: "Well, where
shall I stand?"

I wondered whether there might be some hypocrisy in her
attitude at that moment, and immediately had to admit that
there was not. She had taken her position as a model quite
seriously; even if she also perhaps suspected that it was only
a pretext for a different sort of relationship. But in her mind,
so it seemed to me, there must be a kind of incapacity to connect one thing with another; it was this that permitted her to
be sincere. Quietly I said: "Don't stand anywhere."

She turned around in surprise. "Why?" she asked.

"I'm sorry," I explained, "but I accepted the excuse of painting you rather lightly. Actually I gave up painting some time
ago. And when I did paint, I never painted models or any
other object. I'm sorry."

Without showing any offense, she said in a tone of indifference: "But you told me you wanted me to come and sit for
you."

"Yes, that's true, but forget it."

Slowly, and with an air of attaching no importance to what
she was doing, she took the towel which she had been holding
against her breast and threw it over her shoulders, finally
wrapping it around her body. Then she came over to the divan,
a timid, diffident look on her face, as though I had asked her
to sit down upon it, whereas in reality I had said nothing,
and placed herself at the extreme end of it, away from me.
There was a moment's silence; then, all at once, on her childish

lips appeared the same smile that she used to bestow upon me when she met me in the corridor. Feeling embarrassed, I said: "Now you'll think badly of me."

She shook her head in denial, without speaking. She was gazing at me with her characteristically expressionless look; it was as if her eyes were two dark mirrors which reflected the outside world without understanding it and perhaps without even seeing it; and I felt my embarrassment increasing. It was clear that she did not intend to go away and that she was expecting me to start the second part, so to speak, of the program. As I searched my mind for a common subject of conversation, Balestrieri, naturally, occurred to me. "How long had you known Balestrieri?" I inquired.

"Two years."

"How old are you?"

"I'm seventeen."

"Tell me how you first met Balestrieri."

"Why?"

"Because—" I thought about it for a moment, and then went on, speaking quite sincerely "—it interests me."

"I met Balestrieri two years ago," she said slowly. "In the house of a friend of mine."

"Who was this friend of yours?"

"A girl called Elisa."

"How old is Elisa?"

"Two years older than me."

"What was Balestrieri doing at Elisa's house?"

"He was giving her drawing lessons, as he did to me."

"What does Elisa look like?"

"She's fair," she replied briefly.

I thought I could remember one of the many girls whom I had seen passing across the courtyard. "Fair, with blue eyes," I asked, "with a long neck, and an oval face and tight, full lips?"

"Yes, that's her. Do you know her?"

"No, but I've seen her going to Balestrieri's studio a few times, a little before you started going there. Did Elisa have her drawing lessons at home or at the studio?"

"At home, and at the studio too; it depended on the days."

"You haven't told me what happened that day when you met Balestrieri at Elisa's home."

"Nothing happened."

"I see, nothing happened. But then, in the end, Balestrieri gave drawing lessons to you as well. How did that come about?"

This time she looked at me and said nothing. "Did you hear what I said?" I persisted.

Finally she made up her mind to break her silence. "Why do you want to know these things?" she asked.

"Suppose I'm interested in you," I said, with the consciousness not so much of lying as of telling a lie which, in the very moment in which I told it, became truth.

She looked up in the air, like a school girl on the point of reciting a lesson before an exacting master, and then said: "I saw Balestrieri again at Elisa's because she and I were friends and I used to go there often. One day I asked him to give me drawing lessons too, but he said he couldn't."

I had always thought that Balestrieri ran after all the women he happened to come across; and now, here he was refusing the pretext which the girl offered him. "Why do you think Balestrieri refused?" I asked.

"I don't know, he didn't want to."

"Perhaps he was in love with Elisa?"

"I don't think so."

"Then why didn't he want to?"

Uncompromisingly she replied: "At first I thought it was Elisa who had persuaded him; then I found out that Elisa knew nothing about it. He didn't want to, that was all. I thought he was annoyed at the idea of my coming to the studio and I suggested he should give me the lessons at my home, but he refused again. In fact, he didn't want to."

"But you, why were you so anxious for Balestrieri to give you lessons?"

She hesitated, and then I saw her pale face grow red, in an uneven way, in light patches that succeeded one another. "I had fallen in love with him," she said. "Or rather, I thought I had."

"And he paid no attention to you? But why?"

"I don't know." She hesitated again, then, as though she had succeeded in finally overcoming her last remnant of waywardness, she broke into a kind of loquacity which, though still precise and economical, had in it less reserve than her former manner. "I suppose I didn't attract him, and that was all there was to it. We went on in that way for two or three months, and by then he was positively avoiding me and it made me unhappy. At that time I was really in love with him. In the end I resorted to a trick."

"A trick?"

"Yes. One day when Elisa was due to go to his studio and I knew about it, I asked Elisa to lunch and told her he had telephoned to tell her not to come after all because he was busy, and I went myself instead."

"How did Balestrieri take your trick?"

"At first he wanted to send me away. Later on he became kinder."

"You and he made love that day, did you?"

Again she blushed, in the same gradual, uneven way, and nodded her head in assent, without speaking.

"How about Elisa?"

"Elisa never knew that I had gone in her place. But she and Balestrieri parted shortly afterward."

"Are you still friends with Elisa?"

"No, we never see each other now."

Silence followed. I realized that I was cross-examining her

almost like a policeman, and that she seemed to submit to my examination quite willingly; I asked myself what it was that I really wanted to know. Clearly it was not so much the facts that interested me as something that lay beyond them and constituted their background and their justification. But what was this something? I asked bluntly: "Why did you fall in love with Balestrieri?"

"What d'you mean?"

"What I mean is—why with Balestrieri, a man old enough to have been your father's father?"

"There's no *reason* for falling in love with someone. You just fall in love and that's that."

"There are always reasons, for everything."

She looked at me and she seemed now to be closer to me on the divan. Or was this possibly an optical illusion due to the cross-examination which was making her gradually better known and more recognizable to me? At last, leaning slightly forward and gazing straight at me, she said faintly: "I felt very strongly attracted to him."

"What kind of attraction was it?"

She said nothing, but merely looked at me. "Well?" I insisted.

"Oh well; I'll tell you. Balestrieri was a little like my father, and when I was younger I had a real passion for my father."

"A passion?"

"Yes, I used to dream about him at night."

"So you fell in love with Balestrieri because he was a little like your father?"

"Yes, that was part of the reason."

There was silence again, and then I went on: "Why do you think Balestrieri refused to have anything to do with you at the beginning?"

"I've already told you: I didn't attract him."

"To say that you didn't attract him doesn't explain anything. There are so many reasons why a person may not be attractive."

"That may be so. But I don't know what they are."

"But you might guess them. Do you think Balestrieri refused to have anything to do with you because you were too young?"

"No, not that."

"Or because he had the same feeling about you that you had about him—I mean that he looked upon you rather like a daughter?"

"I don't think so. Otherwise he would have told me."

I paused a moment, engrossed in thought. It had now become clear to me that I was questioning the girl about Balestrieri in order to find out something about myself: I too, in fact, had so far repelled her advances, and with me too she appeared to have fallen in love. "Or don't you think, perhaps," I said, "that Balestrieri was afraid of getting to know you?"

"Afraid, why afraid?"

"Afraid because he foresaw what did in fact happen afterwards: that he would fall in love with you. Love does sometimes frighten people."

"It doesn't frighten me," she said mysteriously.

"You haven't answered my question," I insisted. "Did Balestrieri avoid you because he was afraid?"

"No, he wasn't afraid. In fact I remember now that he once said to me: 'If you hadn't played that trick on me, I should never have paid any attention to you, you didn't attract me.'" She was silent a moment, and then went on: "That's all there is to it, I don't know anything more."

I saw I should make no further headway in that direction, so I abruptly changed my line of approach. "But afterwards," I said, "afterwards he fell in love with you, didn't he?"

"Yes."

"Very much so?"

"Yes, very much."

"Why?"

She bent forward and looked at me. She was quite close to me now. It was no longer a question of an optical illusion; her knees were touching mine.

"I don't know," she said.

"But didn't he talk about his love for you?"

"Yes, he talked about it."

"And what did he say?"

She seemed to be reflecting, and I noticed her drooping over toward me, as if she were going to fall on top of me. Or rather, owing perhaps to the kind of sheath-like wrapping formed by the towel around her body, she seemed like a vessel full of some liquid or other tilting further and further toward me, as though to make it possible for me to drink from it. Finally she answered: "I don't remember what he said. I remember what he did."

"What did he do?"

"He used to cry, for instance."

"To cry?"

"Yes, all of a sudden he would take his head between his hands and start crying."

I thought of Balestrieri as I had always seen him: old, certainly, but robust, broad-shouldered, firm on his legs, his red face full of vitality beneath his white hair; and I could not help feeling disconcerted. "Why did he cry?" I asked.

"I don't know."

"Didn't he tell you why he cried?"

"No, he only said he cried because of me."

"Perhaps he was jealous?"

"No, he wasn't jealous."

"But did you give him reason to be jealous?"

She looked at me for a moment in silence, as though she had not understood, then she replied briefly: "No."

"Did he cry like that in silence, without speaking?"

"No, he always said something."

"Well then, you see, he *did* speak. And what did he say?"

"He used to say, for instance, that he couldn't do without me."

"Ah, then, there was a reason for his crying. He would have liked to do without you and he couldn't."

She corrected me pedantically. "No, he simply said that he couldn't do without me. He never said that he *wanted* to do without me; on the contrary, in fact, once when I wanted to leave him he tried to kill himself."

I was surprised at the complete absence of any change in the tone of her voice, whether she was saying something unimportant or whether she was revealing to me that Balestrieri had tried to kill himself on her account. "So he tried to kill himself? How?" I asked.

"With those pills that people take when they can't sleep. I don't remember what they're called."

"Barbiturates?"

"That's it, barbiturates."

"Was he sick after that?"

"He was sick for a couple of days, then he got better."

"Did Balestrieri suffer from sleeplessness?"

"Yes, he took barbiturates for it. There were nights when he slept for only an hour or two."

"Why?"

"Why didn't he sleep? I don't know."

"Was it because of you?"

"He used to say that everything that happened to him was because of me."

"Didn't he say anything more? Didn't he explain why you were the cause of everything?"

"Yes, now that I think of it, he used to say I was his drug."

"A commonplace, don't you think?"

"What does a commonplace mean?"

"Something not at all original, that anybody might say."

There was silence again. Finally I went on: "But why were you a drug for Balestrieri?"

She in turn asked me, slowly: "Tell me, why are you asking me all these questions?"

I answered, with sincerity: "Because in all this story about you and Balestrieri there is something that makes me curious."

"What's that?"

"I don't know. That's why I ask you these questions. In order to find out why I ask you."

She did not smile, but again gazed at me intently though in an expressionless way, leaning toward me so that it almost seemed to me that the warm, simple smell of her body came faintly to my nostrils. Finally she explained: "I suppose I was like a drug for Balestrieri because he had more and more need of me. He said so himself: 'The dose that was sufficient for me once is no longer sufficient now.'"

"In what sense was he always in need of you?"

"In every sense."

"In the sense of love-making?"

She looked at me and said nothing. I repeated my question. Then she appeared to make up her mind and answered precisely: "Yes, in that sense."

"Did you do it very often?"

"At first only once or twice a week, then every other day, then every day, then twice a day. In the end I gave up counting."

"Why?"

"He was doing it continually"—she seemed more at ease now—"he would make me pose, then he would stop painting and want to make love: and so it went on all day long."

"Wasn't he ever satisfied?"

"He used to get tired. Sometimes he felt sick, too. But it was never enough for him."

"And you, did you like all that?"

She hesitated, and then remarked: "A woman never minds a man showing that he loves her."

"But did he really love you? Wasn't it rather that he needed you as a habit, as a vice, just as, in fact, a person needs a drug?"

With a touch of warmth she replied: "No, he really loved me."

"How, for instance, did he show that he loved you?"

"How can one explain? These are things that one feels."

"Nothing more than that?"

"Well, just as an example, he wanted to marry me."

"But he was already married, wasn't he?"

"Yes, but he said he would manage to get a divorce."

"And would you have accepted him?"

"No."

"Why wouldn't you have accepted him?"

"I don't know, I didn't feel like marrying him."

"Then you didn't love him?"

"I never loved him." She stopped, as if prevented by some scruple, and then added: "Or rather, perhaps I loved him at the beginning, just after I first met him."

There was a long silence. She was very close to me now, almost hanging over me, with her bust inclined forward and her eyes fixed upon me, giving me a feeling of unsteadiness which made me think of her again as a vessel, a beautiful two-handled vase, slim and big-breasted and brimming with desire, on the point of overflowing and submerging me. Finally I said: "I have put you through a full-scale cross-examination and perhaps you're a bit tired?"

"Oh no, you haven't tired me at all," she hastened to reply. "On the contrary."

"On the contrary what?"

"On the contrary you gave me pleasure. You've made me think of so many things that I never think about."

"Don't you ever think about Balestrieri?"

"No."

"Not even today, when they took him away?"

"No, today less than other days."

"Why less than other days?"

She looked at me and said nothing. I repeated: "Why less than other days?"

She answered at last, quite sharply: "Because today I've only thought of you. I followed the funeral for a little, from some way off, then I couldn't resist any longer and ran back to the studio. I was afraid they might have changed the lock."

"What then?"

"Then I shouldn't have had any excuse for seeing you."

I pretended not to attach any importance to this declaration, and asked her: "All the same, Balestrieri did mean something to you?"

"Yes, certainly."

"What?"

She thought for a moment and then replied: "I don't know. Certainly he meant something to me, but as I've never thought about it I don't know what it was."

"Think about it now."

"I can't think about it. You can't think on purpose about somebody or something. Either you just think about them naturally or you don't think at all."

"At this moment what would you be thinking about, as you say, naturally?"

"About you."

I remained silent for a moment. I lit a cigarette and then said, deliberately: "Now, you can rest assured, I've finished cross-examining you and I'll come to the point. While Balestrieri did not mean anything much to you, or possibly nothing, you to Balestrieri were something very real, very concrete. Something he could not do without, according to his own words, in short—something like a drug. Isn't that so?"

"Yes."

"In other words, you, to Balestrieri, were not merely something very real, but actually the only reality that mattered. In fact, when you told him you wanted to leave him, he tried to kill himself. And he tried to do this precisely because you, by going away, would have been depriving him of everything that was real to him."

She looked at me in a gentle, polite, but entirely unconvinced manner; much as a child looks at his mother when she scolds him before giving him a piece of candy, and waits patiently for the scolding, which matters nothing to him and which he does not understand, to be over, so that he can get the candy. She said, however: "Yes, it's true, now that I think of it, I remember his telling me often that I was everything to him."

"Well then, do you see?—Balestrieri, although he was an unhappy lover and a very bad painter, was in a way rather enviable."

"Why?"

"Because he was able to say to someone: 'You are everything to me.' "

She was silent again, as though uncertain of the meaning of my words, and anyhow not very interested in looking for it: it was the candy that she minded about, not the scolding. I resumed: "And now that's enough of Balestrieri, let's talk about you and me."

She seemed delighted at this, in her own highly discreet, almost imperceptible way, making a slight forward movement with her face, as if to show solicitude and attentiveness, and an even slighter movement of her hips on the divan, as though to come even closer to me. "For at least three or four months," I said, "we've been meeting in the corridor or the courtyard, and every time we meet you look at me and smile at me in a way which is, let us say, significant. Isn't that so? If it's not true, contradict me; it'll mean I've had a wrong impression."

She said nothing, she merely looked at me as if waiting for the end of my speech, and as if all that came in between had no interest for her. "You don't answer," I continued, "so I presume that I'm not making a mistake. Besides, what you want of me seems to me pretty clear. Forgive me, I know I'm being brutal: for four or five months you've been wanting to show me that you're ready to do with me what you used to do with Balestrieri. At least, that's what I've understood. Again, if I'm wrong, tell me."

Once more there was silence; her face now expressed a kind of shy satisfaction at having been so well understood. "Balestrieri," I went on, "told you that you were everything to him. And the word 'everything' meant, as far as I can see, really *everything*. Unfortunately I'm in the opposite position. To Balestrieri you were everything; to me you are nothing."

I paused for a moment, looking at her, and could not but admire her impassivity. She said modestly, lowering her eyes: "We've only known each other for half an hour."

I hastened to explain. "I don't want to be misunderstood. It is in fact impossible for you to be everything, or even something, to me, in the sense which is usually given to that expression. It's certainly true, as you pointed out, that we've known each other for barely half an hour. No, this is a question of something different. Do please try and follow me, even if these explanations don't interest you. Well then: I asked you to come here to my studio under the pretext of painting you—isn't that so?"

"Yes."

"It really *was* a pretext; that is, a lie. Apart from the fact that I haven't painted the human figure or other recognizable objects for years, I lied to you because I'm not a painter, or rather, I haven't been a painter for some time. And I am no longer a painter because I have nothing to paint, that is, I have no relationship with anything real."

She answered stubbornly: "But it doesn't matter whether you paint a portrait of me."

I could not help laughing. "I understand," I said; "you don't see the connection between the fact that I've given up painting and the thing that you seem to have so much at heart. But there is a connection. Now listen: I said you were nothing to me, but, I repeat, you must not attribute any sentimental significance to that remark. In other words, you are offering yourself to me in the same way as any object, of any kind. Let's take a concrete example. That glass on the table there has not got beautiful eyes like yours, nor that magnificent bosom nor those rounded hips; if I accepted its offer of itself it would not kiss me or embrace me, and yet it offers itself no more and no less than you do. It offers itself without shame, without reserve, without guile, without calculation, just as you do. And I have to refuse it, as I refuse you, because, like you, that glass is nothing to me. I've given the glass as an example, but I could equally well give any other object, even one that isn't noticeable to the senses."

"But why is it nothing?" She said this in a low, timid voice, as though more in recommendation of the glass than of herself.

I answered briefly: "To explain this thing fully would take me a long way off the point, and in any case it would be useless. Let's say then that the glass is nothing to me because I have no relationship with it, of any kind."

She objected, speaking this time in recommendation of herself. "But these relationships do come into existence, don't you think? It happens constantly that one forms a relationship with people one didn't even know before."

"Do you see that canvas on the easel?" I asked her.

"Yes."

"It's an empty canvas, a canvas on which I haven't painted anything. Well, that's the only canvas I can sign. Look." I rose and went to the easel, took a pencil and signed my name in one corner of the canvas. She followed me with her eyes as I went over to the easel and again as I came back, but she said nothing. Sitting down again, I continued: "So the only relationship there can be between myself and a woman is nothing, that is, exactly the same relationship that there has been so far between you and me, or rather, that there has *not* been. I am not impotent, understand that; but in practice it's as if I were, and anyhow you must imagine that I am."

I had spoken in a sharp, determined fashion, in order to make her understand that there was nothing more to be said. But when I saw her still sitting there, silent and impassive, as though she still expected something, I added rather irritably: "If I feel nothing for you, that is, have no relationship with you, how could I make love? It would be a mechanical, impersonal act, utterly useless and utterly boring. And so. . . ."

I did not finish, but looked at her meaningly, as much as to say: And so there's nothing left for you but to go away. This time, at last, she appeared to understand, and very slowly, with regret, with hesitation, with reluctance, and almost, I think, with a lingering hope that I would stop her by taking her in my arms, she started to rise from the divan, though still appearing to remain seated—that is by gradually raising her hips and keeping her legs bent and the upper part of her body erect. But I did not take her in my arms, and finally she was on her feet in front of me. Humbly she said: "I'm sorry. But if at any time you want me as a model, you can telephone me. I'll write down my telephone number."

She went across to the table and, holding the towel to her chest with one hand, with the other wrote on a piece of paper. "I haven't yet told you my name," she said. "It's Cecilia Rinaldi. I've written it down here, with my address and telephone number."

She stood up again and walked over on tiptoe to the bathroom. She looked as if she were in evening dress, with the towel leaving her arms and shoulders bare, swathing her hips and forming a kind of train behind her. She disappeared, closing the door after her, and as she made this movement the towel slipped from her and I saw again for a moment the body which Balestrieri had painted so often and which it was impossible to divine underneath her clothes.

As soon as she disappeared I started thinking of Balestrieri. I recalled how the old painter had repulsed and avoided her for months, with a kind of animal-like fear or presentiment of what she was destined to be to him, and I wondered what would have happened if he had resisted her instead of yielding the day she presented herself in place of Elisa. Very probably Balestrieri would still be alive, since it was beyond doubt that the not-so-indirect cause of his death had been his love for the girl. But why then had he not rejected her, seeing that he had felt from the very beginning that he ought to do so? In other words, what was it that had brought Balestrieri to accept a destiny he seemed to have been conscious of, even if only in an obscure way? Was it possible for a man to escape his own destiny? And if not, what was the point of knowing what one was doing? Was it possible that there was not some difference between a destiny accepted in a state of unconsciousness and one which was lived out in a state of lucid consciousness?

Thinking over Balestrieri's first, attempted, suicide, an attempt caused by Cecilia's decision to leave him, I seemed to see that the old painter, in carrying on his relationship with Cecilia to its final end, had committed with complete lucidity a second and successful suicide. And so, in a way, he had attempted the first suicide because for a moment it had seemed to him that Cecilia, by leaving him, would not allow him to commit the second.

Even while I was thinking these things, I was surprised at thinking them; or rather, at being driven to think them not so much by idle curiosity as by a disconcerting sense of fascinated attraction, as though Balestrieri's story concerned me directly and the old painter's destiny were linked with my own. If it had not been thus, I should not have put so many questions to Cecilia. No doubt I should have made love with her, just that once, but I should not have questioned her. Instead, I had not made love but had questioned her at considerable length, with an insatiable curiosity which, in effect, had remained unsatisfied. As I had told her, I had questioned her mainly in order to find out why I was questioning her: it seemed like a play upon words but actually was not so. In this way I had learned many things, but my lack of satisfaction made it clear that the thing which really mattered to me had escaped me.

I was so deeply absorbed in these reflections that I did not notice Cecilia, who had come out of the bathroom and was standing near the divan. I started when I heard her voice saying: "Well then, I'll say good-bye."

I rose to my feet with an effort, and shook her hand, stammering automatically: "Good-bye." "Don't bother to come with me," she murmured; and for the last time I had the sensation of her large, dark eyes motionlessly contemplating me. I watched her as she took up her bundle from the table and walked to the door. She moved with a slowness that did not appear calculated; it was as though she felt she was attached to me by a strong, tenacious bond and it was a great effort to her to move her steps in the opposite direction. I was struck particularly by the slight swing of her wide, short skirt and the consequent graceful swaying of the upper part of her body, which rose above her skirt like a rider on his horse. In these two movements, the rotating movement of her skirt and the quivering movement of her body, there was the allurement of a coquetry that was quite unconscious and for that reason all the more potent and irresistible. I followed her with my eyes until she had opened the door and vanished. Then I lit a cigarette and went over to the window.

The courtyard lay deserted in the bleak, subdued twilight of a sultry day. I could see the other big windows opposite; a couple of them were already lit up; also the acanthus bushes, blackish green, all around the flower beds and the dull, chalky whiteness of the pavement. As usual, there were many cats on the pavement, dispersed here and there in a mysterious order that did not seem merely casual: some squatting with their legs folded beneath their bodies, others sitting with their tails wrapped around their feet, others slowly and cautiously prowling, noses to the ground and tails erect; piebald black and white cats, grey cats, cats completely white or completely black, striped cats and tawny cats. I started looking attentively at the cats, as I often did, for it was as good a way as any of beguiling the time. Then Cecilia appeared, carrying her big bundle under her arm. She walked slowly, her head bent, among the cats which did not move as she passed. As she came below my window, I saw her raise her eyes in my direction, but this time without smiling. I lifted my hand to take the cigarette from my mouth, but instead of doing so I gave her a clear signal to turn back, pointing in the direction of the door that gave access to the corridor. Her eyes showed her assent and, without modifying her slow, dragging step, without hurrying, like a person who has forgotten something but knows he will find it again without fail, she turned and came back. I pulled the curtains across the window and went and sat down on the divan.

Chapter 3

After that day Cecilia came to see me a couple of times a week, then every other day, and finally, after we had known one another for a month, almost every day. Cecilia's visits took place always at the same time of day, lasted always for the same length of time, and were spent always in the same way; so that to describe one of them is to describe them all. Cecilia would announce her arrival with one single ring at the bell, a ring so brief that it often left me uncertain as to whether I had really heard it; but it was just this uncertainty that made me know it was she. I would go and open the door and Cecilia would throw her arms around my neck and we would kiss. I wish to say at this point that Cecilia, so expert in the sexual relationship, did not know how to kiss. It may be that the kiss is a symbolic contact, so to speak, in which the pleasure is more psychological than sensual, and psychology was not Cecilia's strong point; or it may be, more simply, that Cecilia did not know how to kiss *me*, that is, that our relationship was not of the kind that can express itself with kisses. Certain it is that Cecilia's lips were inert, cold and formless, like those of a little girl who has been running with the wind in her face and hastily embraces her father. Moreover Cecilia's double nature, at the same time that of a child and of a grown woman, was revealed during the moment of the kiss. She offered me a mouth which was lacking both in eagerness and in abandonment, a mouth which failed to open in response to mine or to insinuate itself into mine, but at that same moment I would feel her straining against me with her body in a forward curve, and then, with her groin, dealing me a strong, sharp stroke that seemed to proclaim the urgent, inarticulate quality of her love. This first kiss lasted only a short time, since I found no pleasure in it and broke it off almost immediately. Cecilia would disengage herself from me, put down her bag and gloves on the table, walk over to the window and pull the cords of the curtains, and then undress, always in the same way and in the same place, between the divan and an armchair upon which she placed her clothes as she took them off.

I had met Cecilia in July, when she was wearing the summer clothes which I have already described—a light, puffy blouse and a wide, short skirt like a ballet skirt; later on, with the autumn, as soon as it began to be less warm, she wore a long, loose, green woolen sweater and a black skirt, very tight, which reached to her knees. Cecilia would slip this sweater over her head, pausing a moment with her arms raised and her head muffled and hidden, and then, with an energetic movement, always the same, she would pull off the sweater and throw it down inside out on the armchair. She was now in her skirt only, naked to the waist, because, indifferent to the rough contact of the wool against her skin, she wore nothing underneath her sweater. She used to say, with little trace of vanity and as though establishing an incontestable fact, that her breasts would stay up without any support; but I always thought she did this out of calculated coquettishness, with the intention that her magnificent bosom should appear, or rather burst forth, the moment she took off her sweater. The sight of her bosom did not in any case dispel the feeling of immaturity that emanated from her: ample and in full beauty, it did not seem to belong to the slender torso from which it rose. This impression was especially remarkable when Cecilia turned around: all I could see then was the thin, white, bony back of an adolescent girl, and the breast that was visible between her arm and her side, beneath her armpit, looked as if it were composed of a warmer, darker, more adult flesh than the rest of her body.

After taking off her sweater, Cecilia would turn slightly on her hip and, bringing her hands together at her waist, unhook and lower the zipper fastening. The skirt fell to the floor and, with an impatient gesture like the movement with which she had snatched her sweater from over her head, she would stamp her feet on it a couple of times before picking it up and placing it on the armchair. Now she was quite naked, or rather she was only wearing what I may call her most intimate trappings: the garter belt around her hips, the triangular veil of the slip over her belly, the stockings on her legs. These trappings, however, were by this time all crooked and in confusion, as though Cecilia in undressing had deprived them of all functional purpose; the slip appeared to be crumpled and rolled up, the garter belt had two of its four garters undone and was hanging slantwise to one side, one stocking was up and the other was dangling below her knee. The disorder was feminine and warlike, and it was curiously out of harmony with the childish, expressionless innocence of her face. In truth, Cecilia always seemed to have a twofold character, to be a woman and a child at the same time; and not only in her body but in her expression and her movements.

This twofold character found particular expression in the contrast between the upper and the lower parts of her body. There are differences of weight which are apparent to the eye even before they are verified by the hands. An object made of lead, for instance, appears to the eye of an observer to be without any doubt heavier than some other object of equal dimensions, made of a lighter material. Cecilia's body, from the waist down, did indeed appear to have the consistency of something made of a very dense, very heavy material. How solid, for example, was the attachment of the legs to the groin compared with that of the arms to the armpits; how different from the delicate thinness of the torso was the vigorous curve of the lower back, the superabundant muscularity of the loins, the massive compactness of the thighs. Adolescent from the waist up, grown woman from the waist down, Cecilia gave rather the idea of one of those decorative monsters which are depicted in ancient frescoes: a kind of sphinx or harpy, a boyish torso grafted with grotesque effect onto a powerful belly and legs.

The manner in which Cecilia conducted herself during lovemaking also reflected the contrast between the two sides of her nature, the childish and the womanly. I have often thought about this; and I have come to the conclusion that Cecilia had no feeling, and possibly, even, no real sensuality, but merely a sexual appetite of which she herself was not entirely conscious although she submitted passively to its urgency. In my arms she would adopt the position of a child obediently opening its mouth to the spoon held out by its mother: only in her case the mouth was her sex and it was her lover who fed her. The poetical, childish fragility of her round, pale face was in continual contrast with the hardness, the exigence, the avidity with which she worked upon herself and upon me, with the object, so it seemed, of bringing me to the point of orgasm and deriving her own pleasure from it to the very last spasm. The movements of her belly which, as the embrace acquired rhythm and force, became more and more frequent, had the strength and regularity of some unharnessed mechanism which neither she nor I had the power to arrest. Languid at first, scarcely perceptible, indolent as it were, in the end these movements seemed truly like those of a piston rising and falling with an automatic, indefatigable force. But all this time her face would remain inert, relaxed, calm, with no curiosity in it and no passion, more childish than ever with the big eyelids lowered and the small mouth half-open; and just a faint redness in the top part of her cheeks served to indicate that Cecilia was not asleep but wide awake and alive to her own sensations.

This dissociation of Cecilia's mind during love-making was especially noticeable at those moments when she suddenly, and apparently without reason, bestirred herself from the avid, mechanical passivity which I have just described and started to return my caresses. Procreative love, as we may call it, is always chaste; hardly ever chaste, on the other hand, are the amatory techniques by means of which lovers endeavor to excite one another. But the way in which Cecilia applied herself to my body was absolutely chaste just because it was so curiously automatic and unconscious. All of a sudden, in the middle of an embrace, she would sit up and bend forward, with her mouth on my belly as though she were browsing; but this sudden impulse had something somnambulistic about it; it was almost as if she had abandoned herself to it in a dream, that is, in a state of complete unconsciousness. Then, when she had satisfied herself, or rather, after she had scrupulously exhausted all the possibilities of her caress, she would throw herself once more into my arms, her eyes closed, her mouth half-open; and once again I would have the strange sensation of having seen a person asleep perform gestures devoid of sense, and then, still without waking, lie down again.

After the orgasm, which shook her body several times like a minor epileptic fit but did not disturb the apathetic stillness of her face, Cecilia would lie exhausted beneath me, one arm behind her head and the other lying limp on the divan, her face turned toward her shoulder and her legs apart, as they had remained after the embrace. For a second, almost immediately after I had withdrawn myself from her, she would smile at me, and that, perhaps, was the best moment of our love-making. The smile, a very sweet smile, in which the sweetness of appeased desire seemed to ebb and die away, did not however belie the childish ambiguity I have already noted: even while she was smiling, Cecilia did not look at me, or rather she did not appear to see me, so that she seemed to be smiling not so much at me as at herself, as though she were grateful to herself for having experienced pleasure, rather than to me for having caused her to experience it. This smile, although impersonal and solitary, was nevertheless the last phase of our embrace, that is, of the communication, the almost fusion, of our two bodies. Immediately afterward there were two of us on the divan, separate from each other, and it became necessary to speak.

At this point I would realize that her sexual appetite—which, even if it did not seem to concern me directly, yet made use of me for its gratification—was succeeded by indifference. When I say indifference I do not by that mean an attitude of coldness or detachment. No, Cecilia's indifference toward me immediately after we had made love was simply a complete lack of contact very similar to the thing which caused me to suffer so much and which I called boredom; only that Cecilia, unlike me, not only did not suffer at all but did not even appear to be conscious of it. It was as though she had been born with the detachment from external things which to me seemed an intolerable change from a very different original state; as though what to me seemed a sort of sickness was, in her, a sane and normal fact.

And yet, as I said, it became necessary to speak. The recent intimacy of physical love inspired in me a desire for another and truer intimacy of the affections which could be achieved only through the spoken word. So I tried to start a conversation with her; or rather, since Cecilia never carried on a conversation but confined herself to answering questions, I interrogated her about herself and her life. In this way I came to know that she was an only child, that she lived with her parents in a flat in the Prati district, that her father was a tradesman, that she had been educated by the nuns, that she had a few girl friends, that she was not engaged to be married—and a few other things of the kind. Told in this way, these may seem summary pieces of information such as might be provided about any girl of Cecilia's age and position; but they were in truth the only facts I succeeded in obtaining, and then only with great difficulty. Cecilia certainly did not appear to wish to conceal anything from me; if anything, she seemed to be ignorant of a great deal of what I asked her, or at any rate to be incapable of describing things or defining them in detail. It might have been thought that she had never stopped to look around, to observe herself and her own world, so that in asking her these questions I was putting her more or less in the situation of someone who is being interrogated about persons and things to which he has never paid any attention. There is a game that consists in showing to someone, for the space of one minute, some illustration or other, and then asking him to name all the objects which are represented in it. In this game, which puts a person's power of observation to the test, Cecilia would certainly have obtained the lowest possible marks, for she appeared never to have seen or observed anything, although she had lived not for one single minute, but for years, in front of the illustration of her own life. Her information, furthermore, was not merely generalized but also inexact; as though these few things—the only daughter, the parents, the tradesman father, the education by the nuns, the girl friends—were by no means clearly established in her mind, as indeed nothing can be which has never aroused our curiosity even though close to us and easily observable. And even when she gave an exact reply, she left me equally in doubt because of the cold, generic, colorless way in which she expressed herself, apparently the result of an unconquerable inattentiveness.

Since Cecilia's family and background did not interest me very much, I fell back of necessity upon Balestrieri, whom I felt to be connected in some obscure way with me and with my relations with Cecilia. In point of fact, even when she was speaking of Balestrieri, Cecilia's laconic manner was never modified, but this did not discourage me; on the contrary, her reserve on the subject of the old painter inspired me with a passionate desire to know more about him, always to know more. Actually, when questioning her about her past and about Balestrieri, I felt, as I very soon realized, that I was questioning her about her future and about myself.

Two months had passed since the day when Cecilia came into my studio for the first time, and I was now beginning to wonder how it was that Balestrieri had been able to entertain so violent a passion for her; how it was, in fact, that Cecilia had come to play the part, for him, of the "fatal woman"—using those two words in the full sense of baleful predestination which they ought to have and normally do not have. I found it difficult to believe because, apart from her noteworthy sexual capabilities—which in any case she had in common with a great many other girls of her age—Cecilia seemed to me insignificant in the highest degree and therefore incapable of arousing a passion as destructive as Balestrieri's. The clue to this character of hers, so devoid of interest and of pretexts for taking interest in it, was provided, as I have already hinted, by her colorless, summary manner of expressing herself. I have often reflected upon the spiritual quality of which this manner was evidence, and I have come to the conclusion that it revealed a great simplicity. Not, however, the simplicity of common sense, which has always something openhearted about it; but rather the troubled, enigmatic, incompetent simplicity of that kind of psychological amputation of which reticence, even if unconscious and involuntary, is the result. Cecilia continually gave the impression not so much of lying as of being incapable of telling the truth; and this not because she was untruthful but because telling the truth would have implied having a relationship with something, and she did not appear to have any relationship with anything. When she really told a lie (and it will be seen that she was perfectly capable of doing so), one almost had the impression that she was saying something true, even in a negative way, simply because of the grain of participation, that is, of truth, which any lie contains within itself.

How, then, had Balestrieri managed to fall so desperately in love with her? Or rather, what had occurred between them to turn Cecilia's very insignificant character—precisely because of its insignificance, perhaps—into a cause of passion? I knew it was never possible to make judgments about other people's love affairs, but after all I had taken Balestrieri's place in Cecilia's life; I myself had taken the drug of which Balestrieri spoke in reference to Cecilia, and I could not help wondering continually, with a feeling of lingering mistrust, as with a danger foretold but belated in appearance, why the drug itself should not be having any effect upon me.

So I questioned Cecilia at length, and gropingly, without myself knowing exactly what it was that I wished to learn from her. This is an example of one of these conversations.

"Tell me, did Balestrieri never say why he loved you?"

"Ugh, the usual question. Always Balestrieri. . . ."

"I'm sorry, but I simply must know . . ."

"What?"

"I don't know what. Something to do with Balestrieri and you. Tell me: did he never say why he loved you?"

"No, he loved me and that was that."

"I haven't explained myself rightly. Love has no reason, it's true, one loves and that's that; but the quality of love, *that* has a reason. One loves without reason; but if one loves with sadness or with joy, with calm or with anxiety, with jealousy or with confidence, there's always some reason behind it. As for Balestrieri, he loved you with—how shall I describe it?—with a kind of mania. You yourself have shown me that. For him you were a vice, a drug, something he couldn't do without—those are his own words. But why this mania?"

"I don't know."

"You're not a woman who could inspire a passion of that kind, at least so it seems to me."

"So it seems to me too." This was said without a shadow of scorn or irony, but with humility and sincerity.

"If I may say exactly what I think, now that I know you better, I simply cannot understand Balestrieri and his passion. If not precisely disappointed, I am surprised. After what you told me of your relations with Balestrieri, I imagined you to be a terrible woman, of the type that can ruin a man. Instead of that, you seem to me a very normal girl. I'm sure you would make an extremely good wife."

"D'you think so?"

"Yes, you give that impression."

"I think so too, on the whole."

"Then how d'you account for the passion, or rather the *kind* of passion, that Balestrieri had for you?"

"I don't know."

"Try and think for a moment."

"Really I don't know. Obviously he was made like that."

"How do you mean?"

"That he couldn't love except in that way."

"That isn't true. For years I saw Balestrieri continually changing women. What happened, happened only with you."

There was a long silence, and then, in a tone of sincerity and good will, she said: "Ask me a precise question, and I'll answer you."

"What do you mean by a precise question?"

"A question about a physical thing, a material thing. You always ask me questions about feelings, about what people think or don't think, and I don't know what to answer."

"A material thing? Well then, tell me: in your opinion, did

Balestrieri know that his relations with you were injuring his health?"

"Yes, he did know."

"What did he say?"

"He said: 'Some day or other this is going to kill me.' Then I told him that he ought to be careful, but he answered that it didn't matter."

"That it didn't matter?"

"Yes." Then, with an air of vagueness and as if she were remembering with an effort, she went on: "In fact, now I come to think of it, I remember one day when we were making love he said to me: 'Go on, go on, go on, I want you to go on without taking any notice of me, even if I protest, even if I feel sick, I want you to make me die, yes, really to make me die.'"

"And what about you?"

"I didn't pay much attention to his words at the time. He used to say so many things. But you've made me think of them."

"So you think he loved you because you made him die, I mean because for him you were a means he made use of to kill himself?"

"I don't know. I've never thought about it."

And so I was continually getting nearer to the truth, or anyhow thinking that I was getting nearer. Nevertheless I always remained dissatisfied. The idea that Cecilia was an ordinary girl like so many others and that Balestrieri had seen something in her that did not exist and had died as result of it, this idea, as a summing-up of the matter, was rather tempting; apart from anything else, it explained why I myself, unlike Balestrieri, had not managed to feel anything for Cecilia beyond a simple physical attraction. And yet, I don't know why, this explanation failed to satisfy me. It seemed that by explaining everything it explained nothing, and anyhow it left unsolved the problem of Cecilia, that is, the problem of the contrast between her actual simplicity and lack of interest and the passion she had been able to inspire.

By this time, however, I realized that I was beginning to be bored with Cecilia, to find myself once more in the state of isolation and detachment in which I had been just before I met her. To say that I was bored with Cecilia may perhaps suggest the idea that she gave me no enjoyment, that is, that she herself was boring. But as I have said, mine was not a case of boredom in the sense normally given to that word. In reality it was not that Cecilia was boring, it was I who was bored, even though I knew in my heart that I might very well not be bored if, by some miracle, I could succeed in making my relationship with her more real. On the contrary, however, I felt it growing weaker and emptier every day.

I became conscious of this change in our relationship chiefly because of the difference in my way of feeling on the subject of physical love—which was, after all, the only possible kind of love between Cecilia and me. At the beginning it had been a very natural thing, inasmuch as I had felt that, in it, nature overcame herself and became human and even more than human; now, on the other hand, it struck me mainly by its lack of naturalness, a sort of act against nature, and therefore artificial and absurd. Walking, sitting, lying down, going up or down, all the actions of the body now seemed to me to have a necessity of their own and therefore a naturalness; but copulation, on the contrary, seemed an extravagant exertion for which the human body was not made and to which it could not adapt itself without effort and fatigue. Everything, I felt, could be done easily, with grace and harmony—everything except copulation. The very conformation of the two organs, the female difficult of access, the male incapable of directing itself of its own accord toward its goal, like an arm or a leg, but requiring to be aided by the whole body, appeared to me indicative of the absurdity of the sexual act. From this sense of the absurdity of the physical relation to that of the absurdity of Cecilia herself was but a step. And so boredom, as usual, destroyed first my relationship with outside things and then the things themselves, rendering them empty and incomprehensible. But the new fact this time was that, in face of a Cecilia reduced to an object of absurdity, boredom—possibly owing to the sexual habit which I had formed and which I did not consider necessary to break off, anyhow for the moment—did not merely fill me with coldness and indifference but went beyond these feelings, or rather this lack of feeling, and was transformed into cruelty.

Cecilia was not a glass but a person; although at the moment when I was bored with her she ceased to exist just like any other object, I nevertheless knew in my mind that she was a person. Now, just as the glass, at the moment when my boredom made it appear incomprehensible and absurd, sometimes inspired me with a violent desire to seize it and smash it and reduce it to fragments so as to have confirmation of its actual existence through destroying it, so, with more reason, when I was bored with Cecilia I was smitten with an impulse, if not to destroy her, at least to torment her and make her suffer. By tormenting her and making her suffer, in fact, it seemed to me that I might contrive to re-establish the relations that had been broken off by boredom; and little did it matter if I succeeded in this through cruelty instead of through love.

I remember perfectly well how this cruelty showed itself for the first time. One afternoon Cecilia, after she had undressed, was coming over to the divan where I was awaiting her, lying down and also undressed, my eyes turned toward her. She was walking on tiptoe with her chest thrown forward and her shoulders and hips held slightly back, and on her face was the expectant, troubled, solemn expression of one who prepares to perform a familiar act which has been performed many times before and is yet, perhaps for that very reason, always new. I watched her as she came toward me and reflected that not merely did I not desire her (though

I also knew that, if only in an automatic way, I should attain a sufficient degree of excitement to have intercourse with her) but that I could not even manage to look upon her as a thing that was in any kind of contact with me. While I was thinking of these things and she had come up to the divan and placed one knee upon it so as to lie down beside me, I suddenly noticed that the curtains were only half drawn across the big window. The white light of the sultry day worried me; besides, there were windows on the other side of the courtyard from which people could look into the studio if they wanted to. So I said, in a casual way: "Look, do you mind drawing the curtains?"

"Oh, the curtains," she said; and as usual she obediently turned away from me and, still walking on tiptoe, went to the window. Then, as I watched her going across the studio, with her strange, significantly shaped figure, half adolescent and half grown woman, I was suddenly seized, for the first time since I had met her, with an impulse of cruelty. It was an impulse which took me back in time to the years of my childhood, to the only occasion in my life when I had been consciously cruel. At that time I owned a large tabby cat I was very fond of but with whom, quite often, I grew bored, especially when I had gone through the few games and tests of intelligence of which the creature was capable. Boredom gave me a feeling of cruelty which led in turn to the following game. I put on a plate a small quantity of raw fish I knew the cat liked and put the plate in a corner of the room. Then I went and fetched the cat and, after allowing it to smell the fish, carried it to the opposite corner and let it go. The cat rushed to the plate, expressing its delight and greed with its whole body, from the tip of its tail to the tip of its nose; but I was ready, the moment it reached the middle of the room, to seize it like lightning by its neck and carry it back to its point of departure. I repeated this game over and over again, and each time the cat became slightly more aware that it was the victim of a mysterious misfortune and in consequence changed its behavior. In its first bounds it had been violent, greedy, sure of itself; then it became more wary, as though it hoped, by pressing its body against the floor and moving its paws with caution, that it might escape my vigilance and perhaps make itself invisible; in the end, all the poor cat did was to make a slight, tentative forward movement in the direction of the plate, an experiment, at the same time both cunning and melancholy, to assure itself without too much effort that I still persisted in my cruel intention. Then suddenly, everything changed: the cat spoke. What I mean is that, turning back its head and looking into my eyes, it gave vent to a long and very expressive mewing, at the same time both touching and reasonable, that seemed to say: "Why are you doing this? Why are you doing this to me?" This mewing, so explicit and so eloquent, made me instantly ashamed. I seem to remember that I even blushed. I took the cat in my arms, carried him over to the plate myself, and left him to eat his fish in peace.

And now, when I saw Cecilia walking away docilely on tiptoe toward the window, it occurred to me to play the same cruel game with her as I had played with the cat. In her case too, it was to satisfy her appetite that she had come over to the divan; and she too, like the cat, had at that moment expressed her appetite—her perfectly natural and legitimate appetite—with her whole body, from her head to her feet. Now I was going to play with her as I had played with the cat; but this time I should be completely conscious of the true motive of the game, which was to re-establish through cruelty my relationship with external things that had been broken off by boredom.

Cecilia, in the meantime, had gone to the window and drawn the curtains and was now coming back to the divan again. Upon her face, which for a moment had worn the diligent expression of a young maidservant (even though she was naked) carrying out an order from her master, there was now, again, that primitive, ritual look, the apologetic, expectant prelude to love. Still walking on tiptoe, she circled around the easel, crossed the room, reached the divan and was on the point of climbing onto it. But I stopped her, saying: "I'm sorry, but I can't bear to make love in front of an open door. Please go and shut the bathroom door."

"How difficult you are!" she murmured. Nevertheless, docile as ever, off she went again across the studio. I saw her disappear into the shadow, a graceful ghost with her spreading, curly brown hair, her slender, bony back, and below her slim waist the two pale, oblong mounds of her buttocks. She closed the door carefully and turned back, ghostly again in the half-darkness which made her eyes look larger and darker, her breasts heavier and browner, her groin deeper and blacker. This time I did not stop her when she placed her knee on the divan, but at the moment when she was laying herself down, a little out of breath, beside me. "Forgive me once more," I said, "but do be kind enough to take the receiver off the telephone. Yesterday it rang just at the best moment. It's true I didn't answer it, but all the same that ringing got on my nerves."

She looked at me for an instant, saying: "That's the third time," in a quiet but not reproachful voice, then she got up and went to the table in the middle of the room to take off the receiver, standing there for a moment in profile against the light. Then she came back again toward the divan, her face assuming, for the third time, its apologetic, expectant expression. I waited until she was close to me and exclaimed with pretended innocence: "How absent-minded I am! Cecilia, my love, do me one more favor: go and fetch my cigarette case from the window sill. . . . You know I like to smoke afterwards. Please!"

She said nothing, but threw me a long, astonished glance. She obeyed, however, for the fourth time; she went again to the window, fetched the cigarettes and came back to me, still ready and willing to give herself to me.

"There are your cigarettes," she said in a cheerfully impatient manner, throwing them in my face and at the same time making a movement to hurl herself upon me. But I stopped her in the act. "What about the matches?" I asked.

"Ugh!" Another walk across the studio, still on tiptoe; as she came back, however, her ritual expression seemed slightly falsified by a shadow of doubt and mortification. She threw the matches in my face as she had done with the cigarettes, but, instead of climbing on to the divan, she stopped at a little distance from it and asked: "Tell me quickly whether there's anything else you want, while I'm standing up."

"Yes," I lied, "I would like you to go into the kitchen and turn off the gas burner. I have an impression I may have left it on."

"And then what?"

"And then, yes, there is one other thing I wanted to ask you to do: go to the entrance door and disconnect the bell. Someone might come and disturb us."

I expected her to obey; instead she sat down deliberately on a chair, hugging one leg in her arms; and curled up like that, in an attitude of distress and doubt, she gazed at me in silence. Surprised, I asked her: "What's the matter, why don't you go and do what I asked you?"

She did not immediately answer. Finally she asked cautiously: "Just those two things, or others as well?"

"Only those two things."

She shook herself, with what seemed like a faint sigh, and then once more made her way across the studio, going first into the kitchen and then to the front door. When she came back I noticed that her face still retained its look of expectancy and desire, and I wondered whether I should ever see her again if I went on with my cruel game. This was love, I said to myself, the only love of which she was capable, and I was on the point of killing it. But when she had lain down beside me, I could not refrain from saying: "I'm sorry, but you'll have to get up again. I want an ash tray; I don't like throwing cigarette ashes on the floor."

This time she did the exact contrary of what the cat had done, in those far-off days of my childhood. The cat had spoken, in a human, reasonable, and I might almost say Christian, way; the pain I had inflicted upon it had raised it to human status. Cecilia, faced with the same cruelty, made a gesture of animal-like humility, at the same time both mute and touching. Instead of getting up as I had commanded, she nestled still more closely against me, hiding her face between my shoulder and ear, entwining her arms and legs about me and as it were imploring me, in silence, like an animal that cannot speak, not to go on tormenting her, whatever the reason for it might be or the satisfaction I might derive from it. This sad, humiliated, suppliant embrace, just as instinctively animal-like as the cat's mewing had been human and reasonable, produced the same effect. Suddenly I was ashamed of my cruelty, which was seeking an evidence of reality in the suffering of another person, and without persisting any longer in my ridiculous requests I returned her embrace. Immediately I felt her body, which seemed to have been waiting only for this signal, clasp itself to mine in a different manner, no longer imploring now, but eager; and she dealt me the usual strong, impatient push with her groin, as if to notify me that she was ready. And thus, I thought to myself with more amusement than boredom, her meal was beginning.

But there remained with me, from that day on, not merely a distaste for cruelty, as a significant symptom of my lack of contact with Cecilia, but also a fear of relapsing in the future into greater and more irreparable and more shameful cruelties. This had been but a preliminary skirmish; I realized that, if boredom and its effects persisted in my relationship with Cecilia, I might really slip into the habit of sadism, for it was precisely toward that that I was being pushed by my need to establish any kind of contact with her. I ought not to be deceived by the fact that Cecilia's touching, animal-like embrace had made me break off my cruel game. In reality I had ceased tormenting her, not so much because I had felt pity for her and shame at my own behavior, as because with that embrace she had admitted that she was suffering, and it was precisely that admission that I had wished to force from her, thus driving away my boredom through the spectacle of her suffering. But along that road, with my own sensibility steadily hardening, I might reach the point of true sadism, of the transformation of my boredom into a vicious mechanism. Boredom inspired me with fear but not with disgust, because it had something frank and essential about it. Sadism, on the contrary, was repugnant to me, especially on account of its hypocrisy (the sadist always claims that he is punishing his victim whereas actually he is seeking enjoyment through the sufferings he inflicts under the pretext of punishment), and also on account of the excitement it brought me, all the more impure because it was chaste, or at least pretended to be, until the moment when, putting aside all hypocrisy, it vented itself in sexual intercourse, thus revealing itself as nothing more than a kind of drug.

Luckily, however, I am not cruel; that first episode was also the last. I thought, on the other hand, that I ought to part from Cecilia before it was too late. I was sorry to do so, not so much on my own account, because I deceived myself into thinking I did not love her, as on hers, for I imagined that, in her own silent and inarticulate way, she was in love. Why I was so certain that I did not love Cecilia and that I was loved by her, it would be hard to say. As far as I was concerned, the fact that I could make use of her—that is, of her body—as much as I wished, every time that I wished, and in every way that I wished, gave me the illusion that I possessed her absolutely, that I had so complete a relationship with her as to make any further continuation of it useless; and this had convinced me that I did not love her. Similarly I was convinced that Cecilia loved me because I always found her so complaisant, so yielding, so docile. Owing to a very common form of male vanity, I attributed this complaisance to love; whereas I ought to have been put on my guard, to say the least, by the inarticulate and almost automatic quality of this love. Thus I felt that while it would be a relief to me to part from her, Cecilia on the other hand would suffer; and for that reason I postponed the separation from day to day, as I wanted to find an excuse that would make it as little galling and painful to her as possible.

Chapter 4

I made up my mind to break with Cecilia on the day when the cruel episode occurred which I have related. I made this decision abruptly, as soon as Cecilia had gone away; then, as I have said, I allowed a couple of weeks to pass in order to find a decent excuse for the separation. Never, in spite of this, have I suffered so much from boredom as I did during that time; it seemed now to have become incarnate to my eyes in the person of my little mistress. I recall that when I heard the bell ring in that familiar, brief, reticent manner, I would heave a deep sigh of impatient forbearance; and then everything that occurred after Cecilia had come into the studio seemed to be plunged in a dull, heavy inertness that nothing could shake, neither the usual operation of undressing, nor the kisses nor the caresses nor the other erotic incitements of which Cecilia was never niggardly, nor even, at the conclusion of the sort of monotonous rite that our love-making had become, the usual epileptic contortion of the final orgasm. Cecilia, whether naked or clothed, whether lying beneath me during our embrace or resting beside me when intercourse was over, whether in the dark or in the full light of day, seemed actually each day to lose, in my eyes, a little more of her substance as a person, in fact as a recognizable object. And since

I did not wish to revert to cruelty, which without doubt would have restored, temporarily, a fleeting reality to our relationship, I saw the day approaching when I should behave toward Cecilia as though she were some kind of object of which one no longer has any need, and should break with her without producing any plausible reason either to her or to myself. It was therefore necessary for me to find an excuse before it was too late.

One morning I went to visit my mother, whom I had not seen since the day I ran away. I headed for the Via Appia in my dilapidated old car and drove out along that ancient road of pagan and Christian times, so much in fashion now with rich people, past walls tumbling with greenery, past iron gates and villas hidden amongst trees; between long straight rows of cypresses and solitary pines, and grassy banks and red brick ruins adorned with fragments of white marble; then I turned between the two pillars and went up the drive of well-raked gravel to the open space surrounded with laurels and holm-oaks and the low, red villa. This time the door was opened to me not by Rita, the maid with the sly, bespectacled face, but by a thickset, bald butler with a plump face like a sacristan, in a striped working coat; and he, after addressing me as "Signor Marchese," informed me that the "Signora Marchesa" was at home. I was startled at this noble title, which was quite new to me, and went into my mother's study. She was sitting at her table, absorbed in the examination of a ledger, her eyeglasses on her nose and a long cigarette holder between her teeth. After the usual ritual kiss on her thin, dry cheek I said to her: "Whatever is this title of 'Marchese' that your butler conferred upon me? And anyhow, where does this butler come from? What's happened to Rita?"

My mother took off her spectacles and fixed her glassy blue eyes upon me for a moment, without speaking. Then, in her most disagreeable voice, she said: "I gave Rita the sack, because she was a bad lot."

"Why, what did she do?"

"All the men," said my mother, "without one exception, both inside the house and out, for miles around. A nymphomaniac."

"My goodness me!" I said. "Who would have thought it? She looked so serious."

My mother was silent again, as if she intended to wait until my mind had recovered the serenity required to receive the news she was going to give me. "With regard to the title," she then said, "a specialist in heraldry came to see me some time ago and explained that we come of a noble house and that we are marquesses. It seems that the title was dropped by your father's family a century ago, no one knows why. I am now going to have the necessary researches made and so quite soon we shall have the right to use it. It seemed to me a pity not to make use of it, seeing that it belongs to us by right."

I said nothing: my mother's snobbishness was well known to me and had long ceased to surprise me. After a moment she went on, in a reproachful tone: "I don't know if you realize that this is the first time you've come to see your mother since your—shall we call it your disappearance?—on your birthday."

"Yes, you're right," I said in an adequately contrite tone of voice. "But I've had a great deal to do."

"Have you started painting again?" she asked.

"Don't worry about that," I replied, "I've been busy for other reasons."

"I don't worry about anything. Personally, in fact, I should prefer it if you were painting."

"Why?"

"Then you'd be thinking less about women," said my mother in an unexpected and exceedingly unpleasant way. Then, looking me in the face, she went on: "What do you think? That one doesn't see?"

"See what?"

My mother did not give a direct answer. "Do you know," she asked, "that you're looking quite completely worn out?"

I did indeed know it. During the last two months I had been overdoing it, sexually; and, above all, I had done nothing else, I had become besotted. "That may be so," I said, "but I feel perfectly well."

"In my opinion you ought to have a rest, get out in the open, take some exercise, breathe some good air. Why don't you go to the mountains for a month or two?"

"Going to the mountains needs money and I haven't any."

Each time I pointed out my poverty, which was voluntary and essentially fictitious, my mother was indignant, as though it were an incomprehensible and fundamentally immoral quibble on my part. It was the same this time. "Dino," she said, "you really ought not to say that."

"Why not? It's the fifteenth of the month and I think I have barely forty thousand lire left of my monthly allowance."

"But, Dino, you haven't any money because you don't want to have any. You're rich, Dino, you're very rich, and it's no good your pretending to be a poor man. You're rich, and whatever you do you remain rich."

It was exactly what I was thinking myself. I replied, stressing each syllable: "If you want me to come and see you, please stop reminding me that I'm rich, do you see?"

"But why? It's only the truth."

"Yes, but it's a truth that depresses me."

"Why does it depress you? Think how many people would be happy to be in your place. My dear son, why must you be depressed by a thing that would make anyone else happy?"

My mother's voice was truly distressed; and I could not help a sudden feeling of irritation and weariness. "There are some people," I said, "who have an idiosyncrasy about strawberries; if they eat them, they break out all over in red spots. Well, I have one about money. And I blush at the idea of having it."

There was a moment's silence. Then my mother resumed, in a tone of good will: "All right, then: you're a poor man. But

113

you're a poor man with a rich mother, at least you'll admit that."

"And what then?"

"Then your mother will lend you the money to go to the mountains—to Cortina d'Ampezzo, for instance."

I was on the point of letting forth the howl of indignation to which my mother's highly foreseeable and conventional advice usually prompted me—winter at Cortina d'Ampezzo, summer at the Lido and spring on the Riviera—when I suddenly realized that she had provided me with the excuse I was seeking for a final break with Cecilia. I would get her to give me the amount needed for a stay at Cortina; with this money I would buy a present for Cecilia; at the same time I would announce to her that I had to accompany my mother to the mountains. The present would soften the parting which, in any case, I would propose as temporary; later on I would write Cecilia a farewell letter. "All right," I said in a submissive tone. "Cortina. Then you must give me the money."

My mother evidently had not expected so rapid a surrender. She peered at me disconcertedly, and then asked: "Why, when do you want to leave?"

"At once. Today is the fifteenth; the eighteenth, for instance."

"But you must reserve a room at a hotel."

"I'll telegraph."

"And how long would you stay?"

"Two or three weeks."

My mother appeared now to be positively regretting her offer; or rather—so it seemed to me—not so much regretting she had made it as that she had failed to make sure she was getting a bargain: the habit of business caution was so strong in her that it did not cease even in her dealings with me. In an irresolute, uncharitable tone of voice, she said: "Of course I'll give you the money you need. I promised it and I shan't go back on my word."

"All right; then give it to me."

"What a hurry you're in! Besides, how much do you need?"

"Say twenty thousand lire a day. Let me have two hundred thousand lire, in the meantime."

"Twenty thousand lire a day!"

"Am I or am I not rich, according to what you said? I won't go to a first-class hotel. Twenty thousand lire a day is only just enough for an unpretentious place."

"I haven't got it here," said my mother, making up her mind at last to oppose my request with a disguised refusal; "I never keep money here."

"All right," I said, rising to my feet, "then let's go upstairs to your room."

"I haven't got it in my room either. I had to pay out money only this morning."

"Then write me a check. You must certainly have your checkbook here."

Oddly enough, she changed her mind at this perfectly reasonable suggestion. "No," she said, "I'll give it to you in cash after all, because I came to the end of my checkbook yesterday. Come upstairs."

She rose and I followed her out of the study, wondering at the reason for this sudden change in the method of payment. I did not have long to wait to discover it. While we were going upstairs my mother, who was in front of me, said without turning around: "I'll give you a first installment—a hundred thousand lire. The rest I'll give you tomorrow. I can't give you any more now because it's all I have."

So my mother had changed her mind because, while she could not have avoided making out a check for the whole amount, in cash she could give me only half, with the excuse that it was all she had. Why this sudden avarice? Probably, I thought, so as not to lose control over me and so as to obtain at the same time something in exchange for the money. I said nothing, but followed her up the stairs and into her bedroom.

It was a large, very comfortable room, modernly styled in various shades of grey and white, with carpets and hangings and curtains in such profusion as to give the rather suffocating impression that there was not a single inch of floor or wall that was not covered with material. In the subdued light which lent an air of mysterious and almost guilty complicity to the reflections of our two figures in the mirrors, my mother went to the door of the bathroom, at the further end of the room, and opened it. I remained standing where I was. "Why do you stand there?" said my mother. "Come along, I've no secrets from you."

"You've no secrets," I said, "because you know that I don't want your money. If I did, you'd have plenty."

"What nonsense," she replied. "You're my son, aren't you?" And she went in front of me into the bathroom. This was a very large room, with the ostentatious, wasteful, useless spaciousness which, in the houses of the rich, is characteristic of places devoted to the care of the body. Between the bath and the wash-basin there were at least four yards of marble floor, and between the basin and the toilet as many of tiled wall. I watched my mother as she went over to the wall, took hold of one of those hooks that are used for hanging towels on, turned it from left to right and then pulled it toward her. Four white tiles opened like a small door, exposing the neat grey surface of a steel safe. "Now let's see," said my mother with schoolteacher complacency, "let's see you try and open it with the secret combination."

My mother had taught me the combination of the safe, and I had learned it almost against my own will, perhaps merely because I had a good memory; but I was most unwilling to make use of it, especially in her presence—rather as one is unwilling to take part in the rites of a religion in which one does not believe. "Why?" I said. "You open it; what's it got to do with me?"

"I wanted to see if you remembered it," said my mother

gaily. Rapidly, with her nervous white hand laden with massive rings, she turned some dials on the quadrant of the safe and then opened it. I had a glimpse of some rolls of stock certificates and a number of white and yellow envelopes lying in confusion inside the deep recess. My mother, changing suddenly from gaiety to suspiciousness, threw me a mistrustful glance. I lowered my eyes in embarrassment. I saw, lying stranded on the porcelain bowl of the toilet, a wad of cotton; I put out my hand and pressed down the lever, and the water came gushing out. When I looked up again, my mother had taken a bulging white envelope out of the safe and was pushing the white tiles back into place. Turning back into the room, she said: "I'll give you fifty thousand lire for today. I've remembered that I need the other fifty thousand to pay a tradesman's bill."

Thus the sum I had asked for was again reduced. I had counted on giving Cecilia a present to the value of two hundred thousand lire; I had resigned myself to accepting a hundred thousand; but fifty thousand seemed to me really a very small amount to alleviate the pain of our parting. I protested firmly. "I need a hundred thousand lire today," I said. "You can pay the tradesman some other time."

"No, I can't." My mother went over to a tall, antique chest-of-drawers and, turning her back upon me, opened the envelope—as far as I could see—on the marble top. Without moving from the middle of the room, I said to her: "In that envelope there are certainly more than fifty thousand lire, perhaps more than three hundred thousand. In that envelope you probably have at least half a million, so why do you tell me all these stories?"

She answered hastily, without turning around: "No, there are only a hundred thousand lire in this envelope."

"Let me see, then."

She turned abruptly, with an unexpected movement, hiding the money with her shoulders and showing me a face which, beneath its usual withered dryness, had in it a trace of emotion. "Dino," she said, "why don't you want to come and live with your mother again? If you were here, you'd have all the money you want."

Such, then, was the bargain that my mother asked of me, and it mattered little that instead of confronting me with a clear-cut dilemma, as she would have done with an insolvent debtor, she presented her proposal in the form of a pathetic appeal. I asked her, in my turn: "What's that got to do with it?"

"I can't help noticing that you've come to see me simply in order to ask me for money, after I've not seen you for two months."

"I've already told you that I've been busy."

"If you came here, you could do just as you like. I wouldn't interfere in your life in any way at all."

"Oh well, give me the money and don't let's speak of it any more."

"You could come and go, stay out late at night, invite anyone you wanted, see all the women you wanted."

"But I've no need to see anybody."

"You ran away that day because you perhaps had the impression that I should have prevented you from having a relationship with Rita. You're wrong: provided you had observed the decencies, I should not have prevented anything."

This left me truly astonished. So my mother had noticed that there was something between me and Rita; but she had held her tongue, hoping, evidently, that an intrigue between the girl and myself would have strengthened my ties with the villa and therefore with her as well. And when had she noticed it? During luncheon? Or later? I had a sudden, unpleasant feeling of guilt, a familiar feeling, as though I were a little boy again and my mother had the right to put me in disgrace. I managed to get the better of it by reflecting that, after all, my feeling of attraction toward Rita had its origin in the sense of despair which a visit to my mother never failed to arouse in me. Looking her straight in the face, I answered, in a tone of resentment: "No, it wasn't because of Rita that I ran away, but because of you."

"Because of me? Why, I even pretended not to notice how you were laying hands on her during luncheon."

This remark and, even more, the tone in which it was spoken, made me furious. "Exactly; and it was entirely because of you that I laid hands on her, as you call it."

"Why, how do I come into it? Now it's my fault, is it, if you annoy the maids?"

"I laid hands on her because you put your feet on me."

"Feet—what ever d'you mean?"

"By telling me not to talk about money affairs in front of servants. And also, let me tell you"—I had moved close to her now and was talking right into her face—"let me tell you, once and for all: all the stupid things I've ever done in my life, I've done because of you."

"Because of *me?*"

"I spent whole years of my youth," I suddenly shouted, overcome by a terrible rage, "dreaming of being a thief, a murderer, a criminal, just so as not to be what you wanted me to be. And you can thank heaven I didn't become one, for lack of opportunity. And all this because I lived with you, in this house."

This time my tone of voice seemed really to frighten my mother, who, as long as it was a question of words, generally showed herself adept in the game of give and take. But now, with a bewildered look on her face, she started shaking her head from side to side in a frightened way. "Oh well," she stammered, "if it's like that, don't come and see me any more, don't come again to this house."

Suddenly I grew calm again. "No," I said, "I'll come to the house again, but don't ask me to love it."

"What is it that's so odious about this house? Isn't it just like any other house?"

"On the contrary, it's a more beautiful and more comfortable house than a great many."

"Well, then?"

I saw that she now appeared a little relieved at my not attacking her more directly. I answered her with a question: "My father didn't like living in this house, either. Why was that?"

"Your father liked traveling."

"Wouldn't it be more correct to say that he traveled because he didn't like living here?"

"Your father was your father, you are you."

It was not the first time that arguments of this kind had taken place between me and my mother. I might shout and I might hurt her, but I always came to a stop in face of the real truth: that the house was repugnant to me because it was the house of a rich person. On the other hand my mother, by provoking and almost defying me, drove me to the revelation of this truth; yet in reality she did not want me to reveal it and there always came a moment when she drew back and changed the course of the conversation. And so it was now. I was on the point of answering her when she went on, rather nervously: "Say rather that you want to live on your own so as to have more freedom. You're making a mistake, but it doesn't matter. Here you are, then, here are your hundred thousand lire."

She held out the money toward me, but only halfway; as I put out my hand, she drew it back again, as though she had realized that I was giving her nothing in exchange; and she added: "By the way, do stay to lunch, anyhow."

"I can't."

"I've invited a few people to lunch. There's the Minister, Triolo, and his wife. A charming, intelligent, energetic man."

"A Minister? How ghastly! Come on, give me this money."

This time she gave me the money, but with a gesture that was both angry and hesitant, as if she wished to take it back at the very moment when she was handing it to me. "Then come to lunch tomorrow," she said. "There'll be no one but you and me. Then I can give you the rest of the amount. If it's really true that you're going to Cortina. . . ."

"Why? Do you doubt it?"

"With you one never knows."

My mother appeared now to be fairly well satisfied. I saw this from the way in which she walked downstairs in front of me, holding her head high and placing her hand on the brass rail. Perhaps she was satisfied, I thought, because she had succeeded once again in avoiding the great explanation between myself and her, the explanation that no one who is rich wants ever to take place, or else he could never again enjoy his wealth in peace. Her satisfaction was so great that, forgetting my recent refusal, she suggested to me when we were in the hall: "Why don't you stay until the Minister arrives? You could have a drink with him and then go away. He's an influential man, he might always be useful."

"Not to me, unfortunately," I said with a sigh. "Besides, I really must run along."

My mother did not insist; she opened the front door and went out onto the doorstep and stood facing the drive, putting her hands under her armpits and shivering in the damp autumn air. "If it goes on raining like this," she said, looking up at the cloudy sky, "it will be the end of my poor flowers."

"Good-bye, Mother," I said, and stooping down I deposited the dry ritual kiss on the no less dry cheek. Then I ran off hastily to my car: I had seen another car appear suddenly at the far end of the drive and turn up toward the villa and I wanted, at all costs, to avoid an encounter with my mother's guests. I sat down at the wheel at the moment when this other car swung around to the open space in front of the house and stopped. My mother was now standing at the front door in an attitude of readiness for the reception of her important guests. I started my engine and went off—just in time to see a chauffeur in a braided uniform get out and open the door of the car, at the same time taking off his cap and bowing, but not in time to see the owner of the black-shod masculine foot protruding from the doorway and feeling for the ground.

It was nearly one o'clock; I drove fast all the way along the Via Appia and reached the Piazza di Spagna shortly before the shops closed. I knew where to go to buy Cecilia's farewell present—to a shop in Via dei Condotti where they sold bags and umbrellas. It was full of smart women shoppers, who drew aside with a faint look of surprise at my appearance. Then, while I was hurriedly choosing an alligator bag, I caught sight of myself in a mirror and understood the reason for their glances. I looked like a tramp, and a rather alarming tramp at that: bald pate encircled with curly fair hair that badly needed cutting, a blur of reddish beard on the cheeks, charcoal-colored sweater showing a shirt without a tie, shapeless, worn-out, olive-green corduroy trousers. Tall, too, very tall in relation to the very low ceiling of the shop, with a forehead that looked like a vizor lowered over blue, bloodshot eyes, a short nose and a prominent mouth: a big ape, in fact. At the same time I realized, as I looked at myself, what a great proof of affection my mother had given me in inviting me to lunch, dressed as I was, in company with the Minister and her other guests. But then I reflected that my mother, with her sensitivity to what she called "good form," must have felt that I was dressed like a painter, that is, I was wearing a kind of uniform which indicated my position, a by no means dishonorable position in a social circle such as hers, where a man had as much right to wear an artist's sweater as a minister's double-breasted jacket. I was startled out of these thoughts by the voice of the shop assistant as she handed me the bag. I paid, took the parcel and went out.

It was one o'clock. The appointment was at five. Strange to say, although I had never been conscious of waiting for Cecilia on other days, when I knew that our relationship was going to continue, now that I had made up my mind to break with her I found that the waiting dismayed me. I therefore did all the things I could find to do until five o'clock as slowly as possible, hoping in this way to make the time pass imperceptibly and painlessly. I had lunch in a nearby restaurant and pretended to enjoy the food and to meditate between one mouthful and the next; I went into a bar and, after drinking a cup of coffee, hung about listening to songs on the juke box; I had a second cup of coffee in another bar and, perched on a stool, read a newspaper from beginning to end; I stood on the pavement for about twenty minutes conversing with a young painter whose name I did not know, pretending to be interested in his long diatribe on the subject of awards and exhibitions. But I succeeded, in this way, in whiling away only two of the four hours until the time of the appointment. In the end, with an aching heart, I went back to the studio.

There, filtering through the white curtain, came a mild, clean, clear light which was very familiar to me, that same light in which it seemed to me that my boredom—the lack of contact between myself and external things—assumed an aspect of supreme normality, although it was none the less painful for that; in fact, perhaps precisely on that account, more painful than ever. When I entered the studio and sat down in the armchair in front of the empty canvas which still glimmered white upon the easel, I said to myself: "I am here and they are there." By "they" I meant the objects around me—the canvas on the easel, the round table in the middle, the screen in the corner to the left behind which the bed was concealed, the terra cotta stove with its pipe going up into the ceiling, the chairs with notebooks lying on them, the bookshelf and the books. They were there and I was here, and between them and me there was nothing, truly nothing, just as, perhaps, in the interstellar spaces, there is nothing between the stars, millions of light-years distant from each other.

I repeated to myself: "I am here and they are there," and then I remembered Cecilia lying the day before on the divan, with her eyes closed and her head thrown back on the cushion, her belly thrust forward and offered in the most explicit, literal manner, like an object with no will of any sort beyond that of being possessed. I remembered also that as I went to her I had thought, as I was thinking today: "She is there and I am here," and I had felt that between her and me there was nothing, and that I had to penetrate, to cross, in fact to fill, that void with the movement of my body throwing itself upon hers. And as I recalled the effort, like the breaking of a barrier, that I had made in order to embrace and possess her, I suddenly realized that my decision to leave her was in reality nothing else than the official confirmation, so to speak, of a situation that already existed. Yes, I would break with Cecilia, but I had in effect left her a long time before—if indeed I had ever had any contact with her.

In the midst of these reflections I began to feel sleepy; I got up from the armchair and threw myself on the divan. I fell asleep almost at once and with such a rush that I had, in my sleep, a sensation of hurtling downward, fists and teeth clenched and all huddled up, into an infinity of space, and the longer my fall continued the more did the weight of my body increase. Then suddenly I awoke, with a taste of iron in my mouth as though I had been gripping a metal bar between my teeth. The studio was almost in darkness, and the objects in it had turned black in the grey half-light. I jumped up from the divan and turned on the light. Immediately it was night at the window. Then I looked at the clock on the table and saw that it was past six: Cecilia was to have come at five.

It did not require a great effort of imagination to realize that her lateness was not a matter of chance and that it was indeed now very probable that she would not come that day. But this was not a normal fact that could be accepted with tranquillity. By one of the many contradictions in her character, even though she seemed incapable of the feelings which prompt us not to cause suffering to the people who love us, Cecilia was always extremely punctual, just as if she had really loved me; and when, for some reason, she could not help being late, she always found means of letting me know in time. Her lateness therefore was abnormal and could only be explained in one way—by some event more important than our appointment, so important that it not merely prevented her from coming but also from letting me know that she would not come.

Nevertheless, the first thought that came into my mind was: "Well, aren't you pleased? You wanted to get rid of her and she hasn't come. So much the better, surely?" But this thought was an ironical one; for I realized to my astonishment that Cecilia's lateness not only gave me no pleasure but seriously troubled me.

I went back and sat down on the divan and started thinking. Why did Cecilia's lateness upset me? I saw that, whereas she had hitherto been nothing to me, as I have already said, her lateness caused her to become something. Furthermore this "something," at the very moment when it was acquiring substance, eluded me in a painful fashion, for after all Cecilia had not come. And so it seemed to me that when she was in the studio and clinging to me, Cecilia was absent; now, when she was not there and when I knew she would not come, I felt her to be poignantly, obscurely present.

I tried to think with greater clearness, although I found it difficult to do so because I was suffering. Cecilia had not come, she had not even taken the trouble to justify herself, therefore she no longer loved me, or anyhow not enough to be punctual or to let me know she was not coming—in other words, she loved me very little. Then suddenly I remembered, with some astonishment, that during the two months that our relationship had lasted Cecilia had never told me that she loved me and I had never asked her. Certainly the fact that she had given herself to me and had shown that she found pleasure with me might be equivalent to a declaration of love. But it was also possible, as I at once realized, that it meant nothing at all.

In any case, the very slight importance that Cecilia gave to this surrendering of her body seemed to prove that it had no meaning. Some things are simply a matter of feeling: Cecilia had given me her body with the same barbaric, naïve indifference with which a savage presents a rapacious explorer with the amulet of precious stones that he wears around his neck. It was, in fact, as though she had never had any wooers to make her understand how desirable a woman's body can be. Balestrieri, it is true, had adored her and had died of his adoration; but Cecilia appeared still to be surprised at it, as at something that seemed to her utterly unjustified.

Suddenly I felt a pang at my heart, and I started violently so that my whole body shook. The thought that had pierced my heart was this: "I can think whatever I like, but in the meantime she hasn't come," and it aroused in me an almost physical feeling of the vanity of any sort of reflection in face of the reality of her absence. I looked at the clock and saw that more than half an hour had passed since I had woken up: certainly Cecilia would not be coming now. And I no longer had any desire to prove to myself that her absence left me indifferent.

I thought she might not be feeling well—the only reason that could explain her conduct without causing me to be suspicious of her—and I got up from the divan to go to the telephone. And then I recollected, with the feeling that I was making a discovery, that I had never, not even once, telephoned to Cecilia. It was she who had telephoned me, every day; I had never telephoned her because I had never felt the need of it. This lack of curiosity on my part seemed to me significant. I had never bothered to telephone Cecilia, in the same way that I had never sought to establish any real contact with her. And so our relationship had been nothing, and boredom had easily corroded it, and I, in the end, had made up my mind to break it.

After I had dialed the number Cecilia's telephone went on ringing for a long time in a mysterious silence. To be more precise, I felt that the silence was mysterious inasmuch as Cecilia, who was in the background of this silence, had from the moment when she failed to arrive become mysterious to me, like an animal which had taken refuge in the depths of its lair. However, although it was mysterious, this silence was not entirely negative. In an insecure sort of way, like a gambler who after many losses still deceives himself into thinking he is going to win, I hoped that Cecilia's voice would become audible. Instead of that a strange thing happened: the ringing stopped, someone took off the receiver but no one spoke; or rather I seemed to hear heavy breathing, or a kind of whispering, at the other end of the line. I called out: "Hello, hello," and several times I asked: "Who is speaking?" Finally I realized that the receiver at the other end had been replaced. In a rage I dialed the number again, was again answered with silence and with that mysterious sound of breathing, and again, finally, the receiver was replaced. The third time, the telephone rang for a long time but nobody replied.

I left the telephone and went back and sat on the divan. For some time, in astonishment, I thought of nothing. The only thing that was clear to me was that, on the very day when I had decided to announce the ending of our relationship, Cecilia, for some reason I still did not know, had for the first time missed an appointment, had in effect—even if only in a provisional way—provoked the separation which I had had in mind to suggest to her. I had the disagreeable sensation of someone who, going down a steep staircase in the dark, expects another step and encounters instead the flat surface of a landing and then loses his balance just because the step is not there.

Deep in thought, I rose and went mechanically to the door, opened it and looked out into the corridor, toward the corner, almost hoping to see Cecilia appear there. I looked also in the opposite direction and my glance, traveling along the wall, came to a stop at the last door, which was that of Balestrieri's studio. It occurred to me that Balestrieri himself must have put his head out into the corridor countless times to see if Cecilia, when she was late, might appear at the corner. I knew that his studio had not yet been let again; in fact it was said that his widow had the intention of going to live there herself. Now Cecilia on the day of our first meeting had left the key of the old painter's studio on my table. She had never asked me for this key, and I had thrown it into the bottom of a drawer, with a presentiment that I might make use of it in the future. I had a sudden desire to look at the place in which Balestrieri had tormented himself through the same uncertainty from which I myself was suffering at that moment.

I took the key, left the door ajar so that Cecilia, if she came, could get in, and went to Balestrieri's studio. When the imitation candles of the central chandelier were lit, the studio looked to me gloomier than ever, with its sham antique furniture and red damask. I went up to the table, walking across the thick carpet and inhaling with distaste the stuffy, dusty, slightly malodorous air. It was a massive, Renaissance style table, its polished top now veiled with the dust of two months' abandonment; the telephone was standing upon it, together with the directories and a green receipted bill. I reflected that the widow was perhaps really intending to come and live in the studio, since she was continuing to pay for the telephone; then my eye fell on a bound address book with a marbled cover: I picked it up and turned over the pages. Balestrieri's handwriting, big and coarse and thick, made me think for some reason of his too-wide shoulders and his too-large feet. I was struck by the great number of women's names without any surnames, on almost every page—Paola, Maria, Milly, Ines, Daniela, Laura, Sofia, Giovanna, etc. etc. Knowing Balestrieri's habits, I had no doubt that they were the names of the accommodating girls who in the past, before his great love for Cecilia, had so often visited him. I went on turning the pages and looked at the letter C. There was Cecilia's name, followed by the same telephone number that I had just been vainly ringing. I stood for a moment with my eyes fixed on this name and number, thinking of the very different feelings Balestrieri must have had on the day he wrote it down and then, successively, on each of the occasions when he went and looked at it before telephoning to Cecilia. No doubt in the end he would not have had to refer to the address book, as he would have known the number by heart, but all the same he would have taken a look, now and then, at the page with the letter C, to revive the memory of that first, fatal occasion when he had written down Cecilia's name and number. All of a sudden the telephone on the table started ringing.

I hesitated, then took up the receiver. I had a strange feeling of being not myself but Balestrieri; and that I should hear Cecilia's voice on the telephone. This feeling had an unexpected confirmation; I did, in fact, hear the well-known voice asking: "Is that you, Mauro?" (Balestrieri's name was Mauro.) In a rush of anguish and nausea, my heart failed. So it really was Cecilia, and she was telephoning not to me but to Balestrieri, to a man who was dead and whom she knew to be dead.

All this did not last more than an instant. In a scarcely audible voice I said: "No, it's Dino," and immediately the other voice, losing all resemblance to Cecilia's and showing itself, in fact, to be very different—as though the resemblance had been created there and then simply by my anxiety—exclaimed in a tone of confusion: "Oh, I'm sorry, am I not speaking to Signor Balestrieri's number?"

"Yes."

"Is Signor Balestrieri not there? You see, I've been away from Rome for four months and I wanted to have a word with him. Are you a friend of his?"

"Yes, I'm a friend of his. And you—who are you?"

"I'm Milly," answered the girl, in a pathetic, hopeful tone of voice which somehow suggested her intimacy with the old painter.

"Signorina Milly, Signor Balestrieri has . . . has gone away."

"He's gone away? And you don't know when he's coming back?"

"No."

"Oh well, tell him, when you see him, that Milly telephoned."

I put down the receiver again and stayed quite still for a time, brooding over the vague, unpleasant feeling that this telephone call had aroused in me. Then I became conscious that it was cold in the studio and that the cold was getting right into my bones. It was a special sort of cold, at the same time both unclean and sepulchral, the cold of a tomb which is also an alcove, or an alcove which is also a tomb. I had sat down to answer the telephone, overcome, it may be, by my agitation when I thought I heard Cecilia's voice. I rose and went out into the corridor.

Back in my studio I looked at the clock and, since I knew I was no longer expecting anybody, I realized that I was looking at it to see how long it was before Cecilia telephoned me in the morning, as she always did. I reflected that it was the first time I had had such a thought; and I knew that henceforward such thoughts would visit my mind more and more frequently.

Chapter 5

Next morning, thinking over Cecilia's failure to arrive, I was convinced, or rather I tried to convince myself, that her absence was due to causes which had nothing to do with our relationship. I still wanted to break with Cecilia, but the Cecilia I wanted to break with was the Cecilia who was in love with me, or whom I imagined to be in love with me, not the Cecilia who no longer loved me and who missed her appointments. This was not a case of that special, perverse kind of love which makes us love someone who does not love us and dislike anyone who does love us; it was because the Cecilia who loved me had proved boring, and therefore unreal, whereas the Cecilia who did not love me seemed, on the contrary, by the very fact of not loving me, to acquire a steadily increasing semblance of reality in my eyes. Nevertheless I preferred to think that Cecilia loved me and that consequently I did not have to alter my decision to get rid of her, because, as I have already hinted, the idea that she had ceased to bore me, in other words that she was becoming real, filled me, fundamentally, with a kind of fear, as though I were confronting a trial that I did not feel able to face.

In the meantime, however, there was a problem, a small but painful problem: should I be the first to telephone, or should

I wait for her to telephone me? Cecilia was in the habit of telephoning me every day, always at the same time, about ten o'clock in the morning, to greet me and confirm our appointment for the afternoon. I could therefore certainly expect her to telephone that day as usual, but at the same time I was afraid lest she might not do so and might go out, in which case, by the time I made up my mind to telephone myself, she would not be there and I should have to spend the whole day in uncertainty as to whether she was coming—an uncertainty which without any doubt had by now become extremely painful. And furthermore I realized that in this affair of the telephone the terms of my greater problem were being repeated in an identical way: I wanted Cecilia to telephone me first so that I could continue to consider her dispensable and therefore non-existent; whereas, if it were I who telephoned, I should have to think of her as of something problematical and elusive and therefore real. At three in the afternoon I was still immersed in these reflections when I heard the telephone ringing repeatedly over at the far end of the studio—gently, querulously, ironically, as if to tell me that the thing that mattered was not my thoughts, however lucid, but its own ringing. I went over and took up the receiver and at once heard Cecilia's voice saying: "At last! Where were you?"

I answered in a very low voice: "I was in the studio, but I hadn't heard you."

There was a moment's silence and then she said: "I didn't ring you this morning because the telephone was out of order. See you today at the usual time, then."

I could not help exclaiming somewhat sharply: "But why didn't you come yesterday?"

I expected her reply, whether sincere or untruthful, to be anyhow precise. Instead, these disconcerting words reached my ears: "Because I couldn't."

"Why couldn't you?"

"Because I had things to do."

"Very well," I said angrily, recognizing, in these answers, Cecilia's characteristic capacity at the same time to avoid both telling the truth and telling a lie. "Very well then. See you soon."

"Yes, soon. Good-bye."

I realized immediately afterward that the fact that it had been she who telephoned first did not bring me the relief I had hoped for. She had indeed telephoned first, but had contrived by her secretiveness to remain just as elusive and mysterious as if she had not done so. Her action in telephoning me, which ought to have meant that I had it in my power to dispose of her, that she was dependent upon me and therefore could be discarded, had in reality meant nothing. And I still had to get rid of her, as I had decided.

In the meantime I had to go on living, by which I mean I had to while away the two hours that still lay between me and the moment when Cecilia would appear in my studio. To give some idea of my impatience I can say that, not knowing what to do, I even took it into my head to start painting, after an interval of more than two months during which I had not touched a brush. I said to myself that if I could perhaps manage to cover the canvas that still stood prominently on my easel I would have, if nothing else, a further reason for parting from Cecilia; I knew, in fact, that painting and painting alone could fill the void in my life which the ending of our relationship would leave. But I only had to look at the canvas standing there on the easel to know that I would be incapable, not merely of painting, but even of lifting my hand to make any kind of a mark upon it. In reality I had at that moment only one relationship—and that a problematical one—with any object of any kind, and that was my relationship with Cecilia, which in any case I was preparing to break off. How the devil, then, could I paint on that canvas, which on the day of my first meeting with Cecilia I had signed as if to underline the fact that painting, as far as I was concerned, was finished? To comfort myself, I reread something that Kandinski had written on this very subject. "The empty canvas. In appearance—really empty, silent, indifferent. Stunned, almost. In effect—full of tensions, with a thousand subdued voices, heavy with expectation. A little frightened because it may be violated. But docile. It does willingly whatever is asked of it, it only begs for mercy. It can lead to anything, but cannot endure everything. A wonderful thing is the empty canvas, more beautiful than many pictures. . . ." Suddenly I hurled the book on the floor and almost ran out of the studio.

I knew what direction I would take, not so much with my mind as by an instinct like that of a sporting dog following a scent through a wood or across a heath. Thus I turned out of Via Margutta, came into Via del Babuino and walked in the direction of the Piazza di Spagna, hurrying along quickly past the shops and through people who knocked against me, just as though I were afraid of arriving late for some appointment. I went on for a hundred yards or so, and then in front of me I saw Cecilia. She too was walking quickly, like a person who knows where he is going and is in a hurry to get there. After thinking for a moment of catching up with her, I slackened my pace and followed her; I had suddenly realized that never had she seemed so real to me as now when I was intending to part from her, and I wanted to enjoy this feeling of reality and at the same time to understand why in the world it had become perceptible to me at this particular moment. So I looked at her attentively and realized that it was as though I were seeing her for the first time in my life, in an atmosphere as fresh as that of the first day of Creation. The details of her figure seemed by some miracle to be more visible than usual, in fact to be visible on their own account—visible, that is, even if I did not look at them and examine them—the light, crisp, brown mass of her hair, more like the intricate, untamed fleece of the groin than a combed head of hair; the motion of her neck, which could not be seen because it was hidden, but which could be felt, at the same time querulous and graceful; the movement of her long, loose, hairy green sweater around the bust which I knew to be naked underneath it, with the full, firm breasts and their delicate points exposed to the friction of the rough wool; her short, narrow black skirt which displayed the rotundities of her hips, shifting and undulating at every step; her whole body, in fact, seemed to attract and swallow up my glances with the avidity with which the dry earth swallows the rain. But beyond these outward appearances which leaped to my eye, I realized that for the first time after a long period I was enabled to perceive a reality—how shall I describe it?—a reality of second degree, that is, something which gave a soul to these vivid, emphatic forms. Finally I understood what this reality was: in every part of that body in movement there was, as it were, an unconscious, involuntary force that seemed to urge Cecilia forward, as if she were a sleepwalker with closed eyes and darkened mind. This force drew her away from me and consequently made her real to me.

When she reached the Piazza di Spagna, Cecilia walked with decision toward the great flight of steps. I stopped for a moment and, my eye leaping from her to the place that she appeared to be making for, I caught sight of the figure of a man who seemed to be waiting for somebody, standing beside a flower seller's big umbrella. He was a young man, tall and vigorous-looking, with two features that I noticed at once: very broad shoulders which seemed to indicate an athletic build, and hair of a false-looking, golden blond that appeared to be bleached with peroxide. Cecilia, meanwhile, had crossed the whole space of the Piazza di Spagna, her head bent, and was now approaching the young man, without quickening her step but with a movement of the hips that was full of irresistible, provoking urgency. She reached him and stopped, and it looked to me as if they shook hands; and then, hastily, I also moved. They were talking now and Cecilia had climbed onto the first step of the stairs, and even so looked shorter than he.

Soon I was quite close to them. I realized that Cecilia had not seen me, so I went almost up to her, at a distance of a pace or so, and even then I was sure that she continued not to see me. I moved up onto the step and walked around her, almost touching her this time: she was talking and laughing gaily with the man with the peroxide hair, and all of a sudden her big dark eyes rested upon me, but even now, although it seemed to me impossible, I had to admit that she had not seen me. I was aware that I was registering these things without thinking at all, and I knew I was not thinking because I was suffering. In the end I went and hid behind the flower seller's umbrella, a few steps farther on.

Now the young man with the peroxide hair had taken Cecilia by the arm, with an eloquent tenderness, and was gently pushing her toward the umbrella behind which I was hiding. They stopped, and then the young man, without letting go of Cecilia's arm, selected a bunch of violets from a jar and handed them to her. Cecilia raised the flowers to her nostrils; the young man paid the flower seller, and then, still holding Cecilia by the arm, went off with her up the steps toward Trinità dei Monti. For the first time I noticed that the young man was wearing a short green overcoat; until then I had not seen it.

For a short time after they had disappeared I remained where I was, looking up the flight of steps. I felt an acute pain which gave me no peace and at the same time an impotent rage at the fact that I felt this pain. I understood, indeed, that until I had suffered I should not be able to part from Cecilia, as I still wished to do. And I also understood that with Cecilia I could only be bored, or suffer: hitherto I had been bored and consequently had wished to leave her; now I was suffering and I felt I would not be able to leave her until I was bored once again.

These reflections and others of a similar kind must have been very intense and very absorbing, for I suddenly found myself, to my surprise, back again in my studio. Wrapped in a cloud of thought I had gone back, without being conscious of it, to Via Margutta, had gone in and thrown myself on the divan. The clock on the central table showed half past four. Only half an hour to go before Cecilia's arrival, but there was nothing more I could do except wait for her. And this half-hour seemed to me to be impassable, as though time itself had stopped and were awaiting a push from me to make it resume its course. Actually it was I who had stopped, arrested by a thought which refused to be displaced, whatever efforts I might make.

What most infuriated me was that, although I did not love Cecilia, circumstances were forcing me to have the feelings and to behave in the ways which are appropriate to love. I wanted to free myself from these circumstances as an ox wants to free itself from the yoke that weighs upon its neck, but I felt that with every movement they oppressed me more and constrained me to behave like the lover which I was now convinced I was not.

I said to myself, for instance: "Now Cecilia and her friend are in some retired corner of the Borghese Gardens and Cecilia is doing with him what she has done so many times with me: she is kissing him awkwardly and coldly, with her childish lips, and at the same time is giving him her customary hard, eager push in the belly with her groin." And immediately afterward I thought: Why do I think all these things and why do I suffer? Obviously because I saw them together. And am I then forced, in spite of myself, by the sole fact of having seen them together, to be jealous on her account and to suffer?

I sat thinking with my head bent and my eyes on the floor. Finally I looked at the clock and discovered that there was only a short time left before Cecilia's arrival. Rising from the divan and stretching my cramped limbs, I reflected that after all I was not altogether sure that she had betrayed me. What, in actual fact, had I seen? An innocent meeting in a place that was far from secret, the gallant but not highly significant gift of a bunch of violets, a walk to the Pincio. Such things happen every hour and every day, without the people who do them being, on that account, bound together by the ties of love. There was, it is true, the fact of the missed appointment of the previous day. But I had to beware of the kind of mental disposition that tends to establish arbitrary relations between separate and dissimilar things. Cecilia had not come to our appointment the day before: that was a fact. I had seen her that afternoon with a young man with peroxide hair: that was another fact. But that did not mean that the two facts were connected; above all, it did not mean that they were connected by a common factor of betrayal.

Strange to say, no sooner had I given shape to these reflections than the figure of Cecilia, which, as long as I had suspected her of betraying me, had been living and real to me, although mysterious (in fact, precisely *because* mysterious)— now that I was doubtful about her betrayal, became unreal and boring again as in the past. And, as in the days past, I felt I must get rid of her at all costs; and I was afraid lest I might not be capable of it; and I strengthened myself in my determination by recalling the cruelty which I had resorted to during one of our last meetings in order to avoid a relapse into boredom.

Cecilia was punctual. At five o'clock I heard the familiar ring at the bell that was so characteristic of her, so brief, so reticent, and at the same time so intimate. I went and opened the door, saying to myself: "The moment I see her I shall tell her I'm leaving for the mountains, and thus, even if I have cause to regret it later, I shall have created an established fact which it will be difficult for me to nullify afterward." I foresaw that the moment she came in Cecilia would as usual throw her arms around my neck, with her customary, mechanically passionate gesture, but this time I would take hold of her hands and pull them down, disengaging myself from her embrace and saying: "First of all I've got to talk to you."

What happened, however, was something I had not foreseen but which I really ought to have foreseen. When I threw the door open, Cecilia did not fling her arms around my neck; on the contrary, she drew back, making a sort of gesture to keep me at a distance and saying: "First of all there's something I must say to you."

I could not help thinking that these were more or less the words I had in mind to say to *her;* and it immediately flashed across my mind that Cecilia wanted to announce a decision similar to my own, that is, that she wanted to leave me. In the meantime she had gone and sat down on the divan. I went over and sat down beside her, saying in a loud, angry voice: "No, first of all you've got to give me a kiss."

Obediently she bent forward and gave me a quick peck on the cheek. Then, drawing back, she said: "The thing I must tell you is that from now on we can't go on meeting every day, but only twice a week."

"Why is that?"

"Keep calm, don't get angry," she said, before answering my question. My voice had indeed been loud and harsh, but I became seriously angry as I heard myself say: "I am calm and I am not angry. I merely want to know the reason for all this."

"They're beginning to grumble at home because I see you every day."

"But didn't you tell them you were taking drawing lessons?"

"Yes, but only twice a week. On the other days I always have to invent some excuse, and now they've found out."

"It's not true, your people don't grumble. They didn't grumble, for instance, when you saw Balestrieri every day."

"Balestrieri was sixty-five, not thirty-five like you: they weren't suspicious of *him.* Besides, they knew him."

"Well, introduce me to them, then."

"All right, I will. But meanwhile we must meet only twice a week."

For a short time we sat silent. I was discovering now that not merely did I no longer want to part from Cecilia, but also that I could not bear to see her only twice in seven days. Then, all of a sudden, I understood. I was even prepared to reduce the number of our meetings; but I had to be mathematically certain that she was not lying to me and that her parents had really made trouble. Since, however, I was not certain, the idea that she was lying to me gave me a feeling of deep distress, as though she had escaped me at the very moment when, thanks to her untruthfulness, she was becoming real and desirable in my eyes. I took hold of her hand. "Tell me the truth," I said. "You don't want to see me any more."

She answered at once: "That's not the point. I said that from now on we must meet only twice a week, that's all there is to it."

I noticed that her tone of voice was completely neutral, equally distant from truthfulness and from falsehood. This was an observation that I had already made on other occasions; but only in order to note a trait in Cecilia's character without attaching any significance to it. In general, she appeared always to be saying simply the things that she was saying, neither more nor less, without the slightest undertone of feeling. The latter, as I knew, was perceptible during sexual intercourse, and only then. But it was absolutely necessary for me to know whether she was lying to me, because I still wished to break off relations with her and her lying to me would prevent this. So I insisted. "What you really want is for us to part. But you haven't the courage to tell me and so you're trying to prepare me. Today you say twice a week, tomorrow you'll say twice a month, and then in the end you'll tell me the truth."

"What truth?"

I had it on the tip of my tongue to say: "That you have another man." But I restrained myself: the connection between her decision to reduce the number of our meetings and the encounter in the Piazza di Spagna was too obvious, and it humiliated me to accept it. Instead, I said brusquely: "Very well then. Let it be as you wish; from now on we'll meet only twice a week. And now let's change the subject."

"What's the matter? Why are you so gloomy?"

"Let's change the subject. Do you know that I passed right under your nose today and you didn't see me?"

"Why, where?"

"In the Piazza di Spagna, near the steps."

"At what time?"

"It must have been about four."

I looked at her closely: her face had its usual uncertain, childish expression and she did not even start. "Oh yes," she said, "I was with an actor called Luciani."

Even her voice revealed nothing in particular: it was expressionless, neutral, unrelated to innocence or guilt. I asked casually: "Why has he put peroxide on his hair?"

"Because he had to play the part of a fair-haired man."

"You seemed very intimate, judging, at least, from the way you walked."

"What way?" she inquired, with genuine curiosity.

I felt that words were not adequate to depict the tenderness with which the actor had taken her by the arm. "Get up!" I said.

"But why?"

"Get up!"

She obeyed. Then I took her by the arm and made her walk about the studio for a little, exactly as I had seen the actor do. "There," I said finally, letting her go again, "that's the way."

She went back and sat down on the divan and looked at me for a moment, then she said: "He always does that"—a remark, I felt, that did not at all signify that she and the actor were not in love. "Have you known this Luciani for long?" I asked.

"For a couple of months."

"D'you see him often?"

"We see each other now and again."

She got up again and started pulling off her sweater over her head. "You had an appointment with him today?" I asked.

"He wants me to work in the films, and we had to talk about that."

I looked up at her: she had pulled up her sweater over her head, showing her white armpits with their few long, soft, brown hairs, but her breasts were still hidden, and only the thin, adolescent torso could be seen. Then, with a violent movement, she gave an upward pull and her breasts burst forth: all at once the torso was that of a grown woman, though it still retained a certain slenderness and immaturity. It crossed my mind that she was undressing in order to interrupt an embarrassing interrogation. "Are you going to work in the films?" I asked her.

"I don't know yet."

"And afterward where did you go?"

"We went to the Pincio and had some coffee."

She had seated herself on the divan again now, bare to the waist, as though to answer me better. Meanwhile she was carefully turning back the sleeves of her sweater. "Yes," I said, "I saw you go up toward the Trinità dei Monti. Perhaps this actor lives close by in Via Sistina, does he?"

"No, he lives in the Parioli district, in Via Archimede."

"And after your coffee what did you do?"

"We walked about in the Borghese gardens until a short time ago, when I left him to come here."

I became conscious that I was looking at her with desire; and I realized that I desired her, not so much because she was naked, as because she was lying to me. She appeared to notice my look, and added, quite simply: "Do you want to make love?"

The idea that she was proposing we should make love in order to conceal the fact that she was lying to me made me suddenly furious. I was certain that only a lover could press a woman's arm in the way Luciani had pressed hers. But now again I avoided mentioning the actor's name. "No," I shouted, "I don't want to make love, I want to know the truth."

142

"But what d'you mean, the truth?"

"The truth, whatever it is."

"I don't understand you."

"Yesterday you didn't come to our appointment and you didn't even let me know that you couldn't come. Today you want to reduce the number of your visits. I want to know the truth; I want to know what there is behind all this."

"I've already told you: my parents are making trouble."

Again I felt it on the tip of my tongue to say: "It's not true, the truth is that you go to bed with Luciani," but at the same time I felt I would not be capable of saying it. So I remained silent and glum, staring at the floor. Then I felt her hand on my cheek and heard her say: "Are you very sorry not to see me every day?"

"Yes."

"Well then, forget what I said. We'll go on as before. Only we shall have to be more careful. We'll meet at different times, according to which day it is. In any case I'll telephone you in the morning to let you know, each day, what time we can meet. Are you content now?"

And so, in a mysterious, unexpected way, Cecilia gave up the idea of reducing her visits to me. I was so surprised that I couldn't go on thinking unkind things about her. It was clear now: Cecilia, in spite of her precocious experience, was a very young girl and afraid of her parents; this fear had prompted her to reduce the frequency of our meetings; in face of my sadness and suspicion, she had changed her mind again and was doing as I asked. So she was not being unfaithful to me, she was not lying to me; she was just a simple, unmysterious girl, torn between her subjection to her parents and her attachment to her lover. It seemed odd that I had not thought of this before; and all at once the way in which the actor had taken her by the arm became an unimportant detail. Perhaps he really did that with all women, whatever his relations with them might be. These reflections lasted only a moment. Then

I became aware of a new fact: not merely was I not pleased that Cecilia had given up the idea of reducing her visits; but also I could see the old boredom reappearing on our horizon, like a tiny but decidedly dark cloud in an otherwise empty sky. "Thank you," I said. "But, if you like, we could perhaps see each other, say four times a week instead of seven."

"No, it doesn't matter, I'll find some excuse."

She had gone back to the chair upon which she had placed her sweater and had started undressing again. I watched her as she put her two hands to the zipper at the side of her skirt and lowered it; I wondered whether the quick, graceful gestures that brought about the gradual fall of her clothes and the gradual unveiling of her body appeared to me, now that I was sure of not being betrayed, as boring and ridiculous as they had in the past; and, after a moment's consideration, I was compelled to admit that it was so. As if, in fact, by a miracle in reverse—a miracle, that is, which instead of introducing something magical into reality had withdrawn it—Cecilia, who had seemed so desirable as long as I had suspected that she was betraying me, now that I was convinced of the contrary had gone back to being an insignificant object, present to the most superficial perception of my senses but not for that reason truly real. I reflected that the whole of her personality was in that action of lowering the zipper fastening, the whole of her, with no margin of independence or mystery, and that she was for that very reason non-existent; that she had been already possessed beforehand, even before sexual intercourse had given a superfluous confirmation to this possession by feeling; possessed and therefore boring. While I was thinking these things I was myself undressing, and that I could not help casting a glance at my sexual organ, almost afraid that it was not in a state of erection, as I might well have feared, judging from my reflections. But it was, and never so much as at that moment had I admired the force of nature which made me desire without any real desire. By this time I was naked. I lay down on my

144

back on the divan, rather as a sick man lies on the doctor's couch, and with the same sense of submitting to an unpleasant ordeal which anyhow was very far removed from love.

Then an unexpected thing happened. Cecilia, who had also finished undressing, went over on tiptoe, as usual, to draw the curtains across the big window, and then, with the joyous movement of one who gains his freedom and runs toward the sea, she rushed to the divan and threw herself on top of me, heavily, violently, and with an inarticulate cry of triumph. Then she raised herself up and sat astride me as I lay flat, and leaning heavily with her two hands on my shoulders, exclaimed: "Tell me the truth, you must confess that you believed just now that I was being unfaithful to you with Luciani?"

I looked at the excited face, red with pleasure, framed in the light, curly hair that had never seemed to me so alive, and I was suddenly convinced of the opposite of what I had hitherto been thinking: yes, Cecilia *had* lied to me; yes, she *had* been unfaithful to me with the actor. There was proof of this, if nowhere else, in her triumphant voice, which in its irresistible artlessness resembled that of a little girl who, after a successful joke, calls out to her companion: "Now admit it, you were caught!"

At the same time I saw her afresh, more real than ever and therefore desirable, with her full, brown, womanly breasts hanging forward from her thin, white adolescent body; with her slim waist; with her compact, powerful hips; and it seemed to me that she appeared real and desirable precisely because she was evading me through her lying and treachery. This thought filled me with anxious, vindictive rage; I seized her by the hair with such force that I heard her groan, threw her off me and hurled myself upon her. Physical possession, usually, was no more than the repetition of a preceding mental possession, that is, it merely confirmed the boredom which made Cecilia unreal and absurd to me. But this time I felt that possession appeared to confirm my inability truly to possess her. However roughly I treated her, however much I squeezed her and bit her and penetrated her, I failed to possess Cecilia and she was elsewhere, God knows where. Finally I fell back exhausted but still angry, withdrawing from her sex as from a useless wound; and it seemed to me that Cecilia, who was now lying beside me with closed eyes, had an expression of irony on her face even in the midst of the composed serenity that follows the satisfaction of carnal appetite. The expression, I said to myself, of reality itself, the reality that evaded me and receded at the very moment when I imagined I had seized hold of it.

I looked at her intently. She must have felt my eyes upon her, for she opened hers and gazed back at me. Then she said: "Do you know, it was wonderful today?"

"Isn't it always wonderful in the same way?"

"Oh no, it's always different. There are days when it's not so good, but today it was very good."

"Why was it so good?"

"It's a thing one can't explain. A woman feels it, you know, when it's good and when it isn't so good. D'you know how many times, today?"

"How many?"

She lifted her hand with three fingers pointing up and said: "Three," then she closed her eyes again, pressing herself lightly against me, and as she made this movement the ironical expression I had already noticed appeared again on her face with its lowered eyelids. And so, I thought, it might even be that I had really possessed her, possessed her totally, possessed her with no margin of independence or mystery. But I was unable to have full consciousness of it, or, therefore, to enjoy it; it seemed that only the one who was possessed could be conscious of possession, not the possessor. Again, and more strongly than ever, I experienced the feeling that I was incapable of achieving true possession, in spite of the fullness of the physical relation. I should have liked to ask: "Was it better with me or with Luciani?", but once again I felt myself unable to utter the actor's name. I asked her instead, for some inexplicable reason: "Is it true that Balestrieri died in your arms, while you were making love?"

I noticed that she wrinkled up her face for an instant, without opening her eyes, as though a gnat had brushed against it in flight. Then she murmured: "Why d'you want to know that?"

"Tell me if it's true."

She was still lying with her eyes closed, and I seemed to be questioning a sleepwalker. "Not exactly," she replied. "He felt sick while we were making love, but he died later, after we had stopped."

"You're not telling the truth."

"Why shouldn't I be telling the truth? I was so frightened. I thought he was really dead; but luckily he managed to get to the bed."

"Then you weren't on the bed?"

"No."

"Where were you, then?"

"What a lot of things you want to know."

"Where were you?"

"On the stairs."

"On the stairs?"

"Yes, he used to want to make love at any moment, so to speak. We'd already done it once in the little room upstairs, and we were going down to the studio because he wanted to paint. I was in front of him. Suddenly he wanted to make love again, and he did it right there on the stairs. But—d'you know what?"

"What?"

"After he felt sick, and I'd helped him to get upstairs to the bedroom again and onto the bed, he lay there for a little, with his eyes shut, quite still. Then, gradually, he recovered,

147

and—just imagine—he wanted to make love yet again, for the third time. It was I who refused. He looked like death already, and I was frightened. He gave up the idea, but very unwillingly, and he was angry. Sometimes I think he died because he got so angry."

So Balestrieri had really wished to kill himself, I thought. I seemed to see those two, separating at the critical moment of their intercourse; and the old painter clinging with both hands to the banister and climbing up painfully, step by step, to the gallery and then going and falling on the bed; and then the corpse-like figure sitting up suddenly and holding out its arms to Cecilia. Following the thread of my thoughts, I asked another question: "Did you use to deceive Balestrieri?"

She made that same grimace of irritation, as if troubled by an importunate gnat; and I realized that what I had really asked her was: "Are you deceiving *me?*" She too seemed to understand the true meaning of the question, for she merely murmured: "Now you're beginning again."

But I persisted. "Tell me, please, did you deceive him?"

Finally she replied: "Why d'you want to know? Yes, I did deceive him, now and then; he was so boring."

This took my breath away. "Boring—how do you mean, boring?"

"Boring."

"But what does that mean, to you—boring?"

"Boring means boring."

"And that is?"

"Boring."

So Cecilia *was* deceiving me, I thought again, and she was deceiving me because I was boring—in other words, as she was for me, non-existent. But between us there was this difference: I knew what boredom was, having suffered from it all my life, whereas for her boredom was simply an obscure urge to take the provoking, irresistible movement of her disdainful hips elsewhere. I looked at her again: she was lying flat on her back, her legs spread out, just as our last embrace had left her, with no sign of modesty, but apparently confident that I would consider her attitude of abandonment as a proof of naturalness and intimacy. As I looked at her I could not help succumbing to the masculine illusion which looks upon physical possession as the only true possession. Yes, I thought, Cecilia evaded me, she withdrew herself from me; but if I took her again—who knows?—possibly I might succeed this time in nullifying the feeling of not possessing her, I might succeed in possessing her truly and decisively. I pulled myself up, and bending over her lightly touched her lips with a kiss. Without opening her eyes she murmured: "I think I ought to be going soon."

"Wait."

And so I took her again without her opening her eyes, although with her body she candidly welcomed and facilitated my embrace in her usual hungry manner—a final proof, if there was need of it, of the fact that she was somewhere else and that what I took possession of had no value for her nor, therefore, for me either. But this time Cecilia opened her eyes wide immediately afterward, and said: "Now I really must be going."

She rose, ran across to the bathroom door and disappeared. Left alone, I fell into a kind of empty reflection. I reflected in the literal sense of the word, that is, I contemplated, in the dark mirror of my consciousness, myself lying naked and inert on the divan, the easel with the blank canvas near the window, the studio and all the things it contained. Then a precise thought insinuated itself into this dead, objective world: namely, that after the second embrace Cecilia had remained more than ever elusive and therefore real, so that, if by some miracle of nature I had been capable of having her, not twice in succession but two hundred times, I should have found myself in the end just as unsatisfied as the first time. In short, the more I had her the less I possessed her, if only because in

149

having her I wasted the energy I should have needed to possess her seriously—in a way, however, that I could not contrive to imagine, at least for the moment.

At this point I heard Cecilia open the bathroom door, and then, rising on my elbows, I said to her: "Look in that cupboard: there's a present for you." I heard her exclaim: "For me?" in a tone of voice which was neither surprised nor really pleased; then, evidently, she opened the cupboard, took out the bag, unwrapped it and looked at it, but I saw nothing because I was now lying on my back, staring up at the ceiling. But after a moment I felt her lips brush lightly against mine in one of those characteristically meager, childish kisses, and I heard her voice murmur: "Thank you." A little later, I hoisted myself on to my elbows again: Cecilia, now fully dressed, was standing at the table in the middle of the room and carefully transferring her various personal objects from her old bag into the new one. I sank down again, flat on my back.

Chapter 6

Cecilia, as I think I have made clear, was not talkative, in fact her natural inclination was to keep silence; but even when she spoke she managed to be silent at the same time, thanks to the disconcertingly brief, impersonal quality of her manner. Words, in her mouth, seemed to lose all real significance, and were reduced to abstract sounds as though they were words in a foreign language that I did not know. The lack of any kind of accent or dialect and of any inflection of social class, the complete absence of revealing commonplaces, the reduction of conversation to pure and simple declarations of incontrovertible facts such as "It's hot today"—all these confirmed this impression of abstractness. I would ask her, for example, what she had done on the evening of the day before; and she would answer: "I had dinner at home and then I went out with Mother and we went to the pictures together." Now these words, as I immediately noticed —"home," "dinner," "mother," "pictures"—which in another mouth would have meant what they usually mean, and consequently, according to how they were uttered, would have made me see whether she was lying or telling the truth—these same words, in Cecilia's mouth, seemed to be nothing more than abstract sounds, behind which it was impossible to imag-

151

ine the reality either of truth or of falsehood. I have often wondered how it was that Cecilia contrived to speak and at the same time give the impression of being silent. And I came to the conclusion that she had only one means of expression, the sexual one, which however was obviously impossible to interpret even though original and powerful; and that with her mouth she said nothing, not even things concerned with sex, because her mouth was, so to speak, a false orifice, without depth or resonance, that did not communicate with anything inside her. So much so that often, looking at her as she lay beside me on the divan after our intercourse, flat on her back with her legs open, I could not help comparing the horizontal cleft of her mouth with the vertical cleft of her sex and remarking, with surprise, how much more expressive the latter was than the former—and with the same purely psychological quality as those features of the face by which a person's nature is revealed.

Furthermore, I had to discover what was concealed behind a remark such as: "I had dinner at home and then I went out with Mother and we went to the pictures together"; whether, in fact, a dinner and a home, a mother and a motion picture were really concealed behind the words, or possibly an appointment with the peroxide-haired actor. Thus I was seized with a furious desire to know Cecilia better; previously I had not taken the trouble to find out anything about her because, being under the illusion that I possessed her through our sexual relationship, I was under the illusion that I knew everything. For example, her family. Cecilia had told me with her usual brevity that she was an only daughter, that she lived with her father and mother and that they were not well off because her father wasn't well and had stopped working. I had been content with this information, almost grateful to her, in fact, for not telling me more, since the thing that mattered to me more than anything else was that she should come every day to the studio and make love with me. But from the moment when I had a suspicion that she was being unfaithful to me, and when this suspicion had suddenly transformed Cecilia from something unreal and boring into something real and desirable, I was filled with curiosity to know more about her home life, as though I hoped that a more thorough knowledge might enable me to achieve the full possession which sexual intercourse denied me. So I started questioning her, rather in the way in which I had questioned her about her relations with Balestrieri. Here, as an example, is one of our conversations.

"Your father is sick?"

"Yes."

"What is he suffering from?"

"He's suffering from cancer."

"What do the doctors say?"

"They say he's suffering from cancer."

"No, what I mean is—do they think he can recover?"

"No, they say he can't recover."

"Then he'll die soon?"

"Yes, they say he'll die soon."

"Are you sorry?"

"Sorry for what?"

"That your father is dying."

"Yes."

"Is that all you can say?"

"What ought I to say?"

"But you're fond of your father?"

"Yes."

"Well, let's go on to something else. Your mother—what's she like?"

"What d'you mean—what's she like?"

"Well, is she short, tall, pretty, ugly, dark, fair?"

"Oh well, I don't know; she's just like lots of other women."

"But tell me, what does she look like?"

"Goodness me, she doesn't look like anything."

"Doesn't look like anything? What ever do you mean?"

153

"I mean she doesn't look like anything in particular. She's just like anyone else."

"Are you fond of your mother?"

"Yes."

"More or less fond than of your father?"

"It's a different thing."

"What does different mean?"

"Different means different."

"But different in what way?"

"I don't know: different."

"Well then, is your mother fond of your father?"

"I think so."

"Why, aren't you sure?"

"They get on all right together, so I imagine they're fond of each other."

"What does your father do all day?"

"Nothing."

"What does nothing mean?"

"Nothing means nothing."

"But people say 'doing nothing' just as a manner of speaking, and then they really do all sorts of things even if they're doing nothing. So your father doesn't work; what does he do instead?"

"He doesn't do anything."

"That is to say—?"

"Oh well, I don't know: at home he sits in an armchair by the radio. Every day he takes a little walk—that's all."

"I see. You live in a flat in the Prati district?"

"Yes."

"How many rooms have you?"

"I don't know."

"What d'you mean, you don't know?"

"I've never counted them."

"But is it a big or a small flat?"

"So-so."

"What does that mean?"

"Medium-sized."

"Well then, describe it."

"It's a flat just like lots of others; there's nothing to describe."

"But I suppose this flat of yours isn't empty? There's some furniture in it?"

"Oh yes, there's the usual furniture, beds, armchairs, cupboards."

"What sort of furniture?"

"Really I don't know; just like any other furniture."

"Take the living room, for example. You have a living room?"

"Yes."

"What furniture is there in it?"

"The usual furniture: chairs, small tables, armchairs, sofas—the same as in all living rooms."

"And in what style is this furniture?"

"Don't know."

"What color is it, then?"

"It hasn't any color."

"What do you mean, it hasn't any color?"

"I mean it hasn't any color, it's gilt."

"I see, but even gilt is a color. D'you like your home?"

"I don't know whether I like it. In any case, I'm not there very much."

I could go on in this way *ad infinitum,* but I think I have given a good example of what I have called Cecilia's abstractness. It may perhaps be thought, at this point, that Cecilia was stupid or at least devoid of personality. But this was not so: the fact that I never heard her say stupid things was a proof, if nothing else, that she was not stupid; and as for personality, this, as I have already said, lay elsewhere than in her conversation, so that to report the latter without at the same time accompanying it with a description of her face and figure would be rather like reading an operatic libretto without music or a film script without the pictures on the screen. But I wished to give an example of conversation mainly in order to convey the idea that Cecilia's way of speaking was thus formal and bloodless for the good reason that she herself was ignorant of the things about which I questioned her, just as much as I was and perhaps more so. In other words, she lived with her father and mother in a flat in Prati and had been Balestrieri's mistress; but she had never paused to look at the people and things in her life and therefore had never truly seen them, still less observed them. She was, in fact, a stranger to herself and to the world she lived in; just as much as those who knew neither her nor her world.

In any case, my suspicion of Cecilia's unfaithfulness, by making her mysterious and elusive and therefore real, finally aroused in me a desire to verify her vague scraps of information, if only in order to abolish at least that portion of mystery which lay outside our sexual relationship. One day I asked her to let me make the acquaintance of her family. I noticed with some surprise that my request did not embarrass her at all, in spite of the "grumblings" that she had put forward as an excuse to justify her intention of reducing the number of our meetings. "I had thought of that too," she said. "My mother is always asking me about you."

"Did you introduce Balestrieri to your family?"

"Yes."

"Did your parents ever get to know that you were Balestrieri's mistress?"

"No."

"If they had known, what would they have done?"

"Who knows?"

"Did Balestrieri often come to your home?"

"Yes."

"What did he do there?"

"Nothing. He used to come to lunch or for coffee and then we'd go off together to his studio."

"Did you ever make love, you and Balestrieri, at your home?"

"He always wanted to, but *I* didn't, because I was afraid my parents would discover."

"But why did he want to do it there, in your home?"

"I don't know, he liked the idea."

"But did you do it, or not?"

"Yes, we did sometimes."

"Where?"

"I don't remember now."

"Try and remember."

"Ah yes, we did it once in the kitchen."

"In the kitchen?"

"Yes, Mother had gone out to buy something, and I had to mind the oven."

"But couldn't you have gone into your room, seeing that you were alone in the house?"

"If Balestrieri had a mind to make love, he did it wherever he was: he liked doing it in odd places."

"Why?"

"I don't know."

"But how did you manage to do it, like that, in the kitchen?"

"Standing up."

And so, one day, Cecilia brought me an invitation to lunch from her parents. That morning I changed my sweater and corduroy trousers for a dark suit, a white shirt and a sober tie, so as to look like the professor I was supposed to be, and went off shortly before one o'clock to Cecilia's address, a street in Prati. To tell the truth, I felt intensely curious and almost excited at going to visit her at her home; this was because every discovery I made, or thought I made, about Cecilia now immediately assumed a sensual quality, as if in discovering aspects of her life that I did not know I had discovered her herself, in a material sense, or had stripped her naked.

I did not have much difficulty in finding the street, a quiet, bleak, straight street flanked by plane trees now leafless, and with rows of shops on the ground floors of the big grey and yellow buildings. The entrance door of Cecilia's block of apartments led into a large courtyard in which a few palm trees planted in the middle of barren flower beds raised yellowed crests like plucked feathers to the garlands of washing hung out to dry from the top floors. There were various staircases marked with the letters A to F; the one leading to Cecilia's flat was staircase E. An "Out of Order" notice hung on the grating of the ancient elevator, so I walked up many flights of stairs, in a wan, cold light, from one landing to another, scrutinizing at each floor the labels on the doors. Flats One, Two and Three; Flats Four, Five and Six; Flats Seven, Eight and Nine; Flats Ten, Eleven and Twelve. This was the staircase, I could not help thinking, as I arrived at last at Flat Thirteen on the fourth floor and pressed the bell, this was the staircase up and down which Cecilia went every day when she came to see me or returned home again. What would I have found out about this staircase if I had asked Cecilia? Nothing, less than nothing. She would have answered me, with characteristic tautology, that "the staircase was a staircase," and that would have been the end of it. And yet upon this staircase she had left a part of her life, and this grey light, these white marble steps, these red tiles on the landings, these doors of dark wood, all these must have remained in her memory—just as others, more fortunate, retain a memory of the smiling landscapes among which they have passed their years of childhood and youth. As I was thinking these things I heard on the far side of the door a step which, though light, made a loud sound on the loose bricks of an old floor. The door opened and Cecilia appeared on the threshold. She was wearing the usual green, hairy sweater that came down below her waist, with the deep, triangular neckline allowing a glimpse of the beginning of her breasts; her short, tight black skirt was stretched in deep, concentric folds over her belly. As I greeted her, she leaned for-

158

ward in the doorway and I was a bit surprised because I thought she was intending to kiss me, and it would not be like her to do so in such a place and at such a moment. Instead she whispered: "Remember it's a lesson day today, and after lunch we go to your studio." For some reason this unusual urgency made me almost suspicious, and it crossed my mind that Cecilia intended to make use of me and of our appointment in order to conceal some other engagement.

The hall was furnished like a room of the same kind in an old-fashioned family boardinghouse at a resort: chairs and table of wickerwork, a rubber plant in one corner and a plaster statue of a nude woman in another. But the chairs and the table looked old and decrepit, the statue, wherever there was a curve or a hollow, was grey with dust and lacked a hand into the bargain, and the plant, of the species called *ficus*, was reduced to a couple of leaves at the end of a long stalk. The walls were white but with a suspicion of dust everywhere, a kind of old, sticky dust which seemed thicker in the corners of the ceiling, where there were little dark, dense cobwebs. It suddenly occurred to me that this was a house of which, rightly or wrongly, any ordinary girl would be ashamed, at a moment when she was bringing in her lover; any ordinary girl, but not Cecilia. Meanwhile she was leading me down a long, empty passage; then she opened a door and beckoned to me to follow her.

I saw a big, rectangular room with four windows, veiled by yellow curtains, in a row along one wall. The room appeared to be divided into two parts by a couple of steps and an arch; the larger part was the living room, and in it was the furniture which Cecilia had once described as being without color, that is, gilded. This furniture, actually, was imitation Louis XV style, as had been the fashion forty years ago, and it was arranged in ghostly groups around little circular tables and meager lamps with shades adorned with beads. With my first glance I noticed white patches where the gilded plaster had peeled off, dirty marks on the flower-patterned arms of the chairs, damp stains on the small pieces of tapestry depicting episodes of gallantry. But the shabbiness of the place was evident not so much in the worn look of its furnishings as in certain almost unbelievable details which seemed to indicate a long-standing, unjustifiable neglect: a long, narrow strip of wallpaper with a pattern of little bunches of flowers and baskets, for instance, hanging down in the middle of the wall and showing the raw plaster behind it; a wide, uneven, rough-edged tear in one of the yellow curtains at the windows; and even a large, black, gaping hole in one corner of the ceiling. Why had Cecilia's parents not taken the trouble at least to paste back the strip of wallpaper, to mend the curtain, to have the ceiling repaired as best as possible? And as for Cecilia—was this, then, the house which was a house, the living room which was a living room, the furniture which was furniture? Was it possible that she lived in a flat which in its own squalid way was so peculiar, and had never become conscious of it? With these thoughts in my mind I followed her into the smaller part of the room, beyond the arch, which was arranged as a dining room, with furniture in the same dark, massive, Renaissance style I had already noted in Balestrieri's studio. From near one of the windows, breaking the silence, came the jerky sounds of popular music on the radio. Possibly because of a certain icy quality in this silence, when I heard these sounds I realized suddenly that although it was already the beginning of December the flat was not heated. Cecilia, who was in front of me, said: "Dad, let me introduce my drawing teacher."

Cecilia's father rose with an effort from the armchair in which he was sitting listening to the radio and held out his hand to me without speaking, at the same time pointing to his throat as if to warn me that, owing to his disease, he was unable to talk. I recalled the strange whispering, breathing sound that I had heard on the telephone some days before and realized that it had been he who had answered me, or rather had tried in vain to answer me. I looked at him as he fell back into his old leather armchair that was all blackened and worn, and then as he bent forward and turned down the volume of the radio. He must have been what is generally called a handsome man, with that slightly vulgar kind of handsomeness that is to be found in some over-symmetrical faces. Of that handsomeness there was now nothing left. Disease had ravaged his face, causing it to swell in some places and contract in others, reddening it here and whitening it there. And there was death already, it seemed to me, in his black hair, which lay flat and lifeless and glued down by an unhealthy sweat upon his brow and temples; in the purplish color of his lips; and, above all, in his round eyes, with their expression of intense dismay. These eyes seemed to say things which his mouth, even if it had not been speechless, would have passed over in silence; and they brought to mind, not merely the dumbness produced by his disease, but, even more, the kind of forced helplessness of one who has been bound and gagged and left, alone and defenseless, to face a deadly peril.

Cecilia told her father to sit down, and she invited me to do the same and to keep her father company, as she had to go to the kitchen: she spoke in a loud voice, mentioning her father as if he were some inanimate object to be disposed of as one liked. I sat down, therefore, opposite the invalid, and, not knowing what to say, began talking in a flattering way about Cecilia's artistic talent. Her father listened to me, rolling his terrified eyes as if, instead of talking to him about his daughter, I were hurling threats at him. From time to time he also talked, or rather tried to talk, as he had done on the telephone that day when he answered me; but the sounds that issued from his mouth, blown forth rather than articulated, were to me incomprehensible. Rather abruptly, without much ceremony and with the involuntary bad manners of the healthy when confronted with the sick, I said I must wash my hands, and I got up and left the room.

I was urged to do this by the same curiosity that had made me ask Cecilia to introduce me to her parents. In the passage I went, at random, to the first of the four doors leading from it, and opened it. A little bedroom of a chilling poverty met my eyes; the cold, subdued light came from the courtyard through the panes of curtainless windows. A black-painted iron bedstead with a consecrated olive-branch tied to its bars and a red coverlet well tucked in under a thin mattress, two kitchen chairs with yellow straw seats, and a small wardrobe of rough wood, constituted the furniture. I was at once sure that this almost empty little room must be Cecilia's; I knew it from the smell that hung in the air, a rather sharp, unsophisticated feminine smell that I had encountered in her hair and on her skin. I opened the cupboard to make more sure, and there I saw on their hangers the few clothes, so well known to me, of which Cecilia's wardrobe consisted—the little ballet skirt she had worn during the summer when I first met her, a two-piece suit of grey wool which she put on in cold weather, a black coat which she wore in the evening, a black dress of the kind known, I believe, as semi-evening dress. On a shelf lay something wrapped in white tissue paper—the bag I had given her on the day that should have been the day of our parting. I closed the cupboard again and looked around, trying to define to myself the feeling which the room inspired in me, and finally I understood: the room was bare and squalid, but its bareness and its squalor were natural and as it were untamed, like those of a place—of some hollow or cave—lived in by wild beasts. It was the bareness, in a word, not so much of a poverty-stricken house as of a lair.

I tiptoed out and opened the next door. Here the darkness was almost complete, but from the vague outline of a big double bed and from a stuffy smell very different from that in Cecilia's room, heavier and less healthy, I concluded it was her parents' bedroom. I closed this door and opened the third.

This was the bathroom, more like a long, narrow passage

than a room, with the window and the half-closed shutters at the opposite end to the door. In a row along one wall stood the bath, the *bidet*, the washbasin and the toilet. The bath was old-fashioned in shape, with deposits of rust on its yellowed enamel, the washbasin was crisscrossed with thin black cracks, the *bidet* had a grey, greasy patina at the bottom of it, and finally my eye, jumping with increasing disgust from one to another of these tarnished instruments of sanitation, detected on the inside rim of the toilet something fresh and dark and shining which had obviously resisted the insufficient rush of water from the antiquated flushing apparatus. I went to the basin, took a tiny piece of soap from the dish and started washing my hands. While I was washing I recalled all the questions I had put to Cecilia about her home and the answers I had received, those formal, abstract answers; and this confirmed what I had previously supposed: Cecilia had not been able to tell me anything about her home because, in point of fact, she had never seen it. Then the door opened and Cecilia herself came in.

"Ah, you're here," she said, without showing any sign of surprise that I was not keeping her father company in the living room, as she had asked me to do. She walked behind me, straight to the toilet and, pulling up her skirt with both hands, sat down and made water. As I saw her sitting like that, her knees bent and her legs apart, her bust thrown forward and her face turned toward me—seeing, especially, her beautiful, dark, expressionless eyes fixed upon me with an innocence like that of an animal which, unconscious of the man watching, quietly relieves the needs of nature—the idea of the wild creature's lair, which had occurred to me shortly before when I was in her room, came back to me again. Yes, I said to myself, this flat made one's heart ache if one considered it as being inhabited by human beings; but the moment one imagined a wild animal living there, a small, graceful animal such as a fox, a stone marten, an otter, it became normal and acceptable.

Cecilia by now had finished. She transferred her bare buttocks from the toilet to the *bidet*, squatted down and washed herself thoroughly with one hand. Then she got up again and, spreading her legs wide apart, wiped herself vigorously with a towel. Finally, pulling down her skirt, she said: "Out of the way a moment, I want to comb my hair."

I stood aside, and she took from the shelf a brush that had lost most of its bristles and a dirty comb from which several teeth were missing, and began energetically doing her hair. I said casually: "Your father is really very ill; I'm afraid the doctors are right."

"What d'you mean?"

"That he hasn't long to live."

"Yes, I know."

"How will you manage?"

"How will we manage what?"

"When he's dead."

"In what sense?"

"What will you live on?"

She answered hurriedly, passing a lipstick over her mouth: "We'll manage as we've always done."

"And how have you managed?"

"We have a shop. That's what we live on."

"A shop? You never told me."

"You never asked."

"What do you sell in the shop?"

"Umbrellas, suitcases, bags, leather goods."

"And who is there in the shop?"

"My mother and my aunt."

"Does this shop pay well?"

She finished painting her lips, then answered conclusively: "No, it pays very little."

I put my arm around her waist and pressed myself against her, my belly close against her back. She threw me a brief glance, whether of understanding or of surprise I could not tell; then she took a black pencil and began touching up her eyebrows. "D'you ever think of death?" I asked her.

I was clasping her tightly and she started moving her hips, slowly and vigorously, from right to left. "No," she said, "I never think about it."

"Not even when you see your father in such a bad state?"

"No."

"Surely anyone in your position would think about it."

"I'm quite well; why should I think about death?"

"But there are other people."

"So they say."

"Why, aren't you sure?"

"No, I was only talking."

"And your father—do you imagine he thinks about death?"

"Yes, he does."

"Is your father afraid of dying?"

"Yes, certainly."

"Does he know he's going to die?"

"No, he doesn't know."

"And do you never think about his dying?"

"As long as he's alive, even if he's sick, I don't think about his death. I'll think about it on the day he dies. All I think about now is that he's sick."

Abruptly I let go of her, saying: "Do you know, I want you?"

"Yes, I realized that."

She finished touching up her eyebrows, put the pencil back on the shelf and pushed me toward the door. "Come on," she said, "Mother must be back by now."

And in fact she had come back. As we came out into the passage, a shrill, discordant voice, like the tinkle of chimes let loose when you open the door of a shop, started shouting: "Cecilia! Cecilia!"

Cecilia started off in the direction of this voice and I followed her. The kitchen door was open, and her mother, still wearing her coat and hat, was standing in front of the stove, spoon in hand, stirring a pot. The kitchen was dark and smoky and of an unusual, triangular shape: the stove stood on the longest side, underneath a hood; the sharp point of the triangle ended in a high, narrow window, a half-window, actually, and obscured by clothes hung up to dry. The room was dirty and extremely untidy, with peelings scattered on the floor, the marble table covered with parcels and paper bags, and piles of dirty plates heaped up in a jumble in the sink near the window. Without turning around, Cecilia's mother said: "The dishes, the dishes have got to be washed."

"I'll wash the whole lot this evening," replied Cecilia, "today's and yesterday's as well."

"And the day before yesterday's too," said her mother. "That's what you say every day and soon we won't have any plates left. I washed the breakfast dishes this morning, but you'll have to wash the dinner dishes because I have to go to the shop."

"Let me introduce Dino, Mother."

"Oh, Professor, excuse me, it's a pleasure, a pleasure, excuse me, excuse me, it's a pleasure." The clanging sound of her voice went on for some time, chiming the words "pleasure" and "excuse me" while I was shaking her hand. I looked at her. She was a woman of small stature, with a minute, wasted face which seemed, however, to have blossomed belatedly into a kind of uproarious youthfulness. Her eyes, black, unsophisticated, and surrounded with fine wrinkles, shone with a reckless light; her cheeks were enlivened by a hectic coloring, whether natural or artificial I could not tell; her mouth, painted and very large, opened in a brilliant smile. She resembled Cecilia, I noticed, especially in the childish look of her brow which jutted out over her wide open eyes, and in the round shape of her face. In her loud, cracked voice she cried: "I didn't know the Professor was here. Cecilia, take the Professor into the living room. I'll see to the cooking."

In the passage I said to Cecilia: "You introduced me to your father as your drawing teacher, and to your mother as Dino. Couldn't you remember my surname?"

She replied, in an absent-minded sort of way: "You may not believe it, but I still don't know it. I've known you as Dino, and I've never thought of asking you your other name. What *is* your other name, then?"

"Well," I said, "if you still don't know it, you might as well go on not knowing it. I'll tell you another time." Suddenly I felt myself to be unnamable, perhaps simply because Cecilia seemed to prefer me without a name.

"Just as you like."

We went into the living room, and I said to Cecilia: "Your mother is very like you, physically. But what sort of character has she?"

"What d'you mean?"

"What is she like—good or bad, calm or nervous, generous or mean?"

"I really don't know, I've never thought about it. She has an ordinary sort of character. To me, she's my mother and that's that."

"And he?" I asked, indicating her father sitting in the arm-chair beside the radio; "what sort of character has he, in your opinion?"

This time she did not answer me at all; she merely shrugged her shoulders, in a strange way, as though I had asked an entirely senseless question. Seized by a sudden irritation, I took hold of her by the arm and, speaking right into her ear, asked her: "What's that black hole up there in the ceiling?"

She looked up at the hole as though she were seeing it for the first time. "It's a hole; it's been there for some time."

"Ah then, you can see the hole."

"Why shouldn't I be able to see it?"

"Then how is it that you can't see your father's and mother's characters?"

"You can see a hole, you can't see a character. My father

and mother are people just like lots of other people, that's all there is to it."

We were now close to her father, who was listening, motionless, to the radio. I sat down on a chair opposite him and shouted: "How do you feel today?"

He jumped in his armchair and looked at me in dismay. Then he said something I did not understand. "He says there's no need to shout, he's not deaf," explained Cecilia who, it appeared, understood her father's whispering sounds perfectly.

She was right, and goodness knows why I had thought that, because he was almost dumb, he was also deaf. "I'm sorry," I said, "I was asking you how you felt." He pointed to the windows and said something which Cecilia interpreted: "There's a *scirocco* blowing, and on *scirocco* days he never feels very well."

"Why don't you go to your shop?" I asked. "It would be a distraction for you, don't you think?"

He made a gesture of humble denial and then answered in a more detailed way, pointing to his throat and face. Cecilia said: "He says he can't go there because customers would be discouraged at seeing him so changed, and sales would suffer. He says he'll go as soon as he's better."

"Are you having treatment?"

Again he spoke and again his daughter interpreted: "He's having X-ray treatment. He hopes to be well again in a year's time." I looked at Cecilia now to see what was the effect upon her of these pathetic illusions on the part of her father; as usual, nothing was perceptible on her round face, in her expressionless eyes. I reflected that not merely did she not realize that her father was dying, but not even—contrary to what she had affirmed—that he was ill. Or rather, she did realize it, she was conscious of it, but in the same way that she was conscious of the black hole in the sitting-room ceiling: the hole was a hole, her father's illness was an illness. Behind us, her mother's voice clanged: "It's ready, please come and sit down."

We took our seats at the table, and Cecilia's mother, apologizing for not having a servant, carried around a tureen full of pasta. As I looked at the tangle of red, greasy spaghetti in the china tureen, it occurred to me that even the food had something about it that resembled the flat; something old, something neglected. I ate this bad pasta with repugnance, using a fork with an unsteady, yellow bone handle and envying the other three, especially Cecilia, who were all devouring their food with appetite. Cecilia's mother poured me some wine which I judged, at the first sip, to have gone sour, and then, when I asked for some cold water, she filled my other glass with mineral water which was also stale; warm and without sparkle. The unpleasantness of the food was, however, surpassed by the unpleasantness of the conversation which Cecilia's mother, the only one who spoke, stubbornly persisted in carrying on with me. Quite logically she had come to the conclusion that, apart from the usual remarks about the weather, the theatres and other things of the kind, the only subject that she and I had in common was Balestrieri, since he was my predecessor in giving drawing lessons to Cecilia. Halfway through lunch, when following the bad pasta I was eating a piece of tough, overcooked meat with vegetables cooked in poor quality oil, she attacked me in her shrill voice: "Professor, you knew Professor Balestrieri, didn't you?"

I glanced at Cecilia before replying. She glanced back at me, but seemed not to see me, so absent-minded and vague was her look. I said dryly: "Yes, I knew him slightly."

"Such a good man, so charming and so intelligent. A real artist. You can't imagine how upset I was at his death."

"Yes, yes," I said casually, "and he wasn't so very old."

"Barely sixty-five, and he looked fifty. We had known him for only two years, and yet I seemed to have known him always. He was part of the family, so to speak. And he had such

a great affection for Cecilia! He said he looked upon her almost as a daughter."

"He ought to have said," I corrected without smiling, "he
ought to have said as a granddaughter."

"Yes indeed, a granddaughter," she approved mechanically.
"And just imagine, he wouldn't even be paid for his lessons.
'Art cannot be paid for,' he used to say. How true that is!"

"Perhaps," I remarked, with an attempt at archness, "perhaps you mean to suggest that I ought to give Cecilia lessons
for nothing, too."

"No, I only meant that Balestrieri was very fond of Cecilia.
For you, it's different. But Balestrieri—really you might almost
say he was dying of love for Cecilia!"

It was on the tip of my tongue to say: "In fact he did die of
it." But instead I asked: "Did you see him often?"

"Often? Why, almost every day. He was like one of the
family. There was always a place for him at table. But you
mustn't think he was inconsiderate—quite the contrary."

"How do you mean?"

"Oh well, he always tried to pay us back. He helped with
the shopping, he used to buy this or that. And then he would
send cakes, wine, flowers. 'I've no family of my own,' he used
to say, 'this is my family now. You must look upon me as a
relation.' Poor man, he was separated from his wife and lived
alone."

Cecilia at this point said: "Professor, give me your plate.
Give me yours, Mother, and yours, Dad." She put the four
plates and the four bowls one on top of the other and left the
room. As soon as Cecilia had disappeared, her father, who,
during the funeral oration upon Balestrieri delivered by his
wife, had merely looked from one to the other of us with his
frightened, imploring eyes, made as though to speak in my
direction. I leaned forward a little and the invalid opened his
mouth and made a vigorous attempt to say something, which
I did not understand. His wife got up, went to the sideboard

without saying a word and fetched a notebook and pencil which she placed on the table beside her husband, saying: "Write it down, the Professor doesn't understand you."

But, with a violent gesture, he swept the notebook and pencil to the floor. His wife said: "We understand him, but strangers hardly ever do. We've told him so many times to write things down, but he won't. He says he's not dumb. He's not, but if other people don't understand him it would be better for him to write things down, don't you think?"

Her husband shot a furious glance at her and then started speaking to me again. In a sad, resigned voice, his wife said: "He says he didn't like Balestrieri." She shook her head in genuine pity and distress, and then added: "Goodness knows what poor Balestrieri did to him!"

Her husband again said something, in a forcible manner. His wife interpreted: "He says that Balestrieri bossed him in his own house."

Her husband was now staring at her with a positively anguished look in his eyes. Then, in the desperately emphatic way of a dumb man who cannot make himself understood, he opened his mouth wide and once more blew his incomprehensible noises into my face. Cecilia had now come into the room again, and I saw her raise her eyes and look at me. Her mother went on: "My husband says ridiculous things. Did you understand what he was saying?"

"No," I said.

I had the impression that she hesitated for a moment; then she explained: "He says Balestrieri tried to make love to me." She uttered these words with an air of anxiety, looking not at me but at her husband, eyeing him with an intensity in which sadness, entreaty and reproof appeared to be mingled. I turned toward him and saw that, in a way, his wife's glance had had its effect. He now appeared crushed and mortified like a dog that has been kicked. Looking already more relieved, his wife said: "Balestrieri liked to pay me compliments—oh yes, indeed,

171

and to have a joke with me too, to flirt a little, in fact. But that was all. That was really all. No, Professor," she went on, speaking of her husband as if he had not been present or had been an inanimate object, rather as Cecilia had done a little earlier, "my husband is a very good, fine man, but his brain goes on working and working all the time—you've only to look at his eyes. It's the thoughts that he turns round and round in his head all day. His brain goes on working and working and working, and then he comes out with something ridiculous."

I glanced at her husband, who was sitting quietly now, hurt and crestfallen, rolling his frightened eyes hither and thither and gathering breadcrumbs together with his fingers; and suddenly a plausible interpretation of his quickly cooled anger flashed across my mind. This was that he had got wind of there being something between Balestrieri and Cecilia; or at any rate that Balestrieri's feelings toward Cecilia were not quite as fatherly as he had wished her parents to believe. This was the accusation which he had shouted in his wife's face; she, however, had hastily substituted herself for her daughter, explaining that her husband was jealous because he had imagined that Balestrieri was trying to make love to *her*.

What I still wished to know was why Cecilia's mother had wanted to conceal the true significance of her husband's words from me. In order not to pass on an accusation which seemed to her false and unseemly? Or because she had always suspected something, and had taken full advantage of Balestrieri's self-interested generosity, even perhaps without realizing that he and Cecilia were lovers? Or, finally, because she had known all the time of the relationship between her daughter and the old painter and had accepted presents and favors in full consciousness of it? These three hypotheses were all equally plausible, although quite different and of varying importance. As I turned these thoughts over in my mind I looked at Cecilia and realized once more that, fundamentally, nothing that I was discovering during my visit concerned her; in other words, even in the worst case—that is, even if her mother had known of the relationship and had derived material advantages from it in agreement with her daughter, I would not be able to say I had learned anything decisive about Cecilia. And this for the good reason that Cecilia, with her family, was like a sleep-walker among pieces of furniture in his own home: she excluded them from her own consciousness.

Lunch ended in an unexpected way. After we had each eaten a small red and green apple, Cecilia's father suddenly rose to his feet and, working his unsteady legs in trousers so wide and loose that they appeared to have nothing inside them, went out of the room, to reappear a moment later wearing an overcoat too big for him, and with his face half hidden by the brim of a hat which looked as if it did not belong to him. He waved his hand to me from a distance, then added some remark or other, pointing to the windows which were now brightened by a feeble round ball of a sun. "He says he's going for a walk," explained his wife, rising in her turn, "and I must go with him. We'll take a little turn and then I'll go with him to the pictures and leave him there, because the shop opens at four. Ah, it's a heavy cross to bear, Professor, a man reduced to such a state." She added a few more remarks of the same kind on the subject of her husband, who meanwhile was waiting for her in the doorway at the far end of the room, looking like a scarecrow. She said good-bye to me, told Cecilia to be careful and shut the door properly when we left, and went out with her husband. After a moment I heard her voice in the hall saying something I could not catch, then the door closed and there was silence.

Cecilia and I had remained in our places, some distance from one another, at the untidy table. After a moment I said: "So these are the parents who, according to you, complained because we saw each other every day?"

She got up and started clearing the table without saying a word. It was her way of answering embarrassing questions. I persisted. "How can you expect me to believe that a father and mother like yours really made trouble?"

"Why, what is there special about my father and mother?"

"Nothing special. If anything, it's something very ordinary."

"What d'you mean?"

"I mean that they're parents who don't seem to me to be too severe."

"And yet it's true, they did complain because we saw each other too often."

"Perhaps your father did, but not your mother."

"Why not my mother?"

"Because your mother knew about Balestrieri. And if she didn't complain on his account, why should she on mine?"

"I've already told you she knew nothing."

"Well then, if she knew nothing, why did she change the words your father said today?"

"Why, when?"

"Do you think I didn't notice? What your father actually said was that he didn't like Balestrieri because he made love to you, but your mother tried to make me believe that Balestrieri was making love to *her*. Isn't that so?"

She hesitated, then admitted reluctantly: "Yes, it is."

"Then let me ask you again: if your mother really knew nothing of your relations with Balestrieri, what need was there for her to make me think that Balestrieri was making love to her?"

"Because it was true," she answered simply.

"What was true?"

"I myself told Balestrieri to make love to Mother. In that way she wouldn't notice that he was in love with me."

"Very correct, and very ingenious too. And did your mother believe in Balestrieri's love-making?"

"She certainly did."

"But your father—he didn't believe in it, did he?"

"No, he didn't."

174

"Why?"

"One day he saw us, Balestrieri and me."

"What did he see?"

"He saw him kissing me."

"And he didn't tell your mother?"

"Yes, he told her, but she didn't believe it, because Balestrieri was making love to *her* all the time; so she told my father he had invented it because he was jealous."

"Did Balestrieri go on coming to your house after that?"

"Yes, he went on coming, but we were more careful. So much so that in the end Dad almost thought he had made a mistake. But he went on hating Balestrieri. When he saw him arrive, he went out."

The table was cleared by now, and Cecilia was putting the chairs back in their proper places. As she passed close to me, I pulled her to me by the arm and made her sit down, reluctantly and absent-mindedly, on my knee. "Shall we go to my studio soon?" I asked.

I noticed that she glanced at her wrist watch. Then she replied: "I'm expecting a telephone call."

"What's that got to do with it?"

"It depends on the telephone call whether I can come to the studio or not."

"Who is going to telephone you?"

She considered me for a moment with an indefinable, thoughtful expression and then answered: "It's a film producer, to make an appointment to see me. If the appointment is in a short time, I'm afraid I shall not be able to come."

I was sure that she was lying. The thing that betrayed her was her tone of voice, which had the excessive naturalness achieved only when a person is lying. "Why not tell the truth?" I said. "It's the actor who is going to telephone you."

"What actor?"

"Luciani."

"I saw him yesterday," she said unexpectedly, seeking to

foist a twenty-four-hour-old truth upon me, I decided, in order to conceal her lie of a moment earlier. "We went together to see a producer. I don't have to see him every day."

"Was it a producer you went to see yesterday, too?"

"It's the same one. It was Luciani who gave me an introduction. The producer couldn't see me yesterday and sent a message that he would telephone me today."

I noticed how plausible it all was. And perhaps it was all true, even in detail, for I knew that Cecilia, on the occasions when she was forced to tell a lie, did so by building up an edifice of falsehood with the materials of truth. "Come on," I insisted, "it *is* Luciani who is going to telephone you. Why shouldn't you admit it?"

"There's no reason why I shouldn't, but it isn't true."

"Well then, if it's not true, let me go and answer the telephone for you."

"All right, if you like."

Her willingness to agree made me think that there might be an arrangement between her and Luciani, as often happens between lovers: if it was she who answered, Luciani would declare himself for who he was; if somebody else, he would say he was the producer. With some bitterness, I said: "No, I don't want to put you to the test. I only want you to understand one thing, just one thing."

"What's that?"

"That I don't want you to love me, I want you to tell me the truth. I would rather you told me you were going to see Luciani today, if it's true that you are, than that you should tell me you're not going to see him, just in order to please me."

We looked at one another. Then, with a gesture that was almost tender, she stroked my cheek. "*My* truth," she said, "is that I'm not seeing Luciani today. Would you rather I told you *your* truth—that I *am* seeing him?"

Thus Cecilia, without intending it, let it be seen that truth and falsehood were for her the same thing, and that fundamentally neither truth nor falsehood existed. Suddenly, from the passage, came the ringing of the telephone. Cecilia jumped off my knee, exclaiming: "The telephone!" and ran out of the room. I followed her.

The telephone was at the far end of the passage and at the darkest part of it, on a shelf. I saw Cecilia take off the receiver, place it to her ear and then immediately say: "Good day." I stood beside her, and she, as though she wished to conceal and protect the black vulcanite instrument into which she was speaking and out of which someone was speaking to her, suddenly turned her back upon me. The conversation continued, but I noticed that Cecilia answered in monosyllables or in words even more insignificant—if that was possible—than those with which she usually expressed herself; and all at once I was convinced that it was the actor at the other end of the line, that he and Cecilia were arranging a meeting, and that Cecilia was unfaithful to me with him. At the same time I became aware that I felt a violent desire for her, lying to me as she was, and therefore evading me and therefore becoming real and attractive; as if, by having her there and then, in the passage, while she was talking to her lover, I might be able to possess her at the very moment when, by means of the telephone, she was withdrawing herself from possession. I stood right up against her, as I had done shortly before in the bathroom; and from the barely perceptible hint of a movement of her buttocks against my belly, I seemed to understand that not merely would she not be opposed to an embrace so inconvenient and so unusual, but would even welcome it, as though to compensate me, by means of a false surrender, for the true surrender of herself which she was at the same moment making to the man who was telephoning to her. I was pressing myself against her, filled with anger and desire, when I recalled that Balestrieri had had her in the kitchen in the same manner, and probably with the same feeling. I drew back abruptly; Cecilia felt that I was no longer standing close against her and threw me a questioning glance over her shoulder; then, still talking on the telephone, she put out her free hand behind her and clasped mine. I allowed her to do this and leaned against the wall behind her, my face bowed down on my chest, my mind in confusion. Finally Cecilia said: "Well, good-bye, see you soon," then she replaced the receiver and stood for a moment deep in thought, her hand in mine. "I'm sorry," she said at last, turning toward me, "but I shan't be able to come to the studio today. I'm expected in half an hour by that film producer."

"Very well, I'll leave you at once."

"Wait a bit—and now come with me."

She walked in front of me down the passage toward her room. She went in first; as soon as I had come in, she carefully closed the door. "Would you like to make love now—here?" she asked. "But we must be quick about it, because I really haven't time."

Faced with this very charming, very cynical proposal, I felt once again that desire for her which seemed never to be satisfied, for the simple reason that it was not her body—always so ready and so docile—which I desired, but the whole of her. However I said: "No, don't think of that now, I don't like doing things in a hurry."

"But we needn't be in a hurry. Only that I shall have to run away right afterward."

"No, I'm not like Balestrieri, it's of no consequence to me to make love in your home."

"How does Balestrieri come into it?"

"Speaking of Balestrieri—there's one thing I want you to tell me."

"What's that?"

"That time you made love in the kitchen, had there been an argument, a quarrel, a disagreement between you shortly before?"

"How can you expect me to remember? It happened such a long time ago."

"Try and remember."

"Well, yes, I think there had been a bit of an argument. Balestrieri was so tiresome, he always wanted to know everything."

"Everything?"

"Yes, everything: whom I saw, where I went, what I did."

"And had you had an argument of this kind on that occasion?"

"Yes, I believe we had."

"How did it finish?"

"It finished in the usual way."

"What d'you mean by that?"

"There came a point when I stopped answering him, and then he wanted to make love."

"Just like me!" I could not help exclaiming.

"No, you're exactly the opposite, you *don't* want to make love. Come on, then, why shouldn't we?"

She gave me a tempting look, as though she felt herself to be in debt to me and wished to pay me back at all costs, so as not to have to think about it any more. I should have liked to reply: "I don't want to make love because I don't want to do the same things as Balestrieri." But instead, kissing her on the neck, I said: "We'll do it tomorrow at my studio, calmly." She shook her head in sign of slight disappointment, then went and opened the wardrobe, took out the parcel containing the bag and removed the tissue paper. "D'you see?" she said, smiling at me, "I'm using your bag."

We left the room and went out of the flat. Cecilia walked downstairs in front of me, and as I followed her I thought over what had happened. I told myself that although the effort had been almost superhuman, I had avoided making love to her in the passage in spite of a furious desire to do so; that is, I had avoided, this time at least, doing precisely the same thing that

Balestrieri had done before me; and yet this was only a tiny episode in a passion which, in its more general development, tended increasingly to resemble the passion which the old painter had felt for Cecilia. I was able, thanks to a clearer consciousness of the situation, to prevent myself from acting like Balestrieri on particular occasions, but it looked as though I was not capable of halting my progress along the road that he had followed before me to the bitter end. When we reached the entrance hall, I said brusquely to Cecilia: "Good-bye, then."

She seemed astonished both by my words and my tone of voice. "Why?" she said, "aren't you going with me?"

"Where to?"

"I've told you already, to that film producer's."

"Very well; come along."

I did not speak during the whole journey. Fundamentally, what most exasperated me was not so much that Cecilia should make me drive her to an appointment with her lover, as that she should do so without malice and without cruel intent, in a vague sort of way, simply, it might be, because she was tired of taking the usual crowded bus, and there was I, ready and on the spot, with my car. I realized that this detached, childish lack of sensitiveness caused me far more pain than any self-indulgent perversity.

I stopped the car in front of the film company's door and watched Cecilia as she disappeared into the darkness of the entrance hall, walking with her usual tired-looking, swaying step. Evidently the appointment with the film-producer was genuine; but either the actor was waiting for Cecilia in the office, or Cecilia was intending to join him at his own home after she had spoken with the producer. In both cases it would have been easy for me to ascertain the truth, either by following her immediately into the building, or by waiting until she came out. But I gave up the idea: I was still at the stage of jealousy when a surviving sense of dignity prevents one from spying upon the person one is jealous of. Nevertheless, as I went away I knew I had merely postponed the moment when I would start watching her. Next time, I thought, I should no longer be able to stand firm against circumstances which encouraged me, which indeed almost obliged me, to spy upon her.

Chapter 7

The events which I am now going to relate may create the impression of a crisis of very ordinary jealousy; and indeed, if my behavior during that time had been observed by a spectator of little perspicacity it might well have appeared to be that of the stock victim of jealousy. But it was not like that. The jealous man suffers from an excessive sense of possessiveness; he suspects continually that some other man wishes to get possession of his woman, and this haunting suspicion gives rise to extravagant imaginings and may even lead him to crime. On the other hand, I suffered because I loved Cecilia (for it had now become a question of love); and my aim in spying upon her was to make certain that she was deceiving me, not indeed to punish her or in any way prevent her from continuing in her unfaithfulness, but in order to set myself free both from my love and from her. The jealous man tends, in spite of himself, to shackle himself in his own servitude; I, on the contrary, wished to release myself from this same servitude, and I saw no other means of attaining my object than by destroying Cecilia's independence and mystery, thus reducing her, through a more exact knowledge of her treacherous conduct, to something well known and ordinary and insignificant.

My first thought was to make use of the telephone. As I have already mentioned, Cecilia used to telephone me every morning about ten o'clock. She had done this, at the beginning, merely in order to greet me. But now that her visits had become rarer (her promise to continue to see me every day had soon been proved unreliable), the telephone had become an essential element in our relationship. It was in fact by telephone that Cecilia now fixed the day and hour of our appointments each time, in an unaccountable, irregular manner. I noticed that the time of these telephone calls had changed recently from ten to twelve o'clock. Cecilia had justified this change by the fact that her telephone was a party line and that the subscriber who shared it had taken to making a great many calls in the early morning. But I was convinced that the reason was a different one and that she no longer telephoned me at ten o'clock because by that time she had not yet spoken to the actor who, like all actors, slept late. Not having spoken to him, she did not yet know what she would be doing during the day, and therefore could not tell me if and when she could see me.

The actor's number was not in the telephone directory; but it was easy for me to obtain it from a film company for whom he had worked in the past. Having found out the number, I ascertained the truth of what I had supposed in the following way: I would first telephone Cecilia at about a quarter to twelve and invariably find that the number was busy; immediately afterward I would telephone the actor and discover that he too was on the line. I would wait five or ten minutes and then repeat the maneuver: both the lines would be free. A moment later, with a punctuality that filled me with sadness, my own telephone would ring and Cecilia, at the other end, calm and precise as a trained secretary, would tell me, according to the situation, whether we could see each other that day or not.

I also made use of the telephone to keep watch over Cecilia's comings and goings. I telephoned methodically (if one can speak of method in relation to the frantic stratagems of jealousy) at various times of day, and either I found no one or I found Cecilia's mother, who often stayed at home, leaving the shop to her sister. Then I would enter into conversation with her. She, on her side, asked nothing better than a few minutes' chatter, and by way of this chatter I would get to know more or less what I wanted. The mother's pieces of information, of course, came almost entirely from Cecilia, who lied to her just as she did to me, and told her only what best suited her; but I had now reached a point when I could decipher these pieces of information fairly well, all the more so because Cecilia, not knowing that she was being spied upon, did not take the trouble to bring them into line with the equally false but different information with which she provided me. Thus I came to know that Cecilia, a creature of habit like all persons who lack imagination, had, to her parents, justified her relations with the actor in the same way as those with Balestrieri and myself: she said she went to see the actor because he had promised to find her work in the films, just as she had said in the past that she visited Balestrieri and me because we gave her drawing lessons. But lessons last only an hour or two, whereas an association with a place of regular work may take up the entire day; and thus I discovered that under the pretext of her film job Cecilia was seeing the actor every day, twice or even three times a day. She saw him sometimes in the morning, especially if the weather was fine, for a walk in the town and an apéritif; she saw him in the afternoon, probably in order to make love; she saw him in the evening, to have dinner and go to the pictures. Her mother was slightly alarmed at this pretended film activity on her daughter's part, and at the same time rather flattered. Taking me into her confidence, she would ask me anxiously if there was not a danger that the motion-picture world, so notoriously free and easy, not to say licentious, might have a corrupting influence upon Cecilia; and then again she would ask, with equal anxiety, whether I thought that her daughter had the right qualities for becoming a star. She spoke with complete ingenuousness; but to me, at the other end of the line, she often gave the impression of knowing everything, both about myself and about the actor, and of amusing herself by tormenting me with refined and conscious cruelty. In reality, as I knew perfectly well, the cruelty lay in the circumstances and in them only.

And so, what with Cecilia's lies on the one hand and her mother's illusions on the other, the telephone neither gave me complete reassurance nor did it furnish me with the indubitable proofs that I needed in order to free myself of my little mistress and of my love for her. Indirect and abstract by its very nature, the telephone now seemed to be the positive symbol of my own situation: a means of communication which prevented me from communicating; an instrument of inspection which permitted of no precise information; an automatic machine, extremely easy to use, which nevertheless showed itself to be almost always capricious and untrustworthy.

Furthermore, the telephone seemed perfectly designed to confirm the elusiveness of Cecilia's character. Obviously it was not the fault of the little black instrument if Cecilia was late in telephoning me or did not telephone me at all; if she lied to me or disappointed me. But since all this took place on the telephone, I had reached the point when I was obsessed with hatred for that innocent object. I never telephoned now without extreme repugnance; I never heard its ringing without a feeling of anguish. In the first case I feared not to find Cecilia— as indeed almost always happened; in the second, that I should hear her, as usual, lying to me—which was also a manner of not finding her. But the telephone, above all, confirmed Cecilia's elusiveness, for by its means her physical presence was replaced by one single part of her, and the most abstract at that—her voice. Even when this voice was not lying to me it remained, to me, ambiguous and evasive, simply because it was only a voice. And all the more so because it was Cecilia's voice, which was always so stubbornly expressionless.

But the thing that drove me on to spy directly upon Cecilia was, more than anything else, my own fatigue. I now spent almost the whole day looking at the telephone, waiting either for the time when Cecilia should telephone me, or for the time at which I knew I could telephone to her with the hope of finding her. Besides this, there were the calls when I found no one, or only the whisperings of her father; and there were the calls to her mother, exhausting and irritating, to reconstruct Cecilia's daily activities. All these telephonic stratagems, growing, as they did, more and more complicated and harassing, in the end canceled out any possible relief that I might derive from the telephone calls themselves. Like a starving man, whose hunger seems unsatisfied even after he has eaten, so I, after I had finally succeeded in speaking to Cecilia, continued to feel just as harassed and angry as before. Moreover the result of all this was a kind of sexual frenzy: after deciding beforehand to question Cecilia calmly and at length and to oblige her to confess her unfaithfulness, the moment she appeared in the doorway of the studio I would forget my cool intentions, throw her on the divan and have her there and then, without waiting for her to undress, without even— as she herself used to say with a touch of childish complacency —giving her time to breathe. It was the usual masculine illusion that possession can be achieved all in a moment and without a word, by the mere physical act, which drove me to this frenzy. But immediately afterward, when I saw Cecilia to be even more elusive than before, I realized my mistake and said to myself that, if I wished to possess her truly, I ought not to expend my energy in an act which had merely the semblance of possession.

An insignificant incident was the immediate cause of my

decision to spy upon Cecilia. It is worth recounting if only to give an indication of my state of mind at that time. One morning, after I had carried out my usual investigation of Cecilia's and the actor's telephones and had found them both to be busy, I asked Cecilia point blank, as soon as she rang me: "Who were you telephoning to? Your number's been busy for at least twenty minutes."

She replied at once, in a perfectly natural way: "I was telephoning to Gianna."

Gianna was a friend of Cecilia's, and by chance I knew her surname and address. I hastily said good-bye to Cecilia and looked up Gianna's number in the directory. Exasperated, I thought that this time I would get Cecilia with her back to the wall. I dialed Gianna's number, and a woman's voice, probably that of Gianna's mother, answered me. "Signorina Gianna?" I inquired.

"She's gone out."

"How long ago?"

"Oh, it must be more than an hour. Who wants her?"

I threw down the receiver and then again dialed Cecilia's number. As soon as I heard her voice, I shouted: "You told me a lie."

"What do you mean?"

"You told me Gianna had telephoned you a minute ago. Well, I've just telephoned her and been told she went out an hour ago."

"That has nothing to do with it; Gianna was telephoning from outside. From a public telephone."

This took my breath away. So I was no longer capable, in my present state of fatigue, of orderly, lucid reflection; and I had thought to catch Cecilia in a trap from which, in point of fact, it was perfectly easy for her to escape. "I'm sorry," I said, with a kind of astonishment, "I hadn't thought of that. For some time now I don't seem to understand anything."

"It seems so to me, too."

This incident, although of minor importance, convinced me that I could no longer trust my own tired, confused mind; and that I must spy upon Cecilia in a direct way, with my eyes. At first this seemed to me the easiest thing in the world. But as soon as I set about doing it in earnest, I became aware that it was not so.

My idea was to telephone to Cecilia from a public telephone as near as possible to the building in which she lived; and, after assuring myself that she was at home, to go and mount guard opposite her door and wait for her to come out, as she usually did, about three o'clock. I was convinced, from a number of clues, that she went to visit the actor at about that time: I would follow her, I would watch her go into Luciani's house, I would wait for her to come out, I would stop her. Of course it was by no means inconceivable that Cecilia, even at that moment and in that place, would find some means of lying to me, or rather, as was more probable, of admitting only a part of the truth—and precisely that innocent part which is never lacking in any guilty action; but I counted on the fact of surprising her and catching her in the act to undermine her duplicity and oblige her to confess. Once I had obtained this confession, I was convinced that the devaluation of Cecilia and my consequent liberation would follow of themselves.

I had noticed that the street in which Cecilia lived was intersected two blocks farther down by a side street, and that at the corner there was a bar. One afternoon I stopped my car in front of the bar, went in and rang Cecilia's number. I realized while the telephone was ringing that I had no excuse for speaking to her. We had already talked on the telephone that morning and had made an arrangement to meet the following day; what then could I say to her? Finally I decided that I would beg her to come to the studio that same day, in spite of our previous agreement, and I also decided that if she accepted I would give up spying upon her once and for all.

The telephone went on ringing for a long time; then at last came Cecilia's voice, neutral, colorless: "Is that you? What is it?"

"I've been thinking it over; I'd like to see you today."

"Today's impossible."

"Why is it impossible?"

"Because I can't."

"Do you have to go and see that film producer again today?"

This time she was silent, as though she were waiting for me to ring off. I waited too, hoping that she would be hypocritical enough to give me a word of affection, as any other woman would have done, seeing herself to be, quite rightly, suspected. But Cecilia had no imagination and never said a word more than was necessary. After a long silence, she concluded: "Till tomorrow, then; good-bye."

I left the bar, got into my car and parked two blocks farther on, in front of Cecilia's door. It was the first time in my life that I had spied upon anyone, and, as I have said, I was under the illusion that it was an easy thing to do. Apart from people who made a business of it, such as detectives and the like, was it not done by silly women through the bars of shutters, by urchins through keyholes, and by idlers in general in order to kill time? But when I began spying, I discovered a simple fact: it is one thing to spy as a profession, like a policeman, or out of idle curiosity, like silly women or street urchins, but quite another to spy for a precise and directly personal reason. Not ten minutes had passed, in fact, before I realized that I was suffering far more than if I had stayed in my studio mentally analyzing my suspicions, without seeking otherwise to verify the basis of them. I continued now to be suspicious of Cecilia in just the same way; but to the misery of suspicion was added that of espionage. If at least I had known the exact moment at which she would come out; then I could have felt easy until, let us say, one minute before she appeared in the doorway. But since I was ignorant of when that moment would arrive, each instant that passed had, for me, the exaggeratedly painful quality of that one single instant when I would see her actually appear. And, instead of being subdivided into a number of easily justifiable periods of delay (the usual delays one concedes to all women, due to the exigencies of the toilet, to a telephone call, a visit, and so forth) sufficiently prolonged to allow of some measure of repose, the period of waiting, and of facing disappointment at every second, increased steadily in intensity, strained and vacant, like a single shrill note rising up and up, or a monotonous pain growing more and more severe.

I waited calmly for the first ten minutes, for I was certain that Cecilia would not come out during that time, since I had mounted guard at ten minutes to three and knew that she never went out before three. These first ten minutes went by without Cecilia appearing, and then I allowed her another ten. These minutes went by, and yet a further ten, and then I decided to wait ten minutes more, though I was quite unable, this time, to imagine what could be keeping her indoors. These empty, but still endurable, ten minutes passed more slowly than the first thirty, seeing that I did not intend to go on waiting and indeed hoped that Cecilia would appear at the third or fourth minute; but she did not come and I found myself faced for the fifth time with an empty period which was as repugnant to me as a huge, deserted square must be to a man suffering from agoraphobia. I waited, nevertheless, telling myself with a kind of mystical hopefulness that this time Cecilia was bound to come. But she did not come, and I resigned myself to waiting a further ten minutes, comforting myself, for lack of anything better, by reflecting that this would make a complete hour, and an hour is the longest time that anyone can wait in any possible circumstances. But naturally (I say naturally, because I now felt that Cecilia's appearance would be a fact against nature, a miracle)—naturally she did not come this time either, and I prepared for the seventh time to wait another ten minutes, justifying my decision with the subtle, arbitrary reflection that, an hour being the longest time one could wait, I must give Cecilia ten minutes over the hour, if only out of politeness. At this point, however, I became aware that my mind was no longer working, and was thus refusing to keep me company while I waited. I was alone with myself, that is, with the misery which at that moment was my only mode of existence, and the only two things that meant anything to me now were the watch on my wrist and the door upon which my eyes were fixed. My plan was to glance at my watch at intervals of three minutes; the rest of the time I kept my eyes on the door as much as possible, as though I were afraid that Cecilia might come out with the speed of lightning and vanish during that one moment when I looked down at my watch. But invariably my impatience caused me to think the three minutes had gone by after only one minute had passed, and that the effort with which I forced myself to stare at the door became suddenly unendurable, as is any muscular tension that is continued for too long. And so I looked too often at my watch and was astonished to see that the minutes of this time of waiting appeared to be infinitely slower than any other minutes I had ever waited in my life; and on the other hand I felt an almost unconquerable longing to take my eyes off the door, the threshold of which seemed deserted only because I was looking at it, as though its stones and bricks and plaster knew of my waiting and maliciously withheld Cecilia's appearance just because I desired it so much.

I waited thus for ten minutes beyond the hour, and then for another ten, because at twenty minutes past four, as I knew, Cecilia's mother went off to the shop which was not far away and which opened at half past four, and Cecilia sometimes waited to go out until her mother had gone. But at a quarter past four, quite suddenly, as though my muscles had given an involuntary jerk, without thinking I started the car and moved away. I did not go far, however. At the bar at the corner I stopped, got out, went in and telephoned. "She must have gone out," replied Cecilia's mother in an uncertain tone. "I've been in the kitchen and I haven't seen her. She may have gone out five minutes ago, or maybe half an hour ago." I rushed out of the bar, jumped into the car and went very fast up and down that street and the adjacent streets, pressing on as far as the bus stop where I knew Cecilia used to wait for her bus, but I found nothing. Evidently her mother had been wrong and Cecilia had not gone out five minutes or half an hour before, but only a minute or so, and thus had come out of the building at the very moment when I was looking for her in the neighboring streets; unless possibly she had come halfway downstairs and then gone back again, for some reason of her own that I could not imagine, and so was now back again in the flat. But I had no desire to make any more telephone experiments; so I decided to go and lie in wait in front of the house in which Luciani lived. This was in the Parioli district, in Via Archimede, a narrow, winding street which circles around the hill between two rows of modern houses. I had already explored this street some days previously, not so much with the purpose of spying as to see the place where I knew Cecilia so often went nowadays; and I seemed to remember that opposite the actor's house there was a bar from which it would be easy to watch it. And indeed, when I got out of the car and looked into the bar, I found I was not mistaken: in the window there were two or three little tables from which, looking through between bottles and boxes of sweets, I could easily watch the door of the house opposite without being observed.

I sat down, ordered coffee and began my spying—an occupation which by this time I hated with my whole heart. The door of the house in which the actor lived was framed in black marble and stood out against the white façade like an obituary notice on the page of a newspaper, but I immediately discovered that a bottle of whisky displayed in the window concealed at least half of it. It was quite possible that Cecilia might slip in or out of the house without my being aware of it, through the half of the door that I could not see. I tried moving my chair, but then I could not see the door at all because it was completely hidden by a large box of English biscuits. I wondered whether I could possibly put out my hand and remove the bottle; but I saw I could not do so without making the barman suspicious. In the end I decided to get rid of the embarrassing object by acquiring it. It was true that the barman might well have a similar bottle in reserve and would therefore not give me the one from the window, but I had no other means of achieving my aim. I called out: "I want that bottle there."

He came over at once, a young, tough-looking man, thin and very pale, with one noticeable feature—a harelip which was ill concealed beneath a drooping black mustache. He asked, in a deep, confidential tone of voice: "The bottle of Canadian whisky?"

"Yes, that one."

He bent forward, cautiously took the bottle from the window and appeared to be making a move to replace it with another standing near it. I said hastily, in a commanding voice: "Let me see it."

Slightly surprised, he handed me the bottle and I pretended to examine it at leisure, in the hope that he would forget the empty place in the window. Fortunately, at that moment a customer came in; the barman left me and went back behind the counter. After an interval he brought me my coffee, but he did not put any other bottle in place of the one he had given me. I breathed freely again and set myself to the task of watching the door which was now entirely visible.

I calculated that Cecilia would have taken the bus because I knew she had no money and that she was never in too much of a hurry to get to her appointments. It took at least twenty minutes to go by bus from Cecilia's home to the Parioli district. All this, of course, depended upon whether Cecilia had really gone out a minute before my telephone call and whether she had really gone to see Luciani. I decided—provisionally, at least—that these two suppositions were correct, and therefore spent about twenty minutes in tolerable ease, though without for one instant taking my eyes off the door.

When these first twenty minutes were over, I waited patiently for a further ten, and then found myself confronted with this dilemma: either Cecilia had arrived before me by taxi (this was not improbable: I had had to stop at three sets of traffic lights), or she had not arrived at all. What ought I to do? Wait for her to come out or go away? I was so sure that Cecilia had gone to see Luciani that day that in the end I decided to wait. Furthermore, I said to myself, if Cecilia had arrived, say, five minutes before me, I should anyhow have thirty-five minutes less to wait.

But, as though to deny me even this modest consolation, suddenly, right in front of my eyes, was the figure of a man in a green overcoat. It seemed to me that there was something familiar about his back, and when he moved to cross the street, I recognized him beyond doubt by his broad shoulders and above all by his artificial-looking, too-bright fair hair; it was the actor. I saw him go in the door and vanish.

So my vigil was only just beginning. Either Cecilia had arrived before Luciani and had gone up to his flat to wait for him, or she had not come at all; but I, in order to make certain, would now have to wait for goodness knows how long. And the thirty minutes I had already spent in spying had been spent in vain.

I realized that if my wait in front of Cecilia's house had been painful, that in front of the actor's house was a hundred times more so. When I waited outside Cecilia's house, I had been waiting for her to finish eating or dressing or talking to her mother—all of them innocent things; but as I waited outside Luciani's house I was actually waiting for her to finish making love. Thus, whereas I had suffered an hour earlier from having to endure a shapeless, empty period of expectation which my imagination had not been able to fill, now, when I knew perfectly well why Cecilia was in Luciani's flat, I had to endure a period of waiting which contained the whole shape and rhythm of the sexual act. Now, in contrast to what had happened earlier, if I looked at my watch I could calculate to the minute what was going on in the actor's flat. At this moment Cecilia is pulling off her sweater over her head. At this moment, naked, she is going over to the bed, is getting on to it, is lying down. At this moment she is having her first orgasm, and after two or three violent jerks of her belly, she throws back her head and lies back exhausted. All these imaginings, naturally, renewed the feeling I had of not possessing, of never having possessed her, since hitherto I had deceived myself into thinking I possessed her simply because I had possessed her body, and that body was now in the arms of Luciani.

Apart from all this, the feeling of Cecilia's elusiveness was further increased by my uncertainty as to whether she was in fact with Luciani in his flat. After all, there was a possibility that they might not be seeing each other that day. In that case my imaginings became truly those of the most ordinary kind of jealous lover, who builds up a whole castle of hypotheses upon the foundation of a small and fallacious clue. Nevertheless, this did not in any way imply that Cecilia was not unfaithful to me; it merely meant that she was not being unfaithful on that particular day.

Finally I thought I would telephone to Luciani; I might possibly be able, by means of some sound or other, to detect Cecilia's presence in the flat. Luckily the telephone in the bar was near the door, so that I would be able to make the call without interfering with my watch on the street door opposite. I went over and dialed the number, and heard the actor's voice. My calculations were not entirely wrong; while the actor was repeating, "Hello, hello," I could distinctly hear the sound of a dance tune, and this made my heart sink, for I knew that Cecilia liked to make love to the sound of music. The actor, after repeating "Hello" once again, added the single word "Idiot!" and hung up the receiver. If the dance music had given me some vague idea of the size and arrangement and look of the room in which it was being played, this insulting word, in which I seemed to detect not only irritation at being disturbed but also male vanity aroused by the nature of the thing which had been disturbed, gave me a glimpse of Cecilia and the actor as they were at that moment—he standing naked beside the little table with the telephone on it, fully visible with his big chest and broad, hairy shoulders, with his muscular belly, and his sexual organ still, perhaps, in a state of erection, with his athletic, over-developed loins and legs; she, naked too, lying languidly on the bed, her eyes turned to gaze with delight at the limbs of her lover. I hung up the receiver and sat in the window again.

I waited twenty minutes longer, and then had another proof of Cecilia's presence in Luciani's flat. The bar phone rang, the barman answered it, listened and then said, in a stupid sort of military voice: "Always at your service, Signor Luciani!" After a short time I saw the waiter, a red-faced youth, go out carrying a tray; on it were a bottle of beer, some sandwiches wrapped in a napkin and a large glass filled with orange juice. I knew that Cecilia, after making love, was in the habit of quenching her thirst with the juice of three or four oranges. I followed the waiter with my eyes, saw him go into the house opposite, and after not more than a minute come out again with the empty tray. The boy came back into the bar, and the barman said to him sardonically: "What's the matter? What did you see? Bowled over, you look. How many times have I told you—what you see in people's houses has nothing to do with you. Come on—get these glasses washed." At that moment, as if propelled by a powerful spring—with the same kind of automatic jerk of the muscles as had caused me earlier to abandon my vigil in front of Cecilia's flat—I put the money on the table, took my bottle of whisky and went out. I saw that to go away after waiting so long meant that all the efforts and sufferings of the afternoon would be thrown to the winds, but for this day, anyhow, I was not capable of waiting any longer. Perhaps, as I thought later, I really wanted to put off the moment when, being completely assured of Cecilia's unfaithfulness, I should feel that I possessed her inasmuch as I was enabled to judge her, and was consequently set free from her and no longer loved her. In any case, the final proof of her unfaithfulness was deferred, and with it the devaluation of Cecilia and the reduction of her from a creature of mystery to an insignificant little adulteress.

I have sought to describe in detail the first day of my starting to spy upon Cecilia, because it was identical, or almost identical, with many others that followed it, of which therefore I may spare myself any extensive description. The only difference was that on that first day I was still capable of acting with a certain method, but as time went on and these wearing vigils were repeated, I did things more and more haphazardly and more and more stupidly. Actually, in order to be a competent spy, I ought, as I have said, to have had the cool, technical detachment of a detective, or the curiosity, for its own sake, of a busybody. Instead of which I was watching Cecilia with the anguished heart of a lover, and little did it matter that I was a lover who was not seeking to keep his own woman to himself but rather to get rid of her.

How many hours did I spend during those days, sitting in my car in front of the building where Cecilia lived! How many hours in that bar, at the little table in the window! In order to show the degree of obtuseness to which I had been brought by jealousy, all I need to say is that, after a week of exhausting vigils, I discovered by chance that it was useless to watch

Cecilia's block of flats because it had two doors, one on to the street where I had been mounting guard, and another on to a parallel, more important street along which the buses passed and where taxis could be found. Naturally Cecilia went out by the latter door, which was more convenient for her. This discovery appeared to me significant. I had become so stupid that it had taken me a week to notice a thing which I ought to have thought of from the very first moment.

After I had discovered this second door in Cecilia's building, I believed that my investigations, now confined merely to the house where the actor lived, would become much easier. But again I was wrong. Apparently, among all the minutes in the day, I always chose those that were never visible on Cecilia's little wrist watch. Time, for Cecilia and her lover, was not the same as for me. Theirs was the calm, sure, regular time of love; mine the furious, uneven time of jealousy. In all probability I took up my station in the bar when Cecilia had already gone into the actor's house, and went away when she had not yet come out. The truth was that I could not manage to overcome my repugnance for the act of spying, which I felt to be both degrading and deceptive. This repugnance made me sluggish when I was preparing to go to the bar and impatient when my period of waiting was drawing to a close.

During this whole time, although I made the most determined efforts to entrap her, I never once saw Cecilia coming out of or going into Luciani's house. This seemed to me an incredible thing, with something supernatural about it; so much so, that it sometimes occurred to me that Cecilia was downright invisible. And so she was, to me at least, with the kind of invisibility of things that are apparent to the senses yet elude the mind.

Cecilia's elusiveness was confirmed not only by the failure of my surveillance but also by that of my investigations into her relationship with Luciani. Knowing well that I could not make a frontal attack upon her because she would be ready to lie to me and would thus become even more elusive than she already was, I tried sometimes to make her talk about the actor in a general way, so as to see if her answers gave a glimpse of a feeling that was more than friendly. Here is an example of how I questioned her.

"Do you often see Luciani now?"

"Yes, I see him sometimes."

"You know him well by now, then."

"Oh yes, I know him a little."

"Then tell me what you think of him."

"What d'you mean—what do I think of him?"

"Well, what do you think of him, what is your opinion of him?"

"I haven't any opinion—why should I have?"

"No, I mean—what's your idea about him, how do you find him?"

"He's very nice."

"Is that all?"

"What d'you mean—is that all?"

"Just—nice?"

"Well, yes, I think he's nice—that's all."

"And you go out with him because he's nice and that's all."

"Yes."

"But I'm nice, you're nice, your father's nice; to say that someone is nice means practically nothing."

"What ought I to say, then?"

"Defects, qualities, good, bad, intelligent, stupid, mean, generous, and so on."

This time she made no answer, replying to my words with a silence that was in no way hostile or offended, the silence, I couldn't help thinking, of any animal. "Well, aren't you going to say anything?" I insisted.

"I've nothing to say. You want to know what Luciani is like, and I can't tell you anything, because I've never thought about it, and I don't know. I only know that I like being with him."

"I'm told he's a very bad actor."

"That may be so, I don't know anything about it."

"Where does Luciani come from?"

"I don't know."

"How old is he?"

"I've never asked him."

"Is he younger or older than me?"

"Perhaps he may be younger."

"Of course he is, at least ten years younger. Tell me—has he a father, a mother, brothers and sisters, a family, in fact?"

"We've never talked about it."

"What do you talk about when you're together?"

"All sorts of things."

"What, for instance?"

"How can you expect me to remember? We talk, that's all."

"I remember almost all our conversations perfectly well."

"I don't; I don't remember anything."

"Well, tell me: if you had to describe Luciani, if you were forced to do so, if you couldn't avoid it, how would you describe him?"

She hesitated, then answered quite simply: "No one is forcing me to, so I haven't any need to describe him."

"Then I'll describe him to you: he's tall, athletic, broad-shouldered, with black eyes and fair hair, small hands and feet, and a fatuous expression."

"What does fatuous mean?"

"It means conceited."

She was silent for a moment, then she remarked: "It's true that he has small hands and feet. Now that you mention it, I remember."

"So, if I hadn't mentioned it, you wouldn't have remembered?"

"I don't look at people in detail, as you do. I only see if they're nasty or nice. That's enough for me."

At this point it occurred to me, naturally, to wonder what Cecilia thought of *me*. I had it on the tip of my tongue to ask her: "And what do you think of *me*?"—but I could not make up my mind to put this question to her, fearing perhaps that she would answer, as in the case of Luciani, that she didn't think anything. In the end, however, I did decide, one day, to ask her: "What do you think of me?"

Rather unexpectedly, she replied: "Oh, lots of things."

I was much relieved, and went on: "Really? And what?"

"I don't really know; lots of things."

"Tell me one of them, anyhow."

She appeared to be considering the matter scrupulously, and then she answered: "Perhaps it's just because you want to know, but at the present moment I can't think of anything."

"What do you mean by that?"

"I mean that at the present moment I can't seem to think anything."

"Absolutely nothing?"

"Nothing."

"But just now you said you thought lots of things."

"Yes, I said so, but I see I was wrong."

"But don't you find it tiresome to think nothing, absolutely nothing, about the man you make love with?"

"No, why should I? What need is there to think anything?"

And so Cecilia did not merely remain elusive herself, but managed to confer an atmosphere of elusiveness upon everything that concerned her; she was like one of those characters in a fairy story who are not only invisible themselves but make everything they touch invisible.

And yet two or three times a week I possessed her, by which I mean that I went to bed with her. Anyone else, faced with the growing inadequacy of the physical relationship, would have sought elsewhere for the explanation of a thirst which increased in proportion as it was satisfied. But I was now set upon a course which I felt to be at the same time both fatal and mistaken; and so I made violent efforts to discover, in that physical possession which I yet knew to be illusory, the true possession I had so desperate a need for. As I threw myself upon Cecilia's willing body, I felt that possibly I was making amends, in those two hours of her delusive presence, for the other days of her absence. Possibly I was seeking, in her unalterable docility, a reason for boredom and thus for liberation. But Cecilia's body was not Cecilia, and what Cecilia was, I did not succeed in finding out. As for her docility, it no longer produced any boredom in me, but rather a profound mistrust, like some trap of nature into which I had fallen and from which I could not contrive to escape.

Anyhow I do not remember ever having loved Cecilia with such violence as I did during the time when I was spying upon her and suspecting that she was being unfaithful to me. I would throw myself upon her as if she were an enemy whom I wished to tear to pieces, a beloved enemy, however, who in an ambiguous way incited me to do this, and I was hardly ever satisfied with only one embrace. Significantly, the feeling that I had not truly possessed her generally used to assail me at the moment when, fully dressed and after saying good-bye to me, she walked toward the door in order to leave; it was as though her departure suddenly revealed to me, in an entirely physical manner, her unchanging power to withdraw herself from me, to elude me. Then I would pursue her, seize her by the hair and hurl her on the divan, disregarding her protests which in any case were not very energetic, and have her again, just as she was, fully dressed, with her shoes on her feet and her bag on her arm, still with the illusory idea that by having her I could nullify her independence and her mystery. Immediately after the embrace I realized, of course, that I had not possessed her. But it was too late; Cecilia went away and I knew that the whole thing would begin again next day—the useless watching, the unattainable possession, the final disappointment.

After more than a month of fruitless spying and of even more fruitless sexual frenzy, I understood what I ought to have guessed from the very first day, that surveillance is not a thing that should be carried out by someone who is directly interested in the results of what he is doing. If I wanted to make any headway, I must have recourse to somebody who carried out such surveillance as a professional duty, that is, a private detective agency. It was Cecilia herself who gave me this idea. Continually, while I was spying upon her, I thought of nothing but Balestrieri. The old painter, whom I had never cared about while he was alive, had since his death become for me an object of horrified and incomprehensible attraction. In reality, I sometimes said to myself, Balestrieri, to me, was rather like a mirror to a sick man—an unanswerable witness to the progress of his disease. I thought especially of Balestrieri each time I suspected that I was doing something he had done before me. And so, during the time when I was spying upon Cecilia, I could not resist the temptation of asking her whether the old painter had also given way to the same weakness. We were in my car; I was taking Cecilia home, in the evening. When we reached the street in which she lived and where I recalled having so often waited in vain for her to come out, I stopped the car and asked her point blank: "Did Balestrieri ever spy on you?"

"What d'you mean?"

"Did he follow you, wait for you, watch you, in fact?"

"Yes."

"You never told me about it."

"You never asked me."

"In what way did he watch you?"

"He stood in the courtyard and waited for me to come out."

So Balestrieri, I thought, had been more intelligent than I;

he had quickly discovered that there were two doors. "And then what?" I asked.

"Then, as soon as I came out, he followed me."

"Did he do this often?"

"During a certain period he did it every day."

"At what time did he take up his position in the courtyard?"

"That depended. Some days, when he knew I would be going out early, he was there by about eight o'clock."

"How did you come to know about it?"

"I used to see him from my bedroom window."

"And what did he do in the courtyard?"

"He used to walk about, or pretend to read the paper, or make drawings in a notebook."

"But what did he do so that you shouldn't see him, when you came out?"

"He went and stood under the doorway, in the shade, or behind a tree."

"And then what?"

"Then he followed me."

For a moment I was silent: I seemed to see the elderly painter, short and square, with his broad shoulders and big feet, his red face and silvery hair, turning up the collar of his raincoat and pulling the brim of his hat down over his eyes as he shadowed the sixteen-year-old girl from the courtyard to the street, and from that street to another; and I felt, recoiling upon me, the now habitual sense of shame at the thought that recently I had been doing exactly the same thing. Then I continued: "But did you notice that he was following you?"

"Sometimes I did and sometimes I didn't."

"And when you did notice, what did you do?"

"Nothing: I went on just as if I hadn't noticed. But once I turned and went back to meet him, and then we went together into a café."

"What did he say in the café?"

"He didn't say anything; he started crying."

I said nothing for a moment. Cecilia, who did not like being questioned, took advantage of this to start getting out of the car. But I stopped her. "Wait," I said. "During the time when he was watching you, were you being unfaithful to him?"

As if amused at the coincidence, she replied: "No, no, at that time I wasn't being unfaithful to him at all. It was only some months later that I had somebody."

"So he was watching you for no reason, unjustly?"

"That's right."

"And by the time that you had somebody, he had given up following you?"

"Yes, because he had had proof that I was not being unfaithful."

"In what way?"

"He had me followed."

"By whom?"

She said somewhat vaguely: "Oh, by one of those agencies —you know—who make inquiries, by a detective. They told him I hadn't anybody except him."

"But how did you get to know that he'd employed an agency to follow you?"

"He told me himself. He made me read a long report—pages of it. It cost him I don't know how much."

"Was he pleased?"

"Delighted."

After a brief silence, I asked: "And you were unfaithful to him immediately after the agency had proved to him that you weren't?"

"Yes, a month later, but I didn't do it on purpose—it just happened."

"And he knew about it?"

She hesitated and then said: "I think he may have guessed something, but he was never really sure about it."

"How do you mean?"

"He saw me two or three times, always with the same boy, and then he started following me again, on his own, without the agency. But he had got rather tired and he did it less often than before. Then he died."

"Why didn't he have you followed by the agency again?"

She said, with a reflective air: "If he had had me followed, he would have found out everything. But he no longer trusted the agency. He said I had always been unfaithful and the agency hadn't been able to discover the truth."

After this conversation, I began to think more and more often of using an agency, as Balestrieri had done. Strangely, whereas in the past I had refrained from doing certain things simply because I knew Balestrieri had done them, now, on the contrary, I felt inclined to employ an agency just because he had employed one. It was as though, having recognized the vanity of my efforts to stop myself on the slope down which Balestrieri had plunged, I had now decided to deliberately do the things he had done before me, as if doing them consciously and of my own free will had now become my only means of distinguishing myself from him, since he had done these things in spite of himself and in a state of unconsciousness bordering on madness.

One day, therefore, I started off to find the "Agenzia Falco," in a gloomy building in Via Nazionale, very solemn-looking outside, ornate and covered with pillars and statues and Latin inscriptions, and dark and dreary inside. I went up to the third floor in a dilapidated, evil-smelling old elevator, stepped out on to a pitch-dark landing and walked toward a glimmer of light filtering through an opaque glass door, on which was the name of the agency and a small, symbolic bird which was, presumably, a falcon. The door rang a bell as I opened it, and I went into an anteroom which was almost entirely bare except for a few wicker chairs. Two men came out of a room at the same moment, tightening the belts of their raincoats and pulling down their hats on their heads; I judged from their behavior and their clothes that they must be detectives, possibly the ones to whom the surveillance of Cecilia would be entrusted. The door having remained open, I walked over to it, and at the far side of a large room, sitting behind a desk reading a newspaper, I saw a dark, bald, thin man with flat temples, a big nose and fallen-in cheeks. I asked where the director could be found. In an earnest, authoritative manner, as though wishing to reassure me, he answered: "I am the director. Please come in and sit down."

I went in, and he rose to his feet, holding out his hand and introducing himself: "Major Mosconi." I sat down and for a moment looked at him, first at his meager face and worn black suit and twisted tie, and then at the old ink stains that speckled the top of the desk. I wondered what all this could possibly have to do with Cecilia and me, and the answer was: nothing. I said, however: "There's a person I want to have watched."

The major answered in a prompt, brisk tone: "That's what we're here for. Is it a man or a woman?"

"A woman."

"Is this woman your wife?"

"No, I'm not married. It's somebody to whom I am bound by special affection."

"Then it's a case of pre-matrimonial investigations?"

"Call it that, if you like."

The major indicated, by a gesture, that he did not wish to insist, that it was not necessary for me to say any more. He asked: "For what reason do you want to have this person watched?"

I looked at him again. For the director of an agency that called itself "Falcon," he had a face which seemed to contradict that sharp-eyed appellation in every possible way. His eyes, deep-set, small, lusterless, expressionless, made one think not so much of a falcon as of a blind finch. With a roughness

207

that gave me a certain satisfaction, I said: "I have very good reasons for believing that this person is unfaithful to me."

It was quite obvious that the major was unwilling to come quickly to the main point of the question by way of the very simple truth; and this, it appeared, was more in order to uphold the decorum of his office than because he had not understood what it was all about. "Is this person married?" he asked.

"No, she's unmarried."

"Are you married?"

"I've already told you that I'm not."

"I beg your pardon, I didn't remember. And so you have the impression that this young lady . . . it *is* a question of a young lady, is it not?"

I could only confirm this, impatiently: "Obviously."

"Excuse me, I didn't explain myself: I wished to know whether it is a question of a young lady of good family or of a woman who lives on her own and leads an independent life?"

"It's a young lady of good family."

"I could have sworn it was," he affirmed mysteriously.

This time I could not refrain from asking: "Why could you have sworn it was?"

"Those are the ones who give us most trouble. Very young girls, of eighteen or twenty. And so you have the impression that the young lady is unfaithful to you?"

"Yes, indeed."

"It's the usual reason. You must excuse my saying so, but ninety per cent of those who come here say the same thing. And alas, in at least sixty per cent of these cases, suspicions are shown to be well founded."

"If their suspicions are well founded, why then do they have recourse to your agency?"

"In order to have a mathematical certainty."

"And you—are you able to provide this certainty?"

The major shook his head with indulgent forbearance.

"Look," he said, "you might perhaps think that anybody can carry out certain inquiries. Even the interested party, you might think, but that isn't so. There is as much difference between the inquiries of an amateur investigator and ours as there is between an analysis made by an amateur scientist, without proper means and without serious knowledge, and an analysis carried out in a scientific laboratory. If you wanted to find out whether you had a definite disease, would you go for an analysis to a charlatan, or to a serious scientific laboratory, accredited and recognized by law? Obviously, the latter. Now the Agenzia Falco is the serious, accredited laboratory, recognized by law"—here the major broke off and pointed to a framed diploma hanging on the wall above his head— "and it is able to provide you with the certainty you require, in a scientific manner."

"In other words," I asked, in order to gain time, "you are able to discover the truth?"

"Always. A case of uncertainty is extremely rare, in fact almost non-existent. Our detectives are honest and trustworthy, all of them ex-carabinieri or ex-policemen, and it is practically impossible for them not to obtain some information."

"And how long does the investigation take?"

The major made a typical office worker's gesture: he replaced a pencil which was not out of place, rested his chin on his hand and fixed me with his little black, lusterless eyes. "I might say two or three weeks," he said. "I might say even longer. But I don't want to run off with your money. By the end of a week we shall know everything. When a woman is in love with a man, she doesn't see him once a week; she sees him every day, even several times a day. Now, if we can prove that the woman we are watching sees a man every day, or indeed more than once a day, our client is in possession of all the proofs he requires. Of course, if our client is not convinced, we can make further investigations, going even more deeply into the matter, if need be."

"What do you mean—going more deeply into the matter?"

"Forgive me, but these are not things that can be stated beforehand. One has to know the case. However, don't worry, a week will be enough. Yours, if I may be allowed to say so, is an ordinary case."

"Why ordinary?"

"It is the simplest kind of case. You have no idea of the complications we are faced with sometimes. A week, then, as I said, will be more than enough."

"Yes, I understand," I said; and I remained silent for a short time. I was thinking that the major, thanks to his so-called scientific investigations, was convinced that he could reach the truth of the matter and I was also thinking that his truth was not mine. Finally I inquired: "What are the conditions of payment?"

"Ten thousand lire a day. With a supplement, according to arrangement, if the person to be watched goes about by car, because in that case our detectives have to have the use of a car too."

I said, meditatively: "She doesn't go by car, she walks."

"Ten thousand lire a day, then."

"And when could you start?"

"Tomorrow. You give me the details, I'll study them and tomorrow morning the detective will start shadowing her."

Suddenly I rose to my feet. "We'll begin in a week's time," I said. "Because the person isn't in Rome at the moment and won't be back for a week."

"As you wish." Major Mosconi had also risen to his feet. "But if by any chance you are hesitating because of the price, you can find out and see that other agencies won't charge you any less."

I answered that it was not a question of price, and repeating that I would reappear in a week's time, I went away.

I went back mechanically to my studio and prepared to wait for Cecilia, for this was one of the two or three days of the week when we saw each other. For some time now I had been suffering from sleeplessness owing to the wretchedness that my relations with Cecilia were causing me. Usually I would drop off to sleep as soon as I had gone to bed, but not an hour would pass before I woke up with a jump, as though somebody had given me a good shaking; and then, inevitably, I would start thinking about Cecilia and would not fall asleep again until dawn, only to reawaken at my usual time, all too early. And then during the day I would drop off to sleep wherever I was, worn out with fatigue, and sleep heavily for as much as two or three hours. And so it happened that day. The window curtain was drawn, and a restful light, warm and yellow, filled the studio. I lay down on the divan and, turning on one side, started looking at the empty canvas still standing on the easel near the window. I reflected that the canvas was blank because I did not succeed in getting possession of any kind of reality, in the same way that my own mind was blank when confronted with a Cecilia who eluded me and whom I could not succeed in possessing. And the physical act, by which I often had the illusion of possessing her, was equivalent to the pornographic painting of Balestrieri—that is, it was not possession, just as the other was not painting. And in the same way as, with Cecilia, I oscillated between boredom and sexual mania, so, in art, I oscillated between bad painting and no painting at all. And now I had turned to the Agenzia Falco in order to find out something certain about Cecilia, but it was as though in order to paint I had read a scientific treatise on the nature and composition of matter. The canvas was empty, I went on thinking confusedly, because Cecilia eluded me; my mind was empty because reality eluded me. Reality and Cecilia were the two words that echoed more and more feebly in my head; evoking two different operations which I felt, nevertheless, to be connected by an undoubted link. It seemed clear to me that this link was the mania to possess, and that both operations were wrecked by the impossibility of doing so. As I thought over these things, more and more wearily, I fell asleep.

I had scarcely fallen asleep when I woke up again. The studio was almost in darkness, and when I turned on the light I realized that in reality I had slept for about an hour; it was half past five, and I had come back from the agency at about half past four. This sleep, so profound as to give me the feeling of not having slept at all, had rested me: I felt unusually clear-headed and, as had sometimes happened to me in the past when I was getting ready to paint, full of precise and conscious creative energy. I looked up at the canvas and thought, almost involuntarily, that it was a pity I had given up painting; this was the state of mind one needed for working. But immediately afterward, in an automatic sort of way, I jumped off the divan and rushed out of the studio. I was sure that Cecilia was in the actor's flat, and I wanted to catch her at the moment when she came out on her way to visit me.

Before this I had set out to watch Cecilia every day except those days on which we saw each other, thinking for some reason or other that she would not go to bed with me and with the actor on the same afternoon. But Cecilia had told me on the telephone that morning that she could not see me before six, and I understood why she had given me an appointment for that time: she was due to visit Luciani before she came to visit me. And so, while I could not know at what time she went to see Luciani on other days, nor at what time she left him, today I at least knew for certain at what time she would be leaving him, because that was the time when she was coming to see me. It astonished me that I had never before thought of a thing that was so simple and, in addition, so completely in conformity with Cecilia's innocently cruel psychology. It was characteristic of her to go straight from the arms of the actor into mine, in the space of barely half an hour; to give herself to me with the same flattering abandonment with which she had given herself to him; to mingle the seed of both of us, with animal-like greed, in her own belly. Why in the world had I never thought of it before?

Fifteen minutes later I was at the house where the actor lived. I found room for the car almost in front of the entrance door, and stayed in it. It was not worth while taking up my position in the bar; according to my calculations, Cecilia ought to be coming out in five minutes at most. I lit a cigarette, never taking my eyes off the ground-floor shutters, through which a light showed. These were the shutters of Luciani's flat, and probably, at that moment, Cecilia was dressing hastily, telling the actor the same childish lie that she generally told me: "I must go, Mother's expecting me." I had a feeling of nausea as I looked at those shutters, and realized that it was not so very different from the feeling sometimes aroused in me, in times past, by the blank surface of a canvas, as the moment when I was preparing to paint: out of that door, framed in black marble, would soon issue something which I desired at the same time both to know and not to know, something for which I felt at the same time both appetite and disgust— Cecilia, or in other words, reality. I knew that I must stay in my car until I saw her appear in the doorway, but at the same time I felt a great desire to go away. Once again, in the light of this twofold, contradictory feeling, I saw that what had so often made me abandon my spying, during these last days, had not been a revolt of dignity but rather a repugnance for Cecilia as she really was—that is, in a word, for reality.

At the end of five minutes, as I had foreseen, Cecilia and the actor appeared together in the doorway. They were holding hands and it seemed to me that they were both staggering a little, as though dazed. I noticed that Cecilia was clasping the actor's hand in a special way, with her fingers between his, as if unconsciously repeating the recent interlacing of their bodies. Still holding hands, they went off along the pavement down the hill.

Everything can be foreseen, except the feeling aroused in

us by what we foresee. One can certainly foresee, for example, that a snake may come out of a hole under a rock; but it is difficult to foresee the quality and intensity of the fear that the sight of the reptile will inspire in us. Countless times I had imagined Cecilia coming out of the actor's house, either in company with him or alone, but I had not foreseen the feelings I would experience when I actually saw her come out of that big door with its black marble frame, into the street, hand in hand with Luciani. And so I was astonished when, at the sight of Cecilia and the actor standing for what seemed an eternity in the doorway, I became conscious of an abominable sensation like that of a fainting fit. I suffered horribly and was at the same time amazed that I should be suffering so much and in so novel a way, when I had been prepared for this moment by so precise an anticipation. I felt that the image of those two was impressed indelibly upon my memory; and I felt a scorching pain, as though that image were a red-hot iron and my memory a piece of sensitive flesh that rebelled against it.

I have said that my suffering was comparable to that of a fainting fit. In reality I had fainted in every part of myself except at the one point in which—as if the whole of my vitality had concentrated itself there—I was conscious of myself to an excessive degree. And it was precisely from this that I suffered; from feeling myself to be everywhere lifeless except at this one grievous point. In the meantime I had automatically started the car, brought it slowly out from its parking place and driven off behind Cecilia and Luciani.

They were walking very slowly, still holding hands, silent and happy, no doubt. Then the actor stopped at a barbershop; Cecilia spoke to him for a moment, held out her hand to him and Luciani kissed it. He went into the barbershop and Cecilia went on her way. Driving slowly, my eyes fixed on her as she disappeared and reappeared on the winding pathway, I went on for some distance down the street. I looked at her, and I looked especially at the movement of her hips under her short, tight dress, a movement at the same time clumsy and lazy and powerful, and I realized that I still felt desire for her—just as though I were not yet entirely sure of her unfaithfulness. And I saw that if I really wished to stop desiring her I must compel her to confess the truth, that truth which alone would irreparably establish her in my eyes for what she was, and would make me cease to love her. Cecilia, meanwhile, had gone to the bus stop farther down the street. I looked at my watch; there were still ten minutes to go to the time of her appointment with me. She had calculated her time well: in a quarter of an hour at most, the bus would put her down in the Piazza del Popolo, a few steps from my studio. At six o'clock, as arranged, she would be able to throw herself into my arms.

I stopped the car abruptly in front of her—she was at that moment fumbling in her bag with her head down—threw the door open and said to her in my normal voice: "Want to get in?" She looked up and saw me, appeared to be on the point of speaking, then changed her mind and got into the car in silence. I started off and asked her: "How do you come to be in these parts?"

"I've been to see that film producer," she replied.

"But isn't his office in Via Montebello?"

"His private house is near here."

I threw her a sideways glance and observed, in spite of being troubled myself, that Cecilia was troubled too, however inappropriate that word may seem when used of a person so expressionless. I saw this from a very slight contraction of her eyebrows, which I knew to be a sign of worry and perplexity. I decided to attack her with a combination of reason and severity, as if this had been a police interrogation. "What's this producer called—quickly now, his name and surname?"

"He's called Mario Meloni."

"Where does he live—quickly, his street number, which floor, and the number of his flat?"

"He lives here, in Via Archimede," she replied, in a grudging tone of voice, like a little school girl being questioned by her teacher, "at number thirty-six, flat six, third floor."

This was the number of Luciani's house, but not his floor nor yet the number of his flat. I realized that Cecilia gave me this number to protect herself from the possibility of my contesting her statement, in case I said I had seen her coming out. But how was she going to explain the presence of the actor at her side? I wanted to see how she justified herself. "I saw you just now," I said, "coming out of number thirty-six, but you weren't alone, you were with Luciani."

"He was at the producer's too. We went there together."

"What for?"

"He wanted to speak to us about a job."

"What job?"

"A film."

"What's the title of this film?"

"He didn't tell us."

"Where did Meloni receive you?"

"In his living room."

"Describe this room, then—quickly—beginning with the furniture and how it was arranged."

I knew, of course, that Cecilia did not notice things nor, generally, places in which she had been. I thought therefore that if, in order to reassure me, she described the furnishings of Meloni's living room with a wealth of detail—that room in which she had never been because it did not exist—I should have a further proof that she was lying to me. But I had not counted upon her unconquerable, negative laziness. She said dryly: "It's a room like lots of other rooms."

Disconcerted and somewhat surprised, I insisted: "Meaning what?"

"A room with armchairs, sofas, little tables and chairs."

These were the same words that she had used to describe the sitting room in her own home. I continued to press her. "What color were the armchairs and sofas?"

"I didn't look at them."

"What color were Luciani's underpants; you must have looked at them, anyhow."

"There you are, I knew you'd begin making insinuations."

By this time we had arrived at Via Margutta. I drove into the courtyard, stopped and jumped out and then, faithful to my plan of systematic intimidation, seized Cecilia by the arm and pulled her violently out of the car. "Now we'll see," I cried.

"What?"

"We'll see if you've told the truth."

I grasped her tightly by her thin, childish arm and realized that I was running purposely in order to be able to give her a violent tug to cause her to stumble and almost fall. "What a way to behave!" she said once, and then: "What's wrong with you?" yet she did not appear to be either surprised or irritated or frightened. I pushed the key into the lock, turned it and kicked the door open, then turned on the light and, with a last, violent shove, hurled Cecilia on to the divan. She fell, her head lowered; I rushed to the telephone and started furiously turning over the pages of the street directory. I fumbled and searched, found what I was looking for, and then, my finger on the list, thrust it under the nose of Cecilia, who had now risen to her feet again. "There's no Meloni at 36, Via Archimede," I said.

"His number isn't in the book."

"Why?"

"Because he doesn't want to be disturbed."

"On the other hand, here's Luciani at No. 36."

"It's not possible, he's not in the telephone book."

"No, but he's in the street directory. Look here, there it is!" She looked with feigned reluctance but said nothing. I commented sarcastically: "What an odd coincidence! Meloni and Luciani live in the same house."

"Yes, Luciani lives on the ground floor and Meloni on the third."

"Very well, then, now we'll go out and drive together to Meloni's."

A long silence followed. Cecilia gazed at me with those eyes, so vague and so poetical, that in reality saw nothing, and was silent. "Come on," I urged her, "get a move on."

I saw her suddenly blush, with an uneven, patchy redness, from her neck up over her cheeks. "Yes," she said, "it's true."

"It's true?—what's true?"

"That Luciani and I see each other."

Again I had foreseen, for some time past, the words of this confession; but there is a great difference between foreseeing with one's mind and hearing with one's ears: once again, as when I saw her coming out of Luciani's house, I had a sickening sensation of faintness. "What do you mean, that you see each other?" I stammered stupidly; "I know you see each other."

"I mean we make love."

"And you say it just like that?"

"How else should I say it?"

I felt she was right: she did not love me, she was unfaithful to me, and her tone, so economical and so colorless, was the correct one. I was still left, however, with an insatiable need to imprison her in her confession as in a cage of shame from which she would never be able to escape. "Why did you do it?" I asked.

She seemed to be reflecting, seriously, scrupulously, before answering. Then she said, quite simply: "Because I liked it."

"But don't you realize you ought not to have done it?"

"Why ought I not to have done it?"

"Because a woman doesn't betray a man she's fond of, and you've told me over and over again that you're fond of me."

"Yes, I *am* fond of you, but I'm fond of Luciani too."

"So you're one of those women who give themselves to everybody—yesterday to a painter, today to an actor, tomorrow, I daresay, to the electrician."

She looked at me and said nothing. I went on again: "You're a good-for-nothing, worthless woman."

Still she was silent. Why did I go on insisting like this? Because I wanted to convince myself that, after the confession she had made, Cecilia was discredited and reduced to nothingness in my eyes, and yet I felt that this was not so. Nevertheless, this discrediting process was bound to occur, I could not help thinking. There had been women who had forfeited my estimation and my affection for no more than a phrase, a gesture, an attitude; all the more reason why Cecilia, who had vulgarly betrayed me, should do so. I concluded angrily: "Do you realize that what one does, one is, and that therefore what you have done makes you into something very different from what you were?"

I should have liked her to ask: "What was I, and what am I now?" And then I should have answered: "You were an honest girl and now you're a whore." At the same time her question would have indicated a need on her part to be well-considered, esteemed, appreciated by me. But I was disappointed in my hope: Cecilia did not open her mouth; and I saw that silence was the only answer I could expect from her. This silence meant that lying and unfaithfulness were, for her, words devoid of significance, not so much because she did not understand them as because they did not denote anything particular in her life. I felt she was eluding me again, and I seized her by her arms and shook her, crying out in a rage: "Why don't you speak, say something, why don't you answer?"

She announced, quite sincerely: "I have nothing to say."

"I have something to say," I shouted, beside myself with rage. "And that is, you're just a vulgar little whore."

She looked at me, but said nothing. I shook her again. "So

219

you allow yourself to be called a whore and you don't protest."

She rose to her feet. "Dino, I'm going away."

Among all the many things I had failed to foresee, there was this—the possibility of her going away. Seized with a sudden anxiety, I asked: "Where are you going?"

"I'm going away. It's better for us not to go on seeing each other."

"But why? Wait. Wait a moment. We must talk."

"What's the use of talking? We don't agree, anyhow. Our characters are too different."

Thus Cecilia was again eluding me, and in two ways—first, by reducing the value of her own confession: between herself and me, according to her, there was merely a difference of character, as though unfaithfulness were a question of individual temperament and not of moral standards; secondly, by leaving me before I could leave her. Passing suddenly from the moral to the physical, I was seized with desire for her; it was as though I should be able to pretend to myself, if I took her at that moment, that I was possessing her through the physical act after psychological possession had failed. I caught her round the waist as she was already moving toward the door and whispered in her ear: "We must make love, for the last time."

"No, no, no," she replied, trying to pull herself away, "that's all finished."

"Come here."

"No, let me go."

She struggled determinedly, but without any hostility, as though she were withholding herself simply because I was incapable of offering her my love in a more efficacious manner. In her enigmatic, unmoving eyes there was an ambiguous hint of allurement; and in her body below the waist, a submissiveness which I did not perceive in its childish, slender upper part. Nevertheless she struggled, and when I succeeded in making her sit on the divan she drew back a little out of reach of my lips. Then an idea came to me, or rather an impulse. That morning I had taken twenty thousand lire, in two notes of ten thousand, out of my drawer and put them in my pocket. I pulled Cecilia violently toward me; and at the same time, as she turned her face away from me and my kiss landed on her neck, I slipped the two notes into her hand. She lowered her eyes to take a quick glance at the unaccustomed object in the palm of her hand; then her hand closed, I felt her body abandon its resistance, and I saw that she had lowered her eyelids as if ready to fall asleep—which was her way of showing me that she accepted my love and was prepared to enjoy it.

And so I took her, without her undressing; with a fury and a violence greater than usual, for it seemed to me that her body had become a kind of arena where I had to compete with the actor in vigor and tenacity. I took her in silence; but at the moment of the orgasm I blew the word "Bitch!" right into her face. I may have been wrong, but it seemed to me that a very faint smile hovered on her lips; I could not tell if she smiled for the pleasure she was feeling or at my insult.

Later, when she was half asleep and I was lying beside her, I reflected as usual that physical possession had in no way satisfied me. The fleeting, ambiguous, possibly ironical smile with which she had answered my insulting word confirmed, if anything, the futility of the carnal relationship. But I had seen her grasp the banknotes in her fist, and during our love-making she had put her hand up to her forehead so that the notes had been in front of my eyes all the time. I said to myself that considering the failure of my previous attempts at possession, money might possibly be the trap in which I could catch her. She had refused herself to me until the moment when I put the money in her hand; so that, contrary to what I had thought hitherto, she was venal. It was now a matter of proving that she really was so, that is, of reducing the mystery of her independence to a question of profit.

Cecilia slept beside me for a little, for her usual length of time and in her usual way; then she woke up, planted a kiss on my cheek with her usual mechanical tenderness, and finally rose to her feet, smoothing down her crumpled dress with both hands. The two banknotes, folded in four, were now lying on the floor where she had dropped them after we finished making love. She picked them up, opened her bag and slipped them, very carefully, into her purse. "Then you still want us to part company?" I asked.

She did not appear to grasp the allusion contained in the word "still"; she answered indifferently: "Just as you like. If you want us to go on, I don't mind. If you want us to part company, let's do so."

And so, I reflected, not without astonishment, the money she had received and accepted had sufficed for one single time only; and it had failed to suggest to her listless imagination the alluring prospect of her being able to earn more in the future, in the same manner. "But," I asked, "if you go on seeing me, why would you do so?"

"Because I'm fond of you."

"If I asked you to give up Luciani, would you do it?"

"Oh no, not that."

I was hurt, in spite of myself, at the firmness of her refusal. "You might answer me with a little less eagerness," I said.

"I'm sorry."

"So from now on I've got to go halves with Luciani?"

She seemed to become more animated, as though I had at last touched a sensitive spot. "But what does it matter to you?" she said. "Why are you so worried about it? I'll come and see you as usual; nothing will be changed."

I repeated to myself: "Nothing will be changed," saying to myself that for her it was the truth. She was gazing at me now with a curious, almost regretful expression. At last she said: "You know, I should be sorry to leave you."

222

I was struck by the undoubted sincerity of these words. "Would you really be sorry?" I asked.

"Yes, I've grown accustomed to you."

"But you would be equally sorry to leave Luciani, wouldn't you?"

"Yes, indeed."

"You've grown accustomed to him too?"

"You're two different things."

I remained silent for a moment. How could we be two different things, seeing that Cecilia asked the same thing from both of us, which was in fact the mere physical relationship? "So you want to have us both?" I asked.

She nodded her head in a mysterious silence, full of impudent, childish covetousness. Then she said: "What fault is it of mine if I like being with both of you? You each of you give me something different."

I felt tempted to ask her: "I give you money and Luciani gives you love—isn't that so?" But I restrained myself, realizing that it was still too early for a question of that sort. Before I asked it, I would have to get to the bottom of her newly discovered venality. The fact that she had accepted money just this once might not have any significance. With a mingled feeling of anger and weariness, I said: "Very well then, you shall have both of us. We'll have a try at it. But you'll see yourself that it's impossible to love two men at the same time."

"Not at all; I tell you it's perfectly possible." She appeared to be extremely glad at having solved the problem of our relationship; stooping, she lightly touched my cheek with her lips and went off, telling me that she would telephone me next morning, as she did every day.

I turned to the wall and closed my eyes.

Chapter 8

I had now to prove to myself that Cecilia was venal. I recalled all the times I had given money to prostitutes and told myself that if Cecilia was really venal I would have the same feeling for her that I had for these women after I had paid them—a feeling of possession, but of a possession depreciated and superfluous, a feeling that the person who had received the money was reduced to the status of an inanimate object, a feeling that, owing to this commercial valuation, she had forfeited all true value. It was only a step from this feeling to the sense of boredom which would liberate me from Cecilia and from my love for her. Certainly it was a degrading kind of possession, for the one who was possessed as well as for the one who possessed; and without doubt I should have preferred a different kind, which would have permitted of my parting from Cecilia as from somebody whom I now knew too well but did not despise; but I had at all costs to relieve my own misery. Indeed, I preferred to know that Cecilia was mercenary rather than mysterious; the knowledge that she was mercenary would give me a sense of possession that mystery denied me.

And so I acquired the habit, at the first moment of our meetings, of thrusting into Cecilia's hand—without a word, as

I had done the first time—a sum of money which varied, according to the day, from five to thirty thousand lire. In this way, I thought, the elusive, mysterious Cecilia, from whom I could not succeed in detaching myself would be replaced in a short time by a Cecilia who was not in the least elusive and who was entirely devoid of mystery. But this transformation did not take place. If anything, it was the opposite that happened: it was not the money that changed Cecilia's character; on the contrary it was Cecilia, evidently the stronger of the two, who changed the character of the money.

Cecilia, when I thrust the folded banknotes into her palm, would immediately clench her fist, but without giving any other sign that she had received and accepted them. It was truly as if this money and the hand that gave it and the hand that received it belonged to a different world from the world in which Cecilia and I existed. Then, while I was embracing her, she would drop the notes on the floor beside the divan, and there they would remain, folded and crumpled, where I could see them easily while we were making love—the symbol, it seemed to me, of a method of possession which I fondly imagined to be more complete and satisfying than the one to which I was applying myself at the same moment. Afterward Cecilia, ready to tiptoe naked to the bathroom, would stoop swiftly and, with the graceful gesture of a runner bending to pick up a handkerchief dropped by his companion, would snatch up the notes with the tips of her fingers and throw them beside her bag on the table. When she was dressed she would go to the table, take up the notes, put them safely in her purse and shut the purse in her bag. Cecilia liked to do things always in the same way, as a kind of ritual. And so this detail of the money came to be included in the customary love ritual with perfect naturalness and even with a sort of grace, without, in fact, any of the meretricious significance which I had thought to be inevitable—indeed, like everything Cecilia did, without any significance at all.

At first, as I have said, I gave her from five to thirty thousand lire, wishing to see whether she would react in any way to these varying sums. I felt that if she said to me: "Last time you gave me twenty thousand lire, today you've given me only five —why is that?" I should have more than sufficient reason to consider that she was venal. But she never showed that she noticed whether the notes I put in her hand were single or double, green or red, as though the gesture of paying her had no particular significance but was simply one of the many gestures I made when I was with her, which I might have made in a different way or not at all, without our relationship being altered on that account. Then I decided to see what would happen if I stopped giving her money. Strange to say, I set about this experiment with a beating of the heart. I did not openly admit it to myself, but since I was almost convinced that these banknotes which I slipped furtively into Cecilia's hand now constituted the chief grounds for our relationship, I was afraid of losing her at the very moment when I hoped to prove to myself that, in losing her, I had nothing to lose.

One day, therefore, I did not put anything into her hand. To my astonishment Cecilia, far from showing disappointment, did not even appear to have noticed the change that had occurred in the customary love ritual. In the clasp of the fingers that received my empty hand there was no feeling of surprise or dissatisfaction; it was exactly the same handclasp with which, on the previous days, she had announced to me after receiving the money that she was ready to give herself to me. That day she behaved during our love-making in the same way as on the days when I paid her; and she went away without alluding in any way to the fact that I had not paid her. I did the same thing two or three times, but Cecilia, childishly impenetrable, again gave no sign of having noticed anything. So I found myself faced with three possibilities: either Cecilia was venal, but was sufficiently superior and elegant in her astuteness not to show it; or she was absent-minded, but with a highly mysterious kind of absent-mindedness—that is, she was as elusive as before and as always, in spite of the money; or again, she was completely disinterested, and in this case too she eluded me and withdrew herself from my possession. I turned over this problem in my mind for some time, and in the end decided to get her with her back to the wall. One day I again slipped two ten thousand lire notes into her hand and said to her: "Look, I've given you twenty thousand lire."

"Yes, I noticed you had."

"It's the first time I've done it, after giving you nothing for a week. Did you notice that too?"

"Of course."

"You weren't annoyed?"

"I imagined you hadn't the money."

Cecilia, completely devoid of curiosity as she was, had never questioned me about my family and did not know that I was rich. She took me for what I appeared—a painter in a sweater and a pair of corduroy trousers, with a very untidy studio and a decrepit car. And so her reply was, as usual, the only one she could give. "It's true," I went on, "I didn't have the money, but I thought you might be annoyed that I stopped giving you any."

"To be left without money is a thing that can happen to anyone," she answered ambiguously.

"Supposing that from now on I couldn't give you any more—what would you do?"

"You gave me some today; why think of the future?"

This was one of Cecilia's fundamental responses: past and future, for her, did not exist; only the most immediate present, in fact only the actual fleeting moment, seemed to her worthy of consideration. I went on insisting, however: "But suppose I didn't give you anything more; would you go on seeing me?"

She looked at me, and then finally replied: "Didn't we see each other before you started giving me anything?" It was, I thought, the perfect answer. But her uncertain, dubious, questioning tone, as if she were not entirely sure of what she was saying, seemed to allow room for the supposition that if I did really stop paying her she would perhaps reconsider the whole question of our relationship. And yet even this was not certain. Cecilia, as I perceived, did not really know what she would do if I ceased to give her money; and this for the good reason that, being attached to the present and quite devoid of imagination, she could not foresee what feeling my financial shortcomings would arouse in her, and above all to what extent, once I had stopped paying her, she would feel the desire to make love with me, whether less or more or in the same way or in a different way or not at all. "Now listen," I said, "I want to make a suggestion. Instead of my giving you sometimes five, sometimes ten, sometimes twenty, sometimes thirty thousand lire, as I do at present, we might agree on a fixed amount which I would give you once a month. What do you say to that?"

She immediately protested, as though she were being asked to replace a cherished habit, slightly absurd but nevertheless poetical, with something more rational but prosaic. "No, no," she said, "let's go on like this, as we've done so far. You can give me what you like and when you like, from time to time, without any rules; anyhow, like that it's a surprise every time."

Thus once again I failed to catch Cecilia in the trap of venality, and also failed to transform her from a creature of mystery and elusiveness into an ordinary, boring, mercenary woman. I came finally to the conclusion that the money one gives to a prostitute has, in reality, a possessive character because not only the one who gives it but also the one who receives it considers it as a recompense for certain very precise services. In other words, the prostitute's client knows that, if he does not pay her, the woman will reject him; the woman, on her side, knows that if she accepts the money she is then obliged to give herself to him. But I was conscious that Cecilia gave herself to me for reasons that had nothing to do with money; and that she, on her side, appeared not to know that the money, once accepted, obliged her to give herself. I had proof of this ignorance one day when, after I had placed the banknotes in her hand as usual, I found myself being rejected with the following words: "Look, I don't want to today; let's be together like brother and sister"—words in which there was no trace of any sort of calculation but merely a quite ingenuous indifference. In the meantime, however, the notes were in her hand, and immediately afterward she put them into her bag. Thus the money which, as long as I had it in my pocket, might seem to me to be the symbol of possession, became the symbol of the impossibility of that same possession as soon as it passed into Cecilia's bag.

On the other hand, the knowledge that each time she visited me she would receive money did not appear to alter the insecure, irregular, unexpected, problematical character of these visits. Not merely did Cecilia now come to see me not more than two or three times a week, exactly as she had done when she was not receiving anything from me; but it also seemed clear to me, from the hesitations and uncertainties in her tone of voice when she telephoned me to arrange an appointment, that our meetings depended, as in the past, upon disinterested and mysterious obligations and opportunities that had nothing to do with money.

The first effect of this frenzy of mine to possess Cecilia through the medium of venality was that, in order to meet the expense forced upon me by my experiment, I again approached my mother, from whom I had hitherto asked nothing more than what was strictly necessary to live on. I could have wished now that I had not been so contemptuous of her money; I was aware that I had accustomed her, by now, to a disinterestedness on my part which I would willingly have discarded and which obliged me to assume a character toward Cecilia which if not actually miserly, was at any rate parsimonious. But there it was: I had wished to be poor, without foreseeing that Cecilia would make me want to be rich, and now it was too late to change my mother's ideas about me, all the more so since these ideas accorded all too well with her own natural inclination toward thrift. I knew, nevertheless, that my mother was prepared to give me a good deal more than she had so far given me; but I also knew that she was not prepared to give me anything without something in exchange. My mother held fast to her desire that I should go back and live with her, and I was not ignorant of the fact that the money which she had so often offered me in vain, and the money which she was now giving me in increasing amounts whenever I asked for it, had the same object always in view, that of putting herself in the position of being able to impose her will upon me. I tried to postpone the clash which I felt to be inevitable by treating my mother, in exchange for her unexpected generosity, with an assiduity and an affection to which I had certainly not accustomed her in the past. Then, seeing that she not only did not refuse me the money but even, apparently, encouraged me to go on asking for more, I suddenly realized that the relationship between her and me was, fundamentally, almost the same as that between myself and Cecilia: my mother, too, was seeking to get control over me by means of money. But here the resemblance ended, for I was not like Cecilia and, above all, my mother was not like me. Money, between Cecilia and me, owing to the lack of importance which we both for different reasons attached to it, seemed no longer to be money at all but a part of our sexual relationship; whereas between me and my mother, just because for her it was not, and could never be, anything but money, it preserved intact its original character. In other words, although my mother certainly loved me, she was not in the least disposed to sink money in me permanently, so to speak, simply because she was fond of me—that is, to do the only thing that could deprive the money itself of its accustomed significance.

I had a confirmation of this difference one day when I asked her for a much larger sum on a pretext which, as will be seen, was extremely unfortunate. It was after lunch; and my mother, as usual, had lain down on her bed in her own room, one arm over her face and her legs dangling. I was sitting in an armchair at the foot of the bed, and asking her questions, I believe, about my father—one of the few subjects which we had in common and which never ceased to interest me. My mother answered more and more briefly and vaguely and appeared on the point of falling asleep. Suddenly, without any preparation, I said to her: "By the way, I'm in need of three hundred thousand lire."

I noticed that she drew her arm very slowly away from one of her eyes and looked at me for a moment with that eye only. Then, with a first sign of unpleasantness in the tone of her sleepy voice, she said: "I gave you fifty thousand on Saturday, and it's only Tuesday now; what do you want all this money for?"

In accordance with the plan I had previously worked out, I replied: "It's only the first instalment of the sum I shall have to spend. I've decided that I must renovate the studio, which is in a shameful state."

"And how much will the total expense amount to?"

"At least three times as much. Apart from plastering and whitewashing, I shall have to redo the bathroom entirely, put up new curtains, repair the floor, and so on."

It had seemed to me a good plan. The studio was really in bad shape; I had good justification for touching my mother for a million or even a million and a half. Furthermore, I knew that my mother, owing to her aversion to my studio—a point of honor with her—would never make up her mind to come to Via Margutta in order to see how I was spending her money.

I awaited her answer, therefore, with confidence. She was lying still now; she appeared really to have dropped off to sleep. Finally, however, from beneath the arm which covered her face, came a perfectly wide-awake voice: "This time I shall not give you the money."

231

"But why?"

"Because I don't see any need for you to give the landlord a present of a million lire when you have the possibility of living in a villa on the Via Appia."

I saw how she intended to parry the blow and realized, too late, that the pretext I had devised to extract the money from her was the very one I should have avoided. Pretending to be surprised, however, I exclaimed: "What has that to do with it?"

"You gave me to understand that you intended to come back and live here," said my mother in a slow, hard, monotonous voice, "and I, as you may have noticed, had the tact to give you as long as you wished to decide. But now you are asking me for money to do up your studio. So I am forced to conclude that you have gone back on your promise."

"I never made any promise," I said, irritated. "On the contrary, in fact, I've never concealed my repugnance at the idea of living with you."

"Well then, my dear Dino, you can hardly be surprised at my saying that this time I shall not give you the money."

Two days before, I had given Cecilia the last thirty thousand lire that I possessed, and Cecilia was to come and visit me in the afternoon. It was possible for me not to give her anything, as so often in the past; but I was suddenly conscious that I would now no longer be capable of that. This was not so much because I felt that by giving her money I possessed her, as for the opposite reason: the money now endowed Cecilia's elusiveness with a new aspect which confirmed and complicated it—that of her disinterestedness. And just because she did not allow herself to be possessed through the medium of money, I now felt myself irresistibly urged to give it to her; in the same way that, just because I could not succeed in possessing her through the sexual act, I felt myself urged to repeat that same act over and over again. In reality, both the money and the sexual act gave me for a moment the illusion of possession, and I could now no longer do without that moment, although

I knew that it was regularly followed by a feeling of profound disillusionment. I looked at my mother lying there flat on her back with her arm over her face, then I thought of Cecilia who, at the same moment that she closed her hand on my money, opened her mouth to my kiss, and I felt that I would be capable of committing a crime in order to have the money I needed. My attention was drawn especially to the hand which my mother held over her eyes; on each of its thin fingers were massive rings with precious stones in them; all I need do was to slip off one of these rings and I should be able to give Cecilia all the money I wanted, at any rate for some months. Then, for some reason, I remembered the favorable, if self-interested, behavior of my mother when I had made advances to the maid Rita; and I changed my plan. I got up and sat on the bed, and said with calculated gentleness: "Mother, I want to be honest with you. I don't need this money for doing up the studio. I need it for another reason."

"And what reason is that?"

"It would be better if you gave me the money without asking so many questions. There are things that it's not easy to say."

"A mother has the right to know in what way her son spends her money."

"A son of sixteen, I daresay; but not a son of thirty-five."

"A mother is a mother, whatever age her son is."

"Well, I want this money for a woman." After I had said this, I looked at my mother again. She was still motionless, and appeared once more to have fallen asleep. Then her voice came to me: "Some bad woman, no doubt."

"But, Mother, if she was a bad woman, do you think I should be asking you for three hundred thousand lire?"

"A respectable woman doesn't expect to be paid."

"But supposing this woman is in real need?"

"Be careful, Dino, there are women who are capable of inventing all kinds of wonderful romances in order to get money."

233

"It's not a case of romance, it's a case of absolute necessities—food, rent, clothes."

"In fact, you have to keep her in every possible way?"

"Not exactly; just to help her a little, for a certain time."

"A piece of riff-raff, I suppose," said my mother. "How much better it would have been, Dino, if you had had a *liaison* with a married lady, someone of your own world, who would not have asked you for anything and would not have been a burden upon you in any way."

I replied, without irony: "My world is not the world in which ladies of that kind are to be found."

"Your world is my world," said my mother. "Above all, Dino, do be careful; you can catch all sorts of diseases with these adventuresses who are going about nowadays."

"I haven't caught anything yet, and I won't catch anything in the future."

"How do you know who this woman goes with when you're not there? I repeat, Dino, be careful. Of course you know that in some cases there are precautions that can and ought to be taken."

"You'll be telling me next how I ought to conduct myself when I make love."

"No, but I want to put you on your guard. After all you are my son and your health is important to me."

"Well, Mother, to come to the point: are you going to give me this money?"

My mother removed her hand from her eyes and looked at me. "And who is this woman?" she asked.

I answered with a phrase worthy of Cecilia. "This woman is—a woman."

"You see—you want money, and then you don't trust me."

"It's not that I don't trust you, but what does it matter to you whether she's called Maria, or Clara, or Paola?"

"I didn't ask you her name, I asked you who she is—whether

she's unmarried or married, whether she works or does nothing or is a student, how old she is, what she looks like."

"What a lot you want for a miserable little three hundred thousand lire!"

"You forget that, if we were to settle accounts and include what I have given you already, we should have to multiply these three hundred thousand lire that you despise so much, several times over."

"Ah, you've kept an account, then."

"Of course."

"Well, Mother, I don't feel like telling you anything more—not for the moment, anyhow; but do answer me, once and for all: are you going to give me this money—yes or no?"

My mother looked at me, and evidently I must have seemed sufficiently determined or even desperate to make her feel that she could not pull the cords of her indiscretion any tighter. Pretending to stifle a yawn, she said: "Very well, then. Here is the key; go into the bathroom, you know where the safe is and you know the combination. Open it and you'll see a red envelope; take it out and bring it here."

I rose and went into the bathroom, turned the hook and opened the panel of tiles, and then the door of the safe. On the top of the rolls of bonds there was an orange-red envelope. I took it out and weighed it in my hand: judging by its weight, I calculated that it must contain at least half a million lire in ten-thousand-lire notes. I went back and handed the envelope to my mother, who was now sitting, thoroughly tired and sleepy, on the edge of the bed. I watched her as she opened the envelope and drew out, with the tips of her fingers, one, two, three, four, five ten-thousand-lire notes. "Here, take these in the meantime," she said.

"But in the envelope," I could not help exclaiming, "there must be at least five hundred thousand lire."

"For that matter, there are even more. But that's all I can give you today. Now go and put back the envelope, close the safe, bring me the key and then leave me. I'm extremely tired and I want to rest."

I did as I was told. But, as I replaced the envelope in the safe, I could not help being surprised at the confidence shown me by my mother, who was usually so mistrustful. After all, I could easily open the envelope again and help myself to some more money. But I realized at once that the reason why my mother trusted me was that I had always behaved in such a way as to inspire confidence in her—ever since I was born— owing to my lack of interest in money, in fact my contempt for it, which was perhaps a little ostentatious but anyhow perfectly serious; and I realized also that it was not my mother but I myself who had changed, for I now felt myself quite capable of stealing the money I needed to pay Cecilia, and I had a presentiment that, if she did not give me enough, I would end by stealing it in sober fact. Yes, I had changed, but my mother had not yet awakened to this change and continued to trust me as she had done in the past. I closed the door of the safe, replaced the tile panel and went back into the bedroom. My mother was lying on her back again now, across the bed, her arm over her eyes.

I stooped and placed the key in her hand, but her fingers did not grasp it and it fell on the pillow. Then with my lips I lightly touched the thin, painted cheek and said: "Good-bye, Mother." She answered with a faint groan: this time she had really fallen asleep. I tiptoed out of the room.

I decided to divide the fifty thousand lire into two parts; twenty thousand lire for myself and thirty thousand for Cecilia, to provide the now indispensable justification of venality for her next visit. But I felt that Cecilia eluded me in proportion to the amount I paid her; the more I paid her, the less did she seem to be mine. Furthermore, to my anguish at not possessing her there was now added the anguish of suspecting that perhaps she let herself be possessed by my rival. More and more, indeed, was I tormented by the thought that Luciani succeeded in possessing Cecilia in earnest, and precisely by means of the simple sexual act which had been shown, in my case, to be so insufficient. I feared that the actor, less intellectual and more a creature of instinct than myself, had succeeded where I had failed. And, reflecting that possession consists not so much in the sexual act itself as in the effect of the act upon the person who was its object, I never tired of questioning Cecilia about her relations with Luciani. Here, as an example, is one of these questionings.

"Did you see Luciani yesterday?"

"Yes."

"Did you just see him, or did you make love together?"

"You know that when I say I've seen him, I mean that we've made love."

"Did you do it much?"

"Just as usual."

"Do you usually do it much?"

"Some days more, some days less."

"Which do you like best, doing it with him or with me?"

"You're two different things."

"What do you mean?"

"Different."

"But what actually is the difference?"

"He's kinder than you."

"Do you like his being kind?"

"It's his natural way."

"But do you like it or don't you?"

"If I didn't like it, I wouldn't put up with it."

"Aren't there any other differences between him and me?"

"Yes, he talks while we're making love."

"And what does he say to you?"

"The things that people say when they're fond of you."

"I've said those things to you, sometimes."

"No, you don't say anything. The only time you spoke, you called me a bitch."

"Did you mind?"

"No, I didn't mind."

"But you prefer the things *he* says to you?"

"When I'm with him I like the things he says to me, and when I'm with you I like your being silent."

"But tell me, what do you feel when he has you?"

"There are some things one can't explain."

"Do you have a stronger feeling than you do with me?"

"I don't know."

"What do you mean, you don't know?"

"I've never thought about it."

"Think about it now, then."

"Well, I feel he loves me."

"Do you like that?"

"All women like to feel they're loved."

"Then it *is* a stronger feeling than the feeling you have with me."

"But with you too, I feel that you love me."

"And you like it?"

"Of course I like it."

"More, or less, than with Luciani?"

"They're two different things."

"Yes, I see. Now tell me: if for some reason you couldn't go on seeing Luciani, would you mind? Would you miss him?"

"It hasn't happened yet, so how can I tell?"

"But if it did happen?"

"Then I should see. I think I would."

"And if you couldn't go on seeing me?"

"That hasn't happened, either."

"Well, try and imagine."

"When I told you we ought to part, I remember I felt sorry."

"Very sorry?"

"How can one measure such things? I was sorry."

"Well, tell me then, are you more fond of me or of him?"

"You're two different things."

Or again, seeing that I had no success in squeezing information out of Cecilia on the subject of her feelings during physical love, I would try introducing a more innocent note into my investigations. "Did you go out with Luciani yesterday?"

"Yes, we went out to dinner together."

"Where did you go?"

"To a restaurant in Trastevere."

"You always refused to go out with me in the evening."

"I hadn't any excuse. You can only have drawing lessons in the daytime. But with Luciani I can always say he wants to introduce me to a film producer."

"But you can't make me believe your parents would have objected. I've met your parents."

"Mother—no, she wouldn't have objected. But Daddy would have. He was so sick, I couldn't go against him."

"Well, never mind. So you went to a restaurant in Trastevere?"

"Yes."

"What did you talk about?"

"All sorts of things."

"Who talked most, he or you?"

"You know I like listening."

"Well, what did *he* talk about?"

"I don't remember."

"Now, try hard to remember; after all, it only happened yesterday evening."

"But I haven't any memory, you know that. I don't even remember the things you said to me five minutes ago."

"All right, then, never mind. What was the restaurant like?"

"It was a restaurant like lots of others."

"What was it called?"

"I don't know."

"Was it big or small, crowded or empty, with one room or several rooms, smart or countrified?"

"I'm afraid I don't know, I didn't look at it."

"While you were talking, did you hold hands on the table?"

"Yes. How did you guess that?"

"Did you like his holding your hand?"

"Yes."

"A lot or a little?"

"I liked it, I don't know how much."

"Were your knees touching, under the table?"

"No, because we were sitting side by side."

"Besides holding your hand, did Luciani fondle you?"

"Yes, he stroked my face and kissed me on the neck."

"You can't remember the conversation, but you can remember the kisses."

"I remember them because I didn't want him to do it."

"Did you quarrel?"

"No, but he always wants me to do things I don't want to do."

"What, for instance?"

"Oh, I can't tell you; if I tell you you'll be angry."

"No, I won't be angry. Tell me."

"Well, he wanted me to put my hand . . . you know where. Do you understand?"

"Yes, I understand. And you—what did you do?"

"I did it for a little, but I couldn't eat with only one hand and so I stopped. What's the matter?"

"Nothing. While you were doing that, did it give you pleasure?"

"It gave me pleasure because it gave *him* pleasure."

"Supposing I asked you to do the same thing to me, would it give you pleasure to give me pleasure?"

"I think it would. There are lots of things one can do with pleasure because one knows they give pleasure to someone else."

"Someone else? To anybody, then?"

"No, I said someone else, meaning Luciani or you."

"Yes, I understand. And afterward what happened?"

"We ate and drank; in a restaurant one eats and drinks, doesn't one?"

"What did you eat?"

"I don't remember, I never look at what I'm eating. The usual things."

"Anything else?"

"Luciani called to the band and they sang us some Neapolitan songs."

"Which ones?"

"I don't remember."

"Do you like Neapolitan songs?"

"I think I do."

"But really now, do you like them or do you not?"

"Oh well, it depends. In a restaurant, yes. But if they started singing them while I was asleep—certainly not."

"After that, what did you do?"

"What did we do? Nothing else."

"I bet Luciani bought you a rose with its stalk wrapped in silver paper, from one of those girls who go around selling them in restaurants?"

"Yes, that's true; how did you know?"

"There are lots of things I know. I know also that you put it to your nose to smell it, didn't you?"

"That's the thing to do when you're given a flower, isn't it?"

"Were you pleased that Luciani gave you a rose?"

"Yes."

"And after dinner where did you go?"

"To the pictures."

"What was the name of the film you saw?"

"I don't know."

"Who were the actors in it?"

"I don't know, I don't know their names."

"But anyhow, what happened in the film?"

"I think it was an American film—you know, one of those with people on horseback, shooting."

"A Western. Did you hold hands in the theatre?"

"Yes."

"Did you kiss?"

"Yes."

"Did you make love?"

"Yes."

"How? You made love in the theatre?"

"We were in seats at the back, behind a pillar, and the place was half empty."

"But how did you manage to make love?"

"I got onto his knee."

"And did you like it?"

"No, I was too frightened. Besides, I don't like doing things in public places."

"Why did you do it, then?"

"Because I wanted to."

"Then you *did* like it?"

"No, I wanted to, but I didn't like it."

"And what else did you do during the evening?"

"We went to a night club."

"Which one?"

"I don't know what it's called. Behind Via Veneto."

"What was it like?"

"It was very crowded."

"No, I mean what was the room like, how was it furnished and decorated?"

"I didn't look at it."

"Did you dance?"

"Yes."

"Much?"

"Yes."

"While you were dancing, did you press close against him?"

"No."

"Why not?"

"Because we were doing dances in which you have to keep apart."

"What more did you do?"

"Nothing more. About three o'clock he took me home."

"Has he a car?"

"He had one but he sold it."

"He hasn't much money, then?"

"Not at present, because he's out of a job."

"Do you give him money, sometimes?"

"Yes, sometimes I do."

"My money?"

"Yes, the money you give me."

"And so the money I give you—you never spend it on yourself?"

"Yes, I buy a few things. But I spend it mostly with him."

"Yesterday evening, did he pay or did you?"

"We each did part of it; he paid for the pictures, I paid the rest."

"In fact you paid almost the whole thing."

"He's paid a good deal on other occasions."

"How did you give him the money?"

"In the restaurant I gave it to him under the table. In the night club he took it out of my bag."

"And then he took you home in a taxi?"

"Yes."

"Did he go into the courtyard with you?"

"Yes."

"Did you go upstairs together?"

"Yes."

"Did you make love on the stairs?"

"We did, a little, on my landing."

"What does 'a little' mean?"

"Without going right to the end."

"Did you like it?"

"Better than I did in the theatre because I wasn't so frightened."

"And then?"

"Then we parted."

"And you went to bed?"

"Yes."

"Did you think about him before you went to sleep?"

"No, I thought about you."

"About me?"

"Yes, about you; I thought about you until I went to sleep."

"What did you think?"

"I don't remember. I just thought about you, that's all."

One day, as if to confirm the feeling of elusiveness that Cecilia inspired in me, there occurred an incident which I wish to relate. Quite often, especially when I knew that Cecilia would not be coming to visit me, I used to go into Balestrieri's studio, which was still in the state as on the day the old painter died. His widow had not troubled to let it again, or—which was more probable—had not yet found a tenant. I was able to get into the studio thanks to the key which Balestrieri had given to Cecilia and which I had taken from her, and I took to wandering about among the dust-covered furniture in that room which smelled of fustiness and squalor, seeking I knew not what. As I lingered in the big, gloomy studio full of black furniture and dull red hangings that had witnessed the amours of Cecilia and Balestrieri, I had a mournful feeling, as though I were not in Balestrieri's studio but my own, and I myself were dead, and had come back in the form of a ghost to visit, as ghosts do, the place of my own amours. This mournful feeling came to me not only from the sickening resemblance between my relationship with Cecilia and that of Cecilia and Balestrieri, but also from the conviction that I, in a way, was dead too, and in a manner perhaps more decisive than the old painter, who at least had never had doubts about his own art and had gone on painting, so to speak, until his last breath. I, on the other hand, as I thought when I looked at the enormous, agitated nudes of Cecilia covering the walls from floor to ceiling, I was dead to painting even before I met Cecilia; and if, like Balestrieri, I had died because of Cecilia, I had merely confirmed in life what had already happened to me in art. And so, as always, I felt that there was a link between the crisis in my painting and my relationship with Cecilia; between my inability to paint on the canvas that stood on the easel and my inability to possess Cecilia upon the cushions of the divan; just as there had been a link between the execrable quality of Balestrieri's painting and the character of *his* relationship with Cecilia. It was an obscure, sinister link; there is a similar significance, for a traveler lost in the middle of a desert, in the white bones scattered on the sand.

One afternoon, while I was contemplating Balestrieri's hideous nudes as one contemplates the mysterious signs of an undeciphered language, the door, which I had left ajar, opened slightly and in the opening appeared the head of a woman. The woman, after making sure that I was there, then entered and came over to me. I recognized her almost at once; it was Balestrieri's widow who, on the day of his funeral, had her face completely hidden by a thick black veil of the kind that you see in village funeral processions, but whom I had happened to encounter on one or two subsequent occasions. She was a tall, well-built woman who had been beautiful and who at fifty still retained her youthful coloring, though it was now diluted and diffused over the slackened flesh of her face—a gleaming whiteness of skin, a clear blackness in her rather cowlike eyes, a vivid red, like that of a ripe cherry, in her full lips. In her youth she had been a model, and was perhaps the only woman, before Cecilia, whom Balestrieri had loved or imagined he loved: indeed he had married her and lived with her for twenty years. Born in a village in Lazio, traditionally famous for furnishing the artists of Rome with models, she had kept intact her original countrified air and her native simplicity.

I noticed that she did not appear surprised nor yet displeased at finding me in her husband's studio. She introduced herself, saying in a warm, low voice, a regular peasant's voice: "I am Signora Balestrieri."

I hastened to offer my apologies. "Forgive me, I found the door open and came in to have a look at the pictures."

She answered promptly: "Please, Professor, do come in here whenever you like. I know my poor husband was a great friend of yours."

I dared not contradict her. Now she was looking at me and smiling; and in her smile there seemed to be a kind of affectionate indulgence which I did not understand. "I came to look for you in your studio, Professor," she said, "because I must speak to you about something that may interest you. I found your door open, saw that you weren't there, and then I thought you might be here."

"Why did you think I was here?"

"Because I knew that you have the key of my husband's studio."

"Who told you that?"

"Why, the caretaker, Professor."

"And you wanted to speak to me?"

"Yes," she said quietly. "I looked for you the other day, but you weren't there." Then, changing the subject, she went on, with awkward, countrified tactlessness: "How d'you like these pictures, Professor?"

Embarrassed, I replied: "Your husband, as a painter, was full of quality."

"They're good, aren't they?" she resumed, starting to walk around the studio and look at the canvases on the walls. "You know, Professor, that they're all done from the same model?"

I said nothing. After a moment she went on, still in that same countrified manner, full of allusions and irony: "What a pretty girl, isn't she, Professor? Look what a chest she has, what legs, what shoulders, what hips! She's really what they call a lovely girl, Professor."

"But you," I said, seeking to turn the conversation, "didn't your husband ever paint *you?*"

"Yes, many, many times in the old days. But there's no picture of me here. When we separated, my husband took down all the paintings of me off the walls and sent them to where I lived. I have them all still. But I was not as pretty as this girl. Mine was a classical beauty, I was made like a statue. But this is a modern kind of beauty, half child and half woman; that's what they like nowadays. Yes," she reaffirmed with a sigh, "really a beautiful girl. Pity she's not as good as she's beautiful."

I could not refrain from asking, not altogether ingenuously: "You know her, then?"

"Yes, of course I know her. How could I fail to know her? My poor husband died because of her, you might say."

"So they say."

"Yes," she corrected with dignity, "I know what they say. The usual disgusting things. And indeed that may have happened, but it could have happened with any other woman just as well. No, I did not mean that. I meant that he died because of this girl from the heartbreak that she caused him."

"In what way?"

"With her wickedness."

"Is this girl so wicked?"

She answered with reason and moderation. "I don't say she's altogether wicked. Women, as everyone knows, are good or bad according to whether they love or not. In any case she was wicked to my husband. With you, I daresay, she's good."

At last I understood the obscure allusiveness of her looks and words; she knew that Cecilia was my mistress. Pretending to be surprised, I said: "How do I come into it?"

She lifted her hand and slapped me on the shoulder, in a gesture of rustic sympathy. "Poor Professor—well, well, well,

247

poor Professor!" Then she walked away from me and, pointing to the wall, asked suddenly: "D'you like that picture, Professor?"

I went up and looked at it. It was a singular picture inasmuch as Balestrieri, who generally limited himself to depicting Cecilia alone, in various attitudes, had here sketched in a kind of composition. Against the usual muddy, sticky looking background Cecilia was to be seen, naked and clothed in a spectral light, astride a dim human shape on all fours. It was one of Balestrieri's worst pictures: in order to convey the idea of Cecilia triumphant, the best he had been able to do was to make her raise one victorious hand in the air, while with the other she grasped the nape of the neck of the shapeless Caliban who served her as a mount. I said dryly: "Yes, it's not bad."

"You know who the man on all fours is?" asked the widow, going up to the picture and looking at it with vindictive intentness. "It's hard to tell because the face isn't clear; but I know. It's he himself, my husband. You may think that by painting himself in that way he intended to show that the girl trampled him, so to speak, underfoot. Not at all. He did it quite seriously."

"But what did he mean?"

"He used to go down on all fours, and she climbed on his back and he jumped about all over the studio. Like little boys playing at horses. And then, believe it or not, he would rear up and throw her on the floor with her legs in the air. I saw them one day, with my own eyes, through the window. Oh, they were enjoying themselves all right!" For a moment she was silent as she continued to look at the picture. Then she added: "If you like that picture, Professor, I'll sell it to you."

So little was I expecting such a proposal that for a moment I did not know what to say; then I understood: the widow knew of my passion for Cecilia and wished to speculate upon it. All of a sudden I had a feeling of shame, like someone with a vice which he thinks he has kept secret and who then finds himself being offered, in the street, a packet of obscene photographs portraying precisely that same vice. I asked, in irritation: "Why the devil should I buy that picture?"

Serenely, she answered: "I asked in case it might interest you. In a few days' time I have to take away the pictures, because I have managed to sublet the studio and the new tenant does not want them. He says they're too daring. So I thought you might like to have one of them as a souvenir."

"A souvenir of what? Of whom? Of your husband? We scarcely knew each other."

Again she made a gesture of roguish compassion, slapping me on the shoulder and shaking her head. "Professor, Professor, let's try and understand one another," she said. "Why don't you want to be honest with me? My hair is white, now"—and she indicated her raven-black hair, combed back in two smooth bands to a bun on the back of her neck, in which a few white threads were visible—"and I could easily be that girl's mother; why won't you be honest with me?"

I now sat down at the table, on which was the telephone; and I made a sign to the widow to sit down too; and then, pretending not to have heard her appeal to my honesty, I said to her solemnly and at the same time rather threateningly: "Signora Balestrieri, kindly tell me exactly what this is all about. You have made certain allusions which I do not understand. I should like you to explain them to me."

Slightly intimidated, she took refuge, like a true peasant woman, in a tone of lamentation. "My husband, alas, did not leave me at all well off. I thought that you, as a painter yourself, would really understand my husband's pictures, and might possibly buy at least one of them. I've tried to sell them but people don't understand them."

"But I haven't any money," I replied. "I'm just a painter, and a painter who doesn't paint, into the bargain."

She was genuinely astonished. "How strange," she said; "I've been told that your mother's so rich."

"My mother is, but I'm not."

"Then forget about it, Professor, forget about it."

"One moment," I insisted; "just now you made a certain allusion. Why, in point of fact, should I acquire this picture as a souvenir? A souvenir of whom?"

She opened her fine black eyes very wide and stared at me. "Of that model, of course," she said.

"And why?"

"Professor, you know why."

"Signora Balestrieri, I don't understand you."

"Well, Professor, you know what people say? That that girl is your mistress."

"Who says so?"

"Everyone. . . . The caretaker, to begin with."

I pretended to be disconcerted. Then, slowly and firmly, I said: "Ah, so that's the reason. Then you're mistaken. That girl is nothing to me."

She gave a little laugh of indulgent complicity. "Ah, Professor! Ah, Professor!" but I interrupted her, raising my voice in a conventional show of annoyance: "If I say a thing, I mean it!"

Again she withdrew into her shell, like a snail. But next moment she peeped out again with the remark: "I believe you, Professor. Well, you know what I say? For your sake, I'm glad."

"Why?"

"I told you: that girl is beautiful but she isn't good."

"In what way?"

She sighed. "My husband could have told you better than I can," she said. "But my husband is dead. I don't know anything precise, you must understand. I know only one thing: my husband owned a five-room flat in the neighborhood of Piazza Bologna, worth several million lire. But when he died, it was discovered that he had sold the flat. However, the millions were not to be found. What *was* found was an account book in which my husband, who was an orderly man, noted down his expenses. On almost every page there was an entry: Cecilia, so much and so much."

"You mean to say that this girl exploited your husband?"

"Exactly, Professor." She sighed again and then went on in a low voice, very hurriedly: "She's a deep one, that girl, Professor. Heartless, false, mercenary. And she was unfaithful to him, into the bargain; she took money from him and gave it to another man."

"Gave the money to another man?" I could not help exclaiming.

"Certainly she did—a miserable creature that she went to see every evening after she'd been with my husband during the day."

"But who was this man?"

"A saxophone player. He played in a night club. They spent my husband's money together. He even bought a car."

"Then your husband gave this girl a great deal of money?"

"Millions, Professor. It's all noted down in the account book. But, do you know, Professor?"

"What?"

"Although we were separated, my husband and I remained friends, so to speak. Well, he used to come and see me sometimes and he always talked to me about this girl. It was too much for him, he couldn't help it, and he took me into his confidence. And do you know? A man like him, who had had so many women, a man with his experience and intelligence—he used to cry."

Recalling that Cecilia, too, had spoken to me of Balestrieri's tears, I said: "But he cried easily, your husband."

"Easily? Don't you believe it. We were together for years and I never saw him shed a tear. He cried because this girl had reduced him to despair. D'you know what he used to say? That this girl would be the death of him. He had a presentiment about it."

"What was the name of the saxophone player to whom Cec—to whom the girl gave the money?"

She understood that I was interested and she wished to make me understand that she had understood. She drew herself up with dignity. "Call her by her name, Professor, call her Cecilia," she said. "The name of the saxophone player was Tony Proietti. He plays at the Canarino, a club in the neighborhood of Via Veneto. Well, Professor, I must go. Again, please excuse me. If the pictures interest you, you can always find me at home. I'm in the telephone book: Assunta Balestrieri. Or possibly you might even make your mother buy one —eh, Professor? Are you staying, or are you coming out with me?"

I did not stay, but said good-bye to her and went back to my own studio, where I threw myself on the divan and fell into deep meditation. The proofs of Cecilia's venality were multiplying, but, strangely enough, these proofs did not prove anything. In fact, no sooner was her venality demonstrated than something came to light to contradict it: Balestrieri's money, according to the widow, was passed on by her to her lover, to Tony Proietti. And the truth of this seemed to be borne out by the poverty of Cecilia's wardrobe and by the fact that she did not possess even the smallest piece of jewelry. If she had not given it to Proietti, where had Balestrieri's money gone?

The day after the widow Balestrieri's visit, as soon as Cecilia appeared at my studio I asked her point-blank: "Who is Tony Proietti?"

Without hesitation she replied: "A saxophone player who plays at the Canarino."

"Yes, but what has he been to you?"

"I was engaged to him."

"You were engaged?"

"Yes."

"And then?"

"And then what?"

"Then what happened?"

Reluctantly she answered: "He left me."

"Why?"

"He liked someone else."

"Did Balestrieri know you were engaged?"

"Of course he knew; I was engaged to Tony when I was fourteen, a year before I met Balestrieri."

I was astonished. "But you told me," I stammered, "that Balestrieri knew nothing and was jealous and for that reason employed a private detective agency."

She answered simply: "Balestrieri wasn't jealous of Tony, because he came after Tony and knew at once that I was engaged to him. He was jealous when he thought I was being unfaithful to him with someone else."

"But did this 'someone else' really exist?"

"Yes, but it was a thing that only lasted a short time."

"Was that at the same time as Tony?"

"No, it was immediately after Tony and I parted."

"Did Tony know about Balestrieri?"

"What are you thinking about! If he'd known he'd have killed me."

"Who, actually, was the first, with you?"

"What d'you mean, the first?"

"The first you made love with."

"Tony."

"At what age?"

"I've told you already. I was fourteen."

"And d'you ever see Tony now?"

"We meet sometimes and greet each other."

"Tell me another thing: did Balestrieri give you money?"

She looked at me for a moment and then replied with her usual mysterious reluctance: "Yes, he did."

"Much or little?"

"That depended."

"Depended on what?"

She was silent again; then she said: "I didn't want it, but he insisted on giving it to me."

"How do you mean?"

"He insisted. He knew that Tony hadn't a penny and that in the evening, when Tony and I went out together, we couldn't even go to the pictures; so he insisted on my accepting the money and giving it to Tony."

"It was he who made you give it to Tony?"

"Yes."

"What happened the first time?"

"I told him that as we hadn't any money we spent the evenings in the streets. Then he took out a ten-thousand-lire note and put it in my hand and said: 'Take this, then you can go to the pictures.'"

"And what did *you* do?"

"I didn't want to take it, but he forced me to. He threatened to tell Tony that I made love with him if I didn't take it, so I took it."

"And then he went on giving you money?"

"Yes."

"Did he give you bigger sums, too?"

"He knew that Tony and I were going to get married and set up house, so he insisted on my buying furniture for it with his money."

"What happened to the furniture?"

"Tony has it in his house, I left it for him."

"And the car?"

"What car?"

"Didn't Balestrieri pay for Tony's car, too?"

"Yes, he did—a small car. Who told you that?"

"Balestrieri's widow."

"Oh, that woman."

"Do you know her?"

"Yes. She came to see me, she wanted the money back."

"And what did you say to her?"

"I told her the truth. I told her that her husband had insisted on my accepting the money and that I had nothing, because I had given it all to Tony, as her husband wished."

"How long did Balestrieri go on giving you money?"

"For almost two years."

"And with Tony—how did you explain the money you gave him?"

"I told him I had a rich uncle who was fond of me."

"And after Tony had left you, did Balestrieri go on giving you money?"

"Yes, now and again, when I asked him."

"But that other man who came afterward—the one that Balestrieri was suspicious of—didn't you give him money?"

"No, he didn't need it. He was the son of an industrialist."

"And did he leave you too?"

"No, it was I who left him, because I had stopped being fond of him."

"Who were you fond of, then?"

"You. You remember when I used to meet you in the corridor and look at you? Well, it was then that I left him."

"Did Balestrieri ever realize that you were fond of me?"

"No."

"Did you ever talk about me to Balestrieri?"

"Yes, once. He couldn't bear you."

"What did he say about me?"

"That you were very conceited."

"Conceited?"

"Yes, he hated your painting. He said you didn't know how to paint."

This conversation left me with the conviction that my attempt to prove to myself that Cecilia was venal had failed: Cecilia was not venal; in other words, her character could not be said to be merely acquisitive. It was clear that Balestrieri had tried to assert his own superiority over Tony by supporting him through the medium of Cecilia, without the saxophone player being aware of it; and that Cecilia, on her side, had lent herself to Balestrieri's psychological maneuver without sharing in it or understanding it. As in my case, therefore, Cecilia had succeeded instinctively in keeping the two worlds of money and of love separate and apart. Balestrieri and I could have certainly affirmed that we had given her money; but she, on her side, could have always made it clear that she had not been paid. And my behavior toward Cecilia tended increasingly to resemble Balestrieri's; with this difference, however, that the old painter had gone further than I had. To counterbalance that, my folly was greater than his; for he had had no predecessor to serve him as a mirror, so that it was more or less understandable that he should not have been able to stop. But I had his example to warn me at every step of the risks I was running, yet in spite of this I was repeating the same mistakes that he had made, and in fact almost taking pleasure in doing so.

Chapter 9

In the meantime Cecilia went on seeing Luciani every day, including the days when she came to see me, so that her elusiveness, after being for a long time a mere hypothesis, had become a certainty, something similar to a fixed character with which I had, one way or another, to settle accounts and to which I had to adapt myself. And I felt that my love for her, originating from my inability to possess her, was now, after oscillating violently between boredom and misery, gradually assuming the aspect of a species of vice with four successive phases: the attempt to possess her otherwise than by sexual means; the failure of the attempt; the angry, futile relapse into the sexual relationship; the failure of this also; and then the same thing all over again. But the only thing of which I was not capable was resigning myself to Cecilia's elusiveness, accepting it, and, in short, calmly sharing her favors with Luciani. I remember that, much as Balestrieri had not been jealous of Tony Proietti because he imagined that Cecilia had been unfaithful to Tony with him, so did I seek to console myself by telling myself that, while I knew that Cecilia went to bed with the actor, the latter did not know that she went to bed with me. In other words, I now found myself, in relation to Luciani, more or less in the position of a lover in relation to an ignorant husband; and no lover was ever jealous of a husband, precisely because knowing, in certain cases, means possessing and not knowing means not possessing. It was a wretched consolation, but it helped me to pass the time with calculations of the following kind: I knew about Luciani and Luciani did not know about me, therefore Cecilia was unfaithful to him with me and not to me with him. On the other hand, he had come after me, consequently Cecilia had been unfaithful to me with him and not to him with me. Finally there was the question of the money, as there had been with Balestrieri: I gave her money and Luciani not merely did not give her any but spent my money with her; therefore she was making me, not him, pay her, and consequently was in a way unfaithful to him with me. However, it was not impossible that she was going with Luciani for love and with me for money, therefore she was being unfaithful to me with Luciani. But Cecilia attributed no importance to money. Money therefore had perhaps a sentimental significance between her and me, and since the actor did not give her any money, perhaps she was being unfaithful to Luciani with me. And so on, *ad infinitum.*

After these agreeable reflections there remained always the bare fact, unalterable and indestructible, that Cecilia went to bed with Luciani and that as long as she went on doing so I should not be able to possess her because incomplete possession is a contradiction in terms. At least Cecilia might have tried to make me forget the incompleteness of my possession! But, confident that she had found a final solution to the problem of the simultaneous presence of two men in her life, not only did she talk to me freely and casually about her relations with the actor, but she did not even trouble to conceal from me the physical traces that Luciani's love-making left upon her. There was no particular self-satisfaction or cruelty in her voice when, in answer to my question, she replied indifferently: "Oh, that was Luciani, he bit me," or again: "Luciani

258

made this white mark on my dress; we made love without undressing"; there was rather the serenity of a person who finds
it easier and more convenient to tell the truth than to invent
lies. Cecilia was so convinced that this sharing of her favors
had now ceased to cause me any pain that she went so far as
to make appointments with Luciani on the telephone in my
presence, and then asked me to go with her to his house. In
the end, one day when I was actually taking her in the car to
Via Archimede, where Luciani was expecting her, she said to
me suddenly: "I should like you and Luciani to meet and make
friends." I said nothing; but I reflected that a world made according to Cecilia's notions would be very different from the
one in which we lived—a promiscuous world, without bound-
aries or contours, shapeless, casual and unreal, in which all the
women belonged to all the men and no woman had only one
man.

But I was suffering. And gradually, through this suffering,
there came to me at last an extravagant idea which I was
astonished not to have had before: possibly the only way in
which I could set myself free from Cecilia—that is, possess
her truly and consequently become bored with her—was to
marry her. I had not succeeded in becoming bored with Cecilia
by having her as a mistress; but I was almost sure that I would
be bored with her once she had become my wife. Thus the
idea of marriage began to attract me more and more, but with
a prospect completely different from the one that generally
smiles upon a man preparing to get married; the latter cherishes
the dream of an endless love; but it was the opposite kind of
dream, a dream of the end of love, that smiled upon me. I
took pleasure in imagining that, once she was married, Cecilia
would turn into an ordinary wife, full of domestic and social
occupations, satisfied, without mystery; that in fact she would
become, as they say, "settled." It was possible that her present
elusiveness was nothing more than an expression of matrimonial ambitions; perhaps she was searching instinctively

259

among her lovers for a husband with whom she might pause and be quiet. I planned to marry her with every sort of religious and social ceremony, and after marriage make her have a large number of children, who would also play a part in ordering her life and confining her to the far from enigmatic role of motherhood.

It may be thought that this idea of employing matrimony where a physical relationship and money had both failed was absurd, and anyhow inadequate. Like burning down one's house to light a cigarette. But I had severed all bonds with any kind of society, especially with the world in which my mother moved. In this lack of all roots and responsibilities, in this utter void created by boredom, marriage, for me, was something dead and meaningless; and in this way it would at least serve some purpose.

Naturally I counted upon going to live, as soon as I was married, in the villa on the Via Appia, with my wife and my mother. Matrimony, the villa, my mother, my mother's world—all these were parts of the diabolical machine into which Cecilia would enter as a charming, enigmatic demon and from which she would issue as an ordinary, middle-class married woman.

Moreover the idea of marriage had come to me spontaneously as the surest means of severing relations between Cecilia and Luciani. I thought, in fact, that she would willingly leave Luciani once she had agreed to marry me. But it was also true that, if Cecilia became my wife, I felt it would not much matter to me whether she went on having Luciani as a lover, or some other man, or no one at all.

At this point I ought to say that, apart from the prospect of freeing myself from my love for Cecilia, the matrimonial solution seemed to give me a gleam of hope that I might start painting again as soon as Cecilia, now installed in my mother's house, ceased to darken my horizon. I imagined Cecilia much taken up with her children and with social life; meanwhile, in the studio at the bottom of the garden, I would devote myself deliciously to my beloved, chaste, highly intellectual painting. Quite a different thing from Balestrieri's foul, hectic nudes. I felt I would paint the most abstract pictures that had ever been painted since abstract painting came into existence. In the end, having planted Cecilia with my mother and a whole nestful of urchins, I would come back and live by myself in Via Margutta.

It will be thought that all this was in contradiction to my previous character and behavior; and furthermore, that the terms of my problem were different. In point of fact, being in love with Cecilia and painting were not two facts depending on each other; rather they were equivalent and independent. It was not my love for Cecilia which prevented me from painting, but rather that I was powerless to paint just as I was powerless to possess Cecilia; and so a release from my love for her did not at all mean that I should be enabled to take up painting again. Moreover, I had always hated my mother's house, my mother's world, my mother's money, and had gone to live in Via Margutta precisely because I had felt that it would be impossible for me to paint at the villa in Via Appia. And now I was thinking of going back to live with my mother, in that same house and that same world that I loathed. I can give no other explanation of all this except that contradiction is the fickle and unforeseeable basis of the human spirit. In reality I was desperate; and it seemed to me that even the kind of suicide that a return to my mother's house meant to me was preferable to my present situation, provided that it served to rid me of Cecilia.

It was summer now, and one day, during our usual morning telephone call, I said to Cecilia that instead of meeting at my studio we might go out of Rome for a drive in my car. I knew that Cecilia liked being in the open air, but I was surprised by the extraordinary warmth with which she welcomed my proposal. "Yes indeed," she added unexpectedly; "and today we can be together all day long, till late this evening. I'm quite free."

"What's happened?" I asked sarcastically, "will that terribly severe father of yours allow you to go out with me?"

She answered frankly, as though astonished at my remembering the lie she had made use of to conceal her relations with Luciani: "It's not that. It's because Luciani and I can't meet this evening. So I thought you would like to spend the whole day with me."

"Please thank Luciani very much from me for his generosity."

"There, you see how it is with you. So it's not true that one can always tell you the truth."

"Very well, I'll come and fetch you about eleven o'clock, and then we can have lunch together."

"No, not at eleven, I can't manage that; I'm lunching with Luciani."

"I thought it was strange that you shouldn't be seeing him for a whole day."

"I'll come to the studio about three."

"All right, three o'clock."

Cecilia appeared at the time arranged. She was wearing a new, green two-piece dress and I told her how well it suited her. She answered promptly, with a grateful eagerness that was vaguely surprising to me. "I bought it with your money, and these too," she said, pointing to her shoes, "and these," she added, stretching out her leg to show the stocking. "In fact," she concluded, "I'm entirely dressed out of your money, underneath and on top."

As I drove the car out of the courtyard, I asked: "Why do you tell me this?"

"Because you once told me that you liked me to tell you these things."

"Yes, that's true. But I would far rather know that you belonged to me, not only underneath and on top, but inside as well."

"Inside where?"

"Inside."

She laughed with her rather childish laugh that lifted her lips above her eyeteeth. "Inside, I don't belong to anybody," she said. "Inside are one's lungs and heart and liver and intestines. What would you do with them?"

She was gay, and I pointed this out to her. She said lightly: "I'm gay because I'm with you."

"Thank you, that's very nice of you."

We crossed the Piazza del Popolo and the Tiber, went the whole length of Via Cola di Rienzo and after circling the sloping walls of the Vatican started off along the Via Aurielia, in the direction of Fregene. Cecilia sat quite still at my side, her head erect, the mass of her thick, curly hair falling about her round face, her hands in her lap. From time to time I cast a sideways glance at her and recognized yet again the characteristics which, in their enigmatic way, made her so desirable to me and at the same time so elusive: the childishness of her face, contradicted by the dry, fine lines that cut into the skin at the corners of her small mouth; the sharp slimness of her shoulders, which seemed belied by the full, heavy prominence of her bosom; the supple slenderness of her waist which did not match the rotundity of her hips and the solidity of her thighs. And, lying in her lap, her big, ugly hands, doubtfully white, yet attractive and even, perhaps, beautiful—if it is permissible to say that an ugly thing is beautiful. Never had I found her so pleasing; and that in a manner so very like herself, both irritating and evasive. As soon as we were outside Rome I began to think I should not be able to wait until six, when we would be returning to the studio. I had ten hours at my disposal, therefore I could make love twice; right now and again at night, after dinner. Now, in any convenient meadow; after dinner, at the studio.

The road went up and down among treeless hills covered with thick, luxuriant grass of an almost blue green, grass which had sprouted from the water-soaked earth after the abundant rains of the last two months. But the sky was still not clear: black clouds, which looked as if they were unable to rise due to the burden of rain they carried, hung in motionless layers above this spring-like green. I kept looking about for a suitable place, although I was driving fast, but failed to find one: either it was too near the road, or too exposed, or too close to a farm, or on too steep a slope. So I went on for some miles, still without speaking, and in the silence I became overburdened with the full force, the anger, almost, of my desire. At last, at the first side road, I turned off. "But aren't we going to the sea?" Cecilia demanded.

"We're going now to a quiet place to make love," I answered, "and afterward we'll go to the sea."

She said nothing, and I drove on as fast as I could along the white, stony country road. After we had bumped along over loose rubble for about half a mile, the landscape, as I had hoped, began to change. No longer were there grassy, treeless hills, but wooded slopes rising behind small fields in which horses and sheep were grazing. It was just what I was looking for. I came to a sudden stop beside a fence and said to Cecilia: "Let's get out."

She obeyed, and stood aside to let me go ahead. I said, for no particular reason: "I'd rather you went in front." She made no objection; and, after pushing open a rustic gate, started off down a path, or rather a track where the tall, thick grass had been trodden down, and then I realized why I had asked her to walk in front of me; I wanted to watch the powerful, indolent movement of her hips. I knew that this movement did not concern me, personally, any more than the sexual appeal of a woman of any kind concerns any particular man. Now if I had been walking in front of her, I might even, perhaps, have had the illusion that I was acting as her guide. But in this way, by making her walk ahead of me, I should be able to persuade myself that this movement was directed not so much at me as at the pleasure that awaited her at some spot in the wood, a pleasure which I should be providing for her, it is true, but of which I should be merely the instrument.

We walked on in silence through the tangled, sticky grass. Above our heads the mass of cloud, low and swollen like a pregnant belly, seemed to be unraveling itself into shreds of mist. The air was damp and warm and humming with insects. I watched Cecilia's hips which, as we gradually drew nearer to the wood, appeared to assert the strength and monotony of their movement like a machine that has found its normal rhythm, and I reflected that there was no difference between this movement which she made as she walked and those she would soon be making as she lay on her back: Cecilia was always ready, so to speak, for the sexual act, just as a machine, nourished with the proper fuel, is always ready to function. She must have become aware of my gaze, for suddenly she turned and asked: "What's the matter, why don't you speak?"

"I want you too much to speak."

"Do you want me always?"

"Do you mind?"

"No, I was just asking."

We walked on for some distance; then the thick grass of the meadow began to be replaced by scantier, taller undergrowth and trees rose from the uneven ground, thinly scattered at first but growing steadily thicker. After a few more steps we found ourselves in a little ravine between two hills, with trees everywhere, and bushes and thickets covering the humps and hollows of the broken ground. I started looking for a suitable place where we could lie down, and finally I found what I wanted—a flat, mossy open space surrounded with tall ferns and big broom bushes. I was about to point it out to Cecilia, when she turned around and said lightly: "Oh, I forgot to tell you, it's not possible for us to make love today."

I felt as though I had put my foot into a trap. "Why?" I asked.

"I'm not well."

"You're not telling me the truth."

She did not reply, but walked on among the ferns and the broom bushes with her usual slow, firm step and climbed up onto a small, round hillock; then she turned toward me, stooped down and, taking hold of the hem of her dress with both hands, pulled it up to her belly. I could see her straight thighs pressed close together, sheathed in their silk stockings, and, at the lowest point of her belly, where usually the transparent stuff of her slip allowed a glimpse of the dark groin, the pale, opaque patch of a wad of cotton. "Now d'you believe me?" she asked.

I answered angrily: "Yes, it's true, with you it's always true."

She pulled down her dress in silence, and then asked: "Why do you say that? On other occasions I've never refused you."

I felt that I was going mad; frustrated desire joined forces with my obsession of being unable to possess her, as though this day's discomfiture were only one of the many impossibilities of a never-changing situation. "I wanted you so much," I said, "and by coming with me and letting me think you were willing, you made my desire twice as great. Why didn't you tell me at once that you weren't well?"

She looked at me with indifference, like a shopkeeper who offers an article of inferior quality in place of another which is out of stock. "But we're going to be together all day," she answered.

"But I wanted to make love."

"We'll do that some other time, perhaps tomorrow."

"But I wanted to do it today—now."

"You're like a child."

Silence followed. Cecilia was walking among the bushes with bent head and appeared to be looking for something. Then she stooped, picked a blade of grass and put it between her teeth. I said furiously: "That's why you suggested that we should spend the day together. Just because you knew you couldn't make love with Luciani."

"Luciani wanted to do it too, and I told him the same thing that I've told you."

"But Luciani had you yesterday and I haven't had you for three days."

"Luciani didn't have me yesterday, he had me three days ago, like you."

She walked on in front of me through the bushes, wandering about, the blade of grass between her teeth. I asked angrily: "Where are you going, what do you want to do?"

"Whatever *you* want to do."

"You know what *I* wanted."

"But I've told you it's impossible."

"Well, if we can't do that, I really don't know what we can do."

"D'you want to go back to town and see a picture?"

"No."

"D'you want to go to the sea?"

"No."

"D'you want to go over toward the Castelli?"

"No."

"D'you want to stay here?"

"No."

"D'you want to go away?"

"No."

"Then what *do* you want?"

"I've already told you: I want *you*."

"And I've already told you—not today."

"Then let's go back to the car."

"And where shall we go?"

"I don't know; let's go, anyhow."

So we went back to the car and this time I walked in front of Cecilia, although, unlike her—for she always seemed to be conscious of her objective, with her body at least, if not with her mind—I was entirely ignorant of where I was going.

When we were in the car I did not even wait for Cecilia to close the door properly before I started off at full speed. I felt an increasing fury which nothing could quench nor satiate, like a fire to whose flames fresh fuel is constantly being added. And this fury filled my mind with continuous, haunting illusions, so that, having failed to make love to Cecilia, I sought her everywhere, in a stupid, stubborn fashion, if even the most remote resemblance permitted it. Thus brief stretches of country, partly mown and partly grassy, made me think of her belly, rounded hillocks of her breasts, irregularities in the ground, of her profile and her hair. Or again I saw the road creeping in between two long, curving hills, and it seemed to me that they were the open legs of Cecilia as she lay on her back, and that between the two hills was the cleft of her sex and that the car was moving swiftly toward this cleft. Then, when I thought I was about to plunge, car and all, into this gigantic Cecilia made of earth, the whole prospect changed, and instead of two hills there were four, and there were no longer any legs or sex or anything but merely an ordinary landscape. Moreover, as I have said, I did not know where I was going; I seemed to be rushing in search of something which, rush as I might, remained unattainable. This something was in front of me all the time—down there in that group of trees, on that hill, in that wide valley, upon that bridge; but when I reached the group of trees, the hill, the valley, the bridge, there was nothing there and I had to rush on breathlessly toward new fictitious goals. And meanwhile, in the midst of this delirium of dull, impotent rage, I still had the feeling that Cecilia was there, at my side, close to me yet at the same time inaccessible.

I do not know how far I went in this haphazard way—along one road after another, branching off at crossroads without any exact sense of direction, turning back, driving for miles and miles along the sea or through woods—for more than an hour, perhaps. Suddenly, on one of these roads, facing a wide stretch of fields bounded by poplar trees, I stopped the car abruptly and turned to Cecilia. "I have a proposal to make to you," I said.

"What is that?"

The idea had never entered my head while I was driving. But I had thought about it during the preceding days and that same morning before seeing Cecilia. And so it seemed to me that I was saying something quite natural. "I want you to become my wife."

She looked at me with quiet diffidence, but without surprise. "You want us to get married?"

"Yes."

"But why d'you say this to me now?"

"I've been thinking about it for some time and now the moment has come."

She was gazing at me, and I, meanwhile, had a giddy, voluptuous feeling, like a man who, after many hesitations, hurls himself headlong into the void. I seized her hands and said hurriedly: "You'll be my wife and we'll go and live at my mother's house. Perhaps you don't know that I'm a rich man."

"You're a rich man?"

"Yes, or rather my mother's rich, and when we're living with her, in her villa on the Via Appia, her money will be mine too —in fact ours."

She said nothing. I went on: "We'll get married with all the proper celebrations. Wedding in church, presents, flowers, wedding cake and refreshments, reception and so on. Then we'll have a fine honeymoon; we can go north to Scandinavia or south to Egypt. When we come back, your whole life will change completely. You'll be a married lady in Roman society, like the ladies you see in Via Veneto or Piazza di Spagna."

Still she said nothing. In a growing frenzy, squeezing her two hands, I went on: "We'll have children, because I want

269

children. And you look capable of producing any number of them. I'll see that you have two, four, six, eight—as many as you like."

Her silence, nevertheless, made me uneasy. Quickly I asked: "Well, what do you think?"

At last she made up her mind to answer. "I can't tell you, like this, all in a moment," she said slowly. "I must think it over."

"Yes, think it over. Will you give me an answer tomorrow, the day after tomorrow? Just as you like. In the meantime," I suddenly added, "let's go at once to my mother's and I'll introduce you as my fiancée." It had occurred to me that Cecilia might be doubting my statement about my mother's wealth and I wanted her to make certain of it with her own eyes. Besides, to introduce her as my fiancée meant compromising her and in a way forcing her to accept my proposal.

"Why go to your mother's now?" she asked. "You can let me meet her some other day."

"No, it's better today; then you'll know her and be able to see what it's all about."

"But you can't introduce me as your fiancée; I'm not that, yet."

"What does it matter? If we decide not to get married after all, I'll tell my mother you changed your mind."

"I'll give you my answer today," she said suddenly, in a strange manner, as though she had already taken the decision which she was to announce in a few hours' time. "This evening."

"Why this evening? Why not now?"

"No, this evening."

I said nothing; I released the brake, started the engine and drove off. I now felt such a desire for her that the marriage I had offered her seemed to me an inadequate price, not for an eternity of love, but even for a single, fleeting embrace. To possess her just once, but really and truly, I would not only have married her but would have made a pact with the devil and damned my own soul. This is a mere phrase, it may be said, and a highly romantic one, into the bargain. Nevertheless, at that moment damnation was for me not a mere phrase but an actual fact which might take place, not in the other world in which I did not believe, but in this world, in which I knew I had to live. Strange to say, however, the sense of such a damnation was not unrelated to a very remote hope of liberation; of that particular liberation which I continually deceived myself into thinking I should attain on the day when I succeeded in possessing Cecilia.

By now it was almost sunset; and at last the cypresses and pines of the Via Appia came into view, black as ink, outlined against the background of a long red streak in the sky which looked like a chink of fire in the dark tumult of the clouds. I started driving slowly up the narrow Roman road, slackening speed where the ancient pavement showed through the surface of the asphalt, lingering now and then to look at the ruins, at the gates of villas, at the cars parked on the grassy shoulders. All the time I was reflecting upon the marriage proposal I had made to Cecilia, and I was conscious that I had made use of matrimony in perhaps too frivolous a way, as a mere means—one among many—of achieving a purpose which was not only foreign to it but actually contradicted it. I feared that I had exposed my own state of mind and my intentions and had thus failed to be convincing, in fact that I had given Cecilia the unpleasant feeling that I wished to marry her simply in order to get rid of her. After all, I thought, it might well be that Cecilia cherished the ideal of marriage in her heart; and perhaps my hasty manner of proposing that she should become my wife had affronted this ideal. After a pause, I resumed: "You're quite right, anyhow, not to want to answer at once. Marriage isn't a thing that ought to be undertaken lightly."

She said nothing, and I went on: "Getting married means

becoming united for life. At any rate, I understand it that way: that's why I want us to get married in church."

Suddenly, and quite unexpectedly, she asked: "Why in church?"

"Because," I said complacently, "if we get married in church we're truly united, without the possibility of ever parting again."

"But you don't believe in it," she said.

"I would do it for your sake."

"I don't believe in it either."

"You don't believe in it? But you told me you'd been brought up by the nuns until you were twelve."

"That doesn't mean anything. Even when I was with the nuns I didn't believe in it."

"What did you believe in?"

She appeared to reflect for a moment; then she replied, in a dry, precise, conscientious way: "In nothing. But I don't mean I didn't believe in it because I thought about it, and realized that I didn't believe in it. I didn't believe in it because I never thought about it. And even now I never think about it. I think about any sort of thing, but not about religion. If a person never thinks about a thing, it means that for him that thing doesn't exist. With me, it isn't that I like or dislike religion, it just doesn't exist."

Slowing down until I had almost stopped, I said: "You may never think about it now, but it's not impossible that you may come to think about it some day."

She sat in silence for a moment, then answered: "I don't think so. I didn't think about it when I was with the nuns, where there was nothing but religion; so why should I think about it outside the convent, with so many other things to think about? D'you know what I used to think about while I was reciting the prayers with the nuns?"

"What?"

"About the clock."

"Why about the clock?"

"It had a pendulum and I used to watch it, and as I recited the prayers I counted the seconds and the minutes."

"Were you so bored, saying these prayers?"

"Yes."

"Why?"

"Because with lots of things, even if they're extremely boring, you at least know that they serve some purpose. But prayer, for me at any rate, serves no purpose at all."

"You never know. Some day perhaps you'll find it does."

"I don't think so. I can't imagine the day when I shall feel a need for religion. It's a superfluous thing."

"Superfluous?"

"Yes—how can I explain? If it exists, things go on in a certain way, and if it doesn't exist, things still go on in the same way. Nothing changes: therefore it's a superfluous thing."

"That could be said of plenty of things in this world."

"What things?"

"Well—art, for instance. Things, as you say, would go on in the same way even if art didn't exist."

"But art is enjoyable to the person who practices it. Balestrieri enjoyed himself. You enjoy yourself. Religion, on the other hand, is boring. At the convent I always had the impression that the nuns were bored, just as priests are bored and indeed all those people in general who are taken up with religion. In the churches, goodness knows how bored people are. You've only to look at them in church, and you can see there's not a single one of them that isn't bored to death."

It was the first time Cecilia had spoken to me on the subject of boredom; my curiosity was aroused, and I could not refrain from asking her: "Are *you* ever bored?"

"Yes, sometimes."

"And what do you feel when you're bored?"

"I feel boredom."

"What *is* boredom?"

"How am I to explain that? Boredom is boredom."

I wanted to say: "Boredom is the suspension of all relationship with reality. And I want to marry you so as to get bored with you, so as to stop suffering and to stop loving you, so as to bring it about, in short, that you cease to exist as far as I am concerned, just as for you religion and a great many other things don't exist," but I hadn't the courage. Moreover, she suddenly interrupted our conversation by raising her hand and stroking my cheek. "Let's go to your mother's now; otherwise it'll be too late."

"Very well," I said. But at the same time I could not help wondering about the reason for this sudden desire to go and see my mother, when a little while before, Cecilia had shown what amounted almost to repugnance at the idea of the visit. It seemed to me, on reflection, that she was suggesting that we should go and see my mother in order to escape a conversation which made her feel uneasy. I knew that she did not like one to talk about her, but I did this continually, and it occurred to me that her stubborn reticence derived from her antipathy to the kind of conversation which I forced upon her. Always ready at any moment and in any situation to surrender herself physically, Cecilia, when it came to a conversation about herself, could be compared to a closed, obstinate oyster which tightens its valves all the more firmly the more one struggles to open them. Usually, as I knew, she contrived to break off this type of conversation by suggesting that we should make love: she would take my hand and bring it to her belly, then close her eyes. Thus she offered me her body in order to distract me from everything else. But that day we could not make love, and so, in her desperate desire not to hear herself talked about, she suggested the first thing that came to hand, the distasteful visit to my mother.

I drove on in silence for a time, thinking about these things, then I asked her: "Did Balestrieri ever talk to you about yourself?"

"No, never."

"What did he generally talk about?"

"About himself, generally."

"What did he say?"

"He said he loved me."

"What else?"

"Nothing else. He went on talking about himself—that is, about what he felt for me. You know, the usual speeches that men make when they're in love."

I could not help thinking that at last I had found one difference between myself and Balestrieri: I was always talking to Cecilia about herself, while Balestrieri, like all erotics, talked about himself all the time. In fact, I decided, Balestrieri had never really loved Cecilia. "And did you like him to talk about himself?" I asked her.

"When he told me he loved me, I liked it for a bit, but then he went on repeating the same things and so I gave up listening."

"Would you have preferred him to talk about *you?*"

"No."

"Don't you like people to talk about you?"

"No."

"Why?"

"I don't know."

"Well, I'm continually asking you questions about yourself —you don't like that?"

"No."

This decided monosyllable almost took my breath away. "Perhaps you reach the point of hating me when I talk to you about yourself?" I asked.

"No, I don't hate you, but I long for you to stop as soon as possible."

"What do you feel when I question you about yourself?"

She thought for a moment and then replied: "I feel I don't want to answer you."

"To stay silent, you mean?"

"Yes, or to tell you something that isn't true, just to satisfy you." She paused for a moment and then went on, with sudden volubility: "Imagine, when I was at the convent and had to go to confession, in order not to talk about myself I used to invent sins I hadn't committed. Then the priest was satisfied and told me that I must repent and say I don't know how many prayers to the Madonna and Saint Joseph, and I said yes, I always said yes, although afterward I never did anything he told me to do, because I hadn't done anything wrong and so there was no need for me to repent."

It occurred to me all at once that this indiscreet priest had wished to do the same thing, fundamentally, that I had so often tried to do—to catch Cecilia, to imprison her in some sin or other, to nail her down to a penalty. I asked in alarm: "Then with me too you've invented things you never did?"

She answered vaguely: "Yes, perhaps I have, sometimes."

"But what do you mean? That you've lied to me? And when?"

"It may be so, but I don't remember now."

"Try and remember."

"I don't remember."

"Did you lie to me, for instance, about your relations with Balestrieri?"

"I swear I don't remember."

"And so everything you've told me about your past may also be untrue?"

"No, that's not so. I've only told you lies when it was necessary."

"When, for example?"

"I don't remember now: when it was necessary."

"And when is it necessary for you to tell lies?"

"How can I explain that? It's necessary when it's necessary."

"Well, now we'll go and see my mother. I'll introduce you as my fiancée and in a month, at most, we'll get married."

We drove on in silence and very soon came to the well-known gate between the two pillars adorned with bits of Roman junk. It was not shut, as it usually was, but wide open; the two lanterns on top of the pillars were lit; and at that very moment three or four cars were on the point of entering. Disappointed, I said: "I'm afraid my mother must be receiving—in other words, giving a cocktail party. What shall we do?"

"Whatever you like."

I reflected that, after all, for the purpose I had in mind, a party might come in useful: Cecilia would in this way be able to form an idea of the world into which I should introduce her if I married her. And if, as I hoped, she was ambitious, this idea could not but be favorable. I said carelessly: "Let's go in, then. I'll introduce you to my mother, you can have a drink and see the house and then we'll go away; is that all right?"

"Yes, that's all right."

I drove up the drive behind the other cars and with some difficulty found a place to stop; the space in front of the house was already almost full. Cecilia got out and I followed her. As she walked toward the front door she put up her hands and lifted her hair from off her neck, arranging it on her shoulders, in a gesture which with her, as I knew, indicated that she felt a timidity which she was trying to overcome. I caught up with her and took her by the arm, whispering: "This is the house we'll come and live in when we're married. Do you like it?"

"Yes, it's a fine house."

We went into the hall and into the first of the four or five rooms that occupied the ground floor. There were already large numbers of guests, standing close together, glass in hand, talking into each other's faces and leering at each other sideways, as always happens at cocktail parties. I thrust Cecilia forward by the arm, cleaving a passage through this haughty, conceited crowd, and as I looked at all these florid, glossy men and painted women dressed in the latest fashion; and as I saw that Cecilia seemed to mingle with the odious multitude to

277

the point of appearing to be one of them; and as I reflected that, if this really happened as in fact it might happen after our marriage, I should not only be rid of her and of my love for her but should actually hate her, as I hated my mother's guests—then I felt a kind of remorse at having planned to lose her among these horrible people, and almost a hope that she would not agree to marry me. I wanted to become bored with Cecilia, but I did not want to hate her. And anyhow I loved her too much to wish to be rid of her at the price of her transformation from a poor and charming girl into a moneyed harpy.

Thus reflecting, I went on pushing Cecilia through the crowd, from one group to another, from one circle of faces to another, through the cigarette smoke and the buzz of conversation, brushing against trays covered with glasses of various sizes and colors which were being handed around by waiters. It was an immensely crowded reception, and it was obvious that my mother was doing things on a grand scale, regardless of expense. But the money my mother had spent in order to receive her guests worthily was a mere nothing in comparison with the money—an almost incalculable total—represented by each one of those same guests. I remembered, for some reason, a question which, at a similar reception some years before, I had heard put, with an air of complacency and at the same time of almost scientific perplexity, by a fat, vigorous, cheerful old man to another old man who was thin and pale and melancholy: "What amount of capital do you suppose is represented within these four walls? What do you think? What's your guess?" To which the other had replied somberly: "How should I know? I'm not a tax collector." Often I had wondered why I felt so profound an aversion to my mother's world; but it was only today, remembering that remark and comparing it with the faces I saw all around me, that I finally understood. As I examined the faces of my mother's guests, I suddenly had a strong feeling that there was not one wrinkle, not one inflection of the voice, not one ripple of laughter, not a single feature, in fact, that was not directly determined by the money which, as the fat old man had said, was represented by the guests in that room, in greater or lesser quantity. Yes, I thought, in that crowd money had turned into flesh and blood; whether earned by honest and successful work or stolen by cunning and arrogance, it produced always the same result—an inhuman vulgarity that was recognizable both in well-fed fatness and in dried-up thinness. And if it was true—as indeed it was true—that money does not allow of any divorce from money, for anyone who is rich cannot make a pretense of not being so; then I understood again that I myself, even in spite of myself, formed part of this society of rich people, and that it was money—which I had renounced without being able to get rid of it—that had caused the crisis in my painting and, in general, in my life. I was therefore merely a rich man who would have liked not to be so; I might dress in rags and eat crusts and live in a hut; but the money at my disposal would transform my rags into elegant clothes, my crusts of bread into delicate and dainty dishes, my hut into a palace. Even my car, old and dilapidated as it was, was more luxurious than many luxurious cars because it belonged to someone who, just for the asking, could have had another one, brand new and of the most expensive kind.

I started as I heard my mother's voice, saying: "Oh, Dino, what a pleasant surprise!"

She was standing in front of me, but I had not seen her, or rather, perhaps I had seen her but had not been able to distinguish her among the crowd of her guests, for at that moment she looked to me like one of them, exactly similar to them in every way and without any kind of connection with me, even of blood. Alone, my mother was my mother, but in the crowd that filled her rooms she became as indistinguishable as a bird in a flock of other birds or a fish in a shoal. Thus the strong business sense which, when my mother was alone, might ap-

pear to be an individual characteristic, revealed her impersonal, generic character among the crowd of her guests. And
as in the case of all the figures thronging the rooms of the villa,
so with my mother one could swear that behind the glassy glint
of her blue eyes and the showiness of her massive jewelry,
behind her nervous thinness, the excessive artificiality of her
make-up and the disagreeable quality of her voice, there was
a conformist attitude toward money, typical of the society of
which she formed part, rather than any originality of private
experiment.

Similar to her guests in physical appearance, my mother also
resembled them in her behavior during our brief encounter.
Usually, when she was alone, she was very attentive; but now,
at this cocktail party—the normal rule for such occasions being,
apparently, a supreme inattentiveness made up of indifference,
haste and thoughtlessness—my mother behaved like all the
other people, looking without seeing and talking without listening. Indeed, immediately after her lively welcoming remark, she murmured a few vague, incoherent words about
how busy she was and how this would prevent her from taking
much notice of me that afternoon; and then, looking around
her all the time, she added, without the slightest sign of curiosity, hastily and as a matter of form, so to speak: "May I point
out that you haven't yet introduced your friend to me?"

Taking Cecilia by the arm, and with a certain solemnity, I
said: "This is Cecilia, my fiancée." And then an unexpected
thing happened. Either my mother did not hear what I said,
or if she heard it she did not take it in, by which I mean that
she was conscious of it as a sound but not of its significance;
the fact remains that, after letting her cruelly sparkling eyes
rest for a moment upon Cecilia, she hurriedly exclaimed: "Forgive me, I'll see you later; there's something I must do now,"
and without waiting for an answer she darted off through the
crowd with the decision of a shark rushing through the depths
of the sea after its prey. I presumed that somebody had ar-

rived; somebody of importance, perhaps; and my mother had not listened to me because, just at the moment when I was introducing Cecilia to her, her eye had caught sight of an eddying movement near one of the doors, the movement caused by an influx of new guests into the crowd at a party.

I took two glasses from a tray handed by a waiter and gave one to Cecilia; then I propelled her across the room into a window. "Well, what do you think about it?" I asked.

"About what?"

I stood for a moment in embarrassed silence. I did not know what it was that I wanted to know from Cecilia; everything, in point of fact, since I knew nothing. I said haphazardly: "About this party."

"Well—it's a party."

"Do you like parties?"

She answered, after a moment, with a slightly troubled air: "Not very much. I don't like the smoke and the noise."

"What do you think of all these people?"

"I don't think anything. I don't know anybody."

"Some of the people who are here might be useful to you. If you like, I'll introduce you."

"Useful in what way?"

"Socially."

"What does that mean?"

"Oh well, they might make friends with you, take a liking to you, ask you to parties like this one, or, if they're men, they might flirt with you. Something useful might come out of any of those things. Lots of people go to parties for that reason. Shall I introduce you, then?"

"No, it doesn't matter; after all I shall never see them again."

"Certainly you'll see them again, since we're getting married."

"Well, in that case you can introduce me later on."

I wanted to turn the conversation to the subject of wealth,

but I didn't know how to manage it. Finally I said: "The people you see here are all very rich."

"Yes, you can see that."

"How can you see it?"

"From the ladies' clothes and jewelry."

"Would you like to be like them?"

"I don't know."

"Why don't you know?"

"I'm not rich; in order to know whether I'd like to be rich, I'd have to become rich. I could only say if I liked it or not after I'd tried it."

"But can't you imagine it?"

"How can you imagine a thing that you don't know about?"

"But you like money?"

"When I need it, yes."

"Aren't you in need of money?"

"Not at present; what you give me is enough."

"Well, if you married me you'd have plenty of money and you'd become like the ladies you see here; what do you say to that?"

I saw her big, dark eyes moving around over the crowd of guests; and once again I wondered what she saw, and whether what she saw in any way resembled what I saw. Then she said, slowly: "There are no girls here; there are only ladies of your mother's age."

"My mother is giving a party for her friends; it's natural therefore that the ladies here should all be more or less of her own age. But you haven't yet answered my question. What do you say, then, to the prospect of marrying me and becoming like these ladies here?"

"I can't tell you, I haven't thought about it."

"Think about it now, then." I saw her look around the room again; then she raised her glass to her lips, took a sip and remained silent. This was one of her ways of eluding me; by silence. "But at any rate," I insisted, "I should like to know what you're thinking about."

Almost brusquely, she replied: "I was thinking that perhaps it might be better for us to go to some quieter place; then I could give you the answer you wanted."

"Which answer?"

"About getting married."

"Where would you like to go?"

"It's all the same to me."

"Let's go upstairs. We can be quiet there. And you can see the house, too."

We put our two glasses on the window sill and I took Cecilia by the arm again and steered her through the crowd toward a door at the far end of the room. I opened the door and led her into the passage. Immediately the din, the smoke, the crowd were replaced by the customary air of the house, clean, deserted and silent. I guided Cecilia to the staircase and started going up with her, one hand on the brass rail and the other on her shoulder. "Would you like to live here?" I asked her.

"Here or in some other place, it's just the same to me."

"But here there's my mother."

"She's charming, your mother."

I exclaimed, in astonishment: "Good Heavens, what do you find charming about my mother?"

"I don't know, she's charming."

By this time we had reached the first floor. "Do you want to see my room?" I asked.

"Yes."

I threw the door open and showed it to her. It had remained just as it was on the day when I ran away, leaving my trousers in the hands of Rita—with the shutters closed and the mattress rolled up on the bed. She gave it a cursory glance, with a complete absence of curiosity, and said: "Does no one use it now?"

"There are some empty rooms upstairs," I said. "We could take them over, if we get married. Don't you think you'd be better off here, in a room like this, than in the one where you're living now?"

Her answer confirmed my conviction that she saw nothing, and that for her there was no difference between my mother's splendid Empire furniture and the junk in her own home. "Why?" she said. "The two rooms are much the same. There's a bed here as there is there, a wardrobe and chairs too, just as there are there."

"At least you'll admit that it's larger?"

"Yes, it's larger."

I shut the door again and said: "Let's go to my mother's room. She's busy with her cocktail party. We can talk there as much as we like."

I led her to the bedroom, opened the door and pushed her forward into the darkness, as I might have pushed her into a prison to shut her up forever. Then I turned on the light. The big, comfortable room, in which there was not an inch of bare wall or uncarpeted floor and where everywhere there were curtains and hangings and rugs, seemed to me suffocating. I went to one of the windows, threw it open and looked out for a moment. The window overlooked the Italian garden, and beyond it the whole garden could be seen, with its avenues and trees, its fountain and pergola. Night had fallen now; the black, starless sky was dimly lit from time to time by flashes of lightning from some far-off thunderstorm, the air scarcely less hot and suffocating than inside the room. Lamps on the ground, concealed among the hedges, threw a false, quivering light upon the feet of the many guests who had gradually moved out from the ground floor rooms and were scattered about the garden. Thus they appeared illuminated up to their knees, in a ghostly sort of way; but from their knees up they melted into the darkness, so that it looked as though the whole garden were populated by male and female legs without any bodies. While I was watching this spectacle, Cecilia's voice made me jump. "Where is the bathroom?" she asked.

"That door over there."

Without a word she went over to the bathroom door. I left the window and went and sat in an armchair at the foot of the bed, and lit a cigarette.

I was struck by a large, old picture hanging to the left of the bed. It represented Danae and the shower of gold, and was probably a recent acquisition of my mother who, as I knew, sometimes "invested" her money in works of art: I did not in fact remember having seen it before. Danae was depicted lying on a bed very like my mother's bed, low and wide, with a canopy decorated with bronze ornamentations. Leaning against a pile of pillows, her bosom drawn back and her belly thrust forward, one leg stretched out along the mattress and the other bent and dangling in the air, she was looking complacently at her lap into which, out of the shadow of the heavy curtains, fell the shower of coins, of a gold as bright and shining as her own wanton hair lying scattered over her white shoulders and rosy bosom. It was an ordinary picture of a mythological subject, and in other circumstances I should not have paid it any attention. But at that moment it struck me as something which concerned me, if only in an indirect, obscure manner. I went on contemplating the picture, wondering why it aroused my curiosity and what the significance of such curiosity could be. Then suddenly the bathroom door opened and Cecilia came back into the room.

She had undressed and had wrapped herself in a short towel which just covered her hips and bosom and looked like one of those abbreviated pieces of material which women in the tropics wind round their bodies. Approaching me on tiptoe, she said: "Do you know, my trouble is all over? So we can make love, if you like."

"Here?"

"Why not? It's so comfortable here."

I had a sudden feeling that this was a treacherous, self-interested piece of generosity, as though Cecilia were intending, by offering herself in this unexpected way when I had already given up the idea, to compensate me in some way, in advance, for a loss of which I was still ignorant. I said brusquely: "Very well, but first you must give me your answer."

"What answer?"

"Whether you'll agree to become my wife."

She said nothing, but wandered about the room for a little and then, with sudden decision, came and sat on my knee. She began to untie my tie and unbutton my collar, and said slowly: "Dino, you're the only man I could marry because with you I can be natural and sincere and not hide anything."

"Really?" I exclaimed, somewhat astonished by this preamble. "I always have the impression that with me you hide everything, or nearly everything. If it's like that with me, whatever happens with other people?"

Bending her head as she pulled off my tie and then, one by one, undid the buttons of my shirt, she went on as if she had not heard what I said. "And this is a lovely house. I should like to live in it with you."

"Well, then?"

"Besides," she continued, trying to pull my arm out of the sleeve of my coat, "you've promised me so many nice things—traveling, clothes, parties."

"Well?"

"But I must tell you I can't marry you. I ought to have told you at once, when you spoke to me about it, but I hadn't the courage, I saw you were so set on it." By this time she had succeeded in taking off my jacket and my shirt too; she folded them and threw them aside, to the bottom of the bed.

I now had a feeling of immense astonishment; it was just as though I had really believed Cecilia would be flattered at the idea of becoming my wife. The fact of the matter, as I at last realized, was that just as in the past I had hoped to possess her by means of money, so this time I had imagined I could achieve the same end by offering her something that women almost always place before money—marriage. I asked angrily: "Why don't you want to?"

"I don't want to because I don't want to."

"But why?"

"Because of Luciani," she said. "I don't want to leave him."

"Do you want to marry *him?*"

"Oh no, I'm not thinking of that. Besides, he has a wife already."

"Luciani has a wife?"

"Yes, and he has to support her, too."

Exasperated, I cried: "What does Luciani matter to me? I'd let you see him as much as you liked."

"No, I said no, and no it is."

"But why?"

Speaking in the same tone with which she had answered me when I had offered to pay her a fixed monthly sum, a tone which suggested that she was attached to a convenient and cherished habit, she said: "No, no, Dino, why should we get married? Let's stay as we are; it all works so well as it is."

With almost unbelievable tenacity, I now clung more and more to the idea of marriage, possibly because Cecilia would have nothing to do with it. "But if I let you see Luciani, or anyone else you like," I said, "if nothing changes except for the better, if instead of living in a wretched flat with your family you come and live in this villa with me, why on earth should you refuse? What is it that makes you refuse?"

"I don't want to get married, that's all," she answered in a decisive manner. Then, getting off my knee and pulling me by the hand, she added: "Come on, come on now, let's make love."

Mechanically, almost in spite of myself, I rose to my feet. And then a ridiculous thing happened: my trousers, the belt of which Cecilia had in the meantime undone, fell down to my feet and I stumbled over them. "No," I yelled, at the height of fury, "no, I don't want to. I only want to know why you won't be my wife."

She stood looking at me, then warned me ambiguously: "As you like. But if we don't do it today we won't be able to do it for some time."

"Why?"

"I'd decided not to tell you, so as not to make you angry. I would have written you a post card and you'd have learned like that. But after all it's best that you should know. Tomorrow morning I'm leaving for Ponza with Luciani and we're staying away for about two weeks."

I was already in a rage, and this revelation, which at last explained Cecilia's behavior that day, redoubled my fury. So she had decided to spend a couple of weeks with Luciani at Ponza; it was for this reason, and for this reason only—that is, in order to console me in some degree—that she had suggested that morning that we should spend the day together; for this reason and for this reason only that she had suggested making love with me; and finally, however strange it may seem, it was for this reason and this reason only that she had refused to become my wife. I knew Cecilia pretty well by now and had had experience of her complete lack of imagination and of her indifferent, apathetic disinterestedness. I knew also that she was incapable of thinking of more than one thing at a time—the nearest and most immediate and most attractive. In this case the trip to Ponza with the actor was the nearest and most immediate and most attractive thing; for the sake of this trip she did not hesitate to refuse a marriage which, at another time, she might have accepted.

I was suddenly aware of the pain this caused me, and that, whereas shortly before I had wanted at all costs that she should become my wife, I should now be satisfied if she did not go to Ponza. I said, in a voice of deep distress: "Don't go!"

She did not answer me; but she went to the bed, got on to it and lay down, slowly, complacently, placidly, her back against the pillows, one leg stretched out on the bed, the other bent, her foot dangling in the air; exactly like Danae in the picture. Then, starting to unwrap the towel from around her body, she said: "Why do you think about the future? Come here now and lie down beside me."

"But I don't want you to go."

"We've already booked the room."

"Well, tell Luciani you don't feel well, and don't go."

"It's not possible."

"Why not?"

"Because I like the idea of going to Ponza and I don't see why I shouldn't go."

"If you don't go, I'll give you a present."

She was naked now, lying in a relaxed attitude with her breasts free and her hips comfortably settled on the bed; and she was looking up in childish curiosity at the hangings. Without lowering her eyes, she asked in an absent-minded way: "What sort of present?"

"Whatever you like."

"But what, for instance?"

"For instance, a sum of money."

She lowered her big dark eyes and looked at me in a vague, expressionless, slightly surprised sort of manner. "How much would you give me?" she asked.

I looked back at her and then, struck by the resemblance of her attitude to that of Danae in the picture on the wall close by, I had a sudden idea. "I'll give you all the money it takes to cover you."

"How do you mean?"

"I mean that you're to lie still there on the bed and I'll cover you with banknotes from head to foot. If you give up the idea of going to Ponza, I'll give you, as I say, all the money it takes to cover you from head to foot."

She started to laugh, flattered and attracted more, it would seem, by the novelty of the game than by the bargain I had suggested. "What ideas you get into your head!" she said.

"Painter's ideas," I said dishonestly.

"Anyhow, where have you got the money?"

"Wait."

I rose and ran into the bathroom, where I swiftly did what I had foreseen that I would eventually do: I moved the tiles, uncovered the steel door of the safe, turned the dials according to the secret combination. Meanwhile I was hoping that the money would be there. If there was no money, I thought, I would cover Cecilia with stock certificates, which anyhow were equivalent to money, as my mother had so often pointed out to me.

But the money was there. On top of the usual two or three rolls of bonds was the well-known red envelope, stuffed to bursting point. I seized it, took out the notes which it contained and went back into the bedroom. As I went toward her, Cecilia looked at me with a kind of leer which, I could not help thinking, was positively mythological—much as Danae must have looked when the first golden coin tumbled into her lap. "Now," I told her with a smile, "lie down flat."

As she lay down she looked at me with curiosity and amusement and also, I thought, with a touch of agitation. The bundle of notes that I had taken from the envelope was a thick one; I calculated there must be fifty notes of ten thousand lire each. I started from the bottom, symbolically, by spreading a single, carefully smoothed note over her dark, curly groin. Then, moving upward, I covered the white, childish belly, the slim waist and the beautiful brown bosom, placing one banknote on each breast. I wrapped another note across her neck; four I put on her shoulders and four on her arms. Then I went down again below her belly, and covered her legs with notes right down to her small feet. Cecilia at first followed this operation with childish, attentive curiosity, just as though it were a game; then all of a sudden she began to laugh, with nervous, uncontrollable laughter. I could not help thinking hopefully that this was the laughter of a woman who finally yields to her lover, after repulsing him for a long time. In such a way, I reflected, must Danae have laughed when she felt the divine shower of gold flooding her with amorous voluptuousness. Still laughing, Cecilia continued to take part in the game, pointing to the places that still remained to be covered: "There's still room here, put one here, and here." Finally she lay still, looking like some strange bedizened animal, flat on her back with her face turned toward me and her eyes wide open. I said curtly: "There are twenty-four ten-thousand-lire notes. If you don't go to Ponza, I'll give you the lot."

She started laughing again and exclaimed: "I thought there'd be more than that."

I thought it might not be enough for her, so I went on: "I'll give you twice the amount, the number that's needed to cover you back and front. That's fair, because after all you have a back and a front."

Lying now beneath the banknotes, motionless and as though afraid of disarranging them and so spoiling the game, she looked at me with an expression of regretful perplexity. Finally she said: "I'm sorry, Dino, but it's not possible." She was silent a moment, still looking at me, then she went on with an unusual gentleness that could not have been feigned: "Let's make love now. Then, when I come back from Ponza, I promise you we'll do it more often than in the past and I promise you we'll see more of each other."

I saw that the gentleness in her voice was due to the excitement that the game with the banknotes had aroused in her. This excitement, according to my intention, should have allowed me to take possession of her through the medium of money; now, on the contrary, after her refusal, it made her once more elusive and unattainable. "You really won't do as I ask?" I demanded.

"No, it's not possible."

She lay still, taking care not to move beneath her garment of banknotes, as though the game were going on and she were awaiting its final phase. Then suddenly I felt myself assailed by the usual blind male impulse, which urged me to take her because I could not succeed in possessing her, as if by taking her I could in fact possess her. I threw myself upon her and covered her body, and the banknotes that covered it, with my own body. Cecilia showed at once that she had expected the game to end in this way, clinging closely to me with her arms and legs, while the banknotes, horribly dirty and incongruous, crackled and slithered between our two ardent, sweating bodies. Other notes had become scattered around us on the bed covers, and yet others on the pillow, among Cecilia's hair.

Afterward, Cecilia lay supine, her legs apart, motionless and sated like a great snake that has swallowed an animal bigger than itself. I lay on top of her, no less motionless; and when I reflected upon our two separate stillnesses, I realized that mine was the stillness that can follow a futile, exhausting effort, while hers had the quality of full, rich satisfaction. I recalled the time when after painting for a whole day I would feel tired, not with an exhausted tiredness such as I felt now but with a satisfied tiredness like Cecilia's; and I said to myself that in our relationship it was she, in reality, who possessed me and I who was possessed, although nature, for her own ends, deceived both Cecilia and me into thinking the opposite. As a man I was finished, I thought; not only would I never paint again, but I should also destroy myself in the pursuit of that species of mirage which seemed to rise up from Cecilia's womb as from the sands of the desert; and in the end, like Balestrieri, I should sink into the darkness of mania.

I was drawn out of these reflections by Cecilia's voice, saying: "At least you must admit that I'm not mercenary."

I asked in surprise: "Why do you say that?"

"Any other woman, in my place, would have taken the money and then gone away just the same."

"And what then?"

"Well, you must admit that in a way I've saved you a lot of money."

"It's not I who have saved it," I said, hoping, almost, that Cecilia had thought better of it and was going to accept my proposal, "it's you who have lost it."

"Just as you like. Now I want to ask you a favor."

"What is that?"

"You were ready to give me nearly half a million lire if I didn't go away. Instead, lend me a small part of that amount, forty thousand."

"But what d'you want it for?" I inquired stupidly.

"Luciani is out of a job, and we have very little money. It would be useful for our trip to Ponza."

Before I realized what was happening, I had leaped forward and fastened my hands round Cecilia's neck, shouting the first words of abuse that came into my head. They say that at certain moments of great intensity a man can think and act in contrary ways. In that second when I clasped Cecilia's neck, my thought was that perhaps the only way of possessing her was by killing her. By killing her I could snatch her away from all the things that rendered her elusive, and could shut her up, once and for all, in the prison of death. And so, for one instant, I thought of strangling her, there on my mother's bed, amongst the banknotes she had refused, in the house in which we should have lived together if we had got married. And I should certainly have done it if I had not realized, in that same lucid, lightning-like moment, that this crime, at least as far as my intended purpose was concerned, would be useless. Instead of achieving full possession of Cecilia and liberating myself from her, I should, in reality, merely succeed in establishing her complete and final independence; wrapped in a mystery doubly sealed by death, she would have then eluded me forever, irreparably. I relaxed my grip and said in a low voice: "Forgive me, for a moment you made me lose my head."

She did not appear to have understood the danger in which she had been. "You hurt me," she said. "Whatever put it into your head to get angry like that?"

"I don't know. Again, please forgive me."

"Never mind. It doesn't matter."

I raised myself slightly on my elbow, quickly collected some of the notes and handed them to her, saying: "Here's seventy thousand lire; is that enough?"

"That's too much, forty thousand would be enough."

"Take them, they'll come in useful."

"Thank you."

She kissed me with ingenuous, disarming gratitude and again I felt desire for her, still for the same old reason that she was there in my arms and at the same time not there, and that possibly, possibly, if I took her once again, possibly she *might* be there and might stay there. And so, with no fury this time, but gently, tenderly, despairingly, I passed my arm under her back, being careful not to hurt her with my wrist watch, and when my hand, encircling her slender waist, almost met my other arm, I insinuated my legs between hers, passed my other arm under her neck, and when I held her closely enveloped and confined, penetrated slowly into her, as though I were hoping, by this slowness, to achieve the full possession which on all other occasions had eluded me. At the end, I asked her: "That was good, wasn't it?"

"Yes, it was good."

"Very good or rather good?"

"Very good."

"Better than usual?"

"Yes, perhaps better than usual."

"Are you happy?"

"Yes, I'm happy."

"Do you love me?"

"Yes, you know I love you."

These were words I had used countless times, but never with a feeling so utterly desperate. As I said them, I was thinking that Cecilia would now go away to Ponza and that her departure, the concrete symbol of her elusiveness, would inevitably give new strength to my love and to my consequent longing to free myself from her by possessing her. When she came back everything would begin all over again, just as it had been before she went away, but worse than before. I felt a sudden desire not to stay with her any longer, to get away from her. I said, as gently as I could: "It's time we went away. Otherwise my mother might come and find us here, and that would be a nuisance."

"I'll get dressed at once."

"Don't be in too much of a hurry. I said it would be a nuisance, but no more than that. It isn't really important. At most, my mother would protest not so much at the thing itself as at the way it was done."

"How d'you mean?"

"My mother attaches great importance to what she calls good form. That's what we've failed to observe, by making love in her bedroom instead of in my studio."

"What is good form?"

"I don't know. Probably it's the result of thinking a great deal about money."

We finished dressing in silence. Then I collected the banknotes that were lying scattered over the bed, went into the bathroom and wrote in pencil on the envelope: "Have taken the 70,000 lire. Thank you. Dino"; and I put the envelope back in the safe. Cecilia was rearranging the bed covers. She asked: "Where are we going now?"

A sudden impulse of rage swept over me. "We're not going anywhere," I said; "it wouldn't be any use now, anyhow. I'll take you home."

I almost hoped she might show displeasure or regret in face of this abrupt change in our program. Instead of which she answered, with indifference: "Just as you like."

"Just as *I* like?" I insisted. "No, it's as *you* like; it's you who is going away tomorrow. It's up to you to say whether you want us to stay together until midnight or not."

"It's all the same to me."

"Why is it all the same?"

"Because I know I shall see you again in two weeks' time."

"Are you sure of that?"

"Yes."

"Well . . . I'll take you home."

During this little discussion we had left the bedroom and gone down to the ground floor. We walked along the passage; an intense hubbub, like the clamor of a disturbed beehive, could be heard on the other side of the closed doors; the party was still going on. We followed the passage into the hall and went out in front of the house.

The unexpected freshness of the summer night made me look up instinctively at the sky as I opened the door of the car: the storm which had been hanging over the city all day long had burst elsewhere; the sky had now cleared and stars were shining brightly, and here and there a few light clouds mingled their whiteness with the luminous whiteness of the Milky Way. Cecilia, I thought, would have fine weather for her trip to Ponza; and again I was conscious of jealousy gnawing at my anxious heart. Yes, I would be counting the days, the hours, the minutes and the seconds as I waited for her to come back, knowing all the time that during those same days and hours and minutes and seconds she would be joking, laughing, strolling about, going on a boat ride and making love with Luciani—eluding me, in fact. And when she came back, I should not be able to restrain myself from starting to run after her again, like Balestrieri, in whose footsteps, it seemed, I was condemned to follow.

I do not think I spoke more than two or three times, and then more and more briefly, during our drive from my mother's villa to Cecilia's home. Once I asked her, stupidly, to write to me, although I was very well aware that Cecilia, so reticent in speech, must be utterly dumb in correspondence and so would not write anything, even a picture post card. We reached the street in which she lived. I stopped and she got out and I said good-bye to her, after kissing her lightly on the mouth. I watched her as she crossed the street and thought: "Let's hope that at least she'll turn around in the doorway and smile and wave to me." But I was disappointed in my expectation. Cecilia crossed the threshold and disappeared without turning around.

As soon as she was gone I realized that I had no desire to go to my studio or anywhere else. The only place I wished to go was Cecilia's home: it seemed to me that I had not finished with her yet. I wanted to go up to the flat, ring the doorbell, go with her to her bedroom and go to bed with her for the third time that day. I knew that this was madness, that by having her again I should not be possessing her any more than I possessed her now—which meant not at all—and that the thing which eluded me was not indeed her almost too complaisant body, but something which had nothing to do with her body. And yet I felt that this was the only thing I wanted to do.

I do not know how long I debated this problem, sitting in my car in the deserted street in front of Cecilia's door. Finally I said to myself that Cecilia, after all, had almost insisted on our being together until midnight, and that therefore there would be nothing strange about it if I, regretting that I had left her so early, telephoned and suggested taking her out to dinner. Cecilia, as I knew, had almost unlimited patience, and when she refused to do something she never refused because she did not want to do it but merely because she could not do otherwise. Suddenly making up my mind, I quickly backed the car to the corner, got out and went into the bar.

But the telephone was occupied by the type of person one could not expect to finish quickly—a modest-appearing girl, a servant girl, perhaps, who was speaking and answering in an extremely low voice and with the long, reflective pauses of one who is engaged in a sentimental conversation. I did not hesitate a moment, but went straight out again and walked resolutely back to Cecilia's door. Why should I telephone? I would go up to the flat, find her there and hurry her into her bedroom.

I ran all the way up the stairs, ran across to ring the bell, then stopped panting on the landing, waiting for the door to open so that I could rush into the flat. But it was not Cecilia who came to open the door; it was her mother, with a troubled expression on her worn, painted face. "Cecilia?" I inquired.

She replied in a voice of distress: "Cecilia's not here, Professor."

"What, she's not here?"

"She went out just two minutes ago."

"But where has she gone?"

"She's gone out to dinner."

"What time will she be back?"

"She's not coming back, Professor. She took her suitcase with her. She's going with a girl friend to Ponza. She's sleeping at her friend's house tonight and she'll be back in a fortnight."

Thus, while I had been debating whether it was advisable to telephone her, Cecilia had run up to the flat, fetched her already packed suitcase, gone out by the usual door which opened on to the other street and made her way to Luciani's. I looked up at her mother's face and saw that she was biting her handkerchief and that her eyes were filled with tears. "But what has happened?" I could not help asking.

"Cecilia has gone away, and her father is dying. She's left me alone in this empty house. My husband was taken off yesterday to the clinic, and there's no hope now."

"There's no hope?"

298

"No, the doctors give him only two or three days to live."

"But isn't Cecilia fond of her father?"

"Ah, Cecilia's not fond of anyone, Professor."

All at once I remembered how Cecilia had come to look for me on the very day on which Balestrieri died. "I'm sorry," I said abruptly, "I'm truly sorry," and after listening impatiently with a set face to a few further laments, I went away.

As I walked back to the car, I realized that I could not endure the idea that Cecilia was with the actor at that very moment. I was faced with the usual impossibility of doing anything at all except what I felt I ought not to do; and this was confirmed and made even more hopeless by my recent disappointment. I jumped into the car and very soon became aware that I was driving in the direction of Via Archimede, where Luciani lived. I say I became aware because I was acting in an automatic manner, with the type of automatism which goes with extreme rage. When I reached Via Archimede, I drove at headlong speed down the narrow, winding street as far as the bar, where I stopped and looked across at Luciani's windows. They were in darkness, and at once I was sure that the two lovers were not there. Nevertheless I got out of the car, entered the building, and rang the bell of the actor's flat on the ground floor. I do not know what came into my mind as I listened to the prolonged ringing of the bell inside the empty flat; I only know that two minutes later I was in the bar dialing the telephone number of a procuress through whom, in the past, I had made contact with girls of easy virtue. When the woman came to the other end of the line, she told me there was a girl available at the usual place, a villa on the Via Cassia.

Back in the car, I reflected that the girl whom I was now preparing to visit was the exact opposite of Cecilia: she was at my entire disposal for a sum of money and I should possess her completely, with no margins of independence or mystery, thanks to that same sum of money. What I had not succeeded in doing in the villa on the Via Appia, with a proposal of marriage and half a million lire, I should now achieve, at small expense, in the *maison de rendez-vous* on the Via Cassia. But the girl was not Cecilia; why, then, was I going to visit her?

I realized to my astonishment, when I tried to answer this question, that at the back of my absurd telephone call to the procuress there was a strange, almost unbelievable hope. In the midst of my fury I hoped, I truly hoped that in the villa on the Via Cassia I should find Cecilia herself waiting for me, ready to give herself to me and to allow me, at last, full possession. I really do not know where this hope came from; partly, perhaps from the alluring words of the procuress who, like all her kind, had made marvelous promises of the very thing she could not possibly provide—that is, love; but partly also from the fact that all rational means of possessing Cecilia having proved vain, my only hope now lay in a miracle.

With these thoughts in my head, or rather, in this raging, almost mystical state of mind, I drove out of the city and started along the Via Cassia. The villa was in the open country; I went on for about twenty minutes or so and then arrived at a rustic iron gate, wide open, with a rough lane leading up from it to the top of a hill upon which could be seen a white building. I drove quickly through the gate and up the road between little stunted trees that appeared to have been recently planted. Leaning forward on the steering wheel, I could see that all the windows in the villa were dark; then one of these windows was lit up. The car came out on to an open, graveled space; I stopped and got out.

The villa was a plain building, with two stories and three windows on each floor, and with an outside staircase going up to the first floor. The staircase led to a little balcony, on which a lantern suddenly appeared as I was getting out of the car. Then a small black figure was outlined against the

300

yellow light of the lantern, a girl with luxuriant hair, a prominent bosom, a slim waist—in fact, I was sure of it, Cecilia.

I thought: "It's Cecilia!" and rushed up the staircase while the dark figure, leaning placidly with her elbows on the balustrade, watched me. When I reached the top, she straightened up and came forward to meet me, saying: "Good evening."

She was against the light and I could not see her face, but her voice seemed to me to be Cecilia's and I took her in my arms. I saw, then, the pretty, plump face of a very young girl, a face covered with the fashionable livid, corpse-like powder, with lilac-painted lips, eyes encircled with black, and fair, straw-colored hair. She had Cecilia's prominent bosom; her waist, around which I had put my arms, was as slim as Cecilia's. But it was not Cecilia.

But, in my stupefaction, I exclaimed: "Cecilia!"

The girl smiled and replied: "My name isn't Cecilia, my name's Gianna."

"But I wanted Cecilia."

"I don't know who Cecilia is, there's no Cecilia here. Well, shall we go in?"

I said: "Cecilia, I came for Cecilia," then I tore myself away from the girl, ran down the stairs, crossed the open space and got back into my car. A moment later I was driving along the Via Cassia, not in the direction of Rome but out into the country.

For some time now I had been conscious, when driving, of a frequent temptation to go off the road and rush at full speed into the first obstacle I encountered. This temptation, singularly hard to resist, was enticing and at the same time reassuring—like the temptation a child feels when he plays with his father's revolver and from time to time raises it to his forehead. And yet I did not think of killing myself, the idea of suicide was never in my mind. The desire for death was, on the contrary, in my body, which was worn out with anguish, so that I often felt that my arm would very easily give the steering wheel the half-turn which was all that would be required to hurl the car against a boundary wall or a white-banded plane tree. It was an almost irresistible temptation, sweet and reassuring, and it made me think of the temptation to fall asleep which sometimes gets the better of us in spite of ourselves, causing us to dream that we are resisting sleep and are awake, when in reality we are already fast asleep. I knew in advance that if I killed myself in my car I would do it without realizing it and without intending it, just as though I had really followed an imaginary road different from the one along which I was driving, a road which took no account of boundary walls or trees or houses, and at the end of which was death.

That evening, as I was driving in a haphazard way along the Via Cassia, out into the country, there flashed into my mind a remark I had once heard: "Humanity is divided into two main categories; those who, when faced with an insurmountable difficulty, feel an impulse to kill, and those who, on the contrary, feel an impulse to kill themselves." I said to myself that I had tried the first horn of the dilemma and had failed in the attempt: I had been incapable of killing Cecilia, shortly before, on my mother's bed. Now there was nothing left but to kill myself. It occurred to me that if I killed myself I should be behaving exactly like any other lover since the world began: Cecilia was going off to Ponza with Luciani and so I killed myself. But it was precisely this reflection upon the banality and normality of my position that inspired in me a destructive fury more intense than ever. At that moment I came on to a straight stretch of road bordered with trees; there was a slow-moving truck in front of me. I shifted gears in order to overtake it, and it was possibly this gear shifting, with its momentary slowing down, that saved my life. Immediately after shifting, just as though I had really seen another road on my left into which I wanted to turn, I drove the car into a plane tree.

Epilogue

In front of the window of my room at the hospital to which I had been taken after the collision there was a great tree in the garden, a cedar of Lebanon, with long drooping branches of an almost blue green. I took to gazing at it for hours, my head turned sideways on the pillow as I lay on my back in bed—during all those hours, in fact, that were not occupied in sleeping or eating; for I was almost always alone, having let my mother and my few friends know the first day that I did not want to be visited. I gazed at the tree and experienced a feeling of absolute but calm and stabilized despair, such as one might well feel after passing through a crisis which, though not decisive, may yet be supposed to be the greatest that one can face. What for lack of a more appropriate term I must call my suicide had resolved nothing, but the fact of having attempted it had made me feel I had done all that was in my power; more than that I could not do. In other words, the fact that I had tried to kill myself confirmed the seriousness of my involvement. I was not dead, but at least I had proved to myself that, rather than go on living as I had lived previously, I should have preferred, and seriously preferred death. All this did not mitigate the feeling of despair that

303

occupied my mind; but it introduced a certain kind of mournful, resigned serenity. I had indeed visited the dim purlieus of death, but I had returned; and now, although without hope, all that was left for me was to go on living.

As I have said, I spent hours gazing at the tree, to the great surprise of the nuns and the servants in the hospital, who said they had never seen a quieter patient than me. In reality I was not quiet, merely I was closely occupied with the only thing that truly interested me at that moment, the contemplation of the tree. I had no thoughts, I simply wondered when and how I had recognized the reality of the tree, had recognized, in other words, its existence as an object which was different from myself, had no relationship with me, and yet was there and could not be ignored. Evidently something had occurred just at the moment when I hurled myself off the road in my car; something which, to put it plainly, might be described as the collapse of an insupportable ambition. I now contemplated the tree with infinite complacency, as though to feel it different from myself and independent of me were the only thing that gave me pleasure. But I knew that chance alone had willed that the tree would be the object of my contemplation; the plaster casing compelled me to lie on my back and forced me to look through the window of my room. Any other object, I realized, would have provided me with the same kind of contemplation, the same feeling of infinite complacency.

And indeed, as soon as I began to think about Cecilia again, I was aware of the same thing happening to me as when I gazed at the tree through the window. Ten days had passed since my collision and Cecilia was certainly still at Ponza with Luciani; I took to thinking about her, therefore, at first cautiously and at rare intervals, then more often and with greater confidence. I realized then that I was able to imagine perfectly well, just as if I had been present, all the things she was doing while I was lying there in bed at the hospital. To say "imagine" is to say too little, for I could see her. As through the wrong end of a telescope, I saw the tiny, remote but brightly clear figures of Cecilia and the actor moving, running, embracing, walking, lying together, disappearing and reappearing in a hundred different attitudes against a background of blue sea and calm, luminous sky. I knew from experience that happiness is to be found with the person whom one loves and who loves one, in a lovely, peaceful place; I was sure that Cecilia, in her own economical, inexpressive way, was happy, and I was astonished to find that I was pleased. Yes indeed, I was pleased that she should be happy, but above all I was pleased that she should exist, away there in the island of Ponza, in a manner which was her own and which was different from mine and in contrast with mine, with a man who was not myself, far away from me. I was here in the hospital, I repeated to myself from time to time, and she was at Ponza with the actor, and we were two different people and she had nothing to do with me and I had nothing to do with her, and she was apart from me, as I was apart from her. And finally I no longer desired to possess her but to watch her live her life, just as she was, that is, to contemplate her in the same way that I contemplated the tree outside my window. This contemplation would never come to an end for the simple reason that I did not wish it to come to an end, that is, I did not wish the tree, or Cecilia, or any other object outside myself, to become boring to me and consequently to cease to exist. In reality, as I suddenly realized with a feeling almost of surprise, I had relinquished Cecilia once and for all; and, strange to relate, from the very moment of this relinquishment, Cecilia had begun to exist for me.

I wondered if possibly, in relinquishing Cecilia, I had also ceased to love her, in other words to experience toward her that same feeling, always delusive and always disappointed, that I had previously had, and which, for lack of a more appropriate term, I must call love. I was aware that that kind of love was dead, but that I loved her all the same, though with a love that was new and different. This new love might or might not be accompanied by a physical relationship, but it did not depend upon it, and in a way did not need it. When Cecilia came back we might or we might not resume our former relations, but I, in any case, would not cease to love her.

At this point I must admit that my ideas became confused. I recalled that from the very beginning it had seemed to me that my relationship with Cecilia had differed in no way from my contact with reality; in other words, that my fundamental reasons for ceasing to paint had been the same as those for which I had attempted to kill myself. But now? In the end I said to myself that, for the moment, I had to remain in bed for more than a month and that it was too soon to come to any sort of decision. Once I was well, I would go back to the studio and try to start painting again. I say that I would try, because I was not at all sure that the connection I had seen for so long between Cecilia and my painting really existed; or that loving Cecilia in a new way would mean starting to paint again. Here again, only experience would be able to provide an answer.

And so, in the long run, the only truly certain result was that I had learned to love Cecilia, or rather, to love her without complications. Anyhow I hoped I had learned. For in relation also to this aspect of my life, doubt could not be excluded. And in order to be completely sure, I had to wait until Cecilia came back from her visit to the seaside.